FREEFALL

Spellkeeper Flight – Book Two

Ken Hughes

Windward Road Press

Los Angeles, CA

Windward Road Press
11923 NE Sumner St Ste 879426
Portland, OR 97250-9601

Publisher's Note: This is a work of fiction. Names, characters, places, and incidents are a product of the author's imagination. Locales and public names are sometimes used for atmospheric purposes. Any resemblance to actual people, living or dead, or to businesses, companies, events, institutions, or locales is completely coincidental.

Book Layout © 2017 BookDesignTemplates.com

Freefall/ Ken Hughes. -- 1st ed.
ISBN paperback: 978-0-9850484-4-0
ISBN e-book: 978-0-9850484-5-7

For Lynn —
whenever the wind blows right, we'll listen for your voice.

CONTENTS

BROKEN AND ENTERING... 1

HEADS AND TAILS 25

GATHERING AND CLOUDS 45

FREEZING AND COLD 65

LABYRINTH AND STRING 81

PRIVATE AND LINE 105

FRIENDS AND CLOSE 121

ENEMIES AND CLOSER 141

COUNSEL AND COUNCIL 167

MOUSE AND CAT 187

GATE AND CRASH 209

THE GIRL AND THE BOX 233

CROSS AND CROSS 255

CRUSH AND WEIGHT 271

LEAP AND BOUND 291

GRAVEYARD AND SHIFT 305

from GROUNDED 331

ABOUT THE AUTHOR 345

CHAPTER ONE

BROKEN AND ENTERING

Dammit, Angie! Where are you?

Mark Petrie swept a glare around the mist-dimmed space above the skyline, but of course his other sense felt none of Angie's magic out there. Why should tonight be any different?

But he sensed no flicker of Winton spying on him either—so this could still be the night he'd track the killer down.

The thought pushed him faster along the November-chilled streets. He left Claremont Road's nighttime crowds behind and twisted up Smithson until its murmurs thinned down to empty sidewalks, and at last he could slip across Teal unobserved.

Olivia Nolan's pale-blue car sat next to a shuttered shop, almost right under the meeting place they'd picked. He adjusted the bag of tools at his side, although nothing he'd gathered for burglary would be as useful as the simple leather belt that the bag hung from, or the other belt hidden under his shirt.

One more glance around. The back street was as deserted as it seemed.

Mark's will tightened around the magic in the belts, and he scampered up a drainpipe.

His fingers barely touched the cold metal; that light grip was all he needed. With his weight all but wiped away by the power, he could *ride* the pipe up the shop wall as fast as his hands could pull him along. If someone came by below he'd be out of their view in moments, and they'd see nothing more than what might have been a person climbing. And nobody did pass by.

Not bad planning, for someone just a year out of high school.

His shoulder barely twinged from the motion. The bullet wound *was* healing faster than the doctors had expected.

When he swung up to the flat top of the roof, he saw Nolan was waiting there. Just a short, middle-aged woman in a dark coat, looking through a pair of binoculars. She stood within the thin lakeside breeze and mist that she'd summoned like she'd been meeting on rooftops all her life.

And she hasn't. The Nolans have had magic for generations instead of my months, but I was watching my back before she even knew she had an enemy. We've fought, I've saved her life—and tonight I need to convince her to do this my way.

Four easy hops at reduced weight brought him to Nolan's side, and he knelt his rangy height down to put his gaze on a level with her. "So, anything out there I should know?"

If his rushing up had startled her, she didn't show it. "It… just looks like a building, from here. There's no sign of whatever the commotion was last night. Nothing online either." She handed him the binoculars.

What they showed him was more the two blocks of vaporous air blocking the view than the East Lavine Youth Center's blur at the end of it. But he could make out that the windows lay unlit, and he knew the place didn't even have curtains to hide what went on inside. Just bars to keep out trouble, and those were only on the first floor.

All set up to promise *the gangs can't reach you here, but we have no secrets.* Except for the fact that Roger Winton only backed the Center to get him influence with the police, while at any time his power could be spying around for the secrets of other people's magic that Winton would kill for. Even now with Winton himself in hiding for months…

Mark forced his clenching fingers to loosen enough to hand the binoculars back. "Well, it's not a trap, because Winton's got no magic in there. Not working now, anyway." That sounded too pushy in his ears, too quick to remind her that without his sense for different energies they'd be fighting blind.

She still didn't ask about his plan. Instead she said "And you did remember *both* belts, yours and the one you took from Rafe?"

"That's right." Both had been drained of much of their tingle of power, but he shouldn't need to stop and replenish them yet. Slowly he began pulling on his gloves. "I can do this just like we did at Winton's other holdings: I jump in, look around, and jump out. *Except,* this time I want to grab any computers I see—with gravity control, why stop at just moving my own weight around? An armful of hardware should give your hacker what he needs."

"An armful?" Nolan's eyes moved to his shoulder, where he'd been shot months ago.

Mark only grinned and stretched his arm out, feeling only a light twinge now. It had to be some effect of the belts' magic over time; nothing else made sense.

Then Nolan said "That just might do it. Winton can't cover up all the clues to where he's hiding. Not if he's still sending as many emails to this place as *she* tells me." She smiled. "Yes, my hacker's a she. Even on the Macs, I keep my hacking PC."

This time Mark had to force his answering smile. Nolan had to know she just couldn't tell a joke right, but she kept trying.

"Their security looks light, too," she went on.

"I know. Joe Dennard said they should have just the basic Steel alarm package. Unless they tripled it overnight."

"You told Dennard?" She raised an eyebrow, but Mark met her gaze squarely, and she shrugged. "All right then. But have you thought about this: the real risk is liable to start after you leave the place. This time we're stealing from an anti-gang center, and Winton already has his friends among the police. That means the authorities will turn over every carpet fiber for a trace of you. This time, you need to use your magic to smash the site up as if one of the gangs had—"

"No."

"What?"

She glared at him. Mark thought of snapping back, about all the weather damage she'd thrown around trying to stop Winton on her own, but by now he knew that wouldn't convince Nolan. He almost wished she *did* have some magic for reading his mind, if it would stop her eyes from constantly searching his face for one crack in his determination.

Then she said "No broken windows? Is that all your revenge for Angie is worth?"

For a moment Mark heard only his own angry gasp of breath in his ears, and the breeze over the rooftop. With tight control, he said "It's 'worth' still being able to live with myself, when we bring her back. I'm not going to trash a place like that to cover my tracks, or because it *might* hurt Winton—"

He'd gestured out toward the Center as he spoke, but as he turned back a new motion below made him freeze. He knew that white Ford.

It pulled up next to Nolan's car. Mark said "That's Dennard down there."

"What?" Her voice buzzed in irritation. "Is he out here trying to help us, or does he want to scare us off?"

"He's got more reason to do this than we do. But I bet you want to ask him yourself, right?"

Mark searched for people on the street below, then held out his hand to her, trying to make the motion look casual. Only a breath later Nolan gripped it. He gave a rushed "Three-two-one," count to ready her, and they stepped off the roof.

He tried to will just enough antigravity into their bodies to let them sink with something like a smooth elevator's drop, with an extra pull up to slow them well before they neared the pavement. Still, he felt Nolan's fingers clench on his once.

Joe Dennard climbed out of his car, and Mark studied the wounded ex-cop and his cane as they walked to meet him. *All those years growing up, I was so sure Angie's dad had turned vigilante for that one night and I never knew how he'd done it. Now I'm wearing his belt.*

"Is your ex coming too?" Nolan asked Dennard.

Mark winced. The idea of Kate Woodward coming out of hiding was Nolan's weakest joke yet.

"Didn't have to," Dennard said. "Kate could be anywhere in the world, but I'd bet her research did more than your hacker to show this place is Winton's pet project." He tapped his cane on the pavement once, and when Nolan only silently studied his face, he went on "So, don't tell me you're about to level the only anti-gang spot in Lavine that works. When we still don't know what happened there last night."

Mark swallowed and fought the urge to step between the two. *Don't make me play peacemaker here.*

"We were just talking about that," Nolan said. "But no, Winton can keep his building. I thought for a moment you might have a problem with going in at all."

"If it would stop Winton, you could blow it away… but without that, no 'freak windstorms.' Not against this place." Dennard's voice roughened, as if he'd felt the irony of a one-time vigilante holding back now—or, he'd learned the lesson all too well.

Mark said "Of course not. And like you said, if we find that it *would* let us take him down, then nothing's saving the place." The words sounded harsher aloud, but with the stakes what they were…

"That does sound impressive," Nolan said, looking between the two men. "But what would you really do to finish a spellkeeper who's a murderer?" Her eyes settled on Dennard. "You saw your proof. After Angie defeated him it was Winton's body, his real body, that had to be hauled away in that ambulance. But you let him go."

Mark saw Dennard flinch. How could he have guessed that would be the last time any of them would see their enemy in person?

She continued "Neither of you talk about it, but are you still trying to catch this man alive? Do you think he can make Angie whole, when her body's gone, and what's left of her stays away from us—"

"Except when she and I saved your life," Mark cut in.

He glanced at Dennard, but Angie's father had gone stone-faced. Like he was losing hope.

It was too much. Mark took a step clear of the two. "Anyway, I know I'm looking for the Center's computers, that and any hidden clues to Winton's magic. I know what its alarms should be. Anything else?"

"Just, stay ready to pull out," Dennard said. "We know something happened there last night—and the fact that we can't find out what, bugs me. And, don't figure you'll sense everything Winton might have set up there. Or, last night could mean that Rafe Martinez is back, and setting up his own moves against Winton."

Rafe. The first enemy Mark had had, even before the magic, the one who'd outmaneuvered him again and again.

Mark forced a smug smile, and tapped the second belt he wore. "Rafe's just a punk from the Blades that Winton used to look for our secrets. I already beat him once, even when he had this belt—maybe I should *hope* he's still alive, at least we could find out how much Winton got from him. Or how there could be a second gravity belt at all."

He glanced at Nolan, hoping that maybe this time she'd say something about how she managed her own weather magic. Seeing how their two forces were alike might get them closer to working out Winton's power as well. But Winton had been spying after all their secrets, and Nolan didn't share.

All she did was turn away and motion back up toward the building they'd dropped from. "I lined the breeze up to blow you right to the Center, if you start from over there. Or I can change it—"

"Don't need it."

This time Mark didn't pretend to climb. He only took one last glance around the street and leaped straight up. *I'm showing off again,* he thought; arguing with his older partners had been wearing him down. His move brought him rushing up through the damp air along the wall of the building. He took a careful look to aim for the broad notch in the skyline two blocks down, and kicked off against the bricks to launch himself toward Winton's center.

It was the strangest trick the belt's magic had, something he couldn't describe even to Dennard, who'd worn it before him. Instead of floating up or pressing down, he could *hold* the forces around him enough to hang in place, or keep himself on a path he leaped along in spite of the damp air trying to slow his momentum. Mark often thought of how much things would have changed if he could truly "steer" gravity—to turn and maneuver in the sky, like a bird. But following one course should be all the flying he'd need right now.

Simpler than the rest of our "war." If Winton stayed hidden, all they'd ever be was on the defensive. Nolan called them all "spellkeepers," and the fact that they'd managed to "keep" the secrets of how to use their two magics away from Winton's spying might be the only reason Winton hadn't picked them off by now.

Or else Winton needed to have his body recover first.

Or both, if he was watching for signs that the belt's magic actually helped Mark heal.

That felt like a fit punishment—since the one time Winton *had* thought he could eliminate Mark and still leave someone with the belt that he could study, Angie had leaped into the attack instead. So if Winton's injuries gave Mark more time to pry a cure for her out of him…

He took a deep breath of cold air. Flying over the city should be a moment to savor—a chance to look past the buildings' painted front faces and the street paths that some forgotten planner had tried to channel the city's life through. Far off to the left, the shapes lay larger and more spread out in the mist, like pieces from a whole different set of building blocks. After months of flying he'd begun to see the walls and roofs below like different crowds of people: those would be hulking factory men, each crowded into their own territories, and they'd each have their own offspring of storehouses and labs somewhere at their elbows within tonight's gray.

The squat little two-story Center building, crouching between the taller walls that flanked it, was sliding nearer on his right. He pulled down his ski mask and released the energies enough to let the breeze push him over towards it, leaving himself just heavy enough to settle downward and drift in toward its front wall.

Its rough brick lines emerged from the mist, and he still saw no lights inside and no shutters to hide them if there were. He felt none of Winton's magic flickering inside either—*but somewhere there'll be clues leading back to where he's gone. There have to be.*

The roof looked too littered with machinery to land on. Instead he let himself fetch up against the wall like a windblown leaf—with enough momentum left to slam his hands and knees and send him rolling to the side, tumbling once around, before he began sliding down the bricks. Then his elbow caught the top of a window frame, and he dangled in place as he tried to take back just enough weight to settle there, hanging by that elbow alone.

Once his breathing steadied, he felt in the bag at his waist. First he drew out a thick block of plastic, built less like his phone than like some old walkie-talkie: the bug sweeper he'd learned to carry at all times. This time, instead of searching his home for any non-magic tricks that Winton might have left for him, he played it over the window. The display's tiny lights never moved.

"Okay." Of course the sensor was meant to catch radio signals, not most alarms' wiring—but that mainly left simple pressure switches that might trigger if the window swung up. That and the motion sensors they had heard the place shouldn't have. He tucked the detector away and drew out the glass cutter.

Breaking in didn't make him a burglar. Not compared to everything Winton had done.

If only the glass would give way as quickly as in the movies. Mark hung on against the wall, listening and looking around the street below, while his gloved fingers scratched away with the tool.

At last he'd cut out an opening big enough for his shoulders, to the point where a movie spy would have slid the glass out with a suction cup... except that no tugging would have coaxed the "detached" section free of the pane that held it. Instead, Mark simply gave it a slow hard *push*—and before it could fall and shatter, a twist of magic through his fingertips left it floating in the air inside. There was still no sound, not below or within.

With a sigh of shame that two months of searching made break-ins so familiar, he slipped his weightless form through the opening.

Sliding out of the night air was stepping down into stillness, and a hint of an odd chemical smell. The dim light from the row of windows caught and glimmered on the floating pane of glass and guided him to set it down in the corner, restoring its weight again. He'd entered near the end of a long corridor, with doors along the side across from the windows, and stairs going down at the far end.

Now, he just needed a quick look around for the Center's office. It'd probably be right on this floor, not down below where the crowds came through.

He played the bug sweeper over the nearest door frame, more because he had the tool than because he expected there to be alarms it could catch. Opening the door showed him nothing but dim shelves; he entered and closed the door behind him, sealing himself in darkness until he flicked his flashlight on. It shone on near-empty racks dotted with cleaning supplies, a few T-shirts, basketballs... the kind of chores and resources a center might use to lure street kids away from gangs. Just like any businessman "giving back" to the community. As if Roger Winton hadn't been the one manipulating the gangs to flush out the secrets of Dennard's magic.

Had the bastard told the young people who came here the same lies that had strung Mark along? How having some fleeting hobby like

Mark's awkward sketches made those kids important, made them worth a busy entrepreneur's attention over the years?

Mark left the first room and kept going, his soft footsteps the only sound. The next room only held more supplies, but a tightening in his gut made him ask himself once again: *if I somehow walked in on Winton himself, could I kill him?* He'd used to dream of revenge, and now the plan was to catch Winton or spy on him and use his magic's secrets to help Angie... but if Winton gave him no choice?

After Angie, her father's stabbing, the Blades' and the 66s' gang war, and a murdered detective? *Yeah, I think I could kill Winton.* The thought felt small, but with deep, cold roots sunk through his mind. As long as he didn't join Nolan in smashing places for no reason at all—

His light caught the great green chunks of what looked like a shattered ping-pong table, piled up on one shelf. The picture-frames on one side looked just as broken, and he saw what could have been a ruined TV screen behind the table's pieces—the picture fell into place for him.

The building lay as silent as ever, and as clear of magic, but when he pulled out his phone he still kept his voice to a whisper.

"I know what happened last night. Someone already attacked here."

"What? Are you alright?" Nolan's outburst in his ear felt too loud in the tight room.

"It's quiet now. It must have been last night—everything's cleaned up now. Maybe it was Rafe."

The guess felt right. Rafe had lost his place in the Blades from being a pawn in Winton's tricks. If he'd recovered from his clash with Mark and Angie, he could have trashed Winton's anti-gang center just to strike at his old boss.

"Hold on," Dennard's voice cut in. "The place was attacked, and all we heard were rumors of *something*? So they hushed it up; why?"

"Must have. I'll see what's left—"

"Quiet!"

Dennard's warning froze Mark in place. He still heard nothing around him except his heart hammering in his ears. The sharp smell he'd caught when he entered, he should have realized it was fresh paint.

Then Dennard spoke again, harsher than ever. "Silent alarm! It's on the police band—get out of there!"

Mark swung the door wide. The window he'd opened waited just two belt-lengthened strides away…

Instead he turned toward the stairs. Glancing down there first would only add another two floating steps to his escape. It was what Angie would have done; she'd already be *at* the stairs by now. He crept toward the corridor's end.

"This is all wrong," he heard Dennard say, from the phone Mark still had at his ear. "It sounds like some special alert, how'd it get on the regular band—Mark? I can't see you getting out—"

Mark lowered the phone and edged down the stairs. A broad, open space stretched below, almost empty except for the light from its windows. He could just make out several doors scattered along the wall, and a kitchen space. A shaft of light from the street made a wall gleam with fresh paint, but under that smell he caught some whiff of garbage lingering somewhere.

Lights moved outside the front door.

He ducked back out of sight before the door opened. He heard feet on the floorboards as he backed away, then a man's clipped voice: "Clear." A cop.

A woman answered "Clear. I'll check the office."

And you'll show me where that is? But Mark forced his curiosity down and padded back up the stairs. He'd pushed his luck too far already.

He almost missed the strange, strangled cry below. Then he heard one cop's feet running toward it—and thought to feel for magic.

Down where the police were, he felt it: the faint, flickering twist resonating against his own belts' power. Winton's magic was controlling one of their minds.

But, neither of those cops had been possessed when they entered, had they? How had Winton been able to get control of one, without someone touching them?

Mark dove back toward the stairs, while the sounds of the running cop slowed to a halt.

As Mark turned the corner he saw the uniformed man reaching his partner's side. She was staggering back through an open doorway, swaying on her feet like some drunk—with Winton's unseen power twisting through her nerves. Mark opened his mouth and fumbled for some kind of warning they'd believe, but the man only glanced at her, then started past her with his gun leveled at the room beyond.

Just as one brushed against the other, Mark felt the magic shift. Within a heartbeat, the energy jumped from the woman through the man's shoulder—

His arm whipped around to *crack* his gun against her skull. Her body crumpled, falling against his—

The magic flickered back to her, *so fast!* She slumped to the floor, and the man caught at her with one arm, waving his gun around with the other. Oblivious to the fleeting second that his body had been stolen from him.

"C'mon, Bennie—" Mark heard him growl at her, all frenzied concern and rage.

And in that moment, Mark felt another pressure against his own magic. A flicker out beyond the walls, a hint of Winton's form of power but with the ragged feel that he'd always sworn he'd get a chance to sense again. *Angie's found me.*

"Hands! Hands up, bastard!"

The cop's eyes and gun locked on him.

Mark flung himself backward around the corner, one move sending him into the cover he should have stayed behind. He slammed back against the wall, then scrambled to his feet. Magic pulsing, he skipped up the corridor in two giant leaps, straight toward the hole he'd left in the window out.

SHREEE!

The screech blasted through the night outside, and he caught one glimpse of the small gray form darting straight across the dimness beyond. Angie, warning him.

Somehow, Mark twisted his step to pivot away from the window and still keep his balance, his hand catching at the doorknob of the last room in the row. He wrenched the door open, darted inside, and swung it shut to close himself in darkness.

Heart pounding, he held his breath, trying to listen. No sound of the cop charging upstairs, so far. Mark's elbow brushed something in the black, and he remembered the empty shelves; it would be all open space in here, nowhere to hide if anyone looked in.

The cop's low snarl came from beyond the door: "You see him climbing out yet?"

Some muffled answer came. Through the cop's radio.

That's from more police out in the street. They're watching the windows, that Angie warned me not to use!

A door rattled open, down the hall, and he heard the cop take a step inside. He was searching the rooms, one by one. Was that four doors he had left before Mark's, or three?

Mark stared at the crack of light below his door, and struggled to think of options. Just dive out the window and hope they'd be slow to shoot? Grab the cop and slam him to the floor with magic—or get shot trying?

A second door creaked open.

He could press himself to the ceiling to hide; even if the cop looked up, the sight might make him freeze for that one instant Mark needed to move. Hell, he could *stay* on the ceiling and show the cop, show the whole police force, what they were really facing—no, not with this cop furious about his partner being hurt...

Through the hush came another sound: another bird cry, right outside again but smoother, less harsh.

Trust her; that's the best signal I'll get. The third door rattled, the room next to him—and Mark opened his own door.

For two whole heartbeats he moved it slowly, holding it tight to keep the hinges quieter than the cop's foot taking that one step into the next room. But when the door was clear of his path, clearing the corridor only took a single lunge.

He dove through the window, into freedom.

As he hit the night air he *wrenched* himself straight up with a burst of raw power. The street plummeted away below, giving him a shrinking image of a pair of police cars with cops, almost under the window and yet looking away. Something had distracted them just when Angie had signaled. Of course.

In another moment the block shrank away below him. Just a patchwork of lines, graying, gray…

He felt his thoughts going sluggish and eased the energy back. The upward force ebbed, leaving him hanging in space while blood thundered back up to his brain again. A glance down showed he could still make out the "notch" of the Center's lower-roofed block, even in the mist, still not so far below.

The last time Angie floated outside a window, it led to our first kiss, when she was still herself. Now…

Mark craned his neck to search the streets below and the air around, but of course she'd be like a hay-colored needle in a haystack as big as the sky; that was *why* Winton used weapons like the body Angie had had to take over. But, he could feel her power arcing along below. She was close.

One small part of him could still remember the plastic square of the phone clenched in his hand, as he tried to match her course against how the breeze blowing on his side could carry him. When his moment came, he let himself sink and drift with the current down to meet her.

Out of the shadows below, the little shape emerged… too far right, out of reach. Slowly she winged on past him.

Biting down on a shout he wanted to send after her, Mark dropped for the roof below, damp air catching at his coat. He thumped down on concrete, then his shoes skidded and he lurched a step to fall against a chimney. He flinched away at once, before the metal cowling over it could burn his hand.

When he looked around, Angie was swooping down toward him.

It was almost his first clear look at the body she was trapped in. Maybe a foot in length and twice that with spread wings, all in gray-brown feathers that nature had designed to disappear into the night. A glint of metal on her leg. The barn owl's white disk face bore in closer.

Mark remembered his phone again—he stuffed it away and held out his hands for her. He still couldn't catch one sound from her wings against the air, but he sensed the magic she carried gathering itself, like how he was holding his breath.

Her weight came down on his gloved hands, so light—

With the touch, pure cold fire swept through his senses and blotted out the world. Buffeting, tangling tides of energy—he couldn't make out more than the quicksilver Angie-presence whirling within it. She spun through some otherspace, brushing against him, again and again.

She can't get her message through. He reached for his other self, the one back with the body and the belt, grappling for that power to resonate with her own energy—

The world *dimmed,* torrents of power fading to streams and pulling back— He broke off his effort and let the storm rise around him again. Be still, let her come… he felt her twisting somewhere in the mingling forces, tried to be ready to let her in.

She was already on him. Pushing, shaking, struggling to reach into his *self* with whatever she had… eager, wild… useless…

He felt the weight lifting from the hands before he felt those hands were his own again. The maelstrom melted away to leave him back in his flesh, but his body moved so slowly now. His eyes couldn't open, his ears couldn't know if she made a sound as her energy drew away.

"Wait!"

When he said it, his world snapped back into sync. He could stare around the misty rooftop again, see her climbing into the night sky. He stumbled over the roof after her. The power she carried, did it feel weaker now?

Then another energy moved in the dimness above. Toward him. *Winton.*

Mark caught his balance and braced himself. He could only dodge at the exact moment that the other bird attacked, so Winton wouldn't know Mark had sensed him.

Then Angie dove straight at the enemy.

Mark felt the other bird twist away from her talons, quicker than Winton's other spybirds had been. It arced around in the air and curved upward. Positioning for its own attack.

Mark leaped up, rocketing after the killer's tool, before the cold thought caught him in midair: *if he triggers his magic as we touch...*

But the bird was already swinging clear of Mark's clumsy path. It turned and closed in on Angie, and she could only veer off along the rooftops. Too slow now.

A wrench of his magic stopped Mark from overshooting them farther, but that cost him his momentum and he could only drop helplessly back through the empty air, tracking as one tiny pulse of power bore down on the other. Angie had to be in the shadows near that roof, and she dove again, spending what altitude she had left to flit down into the concrete gaps below. Where she'd have even less room to dodge, with her enemy close behind her.

She wasn't trying to escape. Was she... keeping Winton's eyes down there to lose sight of Mark?

He tensed as the slope of a roof rushed up, the springboard he could use to leap after them. But he'd only miss them again, he'd *always* miss them if he tried to outfly actual wings.

Trust her. Use the distraction she's fighting to give me.

The Youth Center had been somewhere to the left. Mark broke into a leaping, magic-stretched stride as soon as his feet hit the roof, crossing it in four steps with one more to leap to the next building. Another leap above the street, faster now… each step off concrete or tile or brick was faster, flinging him through the cold mist. His sense of the aerial duel behind him faded out of his range, with Angie's weakened presence dwindling first. But, she'd always beaten Winton before.

Lights moved below. Between the roofs ahead he caught a glimpse of a police car charging away up one street, then as he crested another roof he saw that the other car was already gone. They'd rushed out searching for him, leaving the door open—and he'd only need a minute.

Unless he stopped to think.

One leap forward, one down to the street with a glance around as he dropped, then he hurled himself through the Center's doorway.

Three long steps ahead was the office door the police had found. On the first step, as he squinted through the bright building lights again, Mark saw the injured woman cop, still lying slumped by the wall. *The others have to be near.*

His momentum couldn't slow, but he made his second step come down ghost-light. In the same instant he felt ahead for whatever magic Winton had left to seize intruders in his office—

The power lay *behind* him. His head twisted around, he saw the cop sitting up, gun swinging up in her still-possessed hands.

Too late. Mark tumbled through the office doorway and bounced off a desk, careening to a stop against the wall. He tottered sideways, trying to find cover, but the room barely gave him a few steps either way. No other doors, and no windows.

No flicker of Angie anywhere in range. But she *had* to be alright.

He waited, trapped. And yet… the cop didn't close in. He could hear her shuffling to her feet, and felt Winton's magic starting her toward the door, but so *slowly*. She could have put a bullet in him by now, or called for other cops.

He thought of how fast Winton's control had jumped between the two police officers before, too quick for either of them to realize what had happened… and, he was always trying to spy out the secrets of the belt's magic…

"You *can't* shoot me, can you?" Mark laughed. The sound came out hoarse, and he still moved aside from the doorway. If he was wrong, if Winton *was* ready to explain away Mark's body and find other ways to learn their magic—

He sensed the cop still edging toward the doorway. Mark flexed his fingers, praying he could grab and strike before Winton jumped through that touch. The smell of paint pressed at his nose.

The lights went out.

A flash of memory came: Nolan outside another of Winton's offices, promising *If you need a distraction, I'll freeze the power lines*. He blinked wildly, fighting to push the flood of shadows back and make out where the outlines in the room had been.

Over what had to be the police radio came a sharp "What the hell? Bennie?"

"I'm alright!" the woman under Winton's control answered.

Mark blinked harder. His enemy *was* giving him a moment to work, not calling in the other cop. But that other cop could decide to rush in at any moment. So… there, that blocky shape sitting beside the table's leg would be the computer he'd come for.

One quick step and he reached behind the box to rip a handful of cables from its back, then *snapped* the last wire away, half-expecting to hear sparks popping.

Behind him, the cop moved in.

Mark twisted around to glimpse the woman stepping toward him, her empty hand reaching out—*closing in to touch, ready to grab my mind!* He flung himself backward, and his arm swung out into a scooping motion and slammed into the table.

Pain shot through his knuckles and his injured shoulder, but his magic surged, and he heard the whoosh and the clamor of flying objects and a great *crash* as he flung the near-weightless table at the cop and it glanced off her to clatter against the wall.

It did little more than make her flinch back, but that gave him the moment he needed to stumble to his feet and snatch up the desktop computer, lightening it too. She was already turning back toward him, still blocking the doorway.

He raised the computer like a shield and charged.

He slammed into her and flung her back, and burst on through the doorway to finally stretch his steps into a leaping run that swept him away from her across the room and barely aimed low enough to slide his head under the front doorway to dart through and *out.*

As he burst onto the street he saw a police car parked a block up, and heard a shout from behind him. But out in the open air and with his memory of the block's layout, he only needed to twist to the side and scramble for the corner, fighting the urge to make his steps too long, too obviously unnatural. His hands clutched the weightless computer. Once he rounded the corner and slipped from their sight, he flung himself for the sky.

The buildings fell away, and he saw the police car closing in, far too late to see his escape. At the corner of his mind he felt Winton's grip on the cop *vanish.*

But still, there was no trace of Angie. He could crisscross the whole city for a sign that she had escaped, running the belts dry, but he'd never found her that way before. And Winton had never outflown her; she had to be safe.

Settling on a rooftop, he finally remembered the others again, and pulled out his phone. "Did you get clear?" he gasped.

"*Get* clear?" Dennard snapped. "We're fine—but what the hell happened with you? Did you *stay* in there? Are you out of your mind?"

Could be, Mark thought, as his heartbeat began to settle. But what he said was "It worked. I guess you didn't see what she did—and, I got the computer! And you're..." The map's lines were fresh in his head, from his movement through the air. "Heading north?" he guessed.

"No, back to the lake," Nolan said.

"I'll find you."

The weightless bulk of the desktop in his arms barely slowed him now, as he alternated long jumps across the blocks with higher lifts to scan the streets for friends or pursuit. He kept hoping he'd sense Angie drawing into range behind him, but she still never came to share their victory. *His* victory, with a raid so split-second that even she would have called him insane. His trembling, shocked muscles told him it *would* be madness if he ever ran a risk like that again.

Down below, within blocks of the route he'd predicted, he saw a white car and a blue one inching along a back street. They looked well clear of any search the police might spread out from the robbery site. The first car slowed at a stop sign, and he closed the last of the distance and let his path dip toward them.

And then he sensed the bird. Not Angie's rougher resonance, but one of Winton's spies winging in from behind him.

I could pull up—but, he's already seen me angling for this street. Mark could only drop down to the asphalt and scramble toward his friends.

Dennard's car was the one in back. His window slid down as Mark raced up.

"How close are they?" the ex-cop demanded.

"Not the police," Mark said. "Winton's got a bird chasing us."

Dennard spoke into the phone he had in his hand. "You get that? I'll keep behind you."

Mark heard the click of locks, and he pulled the back door open and dove into the seat, fumbling to set the computer down safely. The moment he shut the door behind him, Dennard started them up, driving with the same cautious glide as anyone who might be out at this late hour. Not that fooling the police was the problem anymore.

"Well?" came Nolan's voice through the phone's speaker. "You're the spotter, Mark: what's the bird doing?"

"Just following us. He could be setting up an attack—or staying with us until we lead him somewhere." Just like with the possessed cop, the real battle wasn't about shooting: they were all chasing hints about each other's magic. "We could find a clear street and outrun him—but we'd need the highway, that's all the way down at—"

"I know," Dennard said. "Sounds too easy. But we make a run for it, and watch for what other tricks he'll have ready."

"Why give him a chance?" Nolan said.

Her car pulled over to the curb ahead. Dennard brought their own to a stop behind it, and Mark could picture Nolan's eyes gleaming as she went on:

"Mark. Just how well can you point that bird out?"

A slow grin spread across his face. He twisted his head to stare out the car window, and tried to overlay the bird's flicker in his mind with the dim shapes he could see.

"Behind us. Closing in—not way up, don't look for movement against the sky. Along the walls across the street, fourth shop back, no, third—"

A rushing sound gathered outside, as if a train had whooshed by but without a single clatter of wheels, and the view through the windows went mad with churning mist. The car *rocked* an inch and then settled back from the great slap of wind. Shapes that might have been trash flew by, and Mark heard spatterings against walls and breaking glass. And Winton's magic...

"He's gone," Mark said. "And not flung away in the wind, I mean the power's vanished."

The mist began to settle, and Nolan stepped out of her car. "Do you think that hurt the real Winton too? I wish I'd called *pull* first."

"From skeet shooting, right?" Mark grinned back. He climbed out, remembering the feel of Angie killing one of Winton's birds and leaving the puppetmaster in an ambulance… but this time… "I think his control magic was still moving when it disappeared, like the bird hadn't crashed yet and he could bail out in time. But I don't know, sensing his power is different from spotting ours, I don't even feel his energy until he's using it. I don't know how he caught that cop in the Center—"

"He possessed one of them?" Dennard said. "Think, did you see anyone else there who could have touched the victim, maybe an animal? Isn't that how he gets them?"

"I always thought so—but I didn't see one. Maybe it's different if Winton had the trap prepared, or something, but I didn't sense it. I never caught any magic on Winton himself either until he used it—except the one time I sensed that trace of it on him, and catching it that time pretty much split my head open…"

Mark's words wound down as he realized he was rambling. Dennard only looked at him, unspeaking, and Mark evaded those eyes to follow Nolan's gaze. She was slowly scanning the battered street, as if hoping to spot the bird's body.

"So you'd seen that Winton had booby-trapped the place, and you went back in anyway," Dennard sighed. "To steal a computer."

"Yeah. Right here." Mark reached back into the car and drew out the battered desktop. "I had to tear the cables out, but it's just the hard drive we want, isn't it?"

Nolan took the computer. "I'd say so. I'm sure Winton will change his passwords and the rest—again—but my hacker keeps telling me it's about finding patterns now. And the Youth Center is the place he stays most in contact with." She set the computer in her car.

Dennard sighed again. "But Mark, you said someone hit the Center before you. This machine might be just a day-old replacement, with no history on it."

"It doesn't matter if it is!" Mark felt the words tumbling out again: "Listen, I saw her! Angie was *there,* she's the one who warned me there were more police outside! And when Winton flew up at me before, she led him away to let me go back and get this."

Her father's face went tight; Mark could *see* the spasm of hope flash across it. "Angie's alright? She's back helping us again?"

Mark stepped closer, leaning nearer to Dennard's window as he went on. "She has to be! This time she even tried to reach my mind again, same as when she showed me she was the owl. We couldn't get through to each other, not really—and then Winton's bird dove in. I should have kept after her…"

"But where is she now?" Nolan was shaking her head, slowly. "Mark, think a moment: if Winton's bird followed us here, and Angie didn't… then either she couldn't get away from him, or she didn't want to join us. That's hardly 'helping us again.' " Her voice softened, but she kept her eyes on his. "And none of us understands how her mind was pulled into the owl in the first place. Or—"

"Or how much of her mind was, is that it? You going to tell me there's not enough of her left to save?"

He heard his voice sharpening as he spoke. Could she really be trying to warn him off, when hope was all that kept him going? From the corner of his eye he saw Dennard watching; it was hard to guess what he believed.

"Well, she came to us tonight, anyway," Mark said. "And what's left of Winton's bird might be lying *right* here somewhere." Changing the subject was easier than arguing.

He stared along the wind-battered storefronts, as the still-settling mists sifted around them, trying to find the shape of a lifeless bird amid all the piled-up litter. Police sirens sounded in the distance, too close for them to linger long.

They found nothing.

CHAPTER TWO

HEADS AND TAILS

The wind whispered along the black, bare streets, and to Mark walking down among them they seemed to stretch forever into the night. But he knew the subway station was waiting one block ahead and to the left, he remembered it as clearly as if he could see it. And of course it would only take a thought to shift upward and close the distance by air.

Pace yourself. Even after a night like this.

Instead he marched on past Lawry Street's near-silent apartments, with his eyes and his magic sense flicking around the night for police cars, or Winton's power, or anyone who might be following him. His feet ached worse than his nearly-healed shoulder—but any corner Mark failed to make a sudden turn around might be the one too-careless move that would let Winton follow him to the park and learn everything he'd need to recharge the belts himself, to learn their magic. And be free to kill them all.

Between glances around, he pulled out his phone and texted Kate: *I saw Angie. She warned us about the police. Winton had them watching his Youth Center.* So few words on the dim screen, launched out to who-knew-where, to tell Kate that her daughter was still alive.

Why was he only slinking back to restore his weakened magic and call it a night, and not leaping every rooftop in the city to catch that flicker of Angie's energy again and *make* her believe they'd find an answer? But he forced a wry smile to stop his teeth from clenching. Following the siren call of the belt again without a proper break would only take him closer to being the shivering, magic-addicted thing he'd once been.

When he reached the subway and the train, the seat was all too soft.

Worse, the rattle of the train fought with his memory's effort to hold onto that brief sense he'd felt of Angie touching his mind. He transferred at the Bend, where he could run across the platform just in time to catch the northwest train and spot if anyone followed him over. The only attention he drew was from a twitching druggie that shuffled toward him from the other end of the new car, and backed away when Mark stood up. Skinny though he was, Mark's height and maybe something in how he carried himself these days had kept more than one troublemaker away.

At last he returned to the streets above, and the air felt colder than ever. Mark wrapped his coat tight and walked faster, plotting turn after turn in his head. A few short hops to the park to bring the belts back to full power, and he could go home and rest at last. Tomorrow they should have data from the computer he'd taken, and maybe more luck in comparing the original magic belt from Angie's family with the one Rafe had somehow gotten. The one that seemed to carry magic with ordinary modern leather, when even Kate had lost the secrets of how their own talismans were made.

His head turned toward a shop window he passed. In its darkened displays he saw a set of jackets… his research into leathermaking should let him recognize their different materials even through the glass.

Again, he checked for other magic around him, and caught the faint pressure winging toward him up above. And with none of that certain ripple he knew was Angie—this bird was Winton's.

Not now, not now! Mark's eyes darted around, looking for cover, but the street was empty. The new spybird must have already seen him.

Useless, strangled rage clenched in his stomach as Mark started to walk. He had been so *close* to the park… he fought to keep each step the exact same brisk pace as the last. His coat covered the fact that he wore two belts, but if he *did* feel the bird start to dive down for a possessing touch…

Neck tense with the strain of not looking up, he paced by the next corner, and the next, before he risked a turn west to begin a twisting route toward his home. *Mustn't be too quick to pull away from Rosewood Park. I have to treat it as just another landmark, and not the pulsing source of the power that made Winton shatter our lives trying to flush it out.*

But soon, somehow, it'll be our turn to get your secrets. For Angie, and to pay you back.

* * *

"—told you I'll call him, just give me one goddamn minute…"

The Golds in the apartment down the hall were at it again; it was Mark's first awareness when his eyes opened. His second was to roll over and glance at the plastic sheeting under the door that screened out any tiny intruders that might be possessed. The tall bookcase shielded his window from aerial spies.

Mark pulled himself to his feet and powered on his ancient computer to sort through its umpteen new security layers. Angie's belt lay with his clothes on the floor near his bare mattress. Touching it let him feel Rafe's belt, also safe, in the drawer where he'd left it… and he realized that he'd already gone a few seconds awake without checking them. Good, a night's sleep had the magic's addictive grip already loosening again.

He pulled a sandwich together from the fridge. The Golds' argument stopped and restarted twice before the Dell was fully online.

At least the risks they'd run at the Center were paying off. One of Nolan's untraceable emails had a huge zip file she called simply *latest raw data*. And it was only mid-morning; her hacker worked fast.

Still…

Mark tried. For more than an hour he scrolled and sorted through the Youth Center's emails and browser history and the wider patterns of use that he tried to follow. But all of Winton's emails were from before he'd vanished. And nothing gave a clue where Winton might go, or even a glimpse into his thoughts beyond helping people stay *out* of gangs.

"Do you really think the girl has a temper, or just a history with this one person…"

"If your friend says nobody hires mechanics, he's not your friend…"

And even when Roger Winton gave advice, he never mentioned anything personal—not about growing up in schools in Europe, not even losing his own father in a fire. But he knew how to get people talking… just like it had only taken him a few dollars and a bit of praise to string Mark along for *years,* until Winton had enough cause to turn that "friendship" into pumping him about the Dennards and their secrets.

Mark's eyes locked on the sketch pads he'd shoved into the corner. Years of struggling to draw, of hanging on the few words Winton dropped, in that rushed, well-meaning tone that made him grateful for a few minutes of his time. All of it just being used.

He let out a slow breath. Why let the past get to him? The files had to bring them closer to making things right.

"And I can fly," he whispered. "Even got a job that uses how I see the city, besides the secret that nobody around me would dream of. That has to count as making something of myself."

And half of it was breaking into buildings and beating back an addiction. But not like his drug-dealer father, not when this fight was to bring Angie back. He forced himself to breathe, slowly, calmly.

When his phone beeped a text, it was a relief to look over up at the screen.

Until he saw the message: *Do you want our fighting to end?*

And the sending address said only *W.*

He stared at that single letter; his gaze tried to skewer the message in place as if he could stab through to the man behind it, but it blurred and swam under his eyes the harder he looked.

So Winton could still use his number, as if he thought Mark would actually fall for any more of his tricks? Mark's fingers strained, only inches from the screen and the taps that could answer the killer and begin sounding out what he was after now… But Dennard and Nolan had both warned him—too many times—not to deal with Winton alone.

The phone's security would hold. It had to.

He shot off some reflexively-tapped alert text to both allies, and his fingers cramped with the effort of touching only their names when Winton's message lay only a twitch away.

Winton sent again: *Be careful who sees how well you're healing.*

Mark dragged his hands away from the screen's temptation. There again, it was the magic being noticed that worried Winton? Also, he'd focused on Mark's shoulder recovering… was that it, had Angie's attack left Winton's body so damaged he wanted the belt to help him heal?

And just last night, Mark had kept Winton away from Rosewood's secret. The thought brought a smile… holding his hands back and leaving Winton to stew in silence was becoming easier, and more satisfying.

Then came: *Do you want her human again?*

His breath locked, then hissed out in a harsh "How *dare* you—" What the hell were Dennard and Nolan doing, ignoring his calls for help, when they were the ones who'd insisted nobody deal with Winton alone?

"One word we tell him would be too much," he sighed; that's how Nolan had put it. Anything would be giving Winton a fraction more knowledge about what they fought for, what they had and what they still needed. Even by showing which bait Mark took.

Instead he hunched in the hard chair, picking through what he would have said—something about Winton having burned this bridge long ago with all his other lies—and watched the screen for the killer's next move. Maybe a treacherous hint at some deal that would restore Angie, or a tease that there'd be less and less of her to save…

The screen was still. Mark sat staring and blinking at it until his slowing heartbeat told him he'd accepted that there would be nothing more. Then he rechecked the phone's security apps, and sent the texts' data to Nolan and Dennard. Maybe Nolan's hacker could find something.

When he picked up the sandwich again, he couldn't taste it at all.

* * *

He had another hour before work, and it seemed to take forever. Staring at Winton's files only tightened the headache left from facing taunts from the killer himself. But soon, driving his cab again would be one more chance to search for Angie and Winton on his own—and, keeping the job was one thing he did for himself.

At last he gave up on Winton's records, and took out a city map, one of the older ones in his collection. The paper spread over most of his table. Was it two or three blocks, that his sense for magic could reach? As he had done so many times, he set a finger on one street corner and another three blocks away on each side, and began moving them to measure the areas he could search at once.

A knock at the door made him whirl. And he'd forced himself to leave the belt at his bedside too.

"Is this a bad time?" Dennard's voice called.

"Checking up on me?" Mark made it a joke, but he knew it had to be true. "Give me a minute." He buckled the belt on, felt for enemy magic around, then opened the door.

Dennard hobbled in, and Mark wondered what the man noticed in the tiny room. The two extra chairs Mark had for guests, both folded up against the wall now? The stack of letters from his father in prison, still unopened and stacked in a corner?

They're a reminder, he wanted to explain.

Instead he set out one chair beside the table and the computer. "I was going to send the Center's files to Kate. If anyone can trace a business to its hidden connections, it's a lawyer living in hiding herself. Or, did you already do that?"

"No," Dennard said; was that a hint of awkwardness in his voice? Then he sighed "I don't *think* Winton had something following me here."

"I don't sense anything now. He tried me last night, before the texts today, but I'm being careful. On the street and on the phone." But Dennard wouldn't have sensed Winton at all, even if he'd had a belt. Mark wondered if that was why he wouldn't take one now, if he was more afraid he couldn't protect its secrets than of how its power made the user want more magic.

"Careful? Are you being careful about Rafe?" Dennard's words broke into Mark's thoughts. "Mark, you look like you're holding up, and this limiting your magic could be working so far. But Rafe won't be playing Winton's waiting games. The last time you got in his way... if his bullet hadn't been a hair off, we'd have nobody who could spot Winton's magic. They'd be free to tear the city apart, and any chance of helping Angie would be long gone."

A fraction later, he added,

"That and, you'd be dead."

Cold twitched and ached in Mark's shoulder, but a worse pain came at hearing Dennard's pause. Was that what Mark was to him now, a tool for saving his daughter—and one that still hadn't delivered?

Mark tried to wave it off with "But we still did save Nolan from them that night, from both of them. So you think the damage to the Center was Rafe? He's making a move again?"

"We have to assume it is." Dennard made a small smile—an apology? "From what I can hear, there's some… sound on the streets… that someone struck the place for standing up to the gangs."

"To get Rafe the attention? Sounds like him, always trying to show he's the best. Plus he's hitting a place that belongs to the man who used to give him his real orders?" Mark sighed. "But, Rafe and Winton—that's the thing that still bugs me. Winton was using Rafe to pressure you and me to bring our magic out where he could see it…"

"We think." Dennard raised a finger. "But it fits with all the moves they've made, and spying's still the best reason why Winton's staying hands-off with us. At least so far, but we—all—have to be ready if that changes."

"All of us, right. But then… how'd *Rafe* get his own belt, and leave Winton still waiting to steal our magic? What's that say about our chance of getting Winton's?"

Mark stood up, and stepped to the battered corner chest to slide open a drawer. He held up Rafe's belt, all new leather that could be a common dress belt. Then he opened another drawer—using separate spaces were Dennard's idea, so if Winton broke in the pieces were too scattered to show a pattern—and pulled up a wallet and a keychain, both samples of different kinds of leather he'd gathered. Dennard had to see he'd been working toward Angie's cure.

Mark explained "Rafe's smart. Sure, maybe he found some whole other spellkeeper to make this for him, but all that seems like too much for us to have missed. What I think is, making them *isn't* some complicated process, not if Rafe figured it out and a real spellkeeper like Winton hasn't. If I can make some of these work as a talisman…" He glanced at the pieces in his hands, then pocketed the keychain for the next time he made it to the park. "If one of them works, it could mean it'll be easier to figure out Winton's own magic too, and *that* puts us closer to bringing Angie back—"

He stopped there, startled by how the words had built up speed as he went. But Dennard only sat there, listening.

"Anyway, it's all worth it if it ends up with an answer for her. And if we find the right body to put her in."

"A lot of ifs," Dennard said. "The more I try to learn about coma patients, the more I know what a gamble it is, picking one."

His body seemed to shrink inward where he sat, just a fraction, and Mark caught an edge of pain in his voice.

I've had the easy part. Dennard had to look at unmoving faces, trying to choose which one might become his own daughter's. Or knowing Angie might end up trapped inside a head that wouldn't have the strength to wake up, ever. None of them knew how they'd explain it, or if this was even possible—

Do not *let that thought in.*

"There's always a way, right?" Mark said. But those words were Angie's too.

Dennard didn't answer, didn't move, for long moments.

Then he leaned back in the chair. "Here's one thing, Mark. I used to argue with Kate that her family could have gotten the belt and the other scraps from some kind of other dimension. That could be why they could pick up its power, when we call out the right words from the place in our world where that one's close enough to pull its energy in. The two of us had years trying to come up with theories like that. Since her parents never gave her the real answers."

"You... never said any of that," Mark said, and settled slowly in his chair. What did that mean? That the *Made in Sha Ta Ruath* stamped on the first belt was a clue about more than what the magic words were?

Then Dennard shook his head. "Not so likely now—Rafe's version looks like it's straight out of any shop. But, Kate's favorite guess was that what we were saying was the name of some spirit. And when we used its power, it was some of its craziness that got into our heads. No surprise that after she lost control with the belt once, she'd never touch it again."

He looked at the floor, then leaned slowly forward.

"And never trust me again, because I still just had to keep the thing," he added. His eyes were too close to Mark, too sharp.

Mark's mouth was dry. "What are you saying?"

"Just, think about that. The next time one of your breaks between magic seems too long, and you think it's safe to go back to it early, think about what kind of presence you could be letting into your head."

"I… I will."

Mark managed a nod, and to keep himself from flinching back from that intense gaze. *No wonder Angie always paced the room.*

He had to say something—for the warning, for how Dennard had talked about his dying, for everything they still had ahead…

All he could say was "Either way, the easier the power is to call, the better we can figure out how to help her."

"Or the more Rafe can abuse it, the same way Winton does his own power," Dennard sighed. The fierceness in his eyes pulled back. "Rafe already knows it better than we do."

And we're back to that. "I said I'll keep an eye out for him. Or…"

He'd known Rafe longer than Dennard had. The scheming street leader *did* know something about the belts, and about Winton too, and he'd turned against Winton already. Mark had tried to bargain with him before, and Rafe had always tried to draw him into the gangs…

Dennard's eyes were narrowing, watching him.

"I'll be careful," he said again.

* * *

Work should have been a release, a chance to show off his eye for the streets. But today, weaving his taxi between the lanes only meant wrenching the steering wheel around again and again, until he could let his passengers out and take a moment to test if his arm was aching from the fading wound. At every block he passed, he took an instant to still his mind and feel for magic around him. Each time might be the one he found himself near Angie or Winton—but it never was.

Push on through.

Still, he found himself near the Fishhook Bar when the afternoon sun began creeping westward. Just on the chance of catching his cousin there, he couldn't resist calling in a break and heading down the street at almost a trot. His rumpled clothes caught an unfriendly look from the business types he rushed by.

He'd expected the visit to be a waste. And yet, when he stepped into the darkness of the bar, almost the first person his blinking eyes saw was Henry.

Mark smiled at his cousin's surprised look. It *had* been a while since they'd met here, before the magic and the fighting, and he knew Henry didn't usually get out of the office so early.

Mark stepped over to the scowling bartender and ordered a coffee, before the graying man could ask for ID about anything stronger, and moved on to Henry's tiny table. Picking his way through the room with its dim lights and black walls would have had him stumbling a few months ago, but now he slipped easily around the mostly-empty tables. Some kind of piping music hung in the air.

I still don't know if I should be seen with Henry, with all the trouble I might have on my tail. Well, I'll have to make it quick.

He dropped into the other chair and leaned over; Henry's bad back kept him from leaning closer himself.

The whispered words burst out of Mark. "Last night—"

"Wait, wait!" Henry frowned through his beard. "You rush in, you're talking so fast... Stop and think. You're keeping *it* with you full-time now; are you sure you're alright?"

"I'm—" Mark broke off, and took a deep slow breath to show he was calm. He'd given Henry enough reason to worry when Angie "died"—of course he was worried Mark might be overdosing on the belt's power again. "I'm okay. I haven't even had a chance to pick up any more of it lately. Today's been more stuck in waiting gear than anything else.

"But the real thing is: last night I saw Angie. She flew right off, but she *is* still helping us!"

Once he'd gotten those words out, he leaned back again, and grinned. He saw Henry smile too… but only for a moment, and then the smile narrowed.

"That's good to hear. But, have you thought about what you're doing next? Besides all the risks—"

"*Whatever it takes* is what I'll do. That's what I promised myself, and—"

Henry glanced past Mark's shoulder, and his face changed. Even in the dimness, Mark could see he'd gone pale.

No magic nearby, Mark sensed in the instant he turned, feet shifting ready to fling himself clear of the table. But he didn't see Winton or Rafe or any threat he knew; instead a dark-haired young woman stood behind him in a fine blouse that almost shimmered in the dim light. Her gaze was fixed on Henry.

And Henry's own suit looked a notch or two more trim than Mark remembered him normally wearing to work… *Did I just barge in on a blind date?*

Mark slid from the chair and stepped to one side, while Henry motioned—suddenly, anxiously—for her not to back away.

Her voice was soft. "No, you two finish—"

"My cousin was pretty much done, right?" Henry said.

"Cousin?" She turned. "This is the 'Mark' you used to put up?"

"For a few years—" and Mark pulled his thoughts back from his startled nerves and frustration at being interrupted; *he* was the outsider here. He glanced between the two again. *I have been out of touch, Henry's already been dating her, but not long enough that my clumsiness can't make it awkward between them.*

He managed a smile. "But, 'put up with' me was more like it," he added.

"This… is Christa." Henry's eyes still flicked between the two, but less nervously now.

Christa took a moment to wave the bartender over, and squeeze another chair in at the undersized table. Then she hesitantly asked "So, what do you do, Mark?"

For an instant Mark thought of answering 'bird science,' just to fit in better with this upscale couple. Instead he looked squarely at Christa and gestured to the coffee in front of himself. "Right now I'm a cab driver."

"Oh? You got the job—" Henry's pleased voice broke off in mid-sentence.

"He means I got the *replacement* job," Mark added, and he whispered behind the back of his hand to give it a conspiratorial tone. "I had problems with the boss of the last cab company—" *since it was Winton*—"so I made the competition hire me."

" 'Made them' hire you?" she said.

Mark winced; now he was bragging to Henry's date? But he answered "The company has an express service, that you call if you simply have to get somewhere on a deadline. I've put in a lot of time learning my way through the streets—" *and seeing them from above*— "so I took on their best driver in a race, and then reminded the boss that if he didn't want me, all I really needed was a ride-sharing app to get fares on my own."

Mark's stomach still clenched at the memory of bullying Charles like that, but it had been easier with the race for proof. And if he could face down Olivia Nolan, he could stand up to anyone.

But Christa smiled, and this time he saw it reach her eyes. "That's a good piece of marketing. If you keep thinking like that you'll own the company someday—if that's what you want," she added quickly.

What I want *is one damn break in hunting down—* Like a weight pressing down on him again, Mark felt his real work squeezing out the pleasant rhythms of chatting. He went for the opening she'd given him: "Not really. I borrowed the whole trick from Henry. Or didn't he tell you how he walked into the office and sketched the pictures for their new campaign before their eyes?"

Christa's eyes turned to her date, and Mark saw his cousin flush.

"Anyway," and Mark stood up, "I should get back to my cab before the rush hour calls come in."

"I see." Christa held out her hand to shake. "It was good to meet you. A pleasant surprise."

"Wait, wait," and Henry stumbled to his feet. "Mark, are you sure you're—"

"I'm doing *fine*. Really, I came by to say I'll be too busy to talk much for the next while, but I'm fine."

Mark took a moment with the bartender to cover their first round; it took a bigger bite from his day's tips than he'd thought, but it seemed like the best way to keep the mood light. Henry deserved that much, and more. He dashed back to his cab.

This time when he sat down, he slid Angie's belt off his waist and tucked it under a newspaper beside the seat, and folded Rafe's up in the glove box. Physically separating himself from the full-sized belts might help their addicting effect wear off faster. And he still had one of the spare strips of leather ready in his pocket.

His next fare was only nine blocks away. After passing the first block he made another instant's test for magic. A second block, a third...

Something flickered down at the next corner. Not one of Winton's birds, but Angie herself.

Practice guided the cab on around the corner, between the cars as smoothly as if his mind weren't racing with *what's she doing? What does it mean that we meet now?* The traffic flowed too thick around him, all part of the busy district and the afternoon hour; the growing crowd on the sidewalks would never let him just step out and float up to meet her.

But her magic was clear, gliding away somewhere above the street ahead. Mark stared up through the windshield for a glimpse of the owl.

Maybe she hadn't seen him. He reached for the horn, but scattered honks were already part of the thick traffic. Instead he revved the engine—loud, sharp, and frustrated.

Did her presence *twitch* in its path, was that her looking back?

Mark slid between two cars trying to gain on her. But the more he watched, the more her energy seemed to drift to the right. By the next block she wouldn't be over the street at all… and that would be the long block with the Ganz department store, he'd have no chance to turn and stay with her.

Angie must be heading toward something, I just have to keep up. He yanked the car rightward before the last turn passed; if the next light wasn't too slow he could dogleg back over and stay close to her path. He could feel the cars pressing tighter around him as she moved further away. If her destination wasn't somewhere near, he'd have to either jump out or let her go.

She turned, swinging around away from him.

No no no— With no chance for a U-turn, Mark swung toward the curb, chased by the burst of honking behind him. He slowed… and she twisted again, circling further away.

The shoppers at the curb looked too crowded, too likely that one of them would dive into his taxi if he stopped. Angie was already nearing the edge of his range.

He pulled the cab out into traffic again, hoping she'd slow until he found a way back around, knowing she wouldn't. She simply hadn't seen him, that had to be it. Those sudden flight changes couldn't be her trying to shake him off, or her flitting around like some simple bird…

He held onto that thought until he wove his way back. Too late.

She was gone, and he could only turn around to pick up his next passenger and try to keep the scowl off his face.

What had Christa asked him, "If that's what you want"? *What I want is some real line on our enemy, not just brushes with Winton or Angie that only melt away and leave me with more searching, more guessing, always watching every move around me.*

"Whatever it takes," he muttered, the same as he'd told Henry. The words made it a little easier to pick up his fare with a smile and a nod. Then the next one. Then came the third.

He was pulling up to the hotel the call had come from when he recognized the hulking man under the ski cap. Waiting for him.

The Eel—Franklin Harris, Dennard had said his name was. The leader of the Blades, the man who'd once competed with his lieutenant Rafe over who could kill Dennard first. Mark's hands ached to swing the taxi into the street and leave his "fare" there at the curb. But if the Eel had used the call to bring Mark to him, the truce between them might still be holding.

Anyway, anything to keep the man away from Dennard, and Henry.

Mark brought the cab right up and slid the window down. *Let him think his disguise fooled me.* "So, the airport? Just buckle up and lean back."

The Eel squeezed himself into the back seat, and Mark felt the car's suspension shift at the weight. But the strip of leather was waiting in his pocket, tingling with enough power to crush at least one enemy if he needed. Mark twisted the car out into traffic.

"Just stay on this street… Mark," and the pale face in the mirror smiled grimly. "I'm thinking we don't need to rush." The Eel's eyes had the dead, unflinching look that even Rafe only showed now and then.

Mark kept the pedal down, and his voice came out steady. "You're paying for speed, and you'll get it. Unless you need all afternoon to say something."

He forced a smile onto his lips. The Eel must be too far from the Blades' territory, to notice they were staying on Zeeb, where one of the smaller police stations would be just two blocks ahead. Pulling over there should make the gang leader keep himself in check.

The Eel's deep voice softened. "Or you're thinking if the cab doesn't slow down, I can't risk it crashing if I shoot you."

Mark felt his eyes widen, just for an instant—and in the mirror, the Eel nodded. The gang leader had angled his head just right to catch that flash of fear in the glass.

Mark's heart pounded faster, harder, as he felt his control of the moment slipping. *Hold on! I keep saying I have to be someone as strong as these killers. Just keep him distracted.*

"Oh, so you *do* need two hours in traffic to talk?" he countered. "And it is to talk, isn't it? I'm not your enemy, we agreed it was your own man Rafe who was trying to start that gang war, and everyone knows it."

"He should have killed you by now."

Even with them in the cab's private world, the Eel's voice had fallen so low Mark had to strain to hear it… and to fight the urge to ease up on the throbbing engine to make the words clearer. He slipped the car through a yellow light.

One block left to safety.

The Eel went on "Rafe always did like to pick the right enemies. Or said he did."

"Except when he picked you, you're saying?" Mark prompted him.

"I'm saying. But now he's got whispers going—one of our buys shot up, a girl chased off her corner, and how it's always Rafe Martinez showing he owns the street, not the Blades. You heard?"

"Maybe." It did sound like Rafe and his plays for influence, his years trying to impress everyone from the gangs to Mark himself. Mark didn't mention the attack on the Center, he'd save that for if he needed a distraction.

Please let the last light stay green a little longer—

"Pull up at the next block." The Eel's grin stretched wider. "By the police station."

Somehow, Mark kept the wheel steady as they eased down the street. The Eel *knew,* about the cops there? At least he did just want to talk.

"See that kid up the alley? And what's across from him?" The pale face nodded left, then right.

"The police, I know. And he's watching them?" Mark brought the cab to the side, next to two parked cars. Even a taxi couldn't stop in the street for long; a cop up the block was already glancing their way.

"No, boy. The *snack* shop," and the Eel nodded again, toward the yellow convenience store squeezed in next to the police station. "The one that boy across the street is staring at, because he can't believe it happened. People come out here a whole *day* after someone hit a place that's *one body's length* away from the cophouse. Just to show he could. And 'maybe' you heard about it."

Mark shook his head, trying to think. *He means Rafe robbed a store* next to *the police?* That was sending a message alright—even more than how he'd once tried setting himself up as a better gang leader than the Eel. And now he was playing the independent, the raider nobody could catch?

Uncatchable. As if he had *another* flying belt?

The cop on the sidewalk was walking toward them.

"And here you are still alive," the Eel rumbled. "You're the one who got that recording of Rafe ratting out our summit—and yet now that he's back and showing his strength, he's still letting you live."

What was he hinting at? Mark's fingers tightened on the wheel. "So, now that Rafe is openly trying to outdo you, maybe that recording only looks like proof of how far he'll go to beat you. Hell, maybe he calls me his publicist."

" 'Maybe,' again." The Eel nodded. "What I think is, you could find Rafe again, just like you caught him once. And 'maybe' you'll have to, now that someone's stalking you." And in the mirror his thumb jerked towards the cars behind them.

It's a bluff—

But Mark's eyes were already swinging toward the side mirror. Two small cars and an SUV behind them… Would he even *know* which one was following them? He didn't feel one flicker of magic on the roads either.

No, it had to be the Eel trying to rattle him. Mark felt his stomach locking up tight; he'd been so careful, there *couldn't* be some untraceable figure who might have been following him to Nolan and Dennard. Or seen him fly. Any of it. And how could the Eel spot a tail with just a glance?

Angie would have.

The Eel chuckled, a sound like grit grinding in a garbage disposal. He held up a finger to his pale lips, and Mark's protests stifled under thoughts that the car might be bugged. Then the Eel twitched his head toward their left.

A battered little black Ford was just sidling by. Mark kept his head facing forward as it pulled past, but he thought the scruffy young man at the wheel seemed to give them the briefest glance as he went by.

"And look—you were right, we *didn't* need long to talk this out."

The suspension creaked as the Eel leaned forward. His pale face loomed right up against the glass partition.

"You've already lost your girl. I think 'maybe' you want to sniff Rafe out for me. Before I start rethinking why I left all you loose ends out there."

So now I'm the Blades' bounty hunter? But Mark choked down his protest, rather than push the Eel to start naming which "loose ends" he had in mind. The Eel dropped a handful of cash on the seat and stepped from the cab, strolling away.

And the skinny cop walked right past the gang lord, to close in on where Mark's cab was stalling traffic in the street.

Mark's fingers clenched on the wheel, but he pulled forward into the traffic again before the officer reached him. Rafe's robbery site and anyone watching it fell away behind him. The black Ford had turned down a side street, out of sight too, for whatever that was worth. Unless the Eel had made it all up.

The cab. That had to be how they'd found him, he thought dazedly. He hadn't used his bug sweeper on it in days, so Rafe could have planted something in it. Or, it might not be Rafe; this tail could be one more spying trick of their real enemy, the one that the Eel didn't even know was out there.

I'm being pulled two ways at once, to chase Winton for Angie's sake and hunt Rafe to get the Eel off my back, and now I don't even know which side is following me! Mark could only keep driving, hoping against hope that he wouldn't see the black car again, that the Eel was only trying to scare him after all.

Four blocks later, the same Ford swung into his mirror again.

CHAPTER THREE

GATHERING AND CLOUDS

Squeezing a hand behind his apartment's bookcase, Mark could nudge a slat in the blinds up to see the black car parked below. The figure of its driver paced back and forth in front of the diner, often stopping to poke under the car's hood. The very picture of a man with late-night engine trouble.

Mark might have believed it, if he hadn't found the tracking bug in his cab, and another on his bicycle.

He looked at his phone again. Nolan's *Get back to you* sounded like she'd barely glanced at his messages, and Dennard's text had advised *Sit tight*—of course. But the tail was keeping him away from the park's energy, after the Eel's demands… He heard the blinds rattle, and realized his hand was shaking.

Think. The man hadn't made a move against him, seemed to be only standing outside to see if he left again tonight. That could make this a new tactic of Winton's to find their secrets; Kate kept warning him there were too many ways to spy on someone that his sense of magic wouldn't catch. Or this spy could be signaling Rafe that Mark was home, ready for Rafe to come after him.

Out there he can't see the building's back exit. Are there more people at the other side? How long will he, they, settle for watching? And I just wait?

Mark grabbed his binoculars and his coat, and darted out the door.

The corridor outside was silent, and Mark strode to the stairs and climbed. A brush of magic kept his feet too light to ring on the metal steps. The master key he'd tracked down unlocked the door to the roof.

He crouched low as he stepped out, both to hunker down against the cold wind and to keep out of sight of anyone below. He usually flew straight up out of the jumble of machines and pipes along the rooftop, but tonight he had to squint against the dimness and creep through them to the roof's edge. The scattered sounds of the night streets hung in the air.

The building's rear approaches looked empty, with no "late drivers" or "homeless" that could have been watching his back door. Maybe Winton—or Rafe—had only sent the one tail.

His phone vibrated in his pocket. Mark grabbed it, eager for advice from Dennard.

Instead he saw one of Kate's aliases on the screen.

"Bad timing," he whispered to her, feeling his way toward the roof's front edge. "But you called it: Winton, or someone, has a man out there to spy on me in person."

"Stop right there!"

Her words rang in his head, and for an instant they seemed to echo across the roof, but of course they were barely a whisper against the wind.

"Mark, you can't be thinking of trying to catch that tail. Think about it: if you make one wrong step he could *shoot* you before you ever saw the gun. Or what if someone saw you go after him, and exactly how you did it?"

"I…" Mark looked around the roof and the open, beckoning sky above; he *had* meant to stay back, hadn't he? "I'm not that crazy. I'm waiting for some backup from Dennard, and a chance to grab more power first. Anyway, whoever this is down there, he's the best lead we've got on our enemy. And on finding the power to help your daughter."

"When someone starts following you, you take it as a good sign? I'd commend your determination, Mark, but are you aware that you can't win?"

I already know where she stands about this fight—in a whole other city somewhere. And here I used to be the one telling her daughter to do the same thing, to get out of town.

Mark drew the phone back from his ear and sank into a crawl to the roof's edge. Down below, his tail was still sitting by his car, but now Mark had a clear view of him with his binoculars. Even with the stranger's collar "pulled up against the cold," the face was clear.

"Got him," Mark grinned. He snapped a picture with his phone, but the lens didn't capture the man's features right. Mark switched back to the binoculars to memorize his face. "Now I just need a pencil," he told Kate, "and some of Dennard's police friends to pass the picture along to. Never tail an artist."

Kate's answer was soft. "And then what? Mark, I said you can't win."

"No?" He tried a small joke. "What's wrong with our odds? We've got Dennard, Nolan, me, any advice you can spare, and now Angie's our lookout again. Besides," and he felt his grin widening, "your daughter already came back from the dead for us, so how can we lose?" He watched as his tail turned to shuffle ignorantly along the street again.

"But she *didn't* come back. Even if you…"

Kate paused then, and when she continued her voice was cold.

"It's only her mind that came back, or part of it. Even if you defeat Winton and take control of his magic, her real body was cremated. Do you honestly think you can find a coma patient who's *just* far enough beyond recovery that Angie can use her body? Or are you going to celebrate your victory with a new birdcage?"

Bitch—

The word strangled in his throat, crushed as his neck muscles clamped tight. A surge of fury burned the shivering out of his flesh—

Then he remembered, and he gave his head a shake to chase some of the tension out.

"You… you know, you're getting predictable, Kate? Right there, the way you try to shock people by playing lightning rod for their outrage." *The same as when you pushed Angie out of your life to 'protect' her*—he managed not to slap Kate with how that had turned out. "Of course I've thought of it. But if there's no way to really help her, it won't be because I wasn't trying. And I won't leave that bastard Winton out there either."

"At the risk of all your lives," and Kate gave a slow sigh. "Was Angela always as stubborn as you?"

"Not 'stubborn,' she was the one who sized things up faster—" *is, not was., she* is *the faster one*— "and she was usually right."

"I see. I—"

She broke off.

A moment later she added "I'm sorry, I have to go. Mark, I'll think about whether I can help, but please, you think about what I said too."

"All right."

And just like that she hung up.

He stared at the phone a moment. "What was it? You're hiding out in the Sahara and had to pull your son back from a sandstorm?" If Kate sent him any help, it would be on her own terms.

And if she kept counting up all the obstacles ahead, she'd lose the only hope that kept them going. Any of them could fall into that trap.

Was Dennard slowing down too? Mark looked at the texts on the phone: their former cop might be too cautious, and too injured, to help turn this tail into the lead it could be. Nolan at least had enough power to help him set a trap—but was she even *reading* their messages?

Mark pressed himself lower on the cold roof, memorizing the face of the man below.

* * *

The Hallington Hotel stood just above Saunders Street, at the other side of the freeway overpass like a castle behind a moat and bridge… some glittering fairy-tale kind of castle, the way its glass front caught what sunlight broke through the overcast skies. *But the sun is already high, I must have spent the whole morning running and twisting my way through the streets to be sure nobody followed me.*

So much for getting in any time at work.

Mark saw the signs for the event Nolan was running, and the gathering crowds, before he passed through the hotel's front door. He shot her another text asking her to meet him just for a minute—but he doubted she'd have time to notice. Not now.

The banquet hall was full of people in business suits, not sitting at the dining tables but mingling and circulating on their feet. The gray-suited North Star Events staff with their headsets mostly moved around the space's edges and near the great windowed wall. At that wall they'd actually set up *mirrors* in steel frames to angle beams of sunlight over to the podium. The beams lit up wisps of dry ice fog that drifted down from nozzles in the ceiling and seemed to be vacuumed away when they reached the floor. And all this played around the podium's banner that read *Solar Power – Brighter Than Ever.*

Mark pulled his eyes away from the effects. He'd never seen Nolan's planning talents up close before, but tracking down Winton and Rafe could be life and death. He circled around the crowd toward two of her uniformed staff standing near the podium, repeating the promise he'd made to himself: he'd tell Nolan to her face that he was *not* leaving until she finished here and they made some real plans to get the hunt moving. No matter how the force of so many uncaring voices flooded his head.

When he reached the two staffers he gave them his best smile. "Quite a show. But, I need to speak to Ms. Nolan."

The younger man mumbled something under his breath that might have been *"Good luck with that!"* before answering "Let's see. Can I help you with that?" And his eyes roamed over Mark, as if taking in his simple, street-stained clothes compared to the high-class crowd. His voice had no welcome in it.

"No, I'll keep looking for her, thanks."

Mark stepped back from the podium and the cool smell of the fog. He only needed a moment with Nolan for now, to show her he wouldn't back down. *We've got to get this in gear, I just need to* find *her.* The crowd was so thick he only caught glimpses through it.

He could still walk out and try following or threatening his tail on his own… why, because that felt easier than getting Nolan to leave a party? He gritted his teeth.

Another two figures in gray stood beyond the fringe of the crowd, and Mark started toward them. Then one turned and he recognized the stocky woman as Olivia Nolan herself.

Next to the two, a long-bearded old man was shaking a finger at her. "I don't know if I told you, but in the solar business we don't usually *like* seeing clouds."

She smiled back. "I thought the winter overcast would be late this year, and when it wasn't, I did what I could to delay it—oh I'm sorry, you meant the fog effects."

The old man frowned. "Delaying… the clouds? That's hardly funny."

Mark winced.

"But look," and the man in gray beside them motioned to the podium. "The reflections on the fog do catch how much sunlight there is, and then when we…"

A moment later Nolan slipped away from the two men. She strode away around the edge of the crowd, gripping her headset as if following some new "crisis."

Mark dodged clear of the crowd and started after her. The conversation he'd heard made his brain twitch: Nolan was the one person who probably *could* have been holding off the November clouds. No surprise that she could use her weather magic to get an edge in planning her outdoor events—and knowing when to switch to indoor ones—but just this week she had said she'd pulled the clouds back in to cover their late-night searches. She could have planned this whole meeting's "fog and sun" theme as a private joke.

"So how can I help you?"

It was the same man who'd been at Nolan's side, youngish but balding, and he flashed a smile so disarming Mark felt a pang of envy. But he was also stepping up beside Mark, and angling around him to cut him off from Nolan.

"It's a quick thing, maybe ten seconds with Ms. Nolan." Mark nodded towards her; she was at the room's corner now, talking to several guests. He only needed to convince her he wasn't leaving.

"Sounds important," the man grinned. Now he was right in front of Mark.

I've seen him before, in her entourage. Mark tried to think, grasping for some story that would let him get by. Why hadn't he had an excuse ready?

Just then, another man in the gray uniform stepped up to them. "The Rev wants to talk to Olivia—"

"Where is—" and the balding gatekeeper moved a step around toward the other worker.

Mark slid past him and broke into a quick trot. He heard a startled *Hey!* behind him, but if all Nolan's people were this protective of her time, this might be the best chance he'd get.

That kind of loyalty might even make them targets, or hostages, the next time Winton or Rafe made a move for her magic's secrets.

Nolan's back was to him, as she talked with two of her finely-dressed guests. Mark stepped straight up behind her to lean over her shoulder, and hissed "We *need* to talk."

She spun around and the guests started at his interruption, and he shifted to face the two staff closing in behind him. The man Mark had dodged looked at Nolan. "Sorry—"

"It's alright, Zeke," she said. "If you step in to help *him* there, and then *you* help with the drinks—" She made two quick gestures around her and in the next second "Zeke" was apologizing to the guests while the other employee was marching off up the hall, dispatched on his own mission.

In another second she swept away up a corridor, motioning Mark to follow.

When the babble of the crowd fell back behind them, the first thing he said was "Don't worry, nothing's on fire. Do what you need to here—but when you're done, we have to talk. So I'm not leaving until we do."

"Is that a threat? Or just a demand?" Her eyes stabbed at him. "And you came *here,* where *people know me,* to force me to rearrange my schedule?"

"Sorry. But… you did read my texts?" When she nodded, he added "And yes, I made sure my new 'friend' didn't follow me here. So you see we need to get a jump on this, *today.* You know I'm right." He glanced past her shoulder to the hotel staff scattered here and there around them, out of earshot but still too near for him to talk about setting traps or hacking computers.

She sighed. "And you know I'm working on it."

"Today," he said again. "I mean *next.* You finish this event, or leave it to your crew, whatever works for you, but then we do this. I know I can't go start one of my own cab shifts right now. This could be my family on the line."

He met her glare, and locked the idea of Angie's survival in his head to steel himself, that and the Eel ready to lean on Dennard and Henry… He remembered his thought about Nolan's own people being at risk, and he was tempted to mention them as well.

A young black woman in baggy green "camouflage" clothes was marching toward them. Mark froze.

She looked deliberately past Mark to Nolan, and said "Now, you wouldn't be talking about the files without me, would you?"

Mark looked closer at her face; probably mid-twenties, and something in the smirking way she spoke the word *files* said *hacker* to him, the woman Nolan had hinted about. And the sidelong glance she gave Mark made it even clearer: she was using secrets she shared with Nolan, and the threat of him overhearing them, to pressure Nolan to talk.

Nolan frowned back at her.

"We'll talk soon." Nolan's tone wasn't the sternest Mark had heard, but something in that cold gaze made him grateful it wasn't aimed at him. "Right now, I need to work. And the rest of my day just filled up," she added, and her eyes flicked toward Mark. So he'd convinced her?

The young woman's smirk *wilted.* "Sure, sure. Nothing that can't wait."

Nolan started back toward the tables. Mark could already see a man in the black hotel uniform moving to meet her… and the man he'd met before, Zeke, starting toward himself and the hacker.

Mark glanced at her again. If she was eager enough to catch Nolan at work, the same way Mark had, just how big a secret had she found?

Even after chasing Mark around the gathering, Zeke didn't show a hint of anger at the two gatecrashers, only a helpful smile. "Now, what's so important?"

His charm didn't soften the hacker. Instead she flashed the arrogant grin from earlier: "Just making sure Miss Nolan got my news. I'm done now." And she spun on her heel and walked away.

Mark stared after her for a moment, but when she passed the first of the giant ferns near the entrance he left Zeke and trotted after her. What to say, what to say to her?

He tried "Did you just threaten Nolan with talking about her secrets in front of me? Maybe I should have tried that."

"And who are—" Then the woman caught herself, and gave him a scowl. "Oh no. Whoever you are, her business with me is just her business."

You mean the hacking you do for her? The words were on the tip of his tongue, but he held them back, then watched as she walked away.

The girl might like showing off her lack of tact, but she had a point—she shouldn't be sharing Nolan's secrets when she didn't know Mark, and he couldn't talk to her either when he didn't even know how much Nolan kept her in the loop. "One more thing we have to start sharing," he muttered. And talking to the hacker alone was no way to smooth things over with Nolan.

I need to start acting like the peacemaker I used to be. I can't have Zeke trying to throw me out, just when Nolan agreed to see me. Mark turned and walked back toward Zeke. Nolan's gatekeeper was still watching both him and the woman, probably to make sure they left.

Mark told him "Sorry about that. I'm still not sure who she's supposed to be," and he nodded toward the hacker; she was just stepping into the revolving doors at the hotel entrance.

"She said she was with you, after she'd already tried to see Ms. Nolan once this morning. Our fearless leader does try to do too much herself… and I wouldn't mind knowing if there's any more we can help you with before you go looking for her again." His voice was still helpful, but Mark thought he saw his eyes narrowing with a hint of suspicion.

"Well, you can let me apologize." He offered his hand. "Mark Petrie."

"Zeke Brent, General Manager for Ms. Nolan," he said as he shook it. "I've seen you meeting with her once or twice before?"

"I'm helping her with a project, sure. The rest, that's really up to her to tell."

"I see." Zeke's face didn't change, but there was some kind of hurt in his voice…

He's Nolan's right hand! Hell, he could be what I *was with Angie, someone that a more driven friend trusts to calm things down around them.* And Zeke had to be better at that than Mark, and yet here Mark was hinting he had special access to Nolan that Zeke didn't. Just what a trusted friend like Zeke hated to hear.

Mark swallowed, and fumbled for a way to repair things. Had she told Zeke about the magic? He felt around him for any faint traces that might mean she'd given him a talisman.

Mark's jaw fell open. *Below us, another belt!*

Instead of anything from Zeke, somewhere below him he felt the same clear, steady pulsing of the park's gravity magic.

And… only Rafe Martinez had ever tapped into that power without one of the original Fletcher talismans. The magic was lurking down on some floor below their feet; that *seemed* like Rafe, just from the cunning way it was keeping out of sight down there.

But Rafe was a wanted murderer. And if it was him here at Nolan's event… he'd tried once before to kidnap her and seize her magic…

Mark's heart hammered; how long had he been standing there staring, whole seconds? *There's no time!*

"Where, where did Nolan go?" he gasped. As he said it he stepped around Zeke to stare at the crowds. Too many people in motion, all he saw were flashes of a few figures in Nolan's company gray, but nobody he could recognize.

Wait, why use his eyes? He reached for his magic again, fighting to steady his racing thoughts to ignore the heavy pulse of the power lurking below them, and catch the faint stillness of Nolan's own energy. *There,* she was somewhere to the left, near the podium, and with that clue his gaze picked her out, again at the edge of the crowd.

"What is *wrong* with you?" he heard Zeke saying at his back.

Right, he must look like a maniac staring around at invisible forces—and Zeke carried none of Nolan's power; he had no reason to believe any of this. Mark pulled out his phone, and said "Just got a warning on this—"

He shot off a text to Nolan: *RAFE is here, with more !!!* and as he sent it he thought he saw her turn slightly toward him. Praying he could draw her notice, he waved the phone wildly over his head.

She twisted to face him fully. Her arm reached inside her jacket, and Mark started to follow up with a call, but she had already glanced at her phone and whirled to grab one of her staff.

Enough for now; Mark spun back to Zeke. "Is there a basement floor? Or an underground lot? Do you know all the ways from it up to here?"

"Will you stop and—"

Rafe's magic moved. It was rising up, straight up. Mark spun around, matching the pulse his mind tracked, against... a row of elevators at the back wall.

Only twenty feet away! He flung himself across in three magic-lifted steps, as the thought hit him in midair: *if he's got a gun I'm running right into his* bullets!

He pulled up just in front of the wall, feeling Rafe's power rising up just behind the nearest door. Mark could only flatten himself to the wall at its side—Rafe couldn't sense him, maybe he could grab at Rafe from behind just as he stepped onto the floor.

But Zeke, and a fat hotel guard with him, were stumbling toward Mark, toward where they'd be right in Rafe's line of fire. Mark waved frantically for them to step aside, just as he felt Rafe draw up level with him—

The power moved on up, past him. The elevator didn't stop.

Zeke stumbled up to him, just as Mark stepped away from his ambush position. "Who *are* you?"

"Special security for Nolan," was all Mark could say, as he felt the power stop on the next floor up.

"And you're straight out of high school? What agency?"

Zeke's questions tugged at his attention, but Mark kept his gaze upward. Rafe was on the mezzanine level above the ground floor; did he want an overview of Nolan at her work? Mark's eyes stared up at the back of the gleaming escalator that led down from that level—

"Mark?" Zeke said again.

Up above, a shrill voice screamed.

In the same moment that Mark dodged around Zeke and the hotel guard, he felt the intruder's power surge and sweep along to rush down the escalator. Mark bolted across the floor toward that moving pulse, knowing he was too late, tracking the magic as it cleared the steps, before he saw the masked figure in the long coat leap into view from it beyond it and turn to take in the crowd before him, the hotel around him.

Mark could only clutch at the underside of the escalator to yank himself back behind its cover, as the attacker brought up two machine guns from under his coat.

Somewhere amid the shrieks and the *baddabadda* bursts fired into the ceiling, Mark thought he heard a *"NO!"* from Zeke behind him. For one instant as the masked man swept his gaze around the floor, he looked straight at where Mark crouched behind the escalator's cold metal. Then the gunman turned back toward the crowd of business-people.

"Freeze! Freeze, and you live!" Of *course* the bellowing, harsh voice was Rafe's.

Half of the one hundred people stood staring, penned in among the tables at the room's center—how many deaths would one spray of those snub-nosed Uzis mean? Mark crouched lower; off behind him he saw someone reach toward a fire alarm, then yank his hand back. Sure, the last thing anyone could risk now was a panic.

"Line up in front of the tables—there! There! Move!" Rafe gestured with one of his guns.

Two or three of the guests began shuffling into place, but the rest were slower to react. Rafe kept his masked face toward them. He wasn't even trying to cover the rest of the hotel? Alerts had to be flying out to dozens of guards and cops, and Rafe had to know that. Out beyond the reach of his guns people had to be shouting and running for help, but the dulled clamor of Rafe's prisoners seemed to drown out any distant sounds.

One of the men in the crowd was stammering "Please God please God please…"

Mark saw Rafe swing in his direction again, and he ducked his head back. Tracking the magic in Rafe's belt told him Rafe wasn't closing in on him—

More magic pulsed, outside. Mark felt a gasp slip from his mouth. Clear as the cold escalator against his shoulder, he could feel *another* knot of gravity magic out there, maybe a block away and barreling straight at them.

The terrified man was still gasping for God. *What's Rafe trying to do here?* What could make him risk seizing all these people so openly, and why was he bringing in even more magic?

No—who is out there bringing the magic? The Eel said Rafe was showing the streets what he could do, so who was listening?

"No, no! Get over there!" Rafe called.

Mark glanced out again. Rafe was waving the crowd to his left, to the tables in the center of the room. And just there, deep within the press of shuffling hostages, Mark caught a glimpse of Nolan again.

She couldn't hide in them for long, not if she and her magic were Rafe's real target. The energy outside grew nearer—Mark glanced around for something to throw at Rafe, but the hostages trapped him and every guard in the place to wait, helpless, as—

A huge van smashed through the front wall of glass.

Howls of terror, storms of splinters, more bursts of gunfire sounded as Rafe shouted to control his captives, *their* captives, as five masked men poured out of the van, waving their own guns and fanning out around the prisoners. All five had weak but very real gravity talismans—down in their shoes, Mark found himself noticing.

"Side by side! Hold out your hands in front!" Rafe yelled at the prisoners. His men were already taking positions where the row of hostages had formed. The first gunman to reach them yanked some bit of jewelry right off a woman's outstretched hand—then in the next second moved to the next victim, and the next.

Mark stared, smelling something sour in the air... *fear?* People were yelping in shock, but the thugs only slowed long enough to snatch visible jewelry from each victim and move on down the line. Was that Rafe's plan, to rush through a robbery before anyone could close in on them? If this *was* just a robbery.

Magic stirred. Somewhere beyond Rafe and his troops, Mark caught the faint, hint-of-a-void sense of Nolan's weather energy beginning to move. *Her power's as useless as mine is right now, with all these people at risk. What's she thinking?* Rafe was moving toward the prisoner line to stand ominously near her...

"Please God please—"

The babbling voice rose to a shriek. That man was cowering away from a thug's demanding hand, and the next moment that hand slammed into his stomach. The victim doubled over and stumbled back against the table.

"You want something to scream about?"

The gun came up.

With all the breath Mark could drag into his lungs, he bellowed "You know you're working for a man who betrayed his gang!"

Heads spun around, but Mark was already dropping back to his cover behind the escalator. He could hear angry voices rising over the sounds of the hostages' fear.

"That's all he is, you know! A traitor!" Mark shouted again. Anything to slow them down—and at least his sense of their magic showed that they weren't closing in around his shelter either. Every second they were listening to him was one more they weren't shooting someone, or grabbing Nolan. Rafe with a magic-bearing army was bad enough without getting the secret of Nolan's magic too—

A different sensation moved, out in the street, and this time Mark didn't freeze. This time the first thought through his mind was a clear, horrified *Oh God don't let that possession magic mean Winton's here as Rafe's partner.*

Somehow, he managed to drag his thoughts away from that new energy, back to the thugs and the one way he could slow Rafe down. His voice had a hoarse note in it now: "You… you know he led you into a trap—"

"Sure, keep stalling us," Rafe's cold voice broke in. "I see an easy ticket out."

Mark couldn't risk looking. But he still did, and just as his head peeped around the escalator he saw Rafe moving toward Nolan. He'd slung one of the Uzis onto his shoulder, to draw a stun "gun" prod from his coat.

So he can call Nolan a hostage and drag her off… Did I just give him the excuse for what he wanted all along?

Still, Mark tried shouting "So you escape by taking something that slows you down even more?" It wouldn't work, nothing he said would work.

Then… *whoosh.*

A gust of air burst from the end of the hall, scattering vapors left and right around the podium's fog machine. The next moment the mist that had been pouring down into the vacuum ducts… thickened, billowed, fed by what had to be Nolan's magic as it began to spill white haze across the back wall and start to spread across the floor—

And Mark saw Nolan dart back under a table.

Her motion was the trigger. Shouts burst through the air: shock, sparks of new terror that started to spread and ripple through the crowd of hostages. Two of Rafe's men yelled and fired at the ceiling again, but it only broke the rise of panic for a second.

Rafe brought up his machine gun. The people nearest to Nolan squeezed back away from it, and she scooted along the floor, under another table. Not much of a hiding place, and less protection from bullets, he thought as he tensed to leap. But if Rafe shot her, he'd lose his chance at her magic's secrets—she wasn't trying to escape, she was refusing to be captured alive. Forcing him to choose.

"Screw this!" Rafe said. "We're out of time!"

With a wave to the others, he dashed toward the getaway van that sat half-in, half-out of the window. Then he ran *past* it, and first one and then the rest of his men pulled away from the hostages and ran for the van.

Two of them spat curses back at the crowd, and one fired a warning shot, but that was all the delay they took. The van's engine roared and the huge vehicle wrenched itself back out of the windows.

The moment it pulled free, Mark ran forward. He could see Nolan getting to her feet, with a shaky, relieved grin that spilled all across her face.

Up the street, a siren blared.

Mark ran past Nolan, past the dazed hostages, leaping through the shattered window onto the sidewalk outside. Cold air stung his face. The van was roaring out of the rounded hotel driveway, smashing a yellow sports car aside with a crunch of metal.

Somewhere up the street to the left, he felt Winton's magic circling above the rooftops.

Off to the right, the chatter of machine guns made him turn to see Rafe firing at an approaching police car. Its tires blew and the car went skidding, to smash to a stop against the railing—that was all that kept it from tumbling down onto the main Saunders road on the level below.

Whole heartbeats later, one cop and then another stumbled from the car. Rafe was already dashing after his van, with a stride twice as long as anything with human weight could clear. Mark held himself back at the edge of the street, crouching low and watching as the van and Rafe behind it pulled out onto the overpass.

Instead of gathering speed, they slowed. Right in the middle of the bridge, the van pulled over and came to a halt.

Mark saw the two police officers run toward it, and started to draw back, knowing he should get off of the narrow, open street before the bullets began flying again. But then, the first of Rafe's thugs stepped out from the van... and flung himself off the bridge.

One cop growled "Holy hell—" as a second masked man and then a third dropped into space. Mark moved closer to the bridge, and he felt the robbers' magic flare to soften their fall. *Just like when I used a bridge to get away from Rafe. I* taught *him this trick.*

Mark reached the edge of the bridge to look over the rail. A huge truck sprawled across lanes in the lower street, with a puffy blue shape spread along its top that the men were landing on. Some kind of inflated stuntman's cushion, maybe, to help—and disguise—how they landed and then ran off unharmed. Even the traffic backed up behind the truck must have blocked any police cars from approaching below. Rafe had it all planned.

Mark was almost at the cops' elbows now. They all watched, unmoving, while Rafe half-dragged a balky thug over the railing, the last of the six.

But the other, softer magic was moving in.

Winton's power didn't circle in the air now. His bird must have struck and possessed someone in the street below, someone down among the cars that were halted behind the truck. Mark leaned out further and searched for whoever was closing in on the reassembling gang.

He spotted a woman in a flowered dress, gray-haired and red-faced, shouting what might have been *Clear the road*—a picture of unlikely road rage, but Mark felt the puppet-master's power sending her running toward the masked group.

The nearest of the thugs watched her rush up. Mark's fingers clenched on the railing and he sucked in his breath to scream a warning… but what could he say?

The masked man backhanded the woman away, and the moment his hand struck, magic jumped. The next moment the robber turned away from the slumped figure of the woman, back to Rafe and the rest of his men as they dashed for a side street. With Winton's newest pawn hidden among their number.

A cop near Mark yelled "They just *hit* her? Damn them!"

More police cars roared up and raced past in search of a way down. Mark edged back and let them go by, scrolling through the maps in his memory. Rafe's planning and his magic would let the gang get further ahead every second. How many more cars did Rafe have waiting just out of sight down there?

So Rafe was raising a magical army, and he'd just proven he knew how to lead one… but he'd never see whatever it was that Winton had just set up behind his back. Rafe's new gang was the least of their problems.

CHAPTER FOUR

FREEZING AND COLD

Mark felt his legs shaking, but he pushed himself to trot after the sirens, toward the next on-ramp down to the lower street where Rafe's gang had gone.

Thoughts of *They could have shot me* dragged at him like hands belatedly reaching out from the past minutes. But he couldn't let himself slow: the police couldn't track that magic, couldn't see how what Rafe's men carried—and Winton's control of one of them—were twisting their way somewhere through what must be the tangle of roads off of Longcor.

But the magic was already fading in the growing distance. He forced his feet to move faster.

Half by reflex, he pulled out his phone and called. He heard Nolan's voice in his ear.

"You okay?" he asked.

"Yes, yes. What's happening?"

"I need help! They're getting away, they all just floated down off the overpass…"

A harsh, strangled sound blasted in his ear, like some wordless curse. Then her voice went still; under the rasp of his own breathing, Mark could just make out a babble of background noise through the line. How many frightened victims and demanding cops did Nolan have around her?

She hung up.

The next moment, the last trace of magic faded beyond his reach. Mark's footsteps slowed, helpless, but he pushed on anyway.

If he just could get ahead of Rafe's route and catch the trace again… or guess even the area they might go to… He called Dennard, but got no answer and all he could do was gasp out a message "Call me! Rafe's made his move."

He slowed to a quick walk, and let his head fill with the routes that would lead him back to Rosewood Park. Rafe was gone, and his own belts' tingle of power was too weak to ignore any longer.

The phone chimed in his hand.

This time Nolan's voice was low and fierce. "Is it true? The whole gang jumped off that bridge?"

"And ran off. And Winton's got his hooks in one of them—there's too many ways this could get so much worse."

"Can you stay on them? The minute I can get out of here, we have to stop them."

"We?" Just hearing the word made Mark feel warmer in the cool air. "Right! Maybe I can catch up to them, then you keep them grounded while we call the cops… or maybe I can…" If Winton attacked Rafe, that could give them some kind of opening…

The corner ahead was the next turn to reach the park, and he moved left. As he turned, he saw a thin figure a block behind him.

"That… *can't* be the man following me," he muttered.

But, the shape had the same awkward walk as he'd seen pacing under his apartment.

"I thought I lost him," he sighed to Nolan. "Unless he already knew about you and guessed where I was headed. If Winton or Rafe sent him, they might have guessed."

"Listen to me: *don't* let him see anything."

Nolan's voice was softer now, and colder than the air… no, the actual air was *growing* colder as she spoke.

"Mark, do *not* let him guess anything of what you can do—one more person who has any hint of it is one too many. Do *not* bring the police into any of this. The few of us may be the only ones in the world who know what really goes on here. And now that idiot gangbanger put everything at risk!"

Mark fought to keep his steps at the same pace, to keep from glancing back at the man behind him. The long storefronts and bright afternoon light seemed to press tighter around him, holding him helpless just when he needed to move.

But, there was something within the outrage in Nolan's voice…

"Did you know Rafe could do this with the magic?" Mark asked. "When we said Rafe got his own belt, did you guess he could make even more of them? Does your own magic let you make talismans left and right, and you never told us we probably could too?" Somehow Mark kept his voice low, forcing all his frustration into the phone.

"You should ask the Dennards. They're the ones who always said their power was limited… but, they're so afraid of it they probably believed that," she sighed. "Mark, the priority is dealing with those… *thieves,* before the whole city sees them flying. Now, where do we look for them—or do you need to wait for me so I can get you away from one single man stuck on the ground?"

"I…" Mark gritted his teeth, trying to force away thoughts of Kate or Dennard lying to his face; of course they hadn't known. "I guess Rafe might be recruiting from his home turf, so we can start… here." He thumbed open the location app and pinged the Oster neighborhood. "And I'll handle the tail myself."

"That's more like it. I'll get down there when I can. But here, I've been working on a present for you."

Mark opened his mouth to ask, but then he saw the sky.

It was graying, swirling. The wind had been up all day, but now he could hear its sound growing louder, and he felt the first flakes of snow sweep in. He glanced around and saw people up and down the sidewalk—even the man behind him—pause and look around. Was Nolan bringing a whole blizzard down on the city?

Nolan said "I'll meet you there."

"Wait, snow? You want me to leave footprints that just vanish?"

"Find a way. At least if you need to get yourself up there you won't be floating in plain sight for everyone." She hung up.

Mark glared at the phone, then pushed down his anger and huddled in his coat to walk faster.

So, I go after Winton and Rafe… after I gather the power to stop them. When me going to the park might be just what this spy is hoping for.

The wind swelled and howled, and snow thickened in the air. Mark tried to focus on the problem right behind him, and his own options. He didn't need to outthink a man who might be making his living shadowing people, he just had to take the time to line up all his own tools and find his moment. Mark knew every street, he could see the air filling with snow and feel the northeast pressure of the wind, and his belts still held enough magic to move. That had to be enough.

Then he reached the long, honeycombed university block and darted off the street between the broad buildings. He caught a last glimpse of the man lunging after him, trying to keep him in sight. But Mark turned the corner whole seconds before his shadow could near it, and the walkways were all but empty in the fierce wind. He grabbed a back door's lever, felt it turn—and the moment he knew it was unlocked he stepped back and with a burst of magic shot himself upward.

Clearing the wall let the icy air smash into him full force. He dropped to the rooftop and took a moment to watch his tail follow his footprints to the door and rush on inside. Then Mark was off, dashing along the snowy roof and dropping down to a sheltered street to scramble on.

Somewhere in the run through the streets he figured out why Nolan had raised the snowstorm: whatever it did to slow him down, it had to do much worse to Rafe's less practiced men, and it might even keep them grounded. So she'd blanketed the whole *city* with power... the force of it dragged at him if he tried to so much as lighten one step.

Finally he launched upward again from a point where the wind could sweep him toward the park. The whistling in his ears dropped to a ghostly murmur, with all but the wildest sounds muted by his riding within the current. Blurred gray shapes flew by where the city lay down below. Mark wondered if this was what clifftop high-divers saw, searching the surf below for half-hidden rocks. But rocks wouldn't race past him and tease him with different half-familiar shapes through the snow.

Power pulsed ahead. The center of the park's magic throbbed in Mark's mind as the perfect invisible beacon for cutting through the blinding air; as it swept up he guessed he'd pass within one or two hundred yards of it. No other magic lurked nearby. Nobody would be out to spot him in the sky today.

He took part of his weight back, and the wind turned savage against him again—worse when the ground drew near enough for him to twist gravity and break his fall, then fight that last distance down through the wind's pressure to reach the snowy grass. "Not bad, not bad," he had to chuckle.

Then he was trotting across the deserted expanse of Rosewood City Park, ducking into the half-fenced-off thicket at its north edge, and shuffling through the trees and bracken with the bug sweeper out for one last check around him. The wood's air smelled empty with the cold freezing away the usual rich scent of the trees. Still, with the sun at least up there behind the snowy sky, this was one time he could *see* the rough slopes he picked his way along. Toward the power.

It was just a space partway down one of the shallow ridges, without even being any barer or more overgrown than any other spot in the thicket. Mark could never have picked it out, even now, without the talismans that resonated with its magic. But this one location, where some kind of natural energies must be aligning, was the first part of the secret Winton would kill for.

Mark whispered the secret's second part:

"Zha-Daruath."

Power surged and flowed and poured through his head, pulsing and aching with the drive to *move* as his will guided it out of the land and air and into the talismans. Angie's and Rafe's belts burned and throbbed to full life around his waist; in his pocket the other scrap of that leather drew in energy as well.

Freedom... power to leap and soar and fling aside anything in my way...

Mark caught the urge to rush away, and waited for his breathing to calm. Was Dennard right? Did this place let these words call some kind of spirit into the leather, so the power-madness that had pulled him in once wasn't even human?

And now Rafe had the whole secret. Somehow he knew the place, the words, and also some way to make *more* bits of leather carry the spirit, or the power, or whatever it was. He knew enough to hand new talismans out like membership badges... and, Winton might already be dragging those secrets out of him, and then be free to wipe out Mark and everyone and leave Angie trapped...

Mark blasted straight up through the trees, back into the storm.

* * *

Am I guessing right? Mark knew not to blunder through a city the size of Lavine, not after months of failed searching for Winton's and Angie's magic. He could only make his way along the streets to the blocks around Oster where Rafe had grown up—all too close to Mark's own high school days.

The cold burrowed into his skin, no matter how much he huddled on the sheltered side of the street, like the few people he passed struggling along. The crammed-together Oster tenement buildings took shape in the snowy air ahead. The weather gave them the same look as the rest of the city for once, covering their dirt and blending their half-deserted state with the blizzard-stripped blocks he'd already passed.

Except for the winds, the streets were oddly still. Twice he saw people rushing indoors with what looked like an anxious glance around; people and cars outside grew rarer by the minute.

Nolan sent a text finally that said she was on her way. So when his phone chimed for a call, he was ready for her voice.

Instead he heard Dennard: "Where are you?"

He pinged his location on Oster again. "You got my messages, about Nolan's banquet? Think about them jumping off that bridge: the whole gang had the same 'thing' as Rafe." Even on an empty street and a triply-secure phone, he found himself avoiding the word *magic* this time. Was the sky getting dimmer now? "I'm looking around Rafe's old turf."

"Looking?"

Dennard paused, and Mark thought he could catch murmurs in the background. When Dennard started again, his voice was lower, half swallowed by the wind around Mark:

"And that body the police found? One of Rafe's friends from his days with the Blades was found in the alley four blocks from where you are."

"Body?" What was happening?

"Yes, body. Was that from you running into them?"

"Not me. Maybe…" Mark tried to think, and the tumble of ideas pushed his feet along faster. "They're making their move, or Winton is—he got himself right in there with them, I'll bet he's trying to get the secret from them. Where was this body? Nolan's on her way."

For a moment Dennard didn't answer, and the voices around him faded as if he'd reached somewhere private. Then: "So it's you two going after them? Did you even think about sending the police? You know you and your senses are the thing we can't risk."

That again! "There has to be a way. We tip the police off, or Nolan keeps Rafe grounded, or something—how do we know what's going to work if we don't find them first? But the city hasn't seen what they can really do yet…"

Wasn't that what Nolan had said? And he remembered something else she'd said.

"Did you really never guess that this stuff could get passed out to a whole gang? Kate never said it was possible?"

"Of course not. Her parents never had a chance to tell her what's possible, remember? But, that doesn't mean we're the only ones who can stop it."

"Tell that to Nolan," Mark sighed. "Look, we've got Rafe's gang, mixed up with Winton trying to trick the secret out of them, and then… Mostly I know that we don't know what we're dealing with. Angie could have sized it up in a moment, but I…"

He took an instant to sweep for magic. The pulse caught at his senses.

Flying? No, the flicker sat still, it must be up in one of the buildings ahead in the snow.

"Mark?"

"They're here!" *They?* Yes, it felt like several of the smaller pulses together. Rafe's full-strength talisman wasn't among them. And it was *above;* hadn't Dennard said that body had been down in an alley?

"Slow down!" Dennard's low, fierce tone stabbed at Mark. "Think! That isn't Winton pulling strings and taking his time. You know it only takes a second to miss one punk and get yourself shot—why do I have to tell you that again? You have more sense than that."

Mark's teeth clenched. Dennard kept trying to make him too valuable to go near the worst dangers. But, Mark felt the shame of all the times he'd barely survived and all those vulnerable moments he kept losing just to size a situation up—and most of them hadn't been against guns. Kate had warned him too.

Except—

" 'Sense'? That's just it, now that they're carrying these things I can *sense* them coming. They've just given me the same edge that I have against Winton. And I know Rafe can't sense me any more than Winton can; I've seen how blind they are." He stared through the white, trying to match the magic to how the nearest building might be screening the next from sight. "Right now, their place is further ahead in the snow, so they can't see me with their eyes yet. I'll try to get closer, but just enough to see what they're doing." He shot off another text and location ping to Nolan.

"Mark, I said…"

"I have to. If I'm really the only one who senses magic this way— how can I waste an edge like that?"

"Mark, you don't need to save us from Rafe, or Winton—this isn't your fault—"

Dennard's warnings continued in his ear as he made his way in. Shifting around the back of the block let him keep out of sight of where the gang was trying to hide.

Finally, Dennard just said "Watch your back," and hung up.

Strange: Winton's subtler power *wasn't* lurking among the gang's. Mark tried to guess if that was good or bad, and couldn't decide. Instead he began looking for a door to duck inside. He should just get out of the cold and wait for Nolan, wait for nightfall…

Except, the gang was all on the far side of the building, out of view, where they couldn't see *him*.

He stole a peek around a corner at the brick shape, and his eyes confirmed it: those presences couldn't be lurking in one of the upper floors, they had to be up on the far end of the roof itself.

Mark pulled back and made his way through the garbage-strewn gaps between the buildings' rears, edging closer. The gang held their place on the roof's far side. If they were keeping watch at all, it would only be toward that direction.

If they'd shifted around just once, he told himself he would have held back. But he reached the base of the wall without sensing a single motion; they must be completely settled in up there. So he took a glance around, then soared up in the shelter of the wall until he was floating just under the rim of the roof.

And still no movement. And the talismans were clustered so close together—were the punks huddling together against the cold? For one moment Mark thought the gang might be lying dead in a pile, all killed by Winton.

He gripped the roof's cold rim, and stole a peek over.

It was empty.

He stared harder, but the roof was flat, and clear, with only the typical snow-coated knots of pipes, wires, and mechanical fixtures—*none* of them large enough to hide a man even with the sun sinking and dimming at the horizon. But the magic was there.

Mark slipped over the rim and crouched down low, to shelter from the wind and from any prying eyes down in the street. The tingle of magic seemed to lie behind a stubby little heating duct, and he picked his way toward it

Leaning against the duct was a bundled-up tarp. He unrolled it slowly, less by sight in the deepening shadows than by touch. Inside it he found sets of running shoes, four pairs, with the magic pulsing somewhere within each one of them.

Yes, right *there.* He shucked off a glove, pulled out his heavy pocket knife and pried up one of the rubbery inner soles. Underneath, his fingers slowly drew out the magic: a square of leather about the size of his thumbnail.

Leather again. His fingertip recognized the same fine-grained feel as the two magic belts, and the stiffness that the newer belt had… He felt in his pocket for one of the bits of leather he carried for his own talisman experiments.

When the leather-fobbed keychain slid from his pocket, the flicker of magic struck his fingers like a sting.

It's full of power now—I forgot it was in my pocket next to the actual strip of Fletcher leather, and after the park I never noticed I had two pulses in there. And now this one random piece of… "genuine horse leather," the ad had said… had drawn in the park's power too and become as real a talisman as any of them.

He drew in a slow breath of cold air. *That's the secret, the* complete *secret of our magic.* No preparation, no special steps. Mark stared at the two pieces of leather in his hands, almost invisible in the dimming light. Shoes with these could give four of Rafe's men their power… no, the magic was there for *anyone* who brought a piece of horsehide to that spot in the park and knew the words to gather the power in…

And Rafe knew, somehow.

Mark swept the shoes back into their tarp and gathered it into his arms. It wouldn't be too bulky to carry away—but then he thought of Winton or the police or anyone stopping him, finding this clue to the secret…

No. He poured lifting force into the bundle, and it leaped out of his fingers, up, and he tilted his head to watch it fade away in the dark sky.

"For all the good that does," he muttered. He sagged in place, picturing—

That sky full of petty crooks that owed their wings to Rafe—

Any leather goods store being better than an armory to his thugs—

No limits, nothing but the three-part secret Angie's family had kept so long, until—

Mark didn't know how long he stayed slumped there, soaking in the cold. When he looked down again, it was to follow *another* fragment of power he felt moving below. Right toward his building.

There, there it was. He peered down through the snow, watching the two figures push through the street. The man with the magic in his shoes looked thin—no, his shape looked small because he was out in the blizzard with only a sweater—and he seemed to be waving at and arguing with the figure in front of him. An even smaller outline, a dark-haired woman, dragging a wheeled suitcase through the snow.

Before she reached the apartment building, the man stepped in front and cut her off. He kept gesturing around, and what little of his voice reached Mark from four floors below sounded desperate.

Mark stared down the side of the building. In the dimming light they'd never look up, and he could just make out the shape of the fire escapes along the brick. *I'll just get close enough to hear.*

Dropping off the roof was easy. Catching himself in the howling air, and hanging from the fire escape two floors above, took the lightest touch of power Mark had. He crawled lower, weightless to keep the metal from clanging. He could follow more of the words now:

"—where? I shoulda met up with them. You call him!" The man stopped waving to wrap his arms around himself.

"My brother stays away from me, don't you get that? But none of you do—I have to get out of here." The woman hugged the bags in front of her, and Mark saw her weight shuffle in the snow, a step toward the door, a step that she halted in mid-move.

The man drew a step closer, voice rising. "But I *saw* Rafe come sneaking this way after training. Right here!"

The bundle of shoes. The punk could be right, Rafe must have come here before to stash the shoes up on… his sister's roof, was it?

She said again "I haven't seen him. Like that's going to save me from all of you now…" Then her voice softened, with what might be a hint of admiration. "That really was you, and Rafe, wasn't it? You got away off that bridge and left the whole city staring."

"Sure. Another day and we'll own these streets, no way the Blades can keep up with us!"

"Gunner, I don't have a day. If you put on a show like that, the Blades *really* need to shut you down, before *all* of them start going over to Rafe—why can't any of you see that I don't know where Rafe is—"

"It was him! Here!" The man, "Gunner," moved closer, and the woman stepped back with her face flinching away. His voice lowered a fraction, like some attempt at a reassuring whisper. "C'mon, it's cool, I just need to find him again. Look at me, freezing, I'm out here halfway naked after dumping clothes so the cops don't track me. If you can't get the word on him, I'll have to go back down to—"

He stopped, and his fists tightened, his face twisted.

"Fuck. I don't mean *down,* I mean—you got me talking, you just sit there and make me say—you selling us out?"

"No, I don't know—"

Gunner's voice rose in a howl. "You think I'm gonna tell you *shit—"*

Mark felt his feet kicking him free of the fire escape. Two stories of cold air and a thousand thoughts of *Stupid, stupid!* rushed by and he only had time to grab one idea before he came down beside them.

Gunner whirled, and his hand dove under his sweater—

"Don't be a fool," and Mark motioned back at the distance he'd just dropped from. Showing off the gang's own high-diving trick was a thin pretense to keep that weapon in the punk's pocket, and Mark's words tightened with contempt for his own recklessness. "You saw me move, right?"

But the punk's wild eyes flashed wide, and his head tilted up to guess at how much distance Mark must have plummeted.

When he looked back again, he frowned. "You... you're one of ours? You've still got the stuff? He let you keep more of it?"

More of it? He's got talismans on his own feet. But Mark held the thought down to answer with a quick "You saw, didn't you? Come on," and turning up the sidewalk before he could hesitate. Giving the punk no time to look for cracks in his "disguise."

A scuffing noise in the snow told him the woman was making a dash for her door. And Gunner fell into step beside Mark, with an eager "Right, right! Back to the boys."

"Sure," Mark said, as he wondered what he'd dropped himself into. Now he was pretending to be one of Rafe's crew—and this thug expected him to *lead* him to the others? As a test, he muttered "So Rafe never told you where to go," with just a hint of pity in it to spur a reaction.

"Go? After Lou started shooting at us? We were *at* the spot, you mean Rafe had *another* place to meet up?"

Mark kept his face turned away, as if hiding his expression would be enough. *Think!* He could still track Rafe's magic and slip away if Gunner just led him to the right area. So, he'd have to make the punk show off what he did know. *At least I've got him on the defensive; he's still the one trying to prove himself.*

The thought must have taken too long.

Gunner added "Y'know… I thought I knew all of us, even the masked ones, but you—"

Then he gasped:

"Fuck! Blades!"

Two men stood up ahead on the street. And Mark's struggling mind must have been looking right past them, even against the gray emptiness of the storm. They might have been simply walking, until Gunner's shout made them whirl. And reach for guns.

"Ohgod my bad they all know—"

"Move!" Mark lunged back for a side street behind them, the one thing he could think of that would keep clear of the bullets. A glance back showed Gunner breaking out of shock to dive after him. No shots cut through the sound of the blizzard yet.

His feet skidded on snow around the corner, and Gunner leaped up behind him.

Gunner's leap tipped, slowed, brought him floating upward three feet, four feet, above the ground with a shocked *whaaa* as he flailed helplessly in the air.

No! Mark sprang upward to catch a thrashing arm, and he forced weight into Gunner, his belts beating down the lifting power of the scraps in those shoes. He caught the glazed, stunned look on Gunner's face before they touched the ground—still light, Gunner was still light enough for Mark to drag his dazed form forward, just bumping over the snow. The shoes' energy faded, used up trying to fight two full-sized belts.

Gunner didn't know about floating?

Mark swept the thug up the street, thoughts spinning as he ran.

Are the Blades right behind us, do we have to jump for the roof—

But if Rafe had taught his men to run without realizing they could fly—

Left, right, which way ahead, what had the view above been—

A huge man stepped around the corner ahead, pistol leveled at both of them. "Stop right there, Gunner."

"Both of you," added a deeper, rougher voice, and the immense shape of the Eel moved into view to dwarf the first Blade. One of his pale hands was clamped onto—

Olivia Nolan's arm.

Mark froze, his grip on Gunner going slack. Nolan's face was pale, barely moving… all her battering, freezing winds were useless with the enemy right on her. What had she done, followed Mark's location ping and walked into an ambush? And Mark had only had to worry about a petty thug before…

Behind them, the other two Blades closed in.

For an instant Mark thought of jumping straight at the Eel and pinning him under a surge of magic, forcing the Blades to back off.

Instead, he willed his clutching fingers to relax, and raised his arms. *Not yet. I have to watch for the moment when I can move.* At least Nolan looked steady enough; he only saw a small trembling in her jaw.

"So we've got one of our traitors that went over to Rafe. And you," and the Eel gave Mark a nod. That single word revealed nothing, nothing about what he thought of finding someone he'd tried to recruit together with Rafe's man.

Gunner squeaked out a *Please* as the Eel's three men—all huge—edged in around him.

Far up beyond them, an old man huddled in a coat stumbled into Mark's view around a corner… and he spotted the gang and backed away out of sight. Terrified.

Then the Eel turned. "And Miss Olivia Nolan, fresh from Rafe's raid at the hotel—oh yes, I know who was there. Why *is* the last person that he robbed coming out here looking for more?"

Mark shifted his feet, his knees making the smallest bend that readied him to leap.

Then Nolan tilted her head back to meet the Eel's gaze, and the tremble faded from her mouth. "Like you said, I was the last one he robbed. I want to make that the last one he *ever* robs."

The Eel… went still. Mark saw one of his men start to grin, then stop and wipe the smirk away.

Then the gang leader laughed, cold and grating. "Sounds like a party."

CHAPTER FIVE

LABYRINTH AND STRING

Why is it always a van? But Mark knew the Eel had the same reason as Rafe had when he launched his robbery. Using vans gave them mobile bases that could bring all their weapons and gear right to a target—or squeeze three enforcers and three "guests" into a space where no outside eyes could see what happened to them.

The Eel's van had no seats behind the front. Instead they sat on the floor with their backs to its sides, and one guard sitting between Mark and Nolan that blocked his view of how they treated her; he could only press himself back against the cold metal and try not to draw their attention to her. And he tried not to look at Gunner across from him, knowing what the Blades might soon do to their traitor.

Can I just sit and watch *that? But I have to put Nolan and me first, that and any chance they can lead us to Rafe and Winton.* Besides, even if Mark tried to use his own power, his two hands couldn't grab all four Blades.

The Eel had only driven them a block or two when the thug next to Mark said "Boss, I know I saw it. Gunner was floating, but there's no wires—"

"Leave it," the Eel said.

Even with the guard between them, Mark thought he heard Nolan give a faint, betraying gasp. And she'd said on the phone, they had to catch Rafe themselves to keep the magic hidden.

Another Blade sneered "So who searches the old lady here?"

No, no, I can't move yet—

"Whichever of you isn't blind," Nolan snapped back. "About a woman's age, or about this."

The thug next to Mark shifted in place—and then *all* the Blades snapped to alert as Nolan slowly handed over a small, gleaming pistol from her coat.

"Uh, Boss…"

The Eel didn't answer, but the van slowed and pulled over to let him clamber around to join them.

"I suppose you'll want this off too," Nolan went on. With the others watching, she slid off her coat, and then unstrapped a heavy gray shape that had to be a bulletproof vest.

One guard said "Who the fuck *are* you—" before the Eel motioned him to silence. A faint smile touched the gang leader, and he stepped over and neatly, impersonally, frisked her body and then the coat.

He kept the gun, the vest, and her phone, but he barely raised an eyebrow at a bamboo-cased tube that had to be some Asian-inspired drinking flask.

Bamboo—like the odd fishing poles in her house when I first met her. Mark thought of the horsehide leather in his and Rafe's talismans, and his eyes went to Nolan's so-still face as the Eel handled the tube. For one breath Mark tried to feel for any of the strange stillness of her magic around it, any sign that bamboo was how she summoned the snow… but with Blades crammed in around him his concentration cramped up.

"Are we done? The night's getting colder." Her voice trembled a fraction as she gathered in her coat, and the flask.

"So who *is* Olivia Nolan, and why's a party planner carry an arsenal?"

"Because I can afford it. Because their attack shut down my business, and I take that personally. You think I'm ex-CIA or something? No. Maybe I come from a tough family," she added.

A spellkeeper family. Stop making secret jokes, the Eel can't miss them all!

The Eel looked at her a moment longer. Then he patted her shoulder like he would a child, waved his men to search Gunner, and moved over to Mark.

Mark kept his muscles limp and his face still. Besides the bug sweeper, he had nothing suspicious to find... except, when the pale hands stripped off the second belt under his shirt, they paused. They paused again when they took out the leather keychain and the scraps of other leather from his pocket.

Does he feel *my magic's tingle in them?*

Then the Eel gave him the same pat he'd given Nolan, and kept only Mark's phone, bug sweeper, and pocket knife. With shaking hands, Mark buckled his leather weapon back around himself.

The Eel turned and crouched down next to Gunner.

"Tomas G., Tommy Gun... 'Gunner' never was a good name for a Blade, was it? Traitor."

He reached out, and his men seized the prisoner's arms. Gunner's face clenched white and looked straight at Mark—his "ally" under Rafe, he still thought. The Eel took the little finger on Gunner's right hand and—Mark forced himself to keep his own hands still—*snapped* it backward.

One thug's grip over Gunner's mouth was all that kept the shrill screams from echoing all down the street.

"Nine fingers left. One chance to talk is more than traitors should—"

"I don't know I don't know!" Gunner gasped, so fast the guard barely had time to release his mouth and let the words out. "You want Rafe? We *split up*—right after the job, Lou tried to shoot us, so we split up, I can't find any of them! That was you, right? You Blades got to Lou, now you know Rafe won't be sticking his head up again—"

"So we don't need you?" The Eel's voice dropped to its grimmest.

"He, he talked about another job. It's Wagon Dogs, Roger Winton's food truck lot—"

"Hot dogs?" the Eel sneered. His hand closed slowly around Gunner's twisted finger.

Mark fought to keep his face still, as the pieces tumbled through his head. If "Lou" had turned against Rafe, then he must be the man Winton had possessed—and meanwhile Rafe was targeting his old patron Winton's property… Mark kept his eyes on Gunner, bracing himself for what the Eel might do to him next. *Nolan and I need to focus on stopping Rafe, and surviving. Somehow.*

"That's what Rafe said!" Gunner howled. "He's gotta call us sometime, just watch my phone!"

The Eel shook his head.

"So you don't know where they are. You want me to trust you with your phone, to get the jump on them—when they're stealing *hot dogs?*" Then he shifted around, to look straight at Nolan. "So you're looking for revenge, woman? Tell me: what would you do with this liar?"

Her eyes widened. Then she frowned back at him.

"I'd send him home with the broken finger. But you don't care what I think, do you?"

The Eel gave a wide, toothy smile. "You heard the lady. Take him on home, safe."

Mark caught the faintest twitch of irony in how the Eel said *safe.* And some other signal must have passed to the guards, as they grabbed Gunner and hauled him to his feet. The last of the strength bled from Gunner's face too.

Gunner babbled "Wait, wait! You don't want Rafe? How about I give you how he's running around town, anywhere he wants? How nobody can catch us?"

This time Nolan didn't gasp, but Mark could almost feel her fury. *Think, think, can anything make Gunner stop talking about the magic? He still thinks I'm one of Rafe's men—*

Mark forced out a clumsy laugh. "Nice bargaining, Gunner. You want to just give it away, are you tired of living—"

The Eel rounded and crouched down right in front of Mark. "Shut. Up."

Mark kept his face still as the pale features loomed near. And the Eel added in the faintest whisper:

"Get him talking later."

Somehow Mark managed not to move. He had to keep them alive, stop Rafe and Winton both, cover up the magic's secret—and now he was supposed to be the Eel's inside man to *get* that secret from Gunner too? His fingers twitched, power ready.

The Eel twisted back to Gunner. "Talk fast. I only need one of you, so why should it be you?"

"Hey, I can't—I mean, I can, I can show you how it works!" Gunner squeaked. "I can take you there, right where we've been training."

A pale hand slammed down on the van's floor. "Faster! The 'secret,' now! And how could you be 'training' when I've got eyes everywhere?"

"You'll *see!*" Gunner could barely hold his voice together, but now he managed to look the Eel in the eye. "You need me! I'm trying to show you all of it—but you'll never find the stash if I don't take you there. Not down in the tunnels."

* * *

It took two Blades and a crowbar to pry the manhole cover up. Partway through hauling it aside, the smell blew out into the snowy air, and the two dropped the metal with a harsh *thunk.*

"Boss, are you sure—"

"Gunner says it's worth it. And watch him. He's going to be more used to the stink than any of us. If he *has* been going down there," and the Eel flashed a tight-lipped grin to their guide.

When they started passing out flashlights, to the Blades only, Mark moved to the Eel's side. "Look, it's got to be cramped down there. You don't need Ms. Nolan in the middle of—"

Nolan cut in "After they brought us this far? Of course I'm coming. Unless it's 'no place for a lady.' "

That got a chuckle from the Eel, and then he gave Mark a small, ominous nod. *She's still a hostage, alright.*

Gunner said "Um, so you know, the place is a ways up from here. I only know the way from this spot, Rafe always took us down from here to see who was tough enough to—"

"Then stop wasting my time. We move."

The smallest of the Eel's three big enforcers climbed down first. As he did, Mark looked at Nolan again—quiet, unflinching, her eyes staying on Gunner as if she could spot the first sign of treachery. Gunner was trembling enough for both of them, trying not to look at Mark, and the Eel was unreadable.

Mark looked up past them to the storefronts all around, dim shapes in the still-tightening snow. It might be his last glimpse of the open streets, but he couldn't even make out if they were on Hastings or Maule. Lost.

Then his turn came.

Climbing down the metal rungs was easy enough, even keeping most of his weight off his weak arm. He'd never been claustrophobic, but the sheer *weight* of all that stone around, with every step bringing him deeper into darkness and the outrage invading his nose…

Moving within the narrow beams of the flashlights, they formed up along the narrow space between the arching wall and the flowing water—he tried to *think* of it as water—in the tunnel's center. The first Blade crept out beyond the others' flashlights, and Mark saw him wearing what looked like a bug-eyed night vision helmet before he vanished in the black. Another Blade came next, then Gunner, and the Eel put Mark next, and followed them holding a gun that looked big enough to shoot through both of them at once. Nolan and the last enforcer brought up the rear.

After a few echoing steps, Mark stopped depending on the darting flashlight beams. Instead he let his elbow slide along the slimy bricks at his left, to help him crowd away from the liquid at his other side. *I've been through worse,* he thought as he *refused* to let his head feel even that first queasiness from the stench.

The two Blades in front led them methodically; at every branch they came to, the one with the light paused until the scout with the goggles had gone up to check it. The group barely needed Gunner's directions, since they kept moving forward, and each side tunnel slanted in from an angle behind them. Like random streams gathering into a river, Mark thought, instead of a city's grid of clean perpendicular lines.

That's just one more way we're out of our element. There's no grid to navigate by, no space to fly in, no light to let me run without cracking my skull, no air to fuel Nolan's weather or even disguise it, but all her snow above is still melting into the drains and rising beside us.

Somewhere in the dimness and the cold, his flailing thoughts caught the magic of Rafe's belt.

Up ahead, maybe a long block away… and the pulses were moving, separate talismans shifting back and forth up the tunnel. This wasn't another stash of abandoned shoes with no one to wear them.

His steps must have slowed. Just at his back, the Eel gave a deep, questioning grunt of *Mmm?* Mark glanced back, and the gang leader's eyes flicked forward, motioning him toward Gunner ahead of him.

Right, he had to "get" Gunner to spill Rafe's secrets so the Blades could wipe out the new gang. As if the Eel with magic would be any less of a threat.

Up in Rafe's group, Mark sensed a different force. *Winton* was controlling one of the people ahead.

Rafe, Winton—Mark looked around again, trying to catch Nolan's eye to give *some* kind of warning. All he saw was the great pale wall that was the Eel, and those too-watchful eyes.

Any warning Mark had faded on his lips.

Two branches later, they heard the Blade in the rear burst out retching. He slumped over to the side, heaving as if he meant to empty every organ inside his skin into the sludge.

Mark took the moment to edge forward to Gunner's side. "You really think they'll let us live?" he hissed.

Gunner answered with a grunt—what was that, doubt? defiance?

Before Mark could follow up, the shaken Blade straightened and waved them on.

The thug ahead of Gunner growled "If this ain't worth it, I'm *leaving* you down here. In pieces."

"You'll see! It's all here—how we got tested, practiced, some of the stuff I stashed—everything you need to work out what it is!"

Mark kept his eyes away from Gunner. The terrified punk had been so *eager* to sell Rafe out. And when Gunner had floated off the ground, he'd been surprised—because of course Rafe wouldn't trust rats like this with the truth of what the magic really was.

But… the Eel wasn't the one who could get Mark closer to Winton, and get an answer for Angie. Rafe knew something, if that Winton-presence lurking near him didn't kill him first.

In the darkness and the cold, that thought put a steadiness to Mark's step.

"Boss… they're up here…"

The leading Blade's low voice slid back down the tunnel like a shiver, and the whole line halted.

The Eel swung up his cannon of a pistol—toward Mark and Gunner both. "So you're just showing us the stash, Gunner? If this is a trap, I'll take *days* finishing you."

Gunner only whimpered.

"It's *him* up there," the scout put in. "Rafe and a couple guys. Looks like they're, I don't know, running races up and down the tunnel."

"Remember, I know where you live," the Eel snarled at Mark, and his light whipped over so Mark had to clench his eyes shut before the beam burned his night vision away.

He heard the gun cock, and all he could do was listen.

"So one trick, or one yell, and you're both dead." The Eel swung the beam away, and he motioned them all onward. Then he muttered "Too many lies."

You have no idea.

One of the Blades' lights clicked off, and the others pressed the lenses against their chests to let only a dimmer glow escape. Each step was more by feel now, inching through the shadows. Every footfall had to be softer than the rippling water at their left.

But, light was swelling in the distance ahead. And as they drew closer, other footsteps echoed there—running steps that stopped a moment later, then started again. Right where Mark felt the smaller talismans.

Keep focused. The Eel's heavy footfalls put him right behind Mark, and Nolan and her guard would be behind them both.

The light shone from around the branch ahead. The closer they drew, the brighter it became.

"...always watch the ceiling, dumbass..."

At that sudden voice up ahead, Mark's back felt the Eel's gun nudge him. "Shh."

The group's pace slowed too, stalking forward as they neared the light. The sound of the water swelled; the tunnel opened onto a wider space ahead, with the flood taking most of the space.

Then a figure dashed across it, into view and out again, magic pulsing in his shoes. The lead Blades froze, and then one turned to cover Gunner as they all edged closer.

"See? You don't slip in these shoes," came a voice up ahead.

"Keep your jumps low." Rafe's answer was calm—the same welcoming warmth Mark had dreaded all through his years of trying to dodge pressure to join the gangs. "You want your head clear when you pop the pill. See what running with small steps does."

Small steps… it all fit.

That's why Rafe trains his recruits in the sewers! They get some drug to "make them faster," the shoes are just "for traction," and training under the low ceiling makes them run with lengthened steps but be afraid to try jumping any higher, so they don't know they can fly… Smart… at least until Gunner got separated and kept the shoes too long and found himself floating…

And Winton's pawn was right there among them, putting the pieces together too.

"Yeah, watch it," one of the others laughed. "If you want to be there the day we finish the Blades—"

A sharp croaking shout tore through the tunnel, as Gunner's voice pushed through its panic: "Rafe! Run!"

I need to move. The thought took Mark a heartbeat—and then he was trying to twist around, but the massive shape at his back smashed him into the wall…

Flashes of light—

A glimpse of Gunner slammed to the floor—

Rafe arching across his view dragging a man through the air, a rescue—

The pain in his head drew back to show that the booming and flashing that flooded the world were real, real guns blasting again and again, and whenever they paused he'd hear a wail from one of the shattered bodies left on the stone.

Then Mark could sense it again: Rafe—and Winton's pawn too—lurked somewhere up in one of the branches from the tunnel's other side. In the darkness that the Eel was waving his men toward.

"Go, go, go!" the Eel bellowed.

Two flashes roared from inside that tunnel's black. One of the Blades dropped with a shriek, and the others crowded back into their own tunnel. Mark stumbled dazedly backwards to keep clear of them.

The Blades glared across the space. Mark caught glimpses between their clustered figures, by the lights Rafe's group had left out for their training—that main tunnel might be just wide enough for two people, between the wall and the current of stormwater and sewage down its center. Moans and some kind of wordless pleading burbled within that space, but the Blades had eyes only for the side opening Rafe was defending.

Rafe's voice called from those shadows. "You want the runner's pills? I'll trade for the men you shot." One of the groaning voices between them went still at his words.

The Eel muttered to his men "More lies. I stall them, you find a way around," and he waved the man with the nightvision visor back down the tunnel where they'd come.

The Eel knows it's not just pills they use, when Gunner was floating. They're both killers, but it's Rafe who knows something about Winton, if Winton at his back or the Eel don't get him first—

"Or how about," the Eel called back, "I finish off this one now." He brought his weapon around, to where Gunner was struggling up onto his knees.

No more!

Mark swung an arm around. Just a wild swing against the gigantic man, but a surge of magic let a simple clutching at the Eel's elbow fling him away like some weightless toy… and Mark's fingers held on just long enough to guide the Eel's path straight into the goggled Blade too.

He turned around as both men tumbled down. The Blade at the back with Nolan, the last one on his feet, was already lifting his gun.

Nolan's foot slammed into that Blade's leg. The huge guard barely stumbled as she pushed clear of him—but that stumble scrabbled, tipped, sent him crashing down as something glimmered on the concrete. A patch of magic-formed ice.

She ran toward Mark. The corners of his eyes saw the Blades all starting to rise, the fury in the Eel's face—

Mark could only reach out to grab Nolan's wrist and Gunner's coat and snatch them all into weightlessness. One leap swept them all to the edge of the training space's lights, and he remembered to yell "Don't shoot!" as his next step yanked them across the air.

Together, the three tumbled to the ground in Rafe's far tunnel.

"You're dead! Dead!" came a shout behind them.

Gunner wrenched away from Mark's grip and shoved him back. "What did you—"

"Just move!" Nolan snapped.

Mark stumbled up the tunnel. The nearest shadows looked empty of Rafe's group, but he could sense their magic lurking some twenty, thirty feet up ahead in the darkness. They had backed away from the Blades—but they stayed unmoving, waiting, probably covering this tunnel's entrance. With Mark, Nolan, and Gunner pinned between them and their attackers.

"Tell your friends, Gunner." His voice didn't want to work. "Don't shoot us, we're not the Blades."

"Rafe? You there?" Gunner managed to say. His face was still wide-eyed with shock… and clear to see in the wash of a beam of light from behind them. The Blades must be probing for targets.

Up at Rafe's position, a light winked on. It showed one brief flash of figures crouching there, guns ready, before it vanished again.

"Get down here," Rafe's voice called from the darkness. "Now."

Mark touched the wall and slid along it, pushing himself to a quick, blind walk through the dark, away from the Blades and toward the sensation of Rafe's magic.

And Winton's. Did I just forget, *our "escape" has us running right into our deadliest enemy's hands!*

He heard Gunner closing in behind him, mumbling pleas for Rafe to let them come, and a clumsier step that had to be Nolan at their back. Both of them could only follow his lead, trapped between their enemies.

Mark slowed as he neared Rafe.

The light flicked on again—just Rafe's phone, enough to let them see Rafe's gun and his lean, scowling face. A second figure huddled behind him, that might be the man Rafe had jumped with to safety.

And Winton's pawn made three. Mark felt that presence a few steps further up the tunnel, but already closing in.

Rafe's voice slashed through the confusion. "What are you playing at? Never mind, just tell me how many Blades are left!"

Back up the tunnel came a rumble of voices, some kind of argument among the Blades.

And Winton's puppet urged "We should run!"

To hear that soft, stolen voice in the dimness so *close,* to have the puppetmaster be only steps away from seizing control of any of them—

All Mark could do was gasp "That one! He's not yours, Rafe!" in the blind hope that it did some good.

And in the next glorious instant, the shadow that was Rafe swung his gun around onto the puppet. Winton's pawn froze, at what looked like all of two feet away from Rafe.

The air went still. Voices filtered in from the Blades behind them, but those might have been in a different world from the clash at their elbows.

Mark pushed on "Think! Has he been talking like himself?"

Gunner said "No no, *Lou* was the traitor—he *saved* us from Lou!"

Mark swallowed. Sure, and if this man had touched Winton's first victim to stop him, he'd given the killer the perfect hiding place to switch himself into.

Rafe's voice was cold, dead, as if the man he stared at had never been alive. "How did we first meet? Say it!" He raised the gun higher.

The thug's face twitched in the dim light.

Behind them gunfire boomed out—but somehow the tumbling thunderclaps were nothing to the sharp stomach-clenching *whing* of bullets ricocheting off the walls behind them. *The Blades aren't lined up to shoot straight down our tunnel, not yet,* he thought as he dropped for the floor.

In the turmoil, one voice gibbered under the bullets: "Huh, how, who are they, whaddawedo *Rafe—*"

"*You* stay where I can see you," Rafe snarled. "We pull back, now!"

The panicked voice came from right where Winton's energy had been—*had* been.

"He let him go," Mark said, feeling a pang of envy for how Winton only had to send out his mind, free to pull out the instant danger pressed too close.

Gunner said "What, what are you talking about—"

"Come *on!*" Rafe broke in. "We find the real Winton later!"

Another bullet glanced off the wall. Rafe shoved Gunner forward, and his men began moving. Their shapes crowded up the tunnel and fell into step... moving along the wall with an ease the Blades had lacked.

Rafe's dim light went out. Mark blinked in the darkness and heard Nolan fumbling up behind him. She brushed his side and he managed to find her arm to guide her.

" 'We' can find Winton? And you want to join these thieves?" There was anger in her whisper.

Mark didn't answer, couldn't answer. Why'd it have to be Rafe?

A light splashed against the wall behind them, and vanished. The Blades must be searching for targets. Closing in.

Mark pushed after the Blades' footsteps, leading Nolan along. Those sounds faded in and out, swallowed by their own stumbling and his breathing in his ears... Jus one hesitant step could slow them enough to let the next beam of light catch them and the Eel's guns cut them down. His only real guide was the sense of Rafe's magic ahead, and he felt every slip that Nolan made struggling to keep her balance. She didn't have his sense for power, or even have his practice flying through ordinary night, he realized, and she had to be more blind than anyone here. She never complained.

He felt Rafe turn, heading up what had to be another branch to the left. Mark twisted them around that corner, and saw a glimmer of light from Rafe ahead, like daring them to keep up. *Maybe we* can *keep a truce with him, now that he sees I'm the one who can spot Winton's spies.* If Nolan would stand for it.

Rafe's footsteps faded, and Mark could only slide his feet blindly on. His world shrank to the rush of water at his feet, the bricks against his one hand, the slimy smoothness of the ground—and each soaking ditch or invisible obstacle that his feet had to react to without tripping, his arm to steer Nolan clear of them—and the magic receding ahead. And the darkness that swallowed the rest was all that kept them out of the Blades' reach.

Then Rafe slowed, and Mark sensed him moving upward to the ceiling. A new sound reached his ears—shoes ringing on steel, like rungs set into in the wall.

A harsh grating sound scraped through the tunnel, iron across concrete. And the darkness ahead split as a shaft of faint, genuine moonlight spilled down and widened. *Opened.*

Mark felt the breath and the tension *whoosh* out of him, and he filled his eyes with that blessed light. He had to blink to make out Rafe's three men clustering under the opening, and the dim gaps around them that must be several tunnels crossing here. One thug pushed the others aside and started up the rungs, with Gunner just behind him.

Nolan scrambled forward, and Mark let her slide past him.

Her feet were loud, and Rafe's group were laughing and grunting as they climbed. But under those sounds, Mark caught more footsteps, back in the tunnel and coming faster. He glanced back.

In the shadows by the last branch, a dim, monstrous shape—the bulging eyes of night goggles with a hand shielding them from the light—leaned into view. Its other hand held what had to be the Eel's huge gun.

The others were on the ladder; Mark could only fling himself backward up the tunnel as the *boom* smashed his ears. He tried to twist in the air, felt stone slam into his arm and shoulder as he bounced off the ceiling. Behind him he caught one glimpse of Nolan's boots disappearing up the shaft, before he wrenched himself upward trying to soften his fall.

The Eel stepped into view behind him.

Mark rolled, scrabbled, dove across for a side tunnel. The open air had been so *close*...

He could only slide himself away around the corner wall, blinking at the light behind him and waiting for the thunder to fade from his ears.

Slowly, echoes formed in the nexus behind him: footsteps, panting, curses. Flashlight beams spilled across the space and flicked out just as quickly. Mark edged back, bracing himself for any sound that the Blades were following him around the corner. He still had the shifting sludge that filled the center of the tunnel—one more sound of pursuit and he could still duck down and hide in it. *In the shit.*

One of the Blades muttered "If they see us stick our heads up there—"

"Move, now!" That was the Eel.

They clattered forward. Mark pressed himself closer to the wall and listened as bodies clambered up the shaft, grunting, muttering grim promises—

The tunnels went dark.

The pale light from above cut off, with some great creaking sound from overhead. In the next instant, gunshots roared out, one, then three, then a rapid fire like a pocket-sized war up in the world beyond the concrete ceiling.

A shout rang out, from close by, still in the tunnels. "Boss, you guys okay—"

Mark peeked around the corner. Only a thin shadow of light stirred there, shining on huge shoulders and the two arms that pounded against whatever had blocked the shaft. Mark ducked back. But if that last Blade turned around and saw him, there'd be nowhere to hide, no way out of the line of fire in time, with the tight darkness of the damn sewers pressing in—

He heard feet thud down onto the concrete, echoing. On the tunnel floor again.

No more hesitating.

Mark flung himself around the corner, aiming more by memory than by what faint light was left. One hand flailed blindly past the thug, but his other caught the gun that swung toward him and he poured weight into it, dragging down the weapon and the hand that held it.

Outside, pulses of Rafe's magic resonating against his power and moved—

An arm smashed into him. He held his grip and fought the spinning in his head as he forced the magic down harder. *Hold on, hold on.*

The thug lurched forward. Somehow he could still totter on his feet with all the weight heaped onto him. A glancing blow sent Mark staggering backward until his feet fetched up against a wall.

He flung his magic into his right hand, into the enemy's arm that his palm pressed against. The Blade's arm plummeted and tipped them both to the stone, but Mark could feel the splintering crash through his enemy's weapon hand.

For long moments he gasped for breath, holding the magic's grip and hearing the thug's howls that proved how small his own pains were.

Then he stepped over to the upward shaft. A sliver of light from it was all he had, but another gunshot fired outside.

"You!"

The pain-soaked voice made him turn. In the dimness, all that the light caught was the wavering gun pointed toward him. The Blade was back up.

Above, another weapon fired, then another. Trying to steady his breath, Mark said "You hear that? Your boss up there is outnumbered, you can't help him, you lose—"

"You! You and Gunner did this. But I *got* you."

The shadows hid the gunman's expression better than any mask. But in that voice, desperation was clawing its way out—

How close were the attackers, to wherever Nolan was? Mark took another breath and felt for the magic again.

His head jerked back in surprise. Up among Rafe's pulses of power, he sensed a different, familiar sense. Angie.

"I got you!" the Blade gasped again. The gun steadied.

No. You aren't stopping me.

"Like you 'got' Rafe?" Mark pushed the words out, trying to stretch them past the gun to the man behind it. "People are dying up there, I've got friends up there, and you still want to—"

"*I got you!*" The Blade stepped closer. The slivers of light caught the pale fear in his face as he stole one glance up. "They ain't helping you now, they stuck a car over the way out!"

Mark stared back, at where the man's eyes darted within the shadows. Another gunshot sounded, but Mark said "That's right, Rafe trapped us. He knew where this shaft comes out, and he used that to turn your attack into his ambush in seconds. So when one side up there wins, and someone pulls the car back and find you down here… you really think it's going to be your Blades that'll be coming down? Now," and he drew a deep breath, "*get*—"

Before he could say *out of my way* the Blade spun and ran off down the tunnel.

For one slow exhale, Mark listened as the footsteps receded in the dark. "Loyalty. Huh."

Then at last, at last, he moved upward. A small step and a twitch of power floated him up to the blocked light. His fingers met the round bulge of a tire sunk into the gap. The Blade had guessed right, Rafe must have moved a car to block the open manhole. There was no way out there.

Except for me.

Mark perched on the rungs in the wall, and searched for the magic above. Rafe's troops were still moving around, a hint of Nolan's soft energy was spreading through the air, and he felt Angie circling over them all. No more threats or lies for him to juggle, all he needed now was power.

He shoved his hand and the force in his two belts upward. The car pressed back, its stubborn bulk mocking him, the tire turning against his grip like a living thing as it first began to move, but he pushed, pushed…

The weight melted away from it. In one move Mark lifted the car and himself and slid out from under it. Light—clean, snow-muffled moonlight—flooded against his eyes, but he was already hurling himself out of any enemy's reach, into the air.

A shift of power held him steady as a world of wind beat at him. Under him was nothing but dimness and whirling gray snow, at what must have been a hundred feet between him and the ground. His magic picked out Angie circling somewhere off by the building on the left, out of sight, and Rafe hung somewhere nearby—but Nolan had to still be earthbound in the chaos down there.

Mark dropped slowly, peering through the snow she must have raised. Another gunshot split the wind. The muzzle flash came from one of the gray shapes below, and the shapes resolved into small trucks lined up across a broad lot… blocky cover that several men were darting between as they advanced, pincering in to catch someone between them.

Rows of food trucks—what had Gunner said about Rafe targeting Winton's lot, was that where he had us falling back to? Where was

Winton's own presence? And, Mark had never seen the place before, but something about it looked shiveringly familiar.

Rows of cars lay below, like the Blades' junkyard. Where Angie had "died."

Closer to Mark's feet, he could see the two figures those men were closing in around, a clear view of their backs as they crouched behind trucks. One lay wounded already. From their bulk those targets were the Eel and his last, bleeding Blade.

Mark watched them—*too hard to reach in time,* he thought, if it meant working his way around more bullets. *But instead I just watch as more people die?*

Then he spotted Nolan hanging two trucks back from the cornered Blades. The advancing killers might move right past her.

One of Rafe's men dodged to the next truck; he had swept in wide enough on the Blades' flank to have almost a clear run at their rear. But the moment he settled in behind his cover, the biggest Blade—the Eel himself—charged forward, seizing the moment to run past several trucks and head his attacker off.

Something moved at the edge of Mark's range. Winton's presence, blocks away and flying in bird-quick. He'd reach the lot in the next minute. Mark turned back toward Nolan.

Then, he felt it before he saw it through the whirling snow. The solid pulse of Rafe leaping out and cutting through the air, toward the Eel. No, soaring in *above* him, unnoticed—

Rafe didn't open fire on his rival. Instead he glided over him and then rocketed straight upward—levitation's fastest way to put distance between himself and where he'd been.

Two breaths after Rafe passed pulled up from the Eel, the ground exploded.

The flash and roar might have burst out of a movie screen, but in another instant the night air itself darkened where the Eel had been, and Mark heard a muffled *smacking* sound showering against the trucks below. The sound could have been a wave of hail, a hail of sharp edges from Rafe's grenade.

Mark pulled upward, blinking back the spots dancing through his vision. That ragged shape lying in the Eel's place would never move again.

After all these months, Rafe gets his shot at his old boss—and kills him. Shouts of confusion drifted up from the oblivious gangs below, and Mark's eyes flicked back to where Rafe hung still in the whirling air. But, Rafe was already settling toward the ground.

To go after the last of the Blades—and that *was* the last, with the rest dead or on the run.

One more death tonight. *And I'm* still *just watching?*

Mark dropped. More shots smashed through the air, but he held that back from his thoughts to track the blurred, too-sudden rush of the ground closing in below him, until his feet touched the truck's roof and kicked him off in a low leap along the row. The Blade had been at one of the trucks up to the left, he thought as he touched the ground.

A scream came from behind him, and a gunshot matching it. Right at his back—

He lunged blindly forward, caught a flicker of Angie diving past him and over to one side—

A kick downward sent him leaping after her, darting between the trucks with barely an instant to aim. He managed to catch himself against one cold metal side… as more footsteps sounded in the row that he'd left.

One of Rafe's men had to have been closing in, and the Blade must have moved back first and Mark had landed right between them until Angie led him out of the crossfire. He gasped for a breath, but the two sides were too close, he had no time.

He hopped up to the truck's roof and pressed himself low. He could see the Blade he'd jumped past, crouching five trucks away and staring wildly left, right, fumbling to load his gun and nearly dropping it. Only two spaces from Mark, Rafe's man—the skinny one Winton had possessed and abandoned—was working his way closer between the trucks.

Mark hauled in a breath. What could he shout: *Let him live... He's the* last *of the Blades here, let him go tell everyone that you won...* yes. He crouched lower to have cover if his voice swung the guns toward him.

He felt a bird-presence sweeping in—*that's not Angie*—

In that instant he could only stare as the hawk struck

...

Stirred. Rippled. The rippling spreads and churns, stillness stirs and stretches, pushed by sparks that pour through him and flow and draw the stillness away.

The touch. Quick, ever-shifting—how had he forgotten?—and pulling back like the feathers from his face, Angie drawing *back* and her tiny weight lifting clumsily away, leaving him only the soft snow around his hands.

Mark pried his head up. The roof under his feet was gone. He lay on asphalt.

Across the row of trucks, two shapes lay on the pavement. The Blade and Rafe's man, both lying still and soaked in red.

And Winton, and Angie... both streaked through the sky. Angie dove and twisted, and Winton's bird slashed after her, faster and fiercer than anything Winton had sent before.

Mark pushed himself to his feet, swaying and leaning against the truck. Somewhere, somewhere in the snow beyond the lot, someone was shouting, sirens were screaming. Winton's sleeping spell had left him, but knocking Mark out had let Rafe's man and the Eel's kill each other after all...

Please, please, let Winton only have put me to sleep, not used me *to kill...*

"What was that?"

For a moment, the sounds made no sense. Then he looked over and saw Nolan running toward him.

"I know that was your owl standing over you," she said. "I thought you were gone."

Except Winton needed him alive. He still did.

Mark shook his head, and the motion made his stomach lurch.

But Winton was gone; his bird and Angie could be halfway across town. He sensed Rafe's belt somewhere up the block, fleeing too.

And the sirens. The police, closing in on the gunshots and worse, somewhere out in the snow.

Nolan's hand closed on his arm. "Can you fly?"

"Can I..." He let out his breath and clapped a hand over hers. The police searchlights might reach out to pin them at any moment.

A thought launched them upward. The rush of cold and motion swept the last of the muzziness from his head, but watching the buildings slide by below did nothing to steady his thoughts.

Winton had *caught* him, until Angie saved him... again... What had she done, used her own mind power to break Winton's sleep? And now the killer had chased her beyond his reach. Rafe was still heading away, but Mark had let Rafe's men die, and the Blades too.

Or he'd done more than that, under Winton's control. *No. No, Angie wouldn't let him.*

He brought them down at the next open roof they blew over, and the fierce wind tore at them while they fell and lurched to a safe stop. Nolan toppled across the roof, and Mark pulled her to her feet.

"Here." Nolan pressed something flat into his hand. His phone, that the Eel had taken. She'd pulled it off his *body?*

Mark looked over the streets below. The snow was finally thinning, and the lights in the black formed patterns, formed streets and landmarks and a world around him again. If there was anywhere to go.

Nolan added "I admit, when I tightened the snow above the tunnels, I was hoping something bigger than an owl would notice. Maybe something Dennard-sized."

Despite himself Mark felt his eyes widen. "That was you? All that floodwater in the drains was what, a signal flare, all the time we were in the sewer?"

"Not a flare. Flares are clumsy, obvious, and weather can't do them." Nolan chuckled.

More of her jokes… sure, after the danger they'd just dodged, why not? Mark managed a smile, as if they were actually any closer to an answer, not dragged even farther away from it.

"But, to be serious, Mark: Rafe and his magic just got more dangerous than ever. Now that his people know he's killed the Eel, he can bring in recruits from anywhere—and those tricks that disguise his magic are already wearing thin. We have to shut him down, *now."*

Mark stared at her, felt the cold in her voice. Too much like the Eel and Rafe when they mentioned their plans for their enemies.

And… stop Rafe? *He's still the* only *one who knows something about Winton. And he hates him as much as we do—more than Nolan does—and I just got him talking about 'us' hunting Winton together.*

Until Winton had grabbed at Mark's mind and Rafe's man had died—

Mark shoved that thought away; that was over, and Rafe didn't know that he'd let his man die. Rafe's magic had been heading east, downwind…

"I can't find him, yet." Mark remembered to turn away as he spoke; faces were where Nolan spotted lies. "I have to… look for Angie, Winton almost got her this time."

"Mark? You always said the birds are too fast to chase—"

"There's your ladder to the street. I have to go, now!"

He flung himself upward, and stole one glance back to be sure the ladder was where he'd said. He must have chosen the landing spot because of it… as if he'd already known he'd have to leave Nolan behind.

CHAPTER SIX

PRIVATE AND LINE

Leap and land, leap and land. Each step down along a roof raised a solid, reassuring thump under his feet, more urgent and real than the muted night traffic below. The biting air and thinning snow he hurtled through dug into his muscles trying to set off a trembling that might never stop… but as long as he reached the next landing he could push it down.

The main street—Collier, that was it—slid by under Mark between the scaffolded glows of the buildings, like a dim river of scattered headlights. He'd last sensed Rafe fleeing this way. And those cars might attract the gang, offering enough traffic to let them drive inconspicuously at night and put quick distance between themselves and the shootout. Just a guess—and they could have gotten enough distance and veered off already.

Nolan would say that was more luck than he deserved, if she knew he wanted to *talk* with Rafe again. He'd just made it away from the gangs alive, leaving some of them dead behind him, and now he was racing to drop himself into their sights again?

A spark of magic moved ahead—not Rafe's, this was Angie.

Low and fast, he felt her cutting through the air toward him. It felt like only moments before she neared him and swung around to fly ahead of him again, weaving left and right along their course. Searching. Guiding him.

She left me on the roof before, but now she breaks Winton's spell on me and comes back to lead me? But the frustration was a small, petty thing, under the warming thrill of flying with her again. On their last real flight together, they—mostly she—had beaten Winton and Rafe in the same few minutes.

The next roof burst out of the dimness at him, too close. He wrenched magic to pull up and skim along it, but the feeble tap of his foot on the concrete mocked him with all the momentum he'd wasted. Just when Angie could see his clumsiness.

He kicked off again for a proper launch forward. *Am I that tired, or is my magic getting a grip in my head again?*

Faster! Angie must have been flying up ahead for a reason. And he only needed to get within a block or two of Rafe's belt to spot it.

The larger patterns of the city began unfolding in his mind, at last. If Rafe started by fleeing along Collier here, what streets or plans might have drawn him off it? The cold air slapping at Mark's face was nothing now. The filtered sounds of the streets below were a soft, comforting rhythm as he flew.

His phone buzzed in his pocket.

He started the next leap as a long, clear arch forward before he risked glancing at the text.

You're running low on new allies—W.

Mark felt the phone's sides bite against his tightening fingers. Winton had helped Rafe and the Blades kill each other, and now he was *laughing* at them?

Somehow, Mark made the next landing and leaped on. No slowing. No stopping to talk with the killer.

Another buzz in his hand:

When your friend woke you up, do you know what it cost her?

What do you think is keeping her alive in that owl?

The night's cold pressed all through him. As if it poured in through his wide-open eyes to freeze his flesh and slow his thoughts.

What it cost Angie... what could it... Winton always lied... but she did break Winton's spell on him, she'd beaten his magic... What "cost"... the cost to Angie's own mind-magic? Was that the energy that held her mind in the owl with her body gone... and, how much did she have left now...

Angie's presence did feel *thinner*.

The roof Mark had aimed for was sliding away below, missed. He flailed in the sky, his arms and legs refusing to obey. Somehow he eased his weight back to let his numbed body dip down toward the next landing.

The phone buzzed again.

It said *She needs real help.*

If Winton knew how to help her—

"Lying backstabber bastard!" Mark spat out, to force his finger off the button that would answer Winton. "We'll *find* you, and we'll *take* the cure!"

He slammed down on the sloped roof and flung himself forward. Up in the snow ahead, Angie's weaving path hadn't even slowed down.

Think, think! If Rafe did leave the main street, would it be north or south? South would be a simple right turn, but north would keep him near more open streets... Mark clenched his teeth against the cold and lunged onward. How far ahead had Rafe already gotten?

A block later the phone buzzed again. Mark beat down the urge to shove it away in his pocket, and glanced at the screen. This wasn't Winton, the call came from Henry.

Henry's scratchy voice sounded rough against the whistle of the air. "Mark? Are you alright?"

"Fine. Kind of busy right now." He watched the flatness of the next roof slide up in the dimness ahead.

" 'Kind of'?" Henry began, and then he started again, hesitant. "Dennard said you were going into... well, he didn't want to give me details."

"So instead you check up on me?"

Mark felt the anger tightening his throat, and he paused a moment to finish the leap and arch his next one up higher, longer in the air.

"Winton killed them, and I was right there! Rafe's men and the Blades were already shooting each other, but he killed the ones that were left, well most of them—and I couldn't stop it, Angie saved me again, and I just got dragged around with them with everyone pointing their goddamn guns at me—"

Was that hoarse, choking sound really his voice? He wrenched down a swallow and tried again.

"But I got one thing right. Rafe knows I tried to help him, and he used to be taking Winton's orders. He has to know something that can get me closer to the killer, and Angie might be fading away on us."

This time, he felt Angie's course ahead slow in the night. He could picture her wings pausing to let her look back at him.

"Rafe?" Henry's voice sounded shocked. "You're trusting *him* now?"

"He needs me! He knows I can spot when Winton comes at him! I have to try!"

"Mark… you know how you sound right now?" Henry said it slowly, as if even naming the problem would push Mark further away.

"Like the magic's made me crazy again? It's not that, I've only been flying one afternoon—and spent half the night being dragged around sewers afraid to use it at all, while people were dying around me."

"Listen to me—"

"Henry, I *wish* this was the madness, then I wouldn't be this sick and guilty and scared. But I have to find Rafe, now!"

Have to. He clung to those words as Henry kept protesting, and he babbled what reassurances he could until his cousin let him go. But it had to be the truth; he had too many real fears still shivering just behind his brain for this to be his self-control slipping away.

A block later, Angie made a sudden swing left, north. As if she'd seen something, or made a decision.

Clearwater Hospital glimmered in the distance. At first it was a pale blur in the snow that his eyes picked out more by expecting it than by what he saw. Then the complex drew closer, and he felt Rafe's magic pulsing somewhere within it.

Clearwater was the place the ambulance had brought Winton, the place he'd disappeared from.

And... Rafe's gang had just been in a shootout, and now he found them at a hospital. *After I couldn't stop it;* Mark bit his lip.

Roofs and buildings edged in and out in front of each other as Angie led him closer, and Mark studied the shapes for a way into the main building. Had Rafe found a neglected window, or just walked in?

The concrete lake of a parking lot still looked only two-thirds empty, even this deep in the night. Here and there, figures were moving back and forth between those cars and the gold-lit entrance. Mark paused at the rim of the last roof before the lot, leaning against a humming bank of machinery. Should he just drop down to the pavement by its back? Angie glided down to sweep over the lot.

Mark crouched lower. Now that he'd stopped moving, the trembling wracked his knees like they'd never hold him up again, even when he bent them tight. Up here out of view he was safe from bullets, from making any more mistakes...

Angie swung in a tight circle, and he could just make out her soft gray shape passing above one parked car—the only car sitting in a pool of its own light. Two shapes moved behind its windows. She circled over it again.

Another shift jerked his head up. Rafe's magic had been moving through the building, but now the pulse drew closer, just matching the figure that stepped out of the hospital entrance. And another shape walked beside Rafe.

The two started across the parking lot, toward the car. The second man's clothes became clearer; not one of Rafe's thugs, he wore the simple green of one of the hospital staff.

And Rafe had pulled him out of the building... Who was in more danger, the doctor or whoever Rafe needed him for? *How can I step in when I don't know who's who—or what else Rafe will try to pull me into?* He could go to the car first, or to Rafe, or pull the doctor out, or watch...

Mark pulled himself in tighter, but the tremors wouldn't leave his clenched knees. Every move he could think of only led deeper into danger.

Now Rafe was *at* the car—Mark knew he'd waited too long. He shoved his hands and numb feet down to fling himself off the roof.

Dropping through the air freed him to glance around again; no, still nobody was too close to the back of the lot where he settled down, not with the night and the snow to hide him. He tapped down onto the pavement and shifted into a smooth walk forward.

Angie circled in the night above. From the corner of his eyes he searched for the few scattered figures walking between the clusters of cars, alert for any sudden, shocked movements of someone who might have noticed him arrive. His shoes crunched over the snow, left-right left-right, easier than thinking how every step brought him closer to the muddy brown car where Rafe and the rest were.

Rafe hasn't looked over. I could still duck away.

The car's door hung open, and the doctor peered inside. But he held himself back from leaning in, enough for Mark to see he was a young man, with pale hair and a paler face.

Rafe nudged the man toward the car... and in the same motion, turned to give a slow, deliberate look right at Mark. Waiting.

Three footsteps closer, another car door opened, and Gunner leaned out to follow Rafe's gaze to Mark. "You again?" Was that suspicion, welcome, or both?

And Rafe... the smug bastard simply nodded, and turned to the doctor and the car. "We'll need blood, and antibiotics and the rest of what you'll need to stitch him up. We get those, and you do your job, and nobody has to know about your little deals."

He's blackmailing the doctor right in front of me, like I'm just another ally to get up to speed on who he's bullying next. And I'm going along with it.

" 'Do my job'?" the doctor said. "You're out of your mind! You think I can work out here?" He reached into the car.

Then he fell back, shoved by a hand that looked stained dark.

"You take me in there, they lock me up." The thug's voice was weak, but fierce as a loaded gun. He huddled in the back seat, teeth clenched, one hand locked over his bloody thigh.

The doctor looked at him, then around at Rafe, at Gunner—and Mark—watching them all with the same wild blinking as if his eyes could break him out of some terrifying dream.

And I'm part of it. Or Mark could grab the doctor and run; Angie could cover him.

Rafe looked right at Mark. "Any ideas?"

Rafe's head turned slowly around the parking lot, nodding to all the scattered people, *daring* Mark to call out to them—just like Mark had threatened Rafe once, trapped near his own apartment, until Mark had seen there'd be no help.

Mark's nose twitched at the *wrongness* of spilled blood. Wrongness he'd smelled again and again since Rafe and everything else tore open his life.

"Listen to me!" the doctor said to Rafe. "He's still bleeding, and he could have a dozen infections already! If you're any kind of friend..." His voice died away, and he looked over at Mark again.

Mark forced down a swallow, and looked right past him. To speak to Rafe.

"You can help him—but you can't spot the man who really got him shot. And I can." Where had that calm, cold voice of his come from? Mark flicked a thought to his magic, and just that instant's effort added certainty to his next words: "He isn't here now."

"Oh, just like that?" Gunner frowned. "And there's no 'he' left in our way now. We got the Eel, we own the streets!"

Rafe's lips moved into a private smile, and he leaned toward Mark—there could have been months, years, of offers and anticipation in the move. "You sound like you want…"

Focus on Angie up there, so I can stand saying it. "A deal. I watch for him, and you help me track him down and get what we need. After we help your friend. And you do need me, you know you do."

Somehow Mark got the words out without his voice breaking. But that scraping on his nerves was nothing compared to standing there in the silence, waiting for Rafe to answer.

A grunt of surprise came from Gunner. "Deal? You're making up rules with our boss? And Rafe *was* your boss too, right?" and he scowled at Mark, then looked at Rafe.

"Later," was all Rafe said.

The doctor cut in "Whatever you're talking about, your friend needs—"

"And we'll help him," Rafe said. "Right after we settle that spy over there."

Slowly, leisurely, he pointed past a patch of cars to a shape standing a distance up in the next row, watching.

Not again! First the Eel spots one tail on me, now Rafe is… what, he tested *whether I saw this guy so he can call me on how blind I am?*

Breath hissed from the thugs, and the doctor stared. Gunner's hand reached into his coat.

"Wait!"

The word burst from Mark and kicked him forward to lunge around the gang and march for the stranger. He could hit him, warn him, drag him away… useless ideas spun in Mark's head. Behind him he heard a shushing sound from Rafe, and the gang falling silent. Waiting for him to handle it.

The watcher leaned against a car, its door open and its engine idling—the same black shape that had been following Mark before.

He leveled a phone and its camera on Mark like a weapon. The face behind it had the same too-young features Mark had sketched from his rooftop. *How'd he find me here?*

"Mark Petrie." The man drew the syllables out into a threat. "The cabbie who got shot by a renegade Blade, and now you're giving rides to the Eel. One of the last people to see Roger Winton before his heart attack—or was that just Winton having to disappear? Disappear from you, maybe? And, you're the man who can vanish on an empty street."

Don't flinch. Mark kept his gaze steady and let each fact roll on over him. The more this stranger knew, the better his answer had to be. Across the lot, Rafe was still watching.

"But now, you're *meeting* with that Blade? Not what I thought I'd find—"

"Find? Someone sent you here tonight?" Mark felt for magic, but he caught no sign of Winton, only Rafe behind him and Angie circling. So far.

"Could be. Or you're not as slick as you think."

The man chuckled coldly, but Mark thought he heard a bluff in that voice—and he *couldn't* have tracked Mark here through the air. He did look only mid-twenties under the warning glare that creased his face. The car's light shone on a blotching that might be freckles.

That young man edged back closer to his car. "What you've got is a choice. You can tell me what you're playing, and start with how you got away from me before. Or I could call the client who wanted you watched, or I just put these pictures out to all the people you're playing and see who bites—"

"Rafe will 'bite' your head off, and having that car running won't save you," Mark said, just to break through the stream of threats. The man knew too much, but Rafe *would* kill him, and Rafe's man was still bleeding and Winton might be on his way. No time to waste.

"I'm talking to you, not him," the spy growled. "I know how you think: a picture of you ready to send the cops is as good as pointing a gun at you. So how did you lose me?"

"I've been dodging Blades, and Rafe, and killers, and… and *that's* going to scare me?" Mark tried a laugh, but it came out shrill and angry. "People are dying, and you want my secrets? I bet I know who hired you, behind all his tricks. And he kills people who get too close to this!"

The man's jaw only tightened, as if threats only made him tougher. "Oh, so *you* know who sent me? How'd you get away—you tell me now!"

"People are dying, while Winton is… and you're still trying to…"

The man only curled his lip.

Mark's hand shot out.

The spy's arm whipped up for some kind of block, but Mark's power was already surging. As the grip locked around his wrist, he launched the two of them into the sky.

His passenger's hands went slack and the phone dropped, but Mark grabbed hold and wrenched them higher. The force slapped at him and dulled the cold rush of the air. When the outlines below began to blur into grayness, he let their flight ease to a stop and locked them in place.

The investigator let out a ragged scream.

One jump and he screams? Really? Mark pressed his free hand over his passenger's mouth, the hand that had been so briefly grabbed.

That left only Mark's head free to motion toward the lights of the cityscape below, where the brightest lights still shone through the snow-sheathed vastness they floated in.

"You see that?"

Stupid, of course he can see it! Mark's hand felt him grunt something, a weak sound that the drifting wind against them swallowed.

Mark tried again, flailing for words that would make this gamble work. "Take a long look at that drop. That's real power, and it's something they tell me they've been able to hide for centuries! I bet you think the snow is natural too, don't you? But some 'client' points you at me, and you think you can make threats? You are in so far—"

He choked back the words *over your head;* no time for jokes.

"Don't you get it, he sent you into this blind, because he's using you! He only needs you because you've got no magic for me to sense. But he sent you after me knowing he can wipe you out if you find anything. You say you know about me—do you know about Detective Lee and his 'accident' when he started asking about me? You have to be next on Winton's kill list, don't you see that? If you want to get through this alive, tell me who you are, and everything you know about him. Help us stop—"

Magic flickered. Like a motion at the corner of Mark's eye, the sense pulled his head around to stare down and over. Somewhere in that space below, one of Winton's birds was slicing through the gray.

A hundred yards away. He felt Angie rising to cut the bird off.

His prisoner was gasping something, and shaking in his grasp.

"—Iskander, Ben Iskander, I'm a private investigator—or almost, so sue me—but it's just a job... you even *hear* me?" In the dim sky, Iskander's face was only a pale gleam of sweat.

"He's already here," Mark said.

Angie's presence shot upward on what must have been a cross-wind, lifting her up above Winton's path to them, ready to strike. Winton's magic edged around, skating along the air currents Mark could only brace against. *And I'm just* hanging *here?*

Iskander's body shook, wracked with the fear that poured out with his words. "Whattaya doing, who's there, who the fuck *are you?"*

"I... sometimes I'm not sure any more."

The sigh released some of the pressure that had driven Mark's pleadings. He felt Iskander's trembling slow, and he went on, quieter:

"I'm sorry if I scared you. Maybe I'm not making sense. But there's someone fighting for our lives right now, and I'm not going to let you fall… you can trust me, I'm trying to help you. But you need to tell me about Roger Winton."

"*Tell* you? Winton was gone before I took the case, nobody's seen him!" Simple surprise held the tatters of Iskander's voice together.

"Winton has to be the 'client' who sent you. We need to know how he contacts you, what he wanted, what you told him about me—everything." The same things Mark had hoped to get from Rafe. "And, maybe a real investigator's just what this team needs—"

Out in the dark, Winton swung clear of Angie and moved closer. Mark tightened the magic to yank them up beyond his path.

The lurch made Iskander shriek and go limp in his hands. Mark let them slow and tracked Winton's bird, struggling up below with Angie closing in.

"I don't know, I don't know!" Iskander was gasping. "He never had a face or a name, there's just the phone—he sent that to me, that's how he reaches me. And I dropped it down there!"

A mysterious anonymous client… *Sure, what could be dangerous about that?* But Mark only said "Okay. Now, hang on and I'll get you safe to the ground. We need that phone—maybe our hacker can get something from it."

But the hacker works with Nolan, and I haven't got Nolan on board with any of this…

Later. Mark tracked Winton circling wide, and he cut the magic and dropped.

Iskander screamed against the whistle of air, and Mark covered his mouth again. "Trust me!"

The lines of the city thickened and formed out of the snow below. Mark watched them through squinted eyes as they unfolded into shapes again, still hard to make out the distance. But Rafe's belt on the ground pulsed like a mental lighthouse to warn when to pull up.

Winton hung back above.

Mark slowed their fall, and watched the shadows resolve into the car-dotted flatness of the hospital lot. Rafe's magic was off to its edge now—had he taken his people away to let Mark work on Iskander in private?

With one last wrench, they dropped softly to the pavement, only a few steps from where they'd launched. Iskander crumpled out of his grip and slumped on the snow, wheezing for breath. But, he was keeping his stomach down.

Winton was still maneuvering, dodging Angie… but it might only take him a moment to dive and strike.

Mark reached out a hand, then pulled it back; Iskander was shaken enough as it was. "Can you walk? We need to get inside, out of sight."

"Out of… what?" the PI managed. "There's nothing there!"

"Can you *walk?* We get the phone and go!"

"I… yes." Iskander stumbled up, and he wiped something from his mouth, then set his jaw. He started for his car, searching the snow around him.

Mark glanced around. The lit front of the hospital lay across the parking lot, maybe the best cover from Winton's eyes for now. And Winton was—

Where was his presence? Not diving on them, not dodging Angie—

Iskander leaned down to scoop up the phone Winton had sent him. *Flicker.*

Iskander didn't break his stride. He straightened smoothly up, his back to Mark, and took another casual step away. Just as Mark had asked him, nothing changed… except that his body simmered with the controlling power that had surged out of the phone.

Mark stared. He took one numbed step toward Iskander, his shoe scraping on the snow.

Iskander bolted.

He ran straight across the lot, toward the lights of the hospital entrance, all his trembling and stumbling wiped away by Winton's possession. He charged past cars, past one startled woman just fumbling with her keys, ignoring them all.

Mark's first steps after him staggered to a halt. *I can't touch him, then Winton would grab me!* But what did Winton want with Iskander's body, that sent him openly running—

NO—

But the shape was right there. A huge pale minivan-SUV thing just pulling away from the hospital entrance. Gathering speed, too big to slow down, no reason for the driver to look to the side as Iskander raced up and flung himself right at the wheels.

In the instant before he dove, his arm swung upward and something arched away into the air. Mark felt the magic leave the victim just before the impact, and sensed Winton's bird—seized by the puppetmaster's control again—swooping over the crash.

To catch Winton's phone that had been tossed away. The bird flew by.

And Ben Iskander himself…

Voices burst out of the night, but Mark could only stagger the other way. His footsteps on the snow were empty muffled things with no power to drown out the screams behind him.

One more dead. Rafe's man and the Blades went before my eyes, and now this man who took Winton's money… I told him that asking about the magic made him a target—

I *made him a target, I made Winton kill him and I made him grab the trapped phone—*

Rafe. Mark remembered Rafe, the other one who'd done the killer's work once, Winton's other target. Rafe's power led Mark across the lot, straight to him and his crew. Four figures stood there, the doctor helping the injured man along. Too late Mark remembered that Winton's bird could be watching him to find the others, but the bird was hanging back again. For now.

"Where'd you go?" Gunner said. "You shut him up or not?"

Mark locked his eyes on Gunner, but the outrage he wanted couldn't seem to push out through the numbness on his face.

"Later." That was Rafe, always in control. "Now we get inside and patch up our boy—and nobody sees," he warned the doctor.

"Right," Mark managed to say. "Inside, out of sight. While we can."

CHAPTER SEVEN

FRIENDS AND CLOSE

The lit entrance and shocked voices drew away, as the doctor led them circling around the pale bulk of the hospital. Mark saw him whispering with Rafe, while Gunner helped the injured man walk despite his dragging leg. A wounded man outside a hospital, and they thought they could hide him from both Winton and the police?

But the doctor led them to a quiet side of the building. A heavy-looking door stood next to a *Loading* sign, and the doctor unlocked it with a shaking hand.

And Winton… hung back. For the whole walk around Mark held himself ready to shout and leap when the bird struck, but he only felt it holding its place on a side corner of the roof, not even moving to their side to keep them in view. What was Winton up to *now?*

Before they stepped inside, Mark stole one last glance up, where the shadow that was Angie passed just over them, as they moved beyond her view.

The hospital corridors looked deserted here. The dull half-light of the fluorescents promised that much, but then a murmur of voices made him whirl to the left, before he took in the muted jumble of voices and hums echoing all around from deeper in the wings. Still Winton held his place above.

The wounded man jerked his head back and forth toward the sounds, his eyes gleaming feverishly. "They won't take me, I won't go back to jail," he muttered. His hand locked inside his coat, one motion short of waving his gun around.

The last time I saw a gang in a hospital, Angie and I were trying *to get them caught.* Mark forced his steps into an even pace and moved past him to the doctor. "You heard him. You sure nobody's going to see us?"

He nodded, too fast. "I, I told you all, nobody uses this supply wing at night—"

Voices sounded just around the turn ahead.

Rafe was already grabbing a door, shoving it open and waving them all inside. *Angie would have been faster,* Mark found himself thinking.

They crowded into what had to be a supply room. Shelves of small boxes lined the walls, with two thirds of the space empty.

Gunner growled "We going to be hiding all night? Why stick our asses out here—we just go to some small-time clinic and make them patch Q up."

"We do what we have to." Rafe said it softly, but something in his tone made Gunner nod and fall silent.

With two gestures, Rafe had Gunner laid their injured friend— "Q"—down. The doctor stepped over, but Rafe waved him back and studied the wound himself. Mark watched them, but the doctor didn't protest, he only observed Rafe as he drew out a roll of surgical tape and covered the wound. A glance through the room's supplies found instruments and machine parts, none of the bandages or medicine they needed. Q's hand never left his gun.

Finally Rafe balled up his coat into a pad and set it down under Q's thigh. "Keep that elevated, and press the corners over the wound," he said. "That's all we can do without real gear."

The doctor sighed "Finally. Right down at the end of the wing they can have him in surgery in—"

"*Nobody* is dumping anyone there." Rafe's hand settled on Q's shoulder a moment. "We need blood, some tools, and something for infection, right? So we bring it to him, you patch him up for tonight, and we're out of your space. It's the only way nobody gets hurt, and nobody knows we were here."

The doctor opened his mouth, then shut it again.

Rafe turned to the door, and motioned to the doctor to follow, and Mark startled to see Rafe beckoning him too.

Before he could move, Gunner pushed past him. He must have meant to whisper to Rafe, but in the tight space of the storeroom Mark caught "—know Q's only slowing us down—"

"Just keep an eye on him. You know we'll be right back." The words sounded calm and steadying, in spite of the warning glare that went with them.

Gunner had already led the Eel to Rafe once, then turned around and tried to warn Rafe, and now the weasel wanted to leave the injured Q... *while Q's bleeding, and there's a whole hospital of security around us, and Winton's still out there too. And I threw myself into the middle of this...*

The doctor paused in the corridor to glance around, before he squared his shoulders and led Rafe and Mark forward. His steps were quick, nervous, echoing in the half-sounds of the hallway.

At the next turn the doctor said "You know he's getting worse. Do you expect me to walk off with a whole ER—"

"In and out," Rafe said. "Just keep thinking that: we're in, we get out. Safe for him, safe for the security he won't have to shoot, safe for your reputation. Nothing you can't cover up, I hear."

The doctor winced.

Sounds echoed and wavered down the hall, through the ceiling, in lurking murmurs that couldn't be all that distant. Mark had to clench his neck to keep from staring around. He tried locking his gaze on the doctor ahead, and listening for any change in their guide's anxious pace.

A door opened ahead, and two women in white stepped out.

Mark tensed, but the doctor simply strode up to them and began talking. His voice was too low to catch… at least he looked casual in how he gestured back at the two visitors, and Rafe only stood there unworried.

And when did I start trusting Rafe Martinez to tell me what's safe?

Mark gritted his teeth and moved closer to the gang leader. Under his breath he said "Winton's still watching outside. And you remember, I'm only putting up with all of you so you can help me track him down."

Rafe's lips twitched in a small, mocking smile. "That's not what Q thinks."

Don't flinch! Mark fought to keep his face clamped still. Yes Q was hurt, same as Iskander had died and the Blades and Rafe's other man had died *when I could've been faster*… The doctor was still chatting with the women, still holding off suspicion.

"So you want a shot at Winton," Rafe said. "What's he want with us?"

Mark swallowed; Rafe needed to know. "The secret of flying, I think. You really didn't let him get it?"

Rafe shook his head.

"Well, you can't. He hinted once he wants the power because it could heal him—he had to be hauled off in an ambulance after Angie killed a bird he was possessing. That and, he'll kill to keep the world from noticing what any of us can do. But the way your people grab for the headlines, you've got everyone worried over that one." The last came out as an accusation.

"Coverups and secrets? Figures." Rafe's grin widened. "I bet you'll like what comes next. C'mon," and he marched after the doctor—who had just turned away from the women and started moving again.

Mark had only just caught up to them when the doctor swung open a door and led them inside.

Another storeroom. But where the first one had been cramped and hemmed in by empty shelf space, this room gleamed with racks of plastic-bagged equipment. Diagrams lined the wall, and a huge refrigerator unit hummed in the back.

"Blood, universal donor." The doctor laid out several containers of the precious dark red next to the room's computer, and began digging through the racks. "And EMT kits… antibiotics for the infection pit that gunshot must be turning into… but I keep telling you, I'm not the guy to do this. I haven't had a GSW since my residency."

Rafe's teeth flashed. "I figured. Not what Lightning React pays you for, is it?"

Lightning React? For a moment Mark only watched the doctor jerk back in surprise, and then the name clicked.

Lightning React. That was the service that had pulled Winton's body out when Angie struck him down, and then let him disappear. *Here I was just telling Rafe how well I knew our enemy, and the whole time Rafe's set this rescue mission up to double as getting a lead on Winton.*

The doctor's voice was weak. "But—you said you *didn't* need to dig into the company… I'm doing what you said, you have to—"

"It's called a lie." Rafe tapped the computer. "Roger Winton, the patient you brought in that nobody can find. Where'd you send him?"

"Winton… I don't know what—"

Rafe held up a hand, and a knife flashed. Mark froze.

Rafe went on "That man back there we're saving got shot on *his* orders. We sit around here and he'll come in after us… You want your secrets kept quiet? Talk. Now." Rafe took a step toward the doctor.

The doctor flung up his hands, face white. Some kind of whine came out of his mouth, that might have been *Okay, okay.*

Rafe tucked the knife away and motioned him to the computer.

Mark heaved in a breath. He'd really just stood there and *watched* Rafe waving a knife at a man, because it might get them a shot at

Winton. Or, was running in Rafe's wake already wearing away his sense of who he was?

"Here. We're all logged in—here's the Lightning transfer records," the doctor said. "Please…"

Rafe glanced at the screen, then back. "Better. Now go bring that blood back to my boy and do what you can—it's the only way to get us out of here with no noise. We'll be right behind you."

The doctor stared, glanced from Rafe to Mark and back. " 'We'? You're just… letting me go? Alone?"

"I can trust you. *Right?* "

That last word was so cold, so fierce, Mark found himself blinking to be sure the knife hadn't reappeared in Rafe's hand. But the gang leader hadn't moved.

The doctor snatched up his supplies and slipped out the door.

Mark stared at Rafe; how could he be so sure his blackmail would keep the doctor under his thumb? Nolan might have seen a dozen signs on his face about whether he planned to run; Angie could have taken a risk trusting she could make a way out if it went bad, but Rafe…

"These look like their ambulance records to you?" Rafe's voice cut through his thoughts.

Can't let my guard down! Mark looked at the screen, and forced the words to come out smoothly. "Days, times, links to other tables… I guess. We tried hacking these once and couldn't get in. We do know the real Winton isn't still in the building." He stepped over and began scrolling back through the weeks.

"If this doesn't work, we go back to Winton's house." Rafe's tone was casual, barely a hint of the life-and-death stakes sharpening its edges. "With enough boys to tear it apart. Something he said: when he was just texts on my phone and he sent me to kidnap himself—still not telling me it was him, crazy bastard—he said not to go near Winton's home. Like I wouldn't see how that 'NOT' was the only time he sent a word in all caps. Ever."

"On your own phone? He didn't send you a private one?" Like the one that killed Ben Iskander?

Rafe shook his head.

"I bet he wishes he had now." Mark let out a breath—

Don't let your guard down, this is still Rafe!

Mark locked his eyes on the gang leader's. "I'm not your friend, you know. I'm here to find Winton, not help you steal, or run the streets. The only thing these hints you're giving me means is that I'm not wasting *all* my time here."

"Is Winton here?"

"No, he—"

As he spoke, Mark felt for the magic again—and his stomach clenched.

"He's in the building! I mean, he's controlling someone on this floor, maybe the far end! He's making his move, whatever it is!" He stared at the paper-covered wall, feeling the deadly tingle far beyond it. How long, how long had it been since he'd checked?

"See? We need that sense of yours. And we've got no time for you to keep saying you aren't in this."

Mark tried to shut the smug bastard's words out, and scrolled on through the hospital records. October, back to September...

The word *August* crowded down into the data column.

"Back up!" Rafe said. "We know they brought Winton here."

Mark could only stare at the months. "It's gone. The whole of September's gone, erased! How'd he know?"

"Who, Winton or the doctor?" Rafe said.

He grabbed out his phone, then snarled at the screen.

"Security. Had to move, Gunner says." Rafe's fingers slashed out an answer, and he muttered it aloud: *"Stay with Q – STAY."*

"Are they okay?" The image in Mark's head was Q panicked and dying, when he should be thinking of the guards Q would shoot at.

Rafe's hands slammed down on the table—hard, from the pain that twisted his face. "What the *hell?* I was sure I owned that doc, but he still ran for help? Move!"

Rafe's outburst passed in a moment and he lunged for the fridge. He yanked out more packets of blood and glanced at their stickers. Mark tried putting two of them in his coat pockets—too big. He had to settle for hiding them under the coat tucked under his arms, shockingly cold.

Rafe grabbed more blood and some packages from the walls, and they rushed for the door.

The corridor carried the same teasing tangle of not-quite-near sounds as it had before. But now Rafe led him skipping forward in a low-gravity stride that cut across the distance. They shot past a side branch—

Are those guards?

Mark and Rafe darted on out of the two figures' view, and the silence behind them told him they must have been looking the other way. One of the bags of blood slipped away from him, but he kept the other in place. He felt for magic again.

He flung himself closer to Rafe's side. "Winton's closing—" Still more than a hundred feet off. Wasn't the sprawling hospital was supposed to hide them?

"No." Rafe said it under his breath, under the lightened touch of their footsteps. He tapped his phone.

Up the corridor a door edged open in response. Rafe bolted for it, settling into a simple trot at his normal weight as he drew near. Mark saw Gunner peering out.

They ducked inside, and Gunner grabbed at Rafe's arm like a frightened child. "I think he's bleeding again. Where's the doc?"

"We got what we need," Rafe said. "Now we get out, and next time I'm listening to you about all those easy unguarded clinics." He leaned down next to Q.

The wounded man wasn't showing more blood on his leg, but Mark thought his face was grayer than ever. He stared at Rafe as his eyes slowly focused. "We… going? Got any pills to help me run?"

"I…"

Rafe hesitated, just for a moment. Mark heard it, the first hint of doubt he'd ever heard in Rafe.

Then: "No, Q. All of you have to make it to the car yourselves. These two have your back, so nothing's going to stop you. And I'll get the guards away."

He gripped the man's shoulder, like he'd done before. Q's face split into a hazy smile of pure gratitude… and when Rafe pulled back it shone on as if Q could no longer notice Rafe was leaving.

Mark felt his mouth move: "Hold on."

His fingers were diving into his pocket on their own, straight to the leather keychain and its tingle of power. *Even Winton thinks my magic can do this…*

Then he was walking over, not letting any more thoughts slow him down. He crouched next to Q, like wading into a cloud of sweat in the air.

"Here's something to bite down on. I hear they've been giving leather to wounded men for ages, and maybe they know something. So you bite, hard—and *think* about biting, just think that the harder you bite, the more strength this will give you to hold on." Just like drawing on the magic had helped Mark's shoulder heal.

He held out the piece toward Q's mouth. The teeth didn't open.

Behind him, Gunner said "Back off! What's that supposed to do?"

"Maybe nothing. If it does, I've got more… Just open up…"

Q's mouth opened and settled around the magic. Rafe sat just on his other side, but his face might have been miles away, impassively watching them as if he had no way to help. Or stop him.

Winton was still at a distance—

Mark sensed the power move, as Q's teeth sank into the leather. The magic in it flickered and faded as Q's mouth sucked it in, in fits and starts. The man's face didn't change, his eyes stayed closed and his skin gray.

Instead he stirred. His limp body trembled and wafted upward by inches, head and torso rising first and effortlessly trailing the limbs below. He floated a half a foot up, a foot…

He dropped, with a soft but undeniable *thump* against the floor. Still no change in his face, not that Mark had expected magic to simply wipe away his wounds.

Something yanked Mark around and flung him to the wall. He bounced back with his fists up, to face Gunner's glare.

"I saw that! I *was* floating too, when the Eel caught us—what did you do? Show me!"

The gleam in Gunner's eyes was hungry, stabbing through Mark and making his hands want to cover the belt by reflex. *Now he knows—*

"Not. Now."

Rafe's voice washed through them… no explanations, no other orders to deflect the moment, just the cold command.

Gunner rounded on him. "You—what do you know—"

"Get Q out. We'll cover you," and Rafe waved Mark to his side.

Gunner's face spasmed like he'd been struck, and it only tightened as he looked from Rafe to Mark, starting for the door together. Without him.

The door closed behind them. Mark followed Rafe up the corridor the way they'd come, trying to picture the ways through, but instead he kept seeing Gunner's face, burning with rage and sheer greed.

This is all tearing apart. Because he'd dived into a tangle of petty thugs and thought he could save them from the world of enemies they'd made? All for one chance to get Rafe's help against the real threat, the real target.

Winton was nearby. Mark glanced up ahead at the corridor they'd passed before; Winton could be just closing in along that. Still, the presence was moving past that, he might come in around them, and the walls already hemmed them in…

Rafe yanked a door open. Mark had no warning, but he managed to duck in behind him, just as the voices came from the branch ahead:

"They dropped a blood bag? This way."

I did that. Shoot me now.

Footsteps clattered up to the intersection, right where Mark had let the bag of blood slip. They didn't speak again, but it sounded like two of them, moving apart to look down different branches.

Rafe turned to their closed door. His feet made no sound, and his voice was softer than a whisper: "Perfect. Losing a body hurt Winton once—which of them is he in now?"

His gun was in his hand.

Mark couldn't breathe. A chunk of something colder than ice was stuck in his chest, freezing his lips and locking his eyes on the gleam of the weapon, while all the while the real Winton presence was moving on past them up some other corridor…

"None of them," he forced out.

"Shh!" Rafe moved a step toward him, and his eyes—*his eyes!*—probed. "Not the time to lie. Which one?"

"But…" Mark gave up looking for words and simply pointed away, off beyond the wall where the actual magic was moving.

But Rafe still crept toward the door.

Rafe wouldn't. He wouldn't just shoot them, he'd never gun down two innocent men in just the hope of catching Winton, and Winton wasn't there, *why doesn't he believe me—*

Mark tried to gather his muscles to strike, but Rafe's eyes were still on him, and he stood just out of reach. Of course.

Then, the footsteps moved. The two security guards drew together and started up one of the corridors… away from Gunner and Q, away from Winton, away from Rafe's ambush.

Mark felt a slow, weak breath slipping in at last, and he realized Rafe hadn't even reached for the door. He motioned numbly toward Winton again, still somewhere up at the other side.

Rafe shook his head. "And you want us to *avoid* him, right? The monster gives us a perfect chance to do the only thing that ever hurt him, and you worry about who he's dragged along…" He shoved the gun into his shirt, hard. "Screw it. If you won't hunt him, I'll stall and you get Q back to the car. *If* you've got the stones for it."

Mark's mouth snapped open… He let it close again. There were no words that wouldn't make the moment worse.

Just as he touched the door, Rafe added "And, try not to tell Gunner the whole story at his first whine."

Mark could only slip out, avoiding Rafe's eyes.

Magic lightened his run, but that silence only made the horror in his head louder. Rafe would have blown those men away at a word if it slowed the real Winton down, and yet Mark was still trying to work with him… *Please let there be* someone *that Winton or Rafe don't kill tonight…*

He heard footsteps, more people out in the corridors. He felt Winton, still off to the side, but too close. How much did he know?

The room was just ahead. He looked in, and Gunner looked up from the supplies piled at his feet. A pistol swung up at him, then halted, quivering in the thug's grip.

"Come on!"

As Mark spoke he realized he'd already stepped around toward Q; Gunner's posturing felt like no threat at all now. Winton was at least a corridor's distance away and seemed to be pulling back. Mark pulled the limp Q up to get a shoulder under his arm.

"Why are you still here?" he added. "The door out is just down there and you take one left."

"You know the turns, do you? That come from riding your routes, Mark?"

The name echoed in the room.

"Yeah, you thought we'd forget your face forever? All us Blades—ex-Blades—knew how Rafe was after you and your girl. What were you, a messenger, a cabbie? And now you've got us floating?" He lowered the gun and pulled out a knife. "What were you doing for Rafe before—"

"Just come on."

Mark scooped up one of the bags of blood with his free hand and moved out the door, trying to block Gunner's threats from his thoughts with simple action.

Winton turned. The presence Mark felt, already moving parallel along what might be the next corridor over, now turned to head off further from their path and the exit. The killer was still bumbling around trying to find them in the building, and he'd never know they'd slipped out behind him.

Mark buoyed Q up and jogged forward. He caught a shocked sound from Gunner behind him, but to be seen running with what looked like the full weight of a man over his shoulder meant nothing compared to missing a chance to slip away.

Winton still drew further away. The turn to the door came clearer in the half-light, and he heard Gunner behind him. Voices and nightly bustle and different speeds of footsteps wove through the hallways, all too far from them now; he felt Rafe's belt on the move somewhere in the thick of it.

Q's lightened weight shifted on his shoulders. He glanced back—and realized he'd somehow shot past the turn for the exit. Gunner must have taken it; he was already out of view behind him. Mark checked on Winton's progress away from them one more time as he backtracked and rounded the turn.

Gunner lay in the corridor. His hand lay under his face, locked around his knife, the knife he'd held to fall on and bury in his own eye.

Numbly, Mark felt Q sliding from his grasp, and his ears caught a shallow breath from the man he'd carried, nothing like the utter stillness of the shape before him.

No sound. There hadn't been one sound after Gunner turned the corner—like he'd simply stabbed himself and dropped, still ten feet short of the exit. The exit.

I can't have lost another one, I can't!

Leaving Q on the floor, Mark dove at the door to face whatever was outside… but when it flew open all he met was cold air and darkness. The cold shocked a thought back into motion: of course the killer hadn't escaped to the outside. Winton's puppet had never come near them… but the killer had seized Gunner's mind all the same, *how?*

The taunting flicker of Winton's magic moved away somewhere into the maze behind him, deep among the sounds of the building. Rafe's power was nearer—closing in on the turn to the way out, to where his surviving man lay, and the other one. Almost here.

I can't face him.

Mark let the wind take him. A moment of shedding his weight, the soaring sense of escape buffeted by all the sensations of how often he'd rocketed away with death and failure behind him…

He tumbled against a hard wall. He huddled there, on some kind of ledge, shaking.

I went to Rafe and his thugs, I swallowed all my fear because of the hope that he could tell me something about the enemy… and all I found out is that brutal lowlifes die like anyone else when Winton wants them gone. Burning anger trembled somewhere in the whirl of pain, too little to warm him.

His senses still worked. That hard pulse of power matched the figure below, Rafe slipping outside with Q on his back. The fainter twitch would be Winton still marching his pawn through the building. He felt Winton's grip leave that body and reappear in the swooping, gloating path of a bird and sweep away through the sky.

Angie flew after it.

She took to the air well after the bird had gone, when Mark's head had already turned away from the departing enemy and sunk back into his hands. Her delay in chasing it should mean something, if his thoughts could work. *She* should mean something.

He tried to pry himself up, and his balance wobbled and he slipped off the ledge, making him kick off to dive after her. Her power darted somewhere among the light-studded shadows far ahead—he leaped hard off a roof, she zigged lower and he dropped blindly to leap again and stay with her. Winton was already out of his sense's range.

Mark leaped faster and let the magic push him on. *Just stay up at the higher roofs, where the path is clear for making straight leaps to close the distance.* Angie was weaving her way forward down among the lower ridges and walls, moving with the same nimbleness that would have kept her dodging Winton's birds. Her route was strangely cautious, with the enemy somewhere up ahead.

Mark hurtled past her toward a cluster of higher buildings, and he felt the target again, still making its way away; at least his magic had the raw speed to close in on a winged enemy. That presence lurked somewhere in the air five hundred feet ahead, four hundred…

Behind him, Angie *slowed.* Mark caught at the corner of a building to let her catch up—

The truth smashed through him, colder than the night air. Angie's low, twisted flight hadn't been hugging cover in case Winton turned back against her, she was staying too low for Winton to see her at all. Following him.

The metal rim of the wall worked coldness into Mark's fingers as he hung still, dangling in plain view if the bird looked back. How long, how long had Angie been searching the city with nothing but an owl's eyes and a hunter's patience, waiting for Winton to let his guard down?

Slowly Winton's bird drew away. Mark held his place, fearing that just one more move from a huge, clumsy human body against the skyline might be the motion that drew the killer's eye. Angie passed below him. Winton's presence grew farther, fainter, lost in the distance… only when Mark felt Angie herself nearing the edge of his range did he start after her.

How many blocks back could Winton's bird see? Mark jumped and twisted his way through the space between the higher and the lower rooftops, straining to see where wires stretched and doing his best to keep the taller buildings in front of him instead of arching himself over them. Too often he had to leave cover just to keep Angie in range… *I always knew these birds could twist on a wingtip and outfly me, and* hiding *myself from one is even more impossible.* Only the sheer range of his sense added to Angie's eyes gave him a chance.

Then Mark realized: Angie had closed in on Winton again, because the enemy's movement had stopped.

Angie had halted too, somewhere up ahead to watch. Mark crept to the next roof and peered down into the wider lots and to the factories half hidden in the falling snow beyond them.

Winton's magic winked away, not sliding over to some other body but as if he'd finished bringing the bird to its destination. Or its home.

Minutes crawled by, and thickened and stacked together. The more still Mark sat, the more his nerves thrummed with the drive to act, to *move* again… anything to kick free of the stink of guilt and failure around himself. All he could hold onto was, if he was seen, this time he'd be risking the chance Angie had fought for. He tried not to notice the hint of light in the corner of his eye, where brightness was creeping across the eastern sky.

The dawn had just begun to brush the chimneys when he felt Angie start toward where Winton had let his bird go. The dimness and the snow still gave Mark cover enough; he dropped down to the street and trotted up the industrial block.

Where had Winton stopped? The fenced-off complex to his right looked too jumbled to be the outline he'd sensed him at, even from that distance. But as he passed it, he felt Angie flitting over the chain fence at his side.

And… he felt other magic. The thinnest hint of Winton's mind energy, deep beyond the factory there.

In his next breath, Mark was soaring up over the fence. If this was their shot at Winton, at the magic Angie needed…

"Careful," he hissed to himself as he dropped to the other side. He forced himself to stand stock-still, between a long chemical tank and some kind of humming generator, for five slow breaths using only his eyes and ears to look around for signs of danger. Nothing moved.

When he reached for magic again, Winton's power felt *stronger.* The distant ripple he'd strained to catch was as firm as Angie's presence ahead, and he felt it thicken with each step he took deeper into the lot. As the squat factory took shape out of the snow, he knew the power lay just on the far side of the building. No, on the *near* side.

Winton's energy has never been so clear—but at only a step back it was fainter. It took all Mark's strength to move across at only human speed. Could it really be Winton's *place,* where all his magic came from?

Angie waited up on the building's roof. Then as he drew near she flew down and settled on the side of the wall. He tried to make out where she was perching, but the wall's shadows and the snow left the upper stories only a faint outline. Instead he floated up to meet her.

His eyes could just make out the owl's shape when she stirred again. A piece of the wall *moved*—some kind of hatch, that she'd dropped open. She darted inside.

Mark caught at the entrance; whatever part of the factory this was, it barely had room for anyone to fit through. At least, it would be tight for any human—and this felt like the same area Winton's bird had gone, and she could have seen it work the hatch. The power thickened somewhere close inside…

He squeezed into the dark.

His fingers touched metal, some tangle of machinery; without light all he knew was that some parts of it hummed, and all of them were cold. The space was wider than his arms could reach, but so low he could barely keep his stomach off the chill floor as he crawled inward. Some kind of sharp, chemical smell hung over it all.

The magic *churned*. He could sense Angie ahead within it, but at this range the other power washed through her presence like a siren swallowing a voice. Mark edged toward the two, scraping elbows and knees on the hard floor. Scraps of light trickled in behind him, not even enough to tease his eyes as the shadows moved.

Angie's presence turned, moving to the right—and fading away in the larger pressure. Mark froze, holding his breath a moment to feel for some last scrap of her within the blaze of power. He could only worm himself to the side, trying to follow her, until his fingers found where the tunnel branched off.

The magic beat against him as he inched in, like some great beast shifting its weight, and he had to remind himself that the floor and ceiling he squeezed between *weren't* trembling with the immaterial force. But if this was Winton's secret, and Angie's salvation—

His shoulders caught in the tunnel entrance. He squirmed in the blackness, but the gap simply had no space for him. Talons pressed against his elbow, right where Angie would be.

Then, in the dark with the last of the light left shining from behind, his sense of magic managed to reach through past the tangle of power to pin down its location. All that force, all that noise, lay clustered in one shape. In his mind, its outline was a blazing shape smaller than a finger.

A… talisman, sucking in power. The mind power that could sustain Angie, or find her a new life.

His hand stretched toward the darkness before the thought: *was this thing what had been inside Iskander's phone?* At the same instant Angie gave a warning rasp, right at his ear.

"No touching, right," he said.

Think, think! Mark lay in the coffin-tight shaft, his sweat thicker than the stench of chemicals now—his fingers had come so *close.* But this was what they'd fought for…

He edged his way backward until he had some room at his sides again. Enough to reach down and draw out his phone.

"I don't have to touch it," he said. He heard a scrabble of Angie moving up in the tunnel, then sensed her emerge from it and slip back past him, giving him more room to work. He smiled toward her in the dark, then held the phone out as he squeezed into the tunnel again.

He was still reaching into utter blackness, but the blazing in his mind lay just ahead. Like a tiny sun he couldn't "look" directly at it… but if he could just pinpoint that shimmering enough…

Holding his phone by one end, he used the other to scrape the talisman toward him.

Inch by inch it moved. Mark edged back to slide his shoulders clear of the tunnel again. A hint of light fell on the shape… a bit of metal, a talisman small enough to build into a phone.

Its magic *wavered.*

Mark's teeth clenched. The power couldn't be that delicate, the tiny sun was still burning… He fumbled on his phone for its light mode.

The button brought a soft, clear glow into the tunnel. Before him lay a fingernail-sized lump of silvery gray, with a tiny hinged door hanging open to show a glimmer of green stone inside, catching the light—

And its power melted away like fire in a river.

Between one heartbeat and the next it was—

He scrabbled through the dimness. Nothing to see, not one scrap of metal left to feel.

"Gone," he breathed. "Its magic's gone, the whole thing's melted away with it—how can *light* kill it? Just because Winton put it in darkness here—God, I didn't know—"

He finally looked over at Angie. She stood near the hatch, silhouetted.

As he watched, she slowly hung her head, and for a moment he was sure the measured motion was no bird's twitch; he could see the human gesture within it, of pure defeat.

"We can fix this," he gasped. "I mean, we lost the magic, but we've got the place that has Winton's power, we watch for him to come back and follow him again—there has to be something, I'm sorry—"

Angie hopped out into the light.

He tried to crawl backward after her, numb and clumsy over the cold metal, but she only scuttled faster. His throat closed up when he tried to call after her.

By the time he squeezed out into the open air, her weakened energy was swallowed up in the distance.

CHAPTER EIGHT

ENEMIES AND CLOSER

The two men at the next table scraped their chairs back and followed the rest of the morning shift out to work. The tiny coffee shop's early crowd had dwindled to Mark and two other customers now, few enough that the smell of the beans wafted undiluted in the air… and he still hadn't sensed one flicker of Winton coming to check on the power that had once been waiting in that factory just up the street.

Mark caught a suspicious look from the cashier. With his sandwich all wolfed down, he took a long sip from his cup, grateful they'd let him in at all with all his stains and filth. The cup warmed his hands again, and the long snowfall was fading anyway: the broad window at his elbow only gave a sighing sound, when yesterday Nolan's storms had been strong enough to make glass rattle.

He set the cup back on the table, and stared at his hand.

He'd had one of Winton's own talismans, right in his grasp… one glimpse of silver and green… and it was *gone.*

Angie had found it, and he'd lost it, the same as he'd lost Gunner and Iskander and everything. Now he could only stare out at the factory, telling himself that finding the site of Winton's magic made it worthwhile, but…

His eyelids dragged against the buzz of caffeine and too much magic. If Winton did come back, would Mark notice? Would it matter, without Angie there to follow the bird?

Beside the cup lay his phone, and he could almost see the text he'd sent, as clear as if he'd left the screen open: *A led me to W's PLACE – I need help watching it. The tail's gone. R's men are gone, the truce is gone.* So few words, along with the location of the factory.

"If they'd just answer, we could save something out of this," he growled to himself. Of course Kate might take days to pick up, and God knew what Nolan was thinking after he'd ditched her. Mark's fingers itched to stab at that screen and dig answers out of… somewhere… not sit probing for magic all alone until its addiction drove him crazy.

Think, think! He pressed his fingertips to the table's wood, and tried again to sort out the different sensations he'd felt. When Winton's power *controlled* a body he could always sense it blocks away—Mark raised his thumb from the table, the same way that possession "stuck out" to his searches. But the talisman Winton had built into Iskander's phone had been different from that, undetectable *until* it was triggered—he left the other fingers lying flat, to represent something hidden. And last night he'd felt what might be a talisman recharging, and yet, even that fierce whirlpool of energy had only resonated as far as the parking lot—his littlest finger traced tiny circles over the wood, an overwhelming presence but detectable within so tight an area he'd never have stumbled across it.

Not without Angie. And now she'd flown away without him.

He shook his head, and pulled his phone from the charger in the wall. A call had come in, just minutes ago? The number was the one Kate routed her calls through.

He called back, and a boy's voice sounded in his ear. "Hey, Mark."

"Hi."

Did James sound sleepy? What time might it be where he and his mother were hiding? His serious, twelve-year-old voice gave little away. But Mark felt his own voice lighten—it still felt odd having a kind of friendship with the boy, after the times James had dragged him into danger in trying to learn about the family magic. Which made James like every other "spellkeeper," or wanting to be like one.

But this time, what James said was an eager "Is *she* really with you?"

"She… led me right here." Mark forced a smile. If James wanted good news about the half-sister he'd never met, Mark could give him a little.

Kate's voice came in then, steadier than her son's, and warmer than she usually sounded. "I'm sure she did."

Then she switched to text, and the message formed so fast he wondered if she'd had the words saved:

So now you're looking for connections between W and the site, and everything we know about him.

Text, now? Kate must be feeling more jumpy than ever, but texting was safer than whispering in the stillness of the near-empty shop. He answered:

right. and: I saw a silver and green talisman before it dissolved in light. don't even know if knowing the place helps

The belts drew their power from the one site in the park… would it kill Nolan to tell them whether her own magic needed a single location too, so they'd have some way to guess whether Winton's did?

Kate replied *You know it takes time. We check every clue against every other. W can't cover them all up.*

I know.

But still, Winton flew his talismans all over the city. How could it be something as simple as light that dissolved that one? The phone seemed to be trembling in his hand.

Another call chimed. Mark saw Henry's name and brought the phone up.

His cousin asked "Are you okay there?"

"Fine. If Dennard wants you to check up on me again, I'm okay. And no, I don't have to come in and clear my head—I haven't used the… you know… since last night." Even talking around the word *magic* now made him lower his voice and pull himself in tighter around the phone.

"Actually, Dennard's with me right now. We're looking at the history of that factory."

Henry, working with Dennard? His cousin should be keeping his distance, not making himself a target. What was Dennard thinking?

And Kate was still on the other line. He glanced at the screen.

Angie's still alright? she had asked.

Mark felt a headache threading into his skull, trying to balance the two calls while his eyes ached and everything he'd done had gone wrong.

He answered Kate:

she flies the city like she built it. anything else?

His question drew only a *When I have something,* and Kate hung up—sure enough, she was the easier one to finish with. He brought the phone back to his ear.

"Mark? Are you there? Hello?"

Was that worry creeping into Henry's scratchy voice, after just a few seconds of him not answering? "Right here. Just finishing a call with Kate. No attacks, no problems, nothing on this end." He huddled in tighter to whisper to the phone.

"That's good to hear," Henry said. "So... you really found the place he makes his talismans at? That must be a breakthrough."

What was that, excitement now? Henry had never even *liked* Angie. "Sure, I found the place—or *a* place, Nolan won't tell me if there's a reason to have just one. All I lost was the talisman."

"But, you found that much."

Was Henry *humoring* him?

"I had a piece of the power that could keep Angie alive, and I lost it. I had Angie flying with me for hours—she's the one who found it, of course—and the moment it's my turn to help, I lost it. *And* I lost Rafe's friends—couldn't save one from Winton so I left Nolan behind for a chance to bring Rafe over to us. Rafe has to know something...

he knew how to make talismans before we did, and he says Winton doesn't know that. But I *lost* his people, I can't face him—God, I think Winton may have—"

The words choked in his throat: *he may have used* me *to kill one, until Angie poured out some of her life to snap me out of it—*

He swallowed and finished with, "And even then Winton got to Iskander and Gunner—I got *everything* wrong."

"But…" Henry tried, slowly, "you still—"

"Everything!"

Just like always, he thought. That was the whisper that never made it to his lips—not when speaking to his so-helpful cousin, or anyone.

"But… Mark, remember what you keep saying? How anything that got you closer to helping—"

"She was right with me. Now she's gone." *And of course it all turns to shit.*

"But you always… you never let…" Henry stopped and hauled in a breath. "Mark, how can I help you if you won't let me?"

"Help?" The raggedness in Mark's voice made him stop, and scrabble for better words. "You… you're with Dennard going through records? Shouldn't you be at work? Go see Christa, be glad you have a real life left." Saying the answer helped steady him, and let him lean back from whispering into the phone. He shook himself.

"A real… no, Mark. Not this time."

Henry's words rasped faster, sharper, sawing in his ear in the quiet room:

"I've kept an eye on you. I've supported you. I've let you brush me off until the moment you hit bottom. Mark, do *not* hang up. *Don't* say we'll talk soon. You get over here and give yourself a rest. What's it take for you to slow down?"

"I'm fine!" The words were a reflex, but they gave him a moment for the excuses to come. "I've been up all night. I lost too much, and I learned a bit too. It's been a long night, is all—nothing I didn't know I'd be getting into."

"Just… this once, will you stop and—"

Henry broke off.

No, he'd been *cut* off, by a sound… it sounded like a crash. A voice shouted, *"Get down."* Mark clutched the phone and held his breath, straining his ears to reach past the murmurs in the cafe and the pounding of his heartbeat.

The last faint sounds vanished as the line went dead.

He jabbed at the screen. No answer, only their location app that placed his cousin at home, and Dennard's phone there with him too. Henry must have hung up, he'd taken a moment to properly hang up and let the phone lock. To keep whoever had attacked them from reaching Mark.

"No no no—" Was it Winton there, Rafe? Whoever it was, *they had Henry and Dennard.*

He lurched to his feet with the chair clattering over behind him. He dodged between empty tables, and a memory flashed, of himself diving off a bridge just to keep Rafe from getting near Henry—dragging a bleeding Dennard through the park—

As he reached for the door, he saw two uniformed cops walking up.

In that moment he watched their eyes snap to him. They spotted the shock on his face… or maybe they'd heard descriptions of the man who'd seen Iskander die… or who'd run after Rafe… or the doctor had told them about someone stinking of sewers and death… *They recognize me, I need to tell them, let them save Henry and Dennard… Screw the magic's secret… Or say it's just Rafe and his guns…*

Then his steps carried him past them and he felt the cold air on his face. He heard a mutter from one cop behind him, but then he was trotting up the street, free.

He dodged around one pedestrian, another, with his thoughts flying on ahead. It would be so easy to run faster, or jump for the sky—no, Henry's place was too far, flying was too slow, the street was too damn crowded and he needed a clear head, not more magic. No good, no good—

A car honked, a savage noise right at the curb beside him that sent him sailing away toward the wall, even as the thought jabbed that an actual enemy could have blindsided him much worse than that. He looked up to see Nolan at the wheel, window sliding down as she pulled up.

Her clipped tone was barely a question: "Henry's?"

Did I… yes, I used the phone's group alert when I tried to recontact them, so the signal went to Nolan too.

He yanked the door open and dove in.

The way Nolan gunned the engine and wrestled their way through traffic, he had to shout directions a few words at a time, between gasps for breath. When they stopped at a light he tried another useless call to Henry, then Dennard.

All because Winton had found his talisman gone…

Or because Mark had let Rafe's man die…

Or because he'd let the gang see the magic and see his face…

The roaring streets settled into the quieter edges of Henry's neighborhood—it had been Mark's own *home* with his cousin for his highschool years, and yet now he had to fight to picture the best pathways to guide Nolan through it.

When they finally pulled over, it was at a corner where they could just see Henry's brownstone ahead. Right out front stood Dennard's white car, and Henry's shiny BMW. And a pickup with a hammer logo on its door.

Sure, they used a "repair" truck to cover someone breaking in. They would.

"I can sense Rafe's talisman right in the apartment, along with a small one that's almost drained. I guess that's the one I gave Q." Mark shifted in the seat, scrambling to get the words out. "And way up in the sky is one of Winton's birds, watching it all—he's not controlling anyone inside, at least not now. Maybe he'll watch us fight and take out the winner, or he's got something even worse in mind. Hell, he could have called *Rafe* here and set it all up!"

Winton would kill to get their magic's secrets, Mark knew. And if he knew Mark had been at his factory… *And Rafe, he'll do worse than kill them, because Gunner died just a few feet from me and I couldn't stop it…*

"Rafe too? Then the *gang's* all here—"

This time Nolan broke off her own fumbling joke before Mark could snarl at her.

Then she turned back to the building ahead, and the humor dropped away. "They've got your friends. It's time to give them a *real* show."

"Show? Why give Winton anything! His bird is about half a block above us; you swat it down, then give me some cover to go in—"

"I can't."

The flat words yanked his head around.

Nolan shook her head slowly. "Mark, don't you get it? Since yesterday I've been burning through magic, and pulling in weather fronts from all over the state for the kinds of air it takes… well, after all that, you don't want to know what it would take to hit a bird way up there. I've got no blizzards, no mist, nothing on that scale."

"You mean, you used up your power trying to ground Rafe—until just when we *need* to freeze them—" He let the curse fade on his lips. Besides, against an enemy like Rafe, any "freak storm" outside would only give away that they were here anyway.

The brownstone waited ahead, curtains closed to hide whatever was happening within. Rafe could lurk anywhere within its two stories, and Henry's rooms were surrounded by a long building full of neighbors on either side and broad daylight that would show anyone moving toward it… the schemer's bird circling over it all…

Rafe's talisman and Q's are down on the first floor—that tells me something. Mark reached for the car door. "The front and back grounds are wide open, anyone watching would see me coming that way. All that leaves me is dropping in through a second-floor window, quiet and fast as I can." And hope Rafe didn't have other men watching up there. He swung the door open.

"Hold on." Nolan held out a gleaming pistol to him.

Of course. Taking it would be the obvious answer. Mark's finger brushed the barrel.

Then he pushed it away. "I think… It's too late for me to pick up a gun now. I should have been practicing with one for months first; that's what Dennard always told Angie. I try shooting now and I'd probably hit him and Henry."

"Or me."

"You? You mean you're—"

"We can catch them between us. I can come in the front, if you distract them and tell me when. I should have gotten more vests," she added. "The Eel took my only one, but keeping us both alive is in my *vested* interest…"

Even for Nolan, the joke fell flat. He could hear a tremble in the back of her voice, the same one she'd let slip at the end of her time under the Eel's gun. Was that what it cost her to give up blasting from the sidelines and let an enemy see her? *And, it's not even her family in there.*

"All right." It was all he could say, before he opened the door; even *thank you* would have cheapened the moment.

Instead he began walking away from Henry's street, feeling the breeze that the blizzard had faded to. The familiar courtyards and fences seemed to press in on him, but the faster he walked, the more he risked *this* jogger or *that* child on the doorstep remembering the face that went with his ruined clothes. None of them seemed to have noticed the murderer who'd settled in behind their neighbor's door, and yet now Mark had to slip past their attention as well as Rafe's, under the damnably bright sun.

After enough turns, he reached the shadowed gap between two old brick walls, upwind of Henry's and out of sight of the street. No faces *seemed* to be peeping out the windows above, so if no eye was watching Mark at right this moment… except for Winton above it all…

No time to hesitate.

A burst of sheer, glorious power ripped the streets away, flung him into clean sky where his teared-up eyes could barely follow the toy blocks, the ridges shrinking below—

Pulse hammering—

Fire in his veins—

He slowed, standing in the dizzy-swaying blue bowl of the sky… but as he clutched at power to hold himself in place, he felt his will flexing ready to squeeze tighter, to *use* the magic more. *And I should be shivering in the cold.*

He'd told Henry he'd taken it slow, safe. But how much magic had he used in the last day—chasing thugs, searching the city? *How* much self-control did he have left? "Great, I need to sneak up on Rafe right when I only want to crush them all. If he'd just given me another day—"

As if in answer, he sensed a twitch of magic entering the airspace between him and the blocks below. Winton. Mark's fists clenched, uselessly trying to fill with power. Enough of the belts' magic could shatter stone, but it was meaningless when he couldn't *touch* the bird's taunting, free-flying shape.

If Angie were here…

Instead he could only study the lines of the streets below, and let the wind push him over above the long building where Rafe's magic pulsed. Winton was keeping his distance so far. Mark gritted his teeth and covered his eyes against the rush of air, and dropped.

When he peeked out and braked, he landed on the sloped roof barely one door down from Henry's. He hunched over, hoping anyone passing by would take him for some roof worker too afraid of falling. Down in the yard he caught a glimpse of Terry the Terrier scratching madly on Henry's back door.

And Winton still held back above, still playing his own games. Henry's bedroom window was just ahead below. Reducing his weight, Mark dangled over to reach for it.

Locked. He forced a wry smile; so Henry did keep some defenses. Or Rafe had sealed the place up.

Somewhere beyond the glass, a voice growled, a human's rage swelled to an animal's incoherent roar.

What are they doing? Fear and the sudden thought that their noise could cover his own entrance locked Mark's hands onto the window frame. His fingers tugged lightly upward but his magic roared, pouring reversed weight into the wood to make it strain upward and splinter and rip around the bolt—

The window slid up, and he managed to pull out of the magic before it tore clean off the frame. He gave himself only one breath to steady his nerves, then swung down to climb in.

"Bastard!"

Mark froze, half through the window, but the hushed, fierce voice was only filtering up from the floor below.

"Don't you close those eyes! Where is he!" the speaker went on, with a strange ragged voice Mark couldn't place.

Another unfamiliar voice said "He don't hear you—"

The *crunch* that followed could only be a full, savage blow landing on flesh and bone.

Mark's fingers clenched, ready to seize something, to grind it to a red smear. He heard a floorboard creak under his feet and cut the flow of magic before he rattled the whole building.

"Where is he?" the wild voice said again.

No answer came, and Mark tried to focus. From the voices, at least two thugs were down in the living room—and both separate from where Rafe and Q stood, if he'd read those talismans right. And they were all down there with Henry and Dennard, *when I must be the one they really want. The one they're asking about.*

With still-trembling fingers, he switched on his phone and whispered "You hear this?"

"Just say when." Nolan's voice was steady now, calmer than his. He slid the phone into his pocket, still live.

No sound came from below now. He turned back and slid the window slowly down again; no point in just inviting Winton's bird to flap in behind him.

He crept forward, and now the room around him edged into his awareness. Henry's bedroom, simple, the walls dotted here and there with landscapes he'd painted—Mark had once thought that his own trying to draw could bring them closer together, but…

Think of the place as just another set of pathways in, and cover. He floated to the open doorway, his feet feather-light where they brushed the floor. Nobody was in the corridor beyond, and he followed the voices to glide down the stairs.

"If the old man doesn't know what hole he crawled into," and that was Rafe, savvy and reasonable, "we still need someone alive to *call* him—"

"Where's the lab? Where's the stuff?"

A flicker of magic jerked Mark's head around. Outside, Winton's bird was descending, closing in—

Control. He had two ways to reach the voices in the living room, and the front hallway was the closer one. They'd only be watching at eye level.

Softly, Mark drifted up until he flattened against the ceiling. He locked his eyes on the ceiling "under" his hands and knees, and spidered around a light fixture and toward the doorway ahead. When he reached the arch under him, he stole a single peek down around it.

Four men gathered around the far corner, one kneeling and shaking a fallen shape—

Mark jerked back out of sight and let his brain register the rest of the image: sure enough, Rafe and three men, a whole army to face, but one had been shaking an unmoving Joe Dennard—

Outside, Winton settled by the front window.

Try the other doorway, around through the kitchen. Mark locked his thoughts on the glimpse he'd seen, better than thinking about whether he'd missed Henry in that instant's glance or about the blood around Dennard or how to get *four armed men* away from him. Rafe and his three were clustered around the room's far corner. That put them closest to the kitchen entrance, with their backs to the kitchen entrance. The only advantage would be to rush them from that direction, and Nolan could take the front door.

Mark flattened himself up tighter and moved backward. Keeping himself silent left him barely pressed against the ceiling, so gently that moving his hands and knees made him bob like a forgotten balloon. He heard the wild-voiced thug again: "Wake up, damn you!"

A *snap*—and a grunt, that must be through Dennard's clenched teeth.

"That hurt? Go on, heal it! Fuck, I should be *dead*—I know the stuff works. Where d'you make it? Where's your boy Mark? Or you, you have to know! You're his cousin."

They do have Henry too. What have they already done to his bad back? My God—they really did come at Henry to find me. A sick, sour feeling burned in his throat.

Rafe's voice was lower, hard to follow: "Q... let me have the gun... any louder and we'll have cops..."

Q. So that hoarse, twisted-up voice was the man he and Rafe had raced to save. And now Q was here for more magic, from him.

Rafe's whispers seemed to be calming them down. So far.

Mark clambered on across the lintel into the kitchen, just one room away from them now. There'd be four of them, and all those guns, and yet he was still creeping closer hoping he could catch them all off-guard. He could feel Rafe's belt—as strong as his own—up ahead. He had to signal Nolan, but they'd hear.

Then, "You want me to back down?" Q snapped. *"You* go get stabbed in a cell—I need to *run,* now! Now you, where is it? I'll give you to three…"

Something clicked. The hammer of his gun.

Mark felt himself settling to the kitchen floor. They'd come here because he'd shown himself and tried to heal Q, and he'd showed Rafe how the magic could do it. *How much more power has Rafe run through Q? Is that what's making him crazy?*

"Two…"

No time left.

Mark shouted "You can't!"

Voices exploded from up ahead. "Shit!" "How the hell—"

Rafe lunged into the doorway, gun first.

The pistol's muzzle loomed in Mark's sight, enormous—but Rafe still kept himself that one safe step back. The gang leader motioned him forward, so slowly. All Mark could do was obey, blood pounding and power burning in him but still trapped a whole helpless world out of reach of crushing an enemy.

Rafe made him stop right in the living room doorway, hemmed in where he could barely move.

One of the punks in the living room stared at him—a pudgy, younger man with darting eyes that Mark didn't know. "That him? He's the one that cut Gunner?"

"See if there's anyone else," Rafe said, and he motioned to the last of his men, the tallest. That one drew a pair of guns and headed up the hallway for the second floor.

"Oh, *now* you're looking out for us?" the plump one glowered at Rafe. He looked straight at Mark. "So, where do we get the pills? Rafe keeps holding out on us, but we know he got them from you, Mark. And we finally ran you down." He spun and kicked out—at Henry, Henry lay on the floor behind them, groaning.

No, his back—

Rafe said "I told you, I can get all the pills we need. Remember what we did last night? We beat the Eel and his Blades, nobody can stop us—"

"It's not just pills!" Q's savage voice broke right through the others. Suddenly he was crouched next to where Dennard lay, slumping in place like a man still weak from his wound. He waved something at Mark—the keychain with its last ergs of energy. "I was flying—I mean, really flying, with this! Rafe wants to hide it, but you know how it works! You show me, or I splatter him!" His gun jammed against Dennard's head.

"You can't shoot him! He's the only one who knows!" Mark threw the words at him, praying the man's lust for more magic would make him stop.

For one breath Mark heard the other thug muttering something, and then Q shoved the gun harder into Dennard. *"This* loser?"

Mark forced his eyes away from Dennard, and scrabbled for words to back up the lie. "Yes, him!" he said. "You kill him and you'll never get the drug supply. That's Joe Dennard there—you guys are ex-Blades like Rafe, you should know your gang's history. The only reason the Blades let Dennard live back when someone shot up the gang, was because they said nobody could have run down the street fast enough. *Fast* enough, don't you get it? You think your 'pills' are something new?"

It was all he could think of, to pour out Dennard's true past and only leave out what the magic was and who else could make it. He locked his eyes on Q's, trying to see past that feverish glaze, the same wildness he'd slipped into himself once... that was burning in his nerves now...

Q's lips spread in a grin. "So Rafe *was* holding out. And you say this guy's the one we need, not you? You hear that, old man?" He spat at Dennard's slack face, then stumbled to his feet.

He staggered as he moved, showing his weakness with every step, but his pistol stayed right on Mark. He swung his other fist, so slowly that Mark had to force himself to hold still, thinking it couldn't be too bad—

Pain exploded through his stomach. Stumbling, lights flashing in his eyes, more pain when he tried to gasp in a breath.

Through the haze he heard "That's for still saying it's some drug. You see that, Dennard? Now, how do we get it?"

Q's head turned back toward their prisoner. Mark's fingers clenched on their own, his feet braced to clear the one step to let him strike.

Then Q was a step back and out of reach. *What? I missed my chance?*

Nolan, are you hearing this? Angie?

Rafe took a step toward Q. "See, we've got all we need. We've got the man with the answers, and we've got his right hand Mark for leverage. Now think: we make any more noise and the cops will be all around us."

Was that *regret* in Rafe's voice? It had command, concern too, but something in that tone faded, as if he were starting to back away from the maddened Q even as his hand reached out to him.

The pudgy younger man added "Hell yeah! We gotta get out—"

Q shoved Rafe aside to lock his wild eyes on Mark. "No more waiting! You see this, Dennard? Tell us how the magic happens, or your right hand has no right hand." He *giggled,* and lined the gun slowly up with Mark's arm.

"Here." Mark reached into his pocket with the slow motion that just might keep the gun from shooting. Not that Mark had a hidden gun to draw, only a strip of leather. *But give me one instant, just let his eyes flicker once and I'll dive at him—*

"Q, slow down!" The younger thug's voice whined in real fear. "He's showing us the stuff—"

The tall fourth thug stepped back into the room, back from his search. "Nobody else there—uh, Q?"

And *still* the black holes that were Q's eyes didn't flicker. He and Mark could have been the only ones in his world now, as Mark drew out the piece of leather that was his other talisman.

Then Q's hand was already reaching out for it. *I blanked out for another instant?*

Back behind Q, the youngest tried again "Just chill—"

"Tell me!" was all Q said.

"C'mon, if they just take us to the lab—"

"It's *not a lab*!" Q burst out.

It could have been an accident, just from the way the youngest stepped in front of his maddened friend. But the gleam in Q's eyes gave a different message, as the gunshot ripped through the room and folded the plump little man up where he stood.

It was so sudden, and the air so *foul* with the reek of blood, that Mark missed the moment to attack—and in another instant Q shoved his crumpling friend away and locked his eyes back on Mark. "You! Look what you did!"

Softly, sadly, Rafe said "Not him. Think: what if it's true, that two of our boys died in prison today? Too many pills—"

"Is that what you tell them?"

Joe Dennard's voice was soaked in pain, but the effort made his deep grunt all the louder.

Rafe took a step back from Q.

Q's eyes stayed on Mark and the bit of leather he'd never taken from him, but his words were for Dennard. *"Knew* you could hear! Now—"

"Now can I tell you who… who's really killing your people." Dennard said.

Rafe's gun darted between Dennard and Mark. It could have silenced Dennard on any word.

The older man didn't flinch. "They're dying on the street, dying in prison. Or is Rafe saying that's about some drug too?"

"No more lies!" Q shrieked.

"Here's the truth," Mark said.

He tossed the leather toward Q, with a tiny, nonthreatening flick of his fingers and a touch of magic to make it fly further. The talisman wafted up toward Q's head and over it, a perfect distraction…

Except Q let it go on by, eyes still right on Mark. The leather landed behind him.

"TELL ME!"

Before Mark could answer, Dennard said "There is no drug."

Something hard and certain resonated in the words, something none of Mark's half-truths had carried. This time Q glanced back… where Rafe stood quiet, helpless to hold the secret in, and Dennard gripped the bit of leather and floated slowly into the air.

"I *knew*—"

Mark slammed into Q. Riding a wave of power and fury, he crashed into the magic-addled thug and twisted the energy to smash him down—not with the bone-crushing force he ached to use, but he let his left hand pin his enemy down while his right poised to pay back all the beatings. The gun and keychain spilled from Q's grip.

Mark turned back to Rafe, mouth opening to bargain for their lives.

Instead, he saw Rafe's face as cold and closed off as the gang leader had ever looked. Even the air felt colder now.

Rafe's gun swung up. The last thug beside him raised his two pistols.

Dennard leaped across the room, to arrow straight into that tall thug's side with a weight-stealing shove that sent him hurtling into Rafe—

…

Mark was tumbling back away from Q's bloody body, flying blindly backward as weapons swung toward him. The gun felt loose in his fingers—*why am I holding a gun*—

The wall slammed into his side, too close too soon, *get up get up*… The room flashed and spun to veil the shapes across from him. One dead, one—Henry—crawling near that one, Dennard crouching stunned, the tall man with two guns stumbling in front of Rafe.

A shot blasted out. The tall thug began to crumple.

Over at the front door… a short, steel-eyed woman lunged in, and the falling man spun and jolted again as Nolan poured more bullets into him.

Rafe dove away, flying out of the room, the last of them. Mark pulled himself to his feet; Nolan paused to put one more shot in the dead man, her knuckles white—

…

Her gun muzzle and her icy eyes blotted out Mark's world, his arm limply lowered his own weapon away from her as someone shouted *"Gone he's gone he's gone"* with a desperation that should have torn the voice open, Henry's voice.

Somewhere a pane of glass shattered.

Nolan's eyes only squinted harder. They could have been triggers, poised far tighter than his own, even tighter than her fingers on the gun she held on Mark.

"Put… the gun down," Dennard's voice came.

Nolan didn't move. Why didn't she move, why didn't Dennard speak again?

Because he's talking to me, not her.

Mark stared at the gun in his hand… when had he raised it toward Nolan? When had he picked it up? Those changes had rushed in without him noticing, suddenly true without him being there when they happened. Blackouts.

When I jumped away from Q, he was spraying blood, and my finger was on the trigger—

The weapon, Q's weapon, fell from his grip. He looked up, but Nolan's gaze was no softer—locked so tight on his face. Had she even seen the gun drop?

"There, see—" Dennard burst into coughing, but he choked it down and swallowed back to tell Nolan, "Henry just said you scared the bastard out of Mark. Now put that away before Rafe comes back!"

Mark heard himself babbling "No, I feel Rafe running up the lawn, didn't you hear the kitchen window smash when he got out—"

Nolan finally spoke, her voice growing colder with every word: "How long has Winton been in your head, Mark? If that's you at all?"

"But…"

Q.

Gunner, possessed and stabbed behind his back in the hospital.

The men in the two gangs' gunfight, where the bird stopped him from saving them.

No, it has to be only that one time, because when that ended Angie broke me free… but then Gunner… And Winton is right out there now, he's controlling another pet at one of the windows, he's still watching us…

"Your pocket, Mark." Henry's voice was thick as if he couldn't spare the effort to control his lips right. His eyes were closed, and his hand clutched the keychain Q had dropped, drawing on its magic. "I think… I know he let go of you, but… I still feel something in your pocket."

Mark's hands brushed at his coat, his pants. Clumsy fingers jammed trying to reach in, so he yanked the pocket inside out and spilled out keys, subway tokens… and a flash of gray metal. Like in the factory. *Two* of them.

"His talismans… Winton's bird must have slipped one onto me when he… left me, sleeping, at the shootout… and I only thought the other vanished in the factory…"

"And Winton's right out there!" Henry said to Nolan. "He's the enemy, remember?"

Mark's eyes couldn't leave the bits of silver. But Henry, *Henry* could use the keychain talisman to sense them, even when they were waiting inertly in his pocket for the puppetmaster to take control again.

He gasped in a breath to swear, but the air screamed first. A roar of wind slammed against the building.

Whatever creature Winton had grabbed, Mark felt it holding onto its perch in the blast. "He's still out there watching—"

"So *you* say," Nolan cut in. "How do we know who's in control of you? Either of you?"

Henry said "I told you it was those talismans! He's clean now."

"Clean? I should trust him, ever?" Nolan's voice rose in the beginning of a shriek… but some of its force leaked away.

Dennard lurched a step toward her, with a hand clutching his stomach. "It has to be about talismans and touch," he said, slowly through gritted teeth. "Our own magic works that way, and I bet you need to carry one around too, and Winton's control always had to pass through what his puppet touches. Or this time he grabbed Mark because he was touching the talisman—it's the only other way that makes sense."

Like the one in Iskander's phone. But Winton didn't even need that to silence Iskander, he could have controlled him through me… no, he used the phone's talisman instead to keep me looking at everything but my own pocket. And if he risked putting any of them on me where I could find them, he must *need them to take control… It has to be… please please please let me be out of his reach now…*

Nolan let her gun droop.

Then: "We took too long." Her breath was a gasp. "Listen."

Listen? The gang's gone, there's nothing left but the blood. Mark forced his eyes up away from the shapes they'd left on the floor. That he'd left.

Then, he caught the sound, out beyond the still cracked-open front door and through the broken window Rafe had left in the kitchen. Police sirens.

"Had to happen," Dennard said. "We're in broad daylight too, no-where to run."

He wobbled a few steps to a corner, one hand gripping the leather strip as if its power was all that pulled him upright with his injuries. Several oversized, heavy shopping bags lay in a corner and he caught one up, then bent down and used the corner of another bag to gingerly scrape the two talismans into it. He held it far away from his body—as if the things could ever, ever be far enough away to be safe.

He had to float himself to his feet again. "Toss these in the toilet, then we tell the police how the gang caught us here."

"We can't!" Nolan waved at the bloody chaos around. "We have three *dead* bodies here, and it's our hands on the guns." She looked at her own weapon, and fumbled it into a pocket. "And you want to let the cops come up with any answer they want, when every hour they hold us Winton pulls more strings on all those people *with guns* around us? I can't. We *can't.*"

Outside, a sharp megaphone voice called "Attention inside! This is the police! We have a report of shots fired."

The sun dimmed. Sudden as an airplane's shadow passing over—but instead of a roar of engines, the air shrieked with wind, shrieked and swelled and sang through the shattered window in the next room as the blizzard slammed down outside.

Henry was the first to speak, his eyes stark and staring at her. "Did you just…"

Snow spattered outside the walls, and Mark felt shivers sweeping through him. He heard the building creak as the wind beat against it. Voices outside shouted and screamed in what must be the air gone mad.

Nolan swayed on her feet. Her face was pale.

Mark rushed to her side. She tottered back from his reach, and her hand groped blindly inside her coat.

He said "What is this? You said the weather was all used up!"

"Not the wind. Used up... me." Her last whisper slipped from her lips, as her eyes closed.

She toppled. He caught at her, and a shape fell from her hand. The same bamboo-cased flask the Eel had found when he searched them. Mark scooped it up.

At first he thought his skin had burst into flame.

No, not on fire, but power raged *through* him, through all the space around him and he had no barrier, nothing to hold himself in as it tore him apart—

Sounds broke through first: shouts and sirens outside pressed underneath the storm, then voices beside him. Finally touch and sight came again, and he saw Henry and Dennard stumbling toward him, as Nolan slumped over against him.

He caught her, absently. As he would have done with the belt, Mark pushed his thoughts against the flask, trying to find what space in his head held the right "muscles" to control it. But at his first touch the wind spun away, wilder than ever, whatever balance there had been now lost. Screams sounded, somewhere outside in the cold storm that was *himself*—

Not cold. He could feel that much; part of it was cold, and part was a soaking wetness of the blinding snow everywhere, all tossed up and down in the driven space. *Hold on, hold it in.*

"...Dying in jail... Mark... listen to me... Rafe's men are dying in jail... If Winton can get at them there, you have to stay free... only you and Henry can track him..." The voice was Dennard, right in Mark's ear.

"We know... too much," Mark managed to force out. He fought to catch his balance, still holding Nolan up; at least she was light. They couldn't risk the police taking them.

Taking *him.* Wasn't that what Dennard had said back in his apartment, that Mark's sense of magic was the one thing they couldn't endanger? Dennard had sounded like he only cared about what Mark could do.

Then Dennard turned to the front doorway and shouted, forcing what must be his aching chest to fling the words out to the police: "Keep back! Please—he'll kill me!"

The first answer was the wind. Then the voice on the megaphone replied "Attention inside! We have you surrounded! Your only way out is to talk to me."

Mark stared at Dennard. "What are you telling them—"

"One of us has to stay here. Someone with gunpowder burns." He held up the gun Mark had dropped. "So I'll say I suckered Rafe's people in here while you were all away. The gangs have been after me so many times, the police will almost buy that, if the rest of you just get *out!*"

He held out the talisman bag and the leather strip out to Mark.

"But… if Winton wants you dead…" Mark stood staring at him. Nolan's weight felt heavier by the moment, and her talisman still made his head spin if he moved—and Dennard wanted to stay, when Mark had been the one who'd shot…

Henry caught at his arm. "Come on!"

Fear. The fear in Henry's voice caught at him. His cousin had just seen murder and twisted-up *wrongness,* and now that he'd shown Winton he could sense the power behind it too, he'd made himself a target. And yet, Henry took the bag with the talismans with his other hand, trembling.

And Dennard wanted them both safe. At any price.

Mark seized the strip from Dennard and drew on it to help with Nolan's limp weight. He wobbled toward the front door, his balance still shaking with the other magic in his head. Through the door's window they saw almost a wall of living white.

Then Henry swung the door wide.

The wind should have sent Mark staggering. But instead, with the weather magic tearing through his nerves, stepping into the storm felt *easier* than balancing in the strange shelter of the building. What felt wrong was looking for the dim outlines of people through the snow, or trying to shuffle onward.

No, the time for walking was over. He felt Henry sliding in under his free arm, trying to help him stand. Mark muttered "Close your eyes."

One burst of magic flung them away from the ground—stretching and tearing at the bonds where the sky-forces flowed through him. Then as he let the upward motion ease, he could feel the three of them again, tumbling upward through the sky.

The sky. He *knew* the sky, he felt the gravity belts thrumming around his waist and more power in his left hand, but a different force that he gripped in his right hand pulled *outward* trying to merge with the air. Even with his eyes shut against the tearing wind, he could see the forces in the air—gone mad, pushed and abused too many ways— thinning and bleeding out—

Focus. Dizzier than he'd ever felt, with one hand's force pulling cleanly upward while the other's swirled and danced, he fought to hold his head together. His arms clung to his two passengers; Nolan's lungs were barely moving, *and how can I handle this?* On his other arm, Henry didn't make a sound.

Mark clutched at his courage, tightened his arms, squeezed his fingers on the talismans. *Balance.* His own magic was a surging and a sweeping upward, while the weather force flowed... *outward?* He felt it streaming out from the bamboo talisman, and other forces streaming *in* from the wider world.

The snow was gone. That knot of sticky power had dropped away below, or thinned out... Mark opened his eyes.

They stood in the sky, within *all* the sky. Below stretched the city, the lake, with the bright clear sun above and the vast blue ring of the horizon circling them. The last of their rising motion settled away... and that motion stirred a recognition in Mark's head, in his bones. That same *rising* air was part of some of the streams around them, while others *sank,* and many more flowed between those two—

To focus he twitched his arms left, as best they could move with their load of passengers and with his body dangling in space. With that motion he tried to nudge the downdrifting forces in the air away to the right, toward the side of space where one hand held the flask, while he gathered some of the updrafts to the other hand's side beside the leather, and let the wind flow between them. His reach was so weak, so short measured against the wide horizon, and these forces felt too different from gravity... *just picture them, pouring between different parts of the sky, flowing like currents of water in the lake... steady, steady...*

He heard Henry gasp in his ear. The twisting in his skin eased, and the air with it. Below, the city began to slide by... Mark should have felt no wind, drifting along within it, but today that motion was *inside* him to match the motion of the shapes below. It was all too bright in the daylight, but if they passed the edge of town they could find some private place to land.

Then the air touched him. Just a feather's brush upward, not part of the wind current, but he felt it begin to grow stronger... he tugged the winds downward to keep balance but it didn't ease how the pressure whipped up against them—

Because we're falling.

The lines in the landscape below spread and blurred, as he struggled to find the power again, but the air blew through his nerves and held his thoughts too open, too wide to hold any gravity power. His eyes fogged, dimmed.

He felt Henry's hand on his belt. Trying to help.

He laughed weakly. *Of course, I just faced all three forces of magic in a few minutes, I'm not going to fail now.*

Mark dragged them upward. "Just a little more now..."

CHAPTER NINE

COUNSEL AND COUNCIL

Even the outside of the police station was too close. Mark stared at the entrance, and at the ragged streams of people flowing in and out, irregular as the twitches of breeze over the pavement that the air had settled down to in the afternoon.

He felt no flicker of Winton's power inside. But he knew one of those talismans could be in position to control anyone in the crowd, and he, Henry, and Nolan needed to get to safety behind Nolan's walls… once they did one thing to help Dennard and stop the police from dragging them back out.

And that meant the lawyer.

"You *had* to be at Henry's home with Mr. Dennard." Todd Gilbert was a rich deep voice in an oversized fine suit, and it resonated even when he spoke softly now. He glanced from Henry to Nolan and finally to Mark. "The fact that the gang came to your own apartment first, Mark, will make your denials all the harder to accept. No matter what I do to head off police questioning, any evidence—"

"Our decision's made." Nolan's voice was tired, her eyes too bright from the pills she'd taken to hold herself awake. "We can't be too near the police now. Not with people dying in their jails."

"Police corruption?" Gilbert frowned. "I owe Kate too much to cut you loose, but she must have told you… the more you let me know, the more I can help."

And the more you're a target of the enemy, or a tool for him. The words almost popped out of Mark's mouth, but he held them in with the same effort of will that kept him on his feet.

When none of them yielded, Gilbert led the way to the station's heavy glass front door. Henry walked close behind him, with Nolan and Mark hanging back a few steps. Mark strained his eyes and his other sense for the first sign of trouble from the people around. Nolan seemed to be keeping herself sheltered behind him.

He and Henry readied the papers they'd brought.

A uniformed cop, a young black man, stepped outside to meet them, just as Gilbert had arranged. He nodded to the lawyer, but his eyes took in the others hanging back.

Before the cop could speak, Gilbert announced "My clients are delivering their statements about the violence at Henry Maes's home."

Mark forgot to move, until he saw Henry signing his own statement under the officer's eye, and moved to sign the paper in his own hand. They handed them over, to a murmur as the people around began to notice the moment of legal theater.

The cop seemed to gather the papers and his wits at the same time. "Thank you, thank you all for coming down. Now right this way—"

Gilbert seemed to swell up, both his voice and the well-padded chest that produced it. "These people have given their statements, and they are not being charged. They have no interest in being harassed over a street gang that died trying to satisfy an old grudge, when you have already begun persecuting the gang's target, Mr. Dennard."

Other police, in plainclothes, were approaching beyond the door as if Gilbert's contact had signaled them. But the lawyer only pressed toward the door into the station, and his momentum held the police back as he gathered volume. Mark and the others edged back, under cover of his words.

Gilbert went on, "Our larger question should be the safety of the man you are holding. I've seen the life expectancy of prisoners connected to this case lately. So if Mr. Dennard is injured in the middle of your persecution, I'll have every reporter in Lavine down here."

The first detective out held up his hand. "Calm down. I don't know where you're getting your rumors from—"

Then another detective, a tall woman, was at Henry's side. "You still say your cousin's friend was in a gunfight *at your home* and you're only coming down here now?"

Gilbert said "These people have been shocked—"

"Of course we're shocked," Mark burst out. "The gang tore up my apartment and Henry's and almost killed Dennard, and we didn't even hear they were looking for me."

"For you? Not Dennard?" The detective closed in on Mark.

God, I'm the one holding our exit up. "For me or him, we don't know. It's all in the statements." Mark fought not to flinch from her gaze, not to let in thoughts of how he'd let Rafe's men come looking for him or about the talisman he'd brought into their midst.

"I think," Gilbert said, "that Mr. Petrie and Mr. Maes have made their positions clear. Any more discussion should wait until tempers have cooled. Unless you do want to haul them into a jail where people *are dying.*" He raised his voice one more calculated half a notch, and murmurs swelled around them.

The male detective growled "Prison's probably safer. Still not as safe as if someone was sick of being caught in the crossfire, and stopped trying to stay alive out there on their own. Not as safe as telling the truth before their luck ran out."

One thought. It would only take one thought to send Mark floating upward and force them to start listening, and bring down dozens, hundreds, of professionals to take over with how to track down an invisible enemy… but all he wanted was to get away from their questions. His eyes ached, fighting to keep from fluttering closed.

Instead he followed Nolan and Henry away, watching people's gazes follow them. At least none of them drifted that one step too close that might be putting one of Winton's tricks within reach.

Nolan's car was just ahead.

A footfall spun Mark around. The woman detective was behind them, too close.

"If that's how you want to play it," she said. "And we *do* have some precautions in place for Mr. Dennard's safety. But, one thing… if you're trying to keep your distance from the gang, why is the target of their most public robbery here with you? Ms. Nolan?"

On the last words she raised her voice and advanced on Nolan.

What did she see? Nolan's pale face and exhausted movements, or the coldness that had made her gun down one man and come within a twitch of shooting Mark?

"So," the detective asked, "what brings Olivia Nolan out here? More about being robbed yesterday? Or are you just partial to people like Mark that have disaster following them around?"

Nolan met her gaze straight on, and her voice was tight with fatigue but still clear. "I'm supporting my employee. You can check with my manager if you like, about how Mark identified himself as security *before* that robbery you're talking about. I'm trying to make him my bodyguard."

Mark managed to keep his face still. *I murdered people without even knowing, and she was ready to shoot me—and now I'm* guarding *her?* Was that one of Nolan's jokes?

She went on "Who'd be better at handling himself than someone who's survived what all the gangs have thrown at him? And I thought the job would help him stay out of trouble… although it turns out it may have only made his enemy notice me too. Now, unless you have any more questions?"

The detective looked at her, and Mark wondered how she could miss the signs of whatever pills were keeping Nolan awake. Had some speck of blood carried over when she'd changed clothes?

Nolan turned back to her car. The detective let them go, and Henry kept pace with the rest as if the beating to his back had been nothing.

Mark had a flash of déjà vu, so strong it made his throat seize up. *Sure we came here once before—when we thought Rafe's people stabbing Dennard was all we were fighting against.* At least this time the supporter was a lawyer Kate knew, instead of Mark innocently calling *Winton himself.*

But that time, it had been Angie walking out beside him. And his hands had been clean.

They reached the car. Nolan sank into the passenger seat, Henry settled in the rear, and Mark took the wheel again—as a sometime cabbie, if not as a "bodyguard."

At least they'd already loaded up a few things from his apartment... what was left of it... and Nolan's home wasn't so far away.

But first...

He closed his eyes, not to rest but to reach for the fear, the pure need to let the world grow still and feel *all* the magic. He'd done this once, long before Henry had. Under the belts' thrumming and the other magic leathers, under the quicksand knowledge of what Winton had made him do, somewhere in the space between one heartbeat and the next...

Winton's talisman. Still back in the trunk where they'd put the bag. When it lay this close, he *could* catch a tiny flicker from the thing even while the killer left it inactive, waiting for some fool to touch it. So they had some defense.

"I only sense one of the two talismans," he told Henry. "I think you're right, the one from the factory really did lose all its energy in the light. Somehow."

He started the car out, and pushed his thoughts further into how the magic might work—better those puzzles than sitting silent.

"You know, he must have had one of these at the Youth Center to get control of that cop—maybe hidden on the office door. Anyway, there's no trace of Winton *doing* anything around here. Or Angie, still."

Henry said "That's what I thought. So it's true? You and I are the only ones who can feel it?"

"That we know. Genetics, I guess. Using the magic can work for anyone, like Rafe's gang… but this trick you get pulled into by birth. Sorry."

Henry shook his head, and turned to Nolan. "So we really leave? You say your home is the safest place to work from now. But Joe Dennard is facing a prison sentence. We can't even wait here and watch for if Winton tries to kill him in the cell?"

Mark clutched the steering wheel to hold himself steady. But Nolan was leaning back on her headrest, eyes closed, so he had to give the maddening answer himself:

"I wish we could. The hell of it is, Winton could just wait us out for days before he made his move. He's always had that option… and, he hasn't made a straight-out attack against any of us. So we have to hope that hasn't changed."

"Oh. Then, it's back to rooting out where he's hiding, before he does this again? Or do we go after Rafe? They're both after us."

"Not both," Nolan said softly. "Rafe Martinez is only… His 'flying gang' were loose cannons. He tried to train them in ways that kept them from being aware of their magic, and you saw how well that ended. He saw it, too. But Winton is still…" She let the sentence fade away.

"So we stop him! And stop Rafe too." Henry's voice trembled as he said it, and Mark saw his face go paler than ever in the mirror, but he still held up the leather keychain talisman in his fist. "We have to. But we need to pick up Christa next—"

"Your girlfriend stays out of this." Nolan said it almost at a whisper, but it stopped Henry in his tracks.

For a moment Henry didn't answer. Then, slowly: "Look, I've been thinking about this. We all know she might be the next one in danger, to get to me. She trusted me enough to get herself out of sight for a few hours, but I can't just *leave* her there with half an explanation. And she's got my dog."

Just like that, my 'allies' are fighting? Mark said "Slow down, nobody's leaving anybody." Wasn't that what Rafe said to his men? He glanced from Nolan, with her drawn face and arms folded tight, to Henry's growing anger.

Nolan spoke first, and the edges softened out of her voice as she said "Henry… we agreed, we have to keep this among ourselves from now on. I understand wanting to go to her. But she—and you, and us as well—we're all safer if she gets herself far away from this." She motioned her hand further back, toward the trunk and the talismans—but the gesture was a small, weak one.

"We're safer?" Henry said coldly. "I think you just insulted her. Or me."

"I don't think that's what she meant," Mark cut in. "Please, we almost got ourselves killed today, all of us. I mean, think about that: Nolan and I have been watching for gunmen and possession around every corner for days, weeks, and that was before we saw how Winton can still have someone like me set up under our nose. Maybe this is the chance you need, to just get yourself and Christa out of this while you can."

Nolan snapped "She goes, not him. We need his 'eyes.' "

In the mirror, Henry's scowl deepened.

"Please!" Mark said. "Just… slow down, all of us. We're all tired, and—"

He glanced at Nolan again, but saw no help in that worn, stretched face. Smoothing things over was supposed to be his job.

Instead of trying again, he said "Look, if we're talking about getting out of danger, that's what Kate did with herself and her son, and she chose that after knowing about the magic all her life. In fact, we owe her a call right about now."

It took a few seconds to find a clear spot on the street to pull over. All that time he could feel Nolan's tight resolve holding her awake, and Henry's bristling.

Kate answered on the first ring, even with what were probably dozens of security apps on her phone. "Mark? So how's Gilbert been for you?"

"A lifesaver, thanks. He knows that the story we're giving out won't hold up forever. But so far, Dennard's safe and the rest of us are free."

"Good."

"It must be some favor you called in, and we aren't going to waste it. We're going to catch up to Winton before he tries to get at Dennard."

"Careful, Mark." She paused, then said gently "You'll want to learn this: the best promises are the ones you know you can keep."

Mark blinked. Winton's trick had slashed through all their defenses, and Kate couldn't even let him have one moment of hope?

Instead of trying to puzzle it out, he said "I'm putting you on with Henry and Nolan here," and tapped speaker mode. "We were talking about getting Henry or his girlfriend out of Winton's reach, like you did, and how to find Winton and get our lives back."

The speaker's tone didn't dilute her sigh. "And you want me to tell you somewhere you aren't already looking. You already know the tools you have: you can keep searching his history for clues to how he might have slipped away, and combine that with narrowing down what places are left that he could be hiding."

"Or where he's fueling his magic," Mark added. "I thought finding that factory meant it was one place we could just wait for him to come back to. But I know we can't assume his power only forms in one spot."

Soft but clear, Nolan said, "Mine doesn't. Careful what you assume."

Six words, that change everything. Mark held his gaze on the windshield, afraid to glance over. After three months, Olivia Nolan was finally admitting something about her magic's limits, and what patterns it might show about their enemy's. She was finally opening up, or just too tired to hold out.

"If he's even still in town," Nolan went on softly. "We don't *know* his magic can't pull strings from the other side of the state."

"Like your weather control does?" Mark tried.

Did Nolan hesitate an instant, before she answered? Then she shifted in the seat to face them, with an audible grunt, and said "My range has its own limits. I have to pull in hot or cold air from some-where, and right now too much of that has already been sucked in and churned up around us. You've felt the toll it takes on me, Mark. Be-sides, if I have to use any more pocket snowstorms to cover us, someday even the weathermen may stop talking about the weather and start doing something about it."

Henry groaned aloud, but Kate said "Twain jokes? Seriously?"

"Serious humor, you mean?" Mark said. *I called Kate to* defuse *the tension between us!* "Or something funny in the air, or something—anyway," and he rushed on, as fast as he could think, "did you two ever think you might be the experts about our other line on Winton? I mean, understanding Winton himself?"

Henry was the first to answer, frowning. "Both of them are? What do you mean?"

"Kate Fletcher Woodward, Olivia Nolan—you have something Henry and I don't. You've both grown up with magic. Spellkeepers, the Nolans would call you." Mark smiled at Nolan, and saw her eyes narrow as he warmed to his thought. "I get that neither of you knew about other kinds of magic, sure, because things like Nolan's weather and Winton's control are just too easy to hide if your family raises you to 'keep' the 'spell' to yourself. But, can you try to put yourselves in Winton's head? And I don't mean the way he jumps into ours."

The last words came out before he thought, and Nolan chuckled "Not bad."

Now I'm making jokes about what he did to me? Well, that's a start, Mark thought as he went on "I mean it. How does he see the world? Do you think he grew up with power, and how would it change him, when it's such an untraceable way to twist people? We're the only ones who can see his work, and I still can't see why we're still *alive* except that he wants to get our magic's secrets before he kills us."

Until today. Winton had aimed Mark and the gun straight at Nolan—

"I can keep him out," Nolan said. "When we get to my home."

Kate mused "It might be the healing that he wants. Our magic does have some enhancing effect on recovery. What's more, Angie killing his bird did hurt him. He stayed quiet for months."

"Right." *Winton's texts did warn me about letting the healing be seen. He's noticed it.*

"Listen—" Henry said.

"That might really be it," Mark rushed on, waving at Henry to let him finish his thought before someone cut it off. "Hell, we know he lost his father in a fire—wouldn't a close call like that make him grab at anything that could heal him now?" *But knowing Winton, he probably killed his father himself—or Edward Winton went after his son first...*

Kate said "It could be he—"

The rest of her words were lost as Henry yelled "He's here!"

Mark twisted in the seat, his eyes darting clumsily around the windows... but in another frenzied heartbeat his belts caught the flicker of Winton's magic. Far, far above, thank God.

"Am I right?" Henry asked. "That's his power there?"

"He—he's up there," Mark gasped, trying to make his lungs work. "Not diving or anything, just another bird watching us, I think." Just another day in their battle of wits. As long as the killer—*that* killer—stayed up there, nobody died. *Please, let that be how it works.*

"Wonderful," Nolan muttered, still leaning against the headrest. "I've got nothing left to hit him with."

"You mean you're tired? If the magic's strong enough—" Mark reached out to offer to take her talisman again, but Nolan glared at him and tightened a protective arm over her coat. The spybird held its slow, lazy circling above them, and he wished Angie was winging in to intercept it.

"So what can we do?" Henry's words had a tremor in them, angry like Mark's own frustration but sharper, still new to the fight.

Nolan answered "Nothing. Except you both stay ready, and get us under my roof."

The next voice was Kate's, and the phone gave it a strange contrast with the three people in the suddenly cramped car: "Then, the last thing you need is me on the line right now. I'll call when I can."

"Okay. And thanks for Gilbert," Mark said, and the call cut off.

Another moment of silence began, as the bird settled on some high place out of view far above the car's roof.

Mark tried breaking the hush this time: "Now he's sitting, like us. I guess he really isn't going after Dennard—since Dennard's not much of a danger in jail."

Henry ventured "Unless… he followed us because he was already coming to the police station."

Nolan said "Or, he just followed the talismans we brought along. They're still his; think about it."

"You mean…" Mark tried to reason it out. "Those things haven't done anything, I'd have sensed them if they did. Unless… God, we don't know *what* else they do, maybe they're always pulling at him without a single sign we can catch—we don't know!" He banged a fist on the steering wheel, not half as hard as he wanted. "But having them is still the first real look we've gotten at his power."

"I know. Anyway, it might only mean that you missed his approach because you weren't searching at every moment; nobody could do that." Nolan gave Mark a smile, and then it widened as she turned toward the back seat. "And now you won't have to."

Henry's own smile was tighter, guarded. "You're welcome."

Nolan looked to Mark again. "Now, back to my home. Rest, plan, and we all stay there until we know our next move."

"Okay then," Henry said. "We can pick up Christa once the bird moves on."

And we're back to this—Mark opened his mouth, but too late.

Nolan said "And then what if she needs to bring a brother in too, and he wants his kids along?"

"That's what my help gets me?" Henry snapped. "And you had to say it now, where that thing can see us fight?"

"That's… not what I'm saying," Nolan said. "If you do have to have her with you, I can't stop you. But think what that means."

"What? I know I'm new at this. So tell me!"

Mark tried "It's not just something we can tell you. I think she means you aren't *used to looking for* how many ways we're all at risk. Or what it's like to keep pushing on through all of this, or ask someone you care about to—"

"I mean," and Nolan turned straight to Mark, "how long was that thing on you? Most of last night? You're the one who already saw how your enemy can jump from one police officer to another and back, so fast that he made one of them *hit* the other without ever noticing the second of time that he'd 'lost.' "

"I know. I know what he did—"

Her weak, relentless voice pressed on. "So how many times did Winton peek through your eyes? A half-second here, a minute there? You ever snap back from your brain wandering a moment? Or longer—when you found the other talisman in the factory, he made you hide it from yourself, and you told yourself it disintegrated. When Gunner turned his back on you—"

"I know!" *Why is she saying this—*

"Can you pin down every moment he could have stolen from you last night? Hidden another talisman under someone's pillow? Just a few touches on your phone? And now we say you're 'clean' because we took those pieces off you, and we pretend we have *any idea how deep his magic goes into your mind.* But still, we *have* to trust you because you're the only one who can *try* to tell us if he's gotten his hooks into Henry. And only Henry can vouch for you."

My God...

Mark felt his breath hitching and coming in struggled gasps. He stared up, through the roof toward where the damn bird was studying them as they spoke—

"I'm sorry, Henry," he heard Nolan saying. "That's what we're fighting against. It's what we need you to be ready for, so Winton *never* catches one of us like that again. And you want to bring someone you care about into this?"

"Did anyone..." Henry gasped, and then he cleared his throat and said again "Did anyone ever tell you, you're a little paranoid?"

Mark's breath steadied, enough to turn and smile at his cousin.

"Nobody's told me that," Nolan said. "Why would I let them see it?"

This time, her voice was so flat, such a perfect deadpan, it was the best joke he'd ever heard from her. If there was any joke in it at all.

With cold, trembling fingers, Mark started the car. And... Winton's bird still moved to follow them.

We need *Winton's talismans, they're the key to helping Angie, if we can make them work.* But even that thought only made Mark wish he knew where she'd gone, that Winton's smug flicker of power wasn't the only one in the sky above them now. He heard Henry on the phone to Christa, speaking whispered reassurances about him calling back later.

The road ahead kept trying to blur in Mark's eyes, the more Nolan's words burrowed through him. He tried to keep his focus moving back and forth between driving and tracking Winton, but lingering ideas kept circling around in his head. If they could make the talismans work for them instead of destroying them… or if they forced Winton out of the shadows… How badly Winton wanted the magic… how long he'd been influencing the gangs, befriending the police…

Finally Winton drifted away in the sky, and Mark realized they'd entered the winding sidestreets and fenced estates of Nolan's Orchard Heights neighborhood. "He's gone," was all he said, and the others had nothing to add.

Still, after another block or two, Mark had to say "Listen…"

"What is it?" Henry said. Nolan only glanced at him, saving her strength.

"When we've gotten some rest, I was just thinking. It may all come down to getting something from his talisman. Or else some way to force him out of hiding. Or bringing the police in on this after all."

"Are you insane?" Nolan said. "Winton's power is *invisible*. All anyone ever sees is someone acting strangely."

Mark met her gaze. "I mean, if we have to. I always think, if I float up to the police's ceiling they'll have to believe us—"

In the mirror behind them, a car sped forward. Mark watched the little blue Honda swing out to pass them, closing in so *eagerly* that his own foot itched to slam on the gas before it got close enough to launch some attack.

Instead the car honked, and he recognized the black woman at the wheel. Nolan's hacker.

"So she wants to talk," Nolan sighed, and waved for him to pull over.

Mark brought the car to the side of the road, and the other driver pulled up behind them and trotted around to the passenger window. She wore what might have been the same casual camo outfit she'd had on when she came looking for Nolan at the banquet, and clutched a laptop under her arm.

When the window slid down, she leaned her head right into the car. "About that hard drive you brought me…" Then she stopped, and swept a deliberate look around at Mark and Henry. "Looks like we're due to renegotiate a few things."

Just like before, the hacker was using the threat of being overheard to force Nolan to make time for her. It hadn't worked then, but now Nolan only said a weak "We might be."

Then Henry cut in, firm but still more tactful than the intruder. "And you are?"

"Irene. And you?"

"My name's Henry—" he began, but Irene pushed right on:

"Henry? The cousin of Mark there? And now you're *both* here to know about Mark's… enemy." Again, she let the hint hang, as a threat.

Nolan sighed "If you want to impress me, don't do it standing in the street. Come on."

Irene glanced at the others again, and raised an eyebrow. "Be careful what you wish for," she said, and marched back toward her car.

As Mark turned back to the road, he realized she had caught up with them just half a block from Nolan's gate. Too well-timed for an accident.

Nolan growled "She tracked me? She hacked *my* GPS?" She said it loudly enough for them all to hear, not only an insight but a warning.

Henry stared. "She what? And what's this about renegotiating— does she already know about magic?"

"She needs to know," Mark said.

He let the car slow. Nolan turned a sharp glance at him, but his words came pouring out:

"We need her. We need every edge we can get, now that Winton's worming his way in around us, and there's Rafe and the cops, and… everything. If that means telling her the whole truth—look, you're the only one who knows her, you'd know if we can trust her, but I'd say

right now we need her all the way in with us, and we need to do anything it takes to keep her—"

Ominous words, he realized, to say to a woman that he'd seen
shoot people.

He added quickly "I say we either bring her in, or send her away
now. In some way that doesn't bring us more problems."

"So, Winton didn't plant something on her too? You checked for
any talismans he's just waiting to activate?"

"Ah. Give me a minute, next time she's in range." *What* is *the
range for spotting one if it's like this? How can we be sure? We have
to be.* "I'll find out."

"Then let me think," was all Nolan said. She dug out a bottle from
her coat and swallowed a pill, at least her third one that afternoon.

Mark dragged his eyes away from that bottle, holding in a warning
about pills or pushing herself too hard. He started the car up again.

The harder part came when he stopped it in Nolan's drive. He had
to open the trunk, and take out his own computer Rafe's that men had
smashed at his apartment… and the shopping bag that could do worse
to him if he was holding it too close. But he brought them inside, into
Nolan's fortress of a house.

Mark remembered standing in Nolan's home during their first en-
counter, when he thought he'd tracked the enemy's magic there. He
remembered the bare style, and the use of solid stone and heavy wood
in all the furnishings… but this time, he understood the *smell*. The
house smelled as if he could close his eyes and forget it had a roof
between it and the open sky, as if Nolan lived with nothing but heavy,
fastened-down objects around her so that she could fling gales through
the corridors without a care.

The others began setting up in a front room, Irene opening a bag of
tools under the TV—that was a huge flatscreen, bolted to the wall of
course. Mark left them there long enough to take Winton's talismans
down to a distant corner of the second floor. The farthest away from
them he could find.

He came back to find Nolan setting a keyboard on her lap and warning Irene to put her own machine away, while Henry watched. Mark took a chair a few feet back from their line of sight, then showed Irene the remains of his own third-hand laptop.

"You think you can hook its hard drive up to some of these?"

Irene sniffed. Then she was grabbing keyboards and clamping wires with some of her tools—she certainly came prepared.

Mark let his eyes go unfocused as she worked. Ignoring whatever they talked about, he had to strain for that tiniest flicker of one of Winton's waiting talismans on her—he could be staking their lives on how sure he was.

Then she began.

"I still can't get a line on that hideaway house of his in Europe. You want to see me hack the FAA to see if that's where he's gone?"

God, if Winton's magic could *reach them from that far—*

Henry countered "Hack the FAA? That's a joke, isn't it?"

"And if I said it wasn't," Nolan said, "you'd ask why we were *that* interested in his location."

"Sure, sure. You're looking for secret properties, but you never ask about moving vans so you *can't* be 'chasing' him, right? He's just some kind of business rival, and you want all this so you can understand how he thinks."

Her sarcasm rang off the walls for a moment, but Nolan only said calmly "And can you understand him?"

"Right there, I called the folder *Investments 4*—" She waited a moment as Nolan followed her instruction, and a table of numbers sprang up on the big screen. "All the little businesses he's known for having a hand in, and then the circles they lead to and..."

She led them on, click by click, and each time Mark stopped straining for talismans he did his best to catch up with her. Most of these charts were the same ones on his own machine that he'd looked at for days, sometimes weeks. Some of them were built from figures he'd struggled to understand himself; the picture they gave of Roger Winton through his activities wasn't so different from the silent, far-reaching web of small operations that Mark already knew. But hearing Irene lead them along, he remembered how he'd never *understood* the layout of the city streets until he began seeing them from above. *It's about perspective.*

But seeing patterns hadn't found Winton so far. Mark tried to hold his mind just far enough out of Irene's rushing stream of reasons and observations, to catch only those Winton projects that might have their own reasons for secrets. He watched for any operation that might be supplying the enemy with animals, or the green stone or silver for the talismans.

When she passed the list of investments again, he searched for the factory he'd discovered—was it really just last night? The letters shimmered in his eyes, too small.

"So that's what makes you pay attention?" came Irene's words, suddenly right at his side.

"I don't know." Too much denial leaked into his voice, but he went on "You ever think you could have missed something of his?"

"Missed? I try not to think of that. But it's not easy; Winton likes holding major shares in all the small, varied operations he can find. Almost like he doesn't want power, just dozens of eyes around town," she added, and the sarcasm thickened in her voice again. "Or did he build a whole other empire using his other hand and a few billion dollars he hid?"

"I guess not." *I hope not.* And Winton wouldn't even need to own a place to fuel his magic, if Nolan was right and he might have a whole set of spots that gave him power.

Irene moved back to Nolan. The more they explored the files, the faster her stream of words came, and the more her abrasive tone grew smoother. Nolan only grew more pale and quiet, chasing Irene's words with rapid clicks trying to keep up with her. Mark let fewer and fewer of those words stay with him: "police," "family," "influence."

No, Winton didn't own a pet shop or a zoo to get his birds. He had some small dealing in minerals, so that might relate to what was in the talismans—

The next time Irene walked toward him he tried to look unimpressed, but she still glanced over at the screen. "Imports, is that what you notice? If Winton does turn out to be a diamond smuggler, and you're all in the same racket, you could pay me better."

She glared a challenge at Nolan, but the older woman ignored the bait.

Irene pushed on "And we all know it's some kind of racket. Sure, some boys lose their dads in a fire. But how many burn their hands and get patched up just enough…"

She tapped a key, and a new image filled the TV screen—

"—to lose most of their fingerprints."

Mark felt his jaw falling open. He stared at the images, close-ups from some ID file that showed ten huge prints, some twisted into mad moonscapes, and all of them mostly swallowed by pale, barely-lined regions that could only be some kind of replacement for his skin. *Winton's* fingerprints? *This has to mean something. What's he been up to?*

Irene folded her arms, and swept a smug look around the room. "So what kind of man got rid of his fingerprints? Did you know that? Did you *all* know that?"

"Make up your mind," Nolan said suddenly.

She pulled herself up from the chair, stumbling a moment as she did—so much of her strength sapped by her magic, and whatever pills she'd popped to stay awake. But she glared at Irene as if she hadn't used up her endurance, only her patience.

"So you want to pressure me. Just tell me, do you want my guests here when we compare my dirty laundry, and yours?"

"Do *you?*" Irene's answer didn't hesitate, but her voice trembled under that gaze. "B-but, if you want to get to the bottom line faster—"

Nolan smiled thinly, and turned to Mark. "You heard her. Can you two give us a few minutes?"

Mark blinked, stared. In just a few words, Nolan was trying to force him out of the conversation that he'd pushed her to have. He opened his mouth, to demand that Irene joining the team had to be a team decision.

Then he looked at Irene again, at how she'd just stood quiet for whole seconds longer than she had in the last hour. *I told Nolan to deal with her; I have to let her do that.*

"Sure," he said. "And you know where I stand on this. Henry?"

"I think you said it best." His cousin got to his feet. "Mark, why don't you show me around here?"

Mark was just turning away, when Nolan said "And, that other question I asked you?"

Meaning if Winton had planted any tricks on Irene. Mark scowled; he'd sensed nothing, but any trace of it would be *so* faint... and he was so tired...

Trust myself too. "It's fine."

CHAPTER TEN

MOUSE AND CAT

Mark led his cousin through the rooms. About the time he scooped up the bag with the talismans from where he'd left it, he realized he'd retraced the path he'd taken when he first broke into this house. The large, overstuffed couch Henry eased himself down into was the same one Mark had once hidden behind thinking he could ambush Nolan. Instead she'd come within one second of shooting him… a little like today.

Henry sighed "And so she pushes us aside all over again. But I suppose a gatecrasher like Irene doesn't need to know that Nolan's taken us on as full partners yet. Or else those two are the ones hiding things from us, or… And you've been keeping all this straight for three months?" He spoke in a whisper, to keep the words from echoing down to Irene.

Mark shook his head, grinning sadly. "I wasn't standing right in the middle of those games, most of the time. It's been more about ignoring most of them and picking one thing at a time to look at. Like these." Carefully, he tipped the pair of talismans onto the carpet.

"You think so?" Then Henry's eyes opened wider. "Wait, you're *not* going to try using those to find Winton. You've seen how he controls… them. That's crazy!"

Touch those things? Mark made himself laugh against the chill the idea stirred. "Of course I won't. I just want to look at what we have. Because, getting them brings us a little closer to helping Angie."

He stood over them, and closed his eyes, not for the sleep his body ached for but to lock his thoughts in with the danger, the possibility, right at his feet. The belts were a solid *thrumming* at his waist, and Winton's power in use would have been like a flickering scratch resounding against some silent floorboard, but these…

When he'd first gotten his apartment—*the one that Rafe's men had just torn apart*—

Focus. In his apartment, there had been cobwebs laced through the radiator. He remembered staring deep into the tangle, for a glimpse of whether the spider was still within… buried in the dim shapes without even a motion to show if it was gone or simply waiting to rush out…

"There's still some power in one of them, just one," he said. "If the other's the one from the factory, I think it really did lose its magic, even before Winton made me pocket it." Being possessed sounded almost bearable, the way those words came out.

"Why would he do that, if the talisman was no good to us?" Henry said. "So you wouldn't try deep-sense testing the dead talisman and catch the one that was already on you?"

"That sounds right—and to stop me seeing what it's made of, of course. But did he make it go dead too? Or was that the light hitting it…"

He knelt down, just close enough to study the two pieces of silver. On one side, clear square grooves and a hinge showed their miniature door. That door had been hanging open in the factory.

He drew out his keys; maybe the tips could pry at some catch on the silver, if he could find tongs or something to hold a half-inch-sized piece of metal still. If he could make himself reach that close to it.

Henry's voice cut in: "Winton's back."

Mark twisted to his feet, but the presence approaching in the air… He let out a sigh. "Not Winton. That's Angie up there."

"It is? Is that how you tell, because her aura's so much fainter than when it's him controlling something?"

He noticed it right off—so she really is weaker. Winton's damn text was the truth. Mark tracked the owl closing in, trying to remember how strong her magic had been before she'd used up some of it on him. If he could always sense her energy, did that mean Angie had to be drawing on it just to hold herself together, and she'd been burning it away for three months even before…

To push the fear back, he told Henry "You know, this room we're in was where I was the very first time she flew in to save me." He stepped over and slid the window up for her. "Come on in."

She didn't respond.

Angie only hung in the air, some hundred feet up, circling slowly over Nolan's property. Once, twice.

Henry spoke then, at the same quiet level but with his words more hesitant. "Angie? Mark's fine. We found Winton's talismans on him. He's free now."

She only circled around again.

Mark stared at the ceiling she drifted beyond. That had been his hope, that when Angie heard they'd freed him from Winton, she'd come back. But this *was* coming back, the same way she'd been keeping her distance ever since she lost her body. Even here, even when they had a taste of the magic that might help her, except they didn't dare open it—

He spun around and dropped to the carpet beside the glint of silver. The key in his hand clicked the clasp open, and he was staring at a piece of pale, green-veined stone before he remembered he was *holding* the talisman. He snatched his hands back.

I actually touched the thing again, just out of the hope that it's as drained as it feels? I'm that *wrecked?*

He tried to steady his voice, into a casual "Well, that's what I remember was inside."

Henry knelt slowly, easing his bad back down. "Is that… jade? We can find out."

"The cover could be to protect the energy," Mark mused. "You open it to charge it, but you only do it in darkness. If we just buried this thing for a day, would it start filling up again?" No, it couldn't be that easy, there had to be more to why Winton had put it in the factory—and it was far too soon to risk giving a talisman to Angie anyway. "But, we're closer. We're closer, and we haven't even caught Winton yet!"

"Can she hear you?" Henry said. "She's pretty high up."

"I…" Mark wanted to shout, but Irene would still be downstairs. He glared at the window. If the afternoon sun wasn't flooding the air he could soar up and speak at her altitude, to remove all doubt. "Owls' ears are supposed to catch everything. I always thought she could."

Then Henry looked up, and his bearded face nodded. "If all this is how this game is played, I know what I'm doing next: practicing this sense of magic. We lookouts need to work in shifts, don't we?"

He held the keychain up in front of his eyes—

Then he stopped to look at Mark again. "And now I'm doing it! I almost *forgot* what your own magic does to us if we don't spread out our time using it. You said it's safest to look only a couple of times in a minute?"

Was this how it felt, to have a partner to help keep watch, and have to bring someone up to speed instead of being the one trying to catch up?

A memory touched Mark, and he reached down and pulled Henry carefully to his feet. "Work on one other thing first. If you want to fly—"

"Fly?" Henry shook his head. "But you need me to stay with Nolan, don't you? I can't learn to outrun killers. The way my back is I can't even walk right…"

But as he spoke, a light was growing in his face, and Mark watched the world start to open up for him. *I don't even need to say the magic might heal him.*

First, they had to be sure Irene couldn't wander in. A surge of magic let Mark heft the couch and set it to block the door closed.

Then he smiled back to Henry. "You already sense the power— that's better than Kate thought was possible. Now you just need to practice one thing before you try this in the air. This is how Angie tested me."

He brought himself floating to the ceiling. In Nolan's home that felt maybe a foot lower than in other houses.

Just right to make this a challenge.

"That keychain's almost empty. Try this." Floating with Angie's belt, he unbuckled the other and held it down to Henry.

His cousin looked at Rafe's belt a moment. In the next he gripped it, twitched and then rose, slowly, slowly drifting up until he had to raise his hand to stop his skull from brushing the ceiling. He had none of Mark's control, yet.

"It's all about how close you get to the ground, before—"

Mark let the power flicker, enough to drop and then pull himself to a halt a moment later. Tilting a foot down, he tapped a toe on the floor inches below him.

"Once you know you have enough control to break your fall, we can work on the rest of flying any time. Because then you'll know you *can* fly, and that flying can't hurt you."

Except for drifting into electrical lines, or getting shot, but he didn't need to mention that just yet. He watched as Henry dropped— and instantly bobbed up again, banging off the ceiling with his up-raised hand. Henry dropped again and thumped onto the floor, but the embarrassment left his face before the sound faded and he was already looking upward again—

Henry stopped there, and eased himself back to the couch. "What was I saying before? Maybe I'll try once every *couple* of minutes. I wouldn't want the power to break my mind on my first day as a spellkeeper."

The word made Mark's grin stretch even wider. "I guess not. And I should see how Nolan's doing." He slid the couch, and Henry still on it, to the side enough to open the door again. As he stepped out, he heard a mutter from his cousin that could have been "Showoff."

Henry was probably right, he thought as he walked. But, making the couch weightless was nothing, compared to staggering for the stairs. They all needed rest, and then they needed *answers*. About how to use Winton's magic or find him or just what would force him out of hiding.

Maybe look for some small tie between Winton and Nolan, or Kate... If it even was *their magic Winton was after, but why else would he spy and manipulate but never try to kill* us—

Then he reached the front room again and saw Nolan, slumped and motionless in her chair.

No! His fists clenched, his senses felt for enemy magic at the same moment his eyes locked on Irene... but the hunched way Irene sat, so *uncertain* in how she looked at Nolan next to her, reminded him there could be answers besides an attack.

Irene looked up at his footsteps. "It wasn't me! She just closed her eyes, that's all. Or it's her idea of a test, to try to catch me spying on something." The worry in her voice sounded real too.

He reached them, and saw Nolan's chest moving in slow breathing. *We all knew she was worn out, and she did trust Irene enough to talk to her alone.* He settled for frowning down at the hacker and saying "I *could* believe you."

"It's true! I was just showing her how I'd checked out whole generations of Wintons." She began talking faster now, awkwardness taking refuge in the familiar. "Even found her a formula or two for which industries would show up *less* on my crawlers because they were slower to get their records off of paper and online—and then she shows why she really wanted all that, smart—"

"Oh?" Mark growled.

"Yeah, it would have been. Once we factor out older investments having different digital footprints, we could compare how Roger Winton's moves were different from his father's and zero in on what are his own priorities—too bad they barely changed at all, though, my filters showed that. Anyway, she was just looking through the Winton family's pictures, and then she started snoring. Are you going to wake her up now?"

The bullying, taunting hacker's voice lowered with what felt like real anxiety when she glanced at Nolan again, and Mark let his scowl ease. "I think she needs her rest. Did you two make a deal?" He glanced at the computer screen; Irene hadn't *looked* like she was peeking into private files there.

Then he frowned. On the screen, Roger Winton stood in a publicity photo, but there was a woman hovering behind him. The picture was of him at his home, and she was serving drinks to his guests, her face as pale as the maid's apron she wore. They'd already researched what employees Winton had, but what was it Rafe had said in the hospital? Something about Winton being off-limits to attacks in his home?

"Her?" Irene jabbed a thumb toward the screen Mark had been watching. "I know. Her aunt worked for Edward Winton and disappeared, now she gets the same job with his son. Weird? —But no, no deals, our boss there said thanks for it all and I should come back to settle that later."

Disappeared?

But, Mark tore his thoughts away from the screen, back to Irene's words. "You… you sure she said to leave? You keep saying you know we're into something dangerous, but you think it's safe for you to go back home alone—"

"You gonna stop me?" She stood up and grabbed her laptop. "I came here to do what I'm paid for. I didn't spy on her, I didn't touch her, I'm not gonna sell your secrets to Winton. She knows that. Now I'm going home."

Irene sounded honest. Mark strained to catch any echo of deception in the abrasive outrage of her voice, or in how she glared straight at him. He fumbled for words to make her stop, and none came.

Unless he just grabbed her. That was the only way to make sure Winton never got at what she knew. One long step, one touch, and she'd be too heavy to walk.

—And then she'd never be their ally, just their prisoner, no matter what Nolan said to her. But even that would be *easier* than weighing one more set of risks when his eyes ached for sleep… No.

"Okay. I don't think we're being watched now anyway." He could tell that much, at least none of Winton's creatures were nearby.

"Glad I have your permission."

Irene flung the words with her usual harshness, but Mark heard a hint of warmth in it this time. Maybe they *had* dodged past some of their suspicion after all.

He smiled back, and walked behind her to the door. He tried not to think of the risk he was taking… *Oh, I guess it's a blow against what Winton did to me. He is* not *taking away my ability to have faith in people.*

He stood in the doorway until the estate gate swung open on its own to let Irene drive away, and closed again.

Then he moved back inside, to check on his friends—and that photo's unlikely face. And find a bed.

* * *

It was a long night, a different kind of length from the hours of searching he'd spent in the past. Something about the sitting still, learning to manage Nolan's security screens while testing his own sense just often enough to be sure… it took a new kind of toll on Mark.

Winton did come circling in, every few hours. Twice Mark thought standing guard was a waste of sleep time, only to spot their enemy sneaking in again. He learned that the estate's motion sensors were good enough to spot a squirrel creeping outside a curtained window, and let him spend seventeen taut minutes tracking the magic piloting the scurrying spy for the first sign that it might do anything more than observe.

When the hour came to wake Henry and leave him on guard, Mark was sure he'd never be able to sleep. Not with Henry up alone, not with Angie keeping her distance… but he still slipped away.

* * *

The next day was longer yet. They poured over maps and reports, trying to see them in the dimensions Irene did to narrow down a whole city's worth of possible hiding places. Nolan made three calls to the hacker, and she never let Mark or Henry hear what they debated.

But Mark couldn't see anything new. He never thought he could get tired of maps, but now the fast-shifting digital copies on Nolan's screens only fed his growing sense that no cage of facts was going to trap Roger Winton. And watching Winton's beasts come sniffing around, again and again, while the three could only *sit*… Mark kept glaring toward the far room where they kept the captured talismans, wishing he had some clue how to tame them and blast Winton with his own weapon.

When they spoke about the enemy, the conversation always stuck at one of the same impasses, depending on who was there to argue. Mark would push his point that Winton might spend days or months just observing a target, then spring some vicious new trick. Henry would run through the facts and the reasoning on all sides willingly enough, but have nothing to add but his own share of frustration. Nolan said even less, but if Mark argued they had no choices left besides baiting Winton into some trap or bringing in new allies, she'd say there was no need to turn desperate.

Except how Angie comes and goes here with no way for us to know why, or how long before Winton or Rafe pick another victim to sic on us.

What leads they found always locked up into the same debate. Any guesses about the two Wintons' maids were waved away by Nolan, pointing out how many records showed the "disappeared" aunt leaving town for a different job. The idea that her niece was some secret child of either Winton was hushed by one look between her face and theirs.

Nolan found her own favorite lead: a psychologist who'd had some mild partnership with the previous Winton, and whose articles about restorative sleep had made several mentions of using jade, the same material that the talismans used to overwhelm the mind. Dr. Chung was long dead, but his work still gave them a second path to follow.

At least Gilbert's calls told them the lawyer had impressed the police about what would happen if Dennard were the next "jailhouse accident." And Henry somehow convinced his girlfriend to stay out of sight a while longer, and he pretended he didn't worry over leaving her alone.

Slowly their plans took shape.

And then there were the winds. Nolan never spoke about it, but the only time any of them went to a window was at moments when the insistent brush of the air over the walls moved to a new pace. The more glances Nolan stole at the clouds and trees outside, the more certain Mark was that she guided the weather to restore her own magic—and her strength with it.

When night came again, she had the wind howling, just enough to challenge the spybirds that tried to keep watch on them. But it never kept them away for long.

* * *

It was late morning when they made their move.

It began when the call came in—a simple confirmation of a delivery. With the siege starting a third day, Winton might see Nolan ordering a supply of groceries as either a natural step, or an obvious cover for bringing in equipment for some secret plan.

After she hung up, Nolan looked around the table at the others. "So Winton's gone, for now?"

"Feels like it. He can't be here for everything." Mark took a moment to think. "He keeps switching up his visits, but it still averages about every… two hours?" He looked at Henry.

"That's about right. But you can't just walk out. The more I look through the cameras… well, I think he *has* to have something watching us besides magic. I still feel like he's looking right back at us."

"And he'd still have time to set up some plot somewhere else, I suppose," Nolan sighed. "Unless one of you has a clue what that is, we have to hope he's still playing a waiting game. And that we'll have more luck changing the rules than we've had so far."

Henry smiled. "Our side of it will be fine, Mark. He'd need a bulldozer to break into this house, or something better than he's got to sneak in with. See?"

He waved at the flatscreen. On one corner they could just see the big delivery truck trundling around the street's bend into the security camera's view.

Nolan took a hard look at it. "They're early. But you're right, we have to trust what we've got here to hold out… especially you, Mark." She leaned across the table to him, and her eyes narrowed warningly. "We're trusting you to leave this side of things to us, no matter what Winton might have in the works. Our best advantage is if he never knows you're out there following leads—you can't get careless and let him spot you. And don't let that hope of finding more allies make you do something that goes on to change the whole world, for all of us. Not unless the rest of us agree."

She's really worried I'll let the magic's secret slip out, after all this time. Mark met her eyes. "I know."

"Ready?" Henry asked. Nolan's gate was swinging open, and the red and white truck began rolling inside.

Nolan actually had to scramble, to get to her garage in time to beckon the truck partway inside… and stop it at just the spot she'd picked out. It halted half-in and half-out of the garage, where any opening of its doors should be clear to anyone watching from outside.

What an observer *shouldn't* see was the moment Mark ducked away from helping the driver unload, and dove straight under the front of the cab to float himself up against its underside.

The motor smell was thicker than a dozen garages. Nolan had chosen the delivery service for the size of its trucks, to give him room. But still, to press himself up near the metal's *heat,* and know it would be nothing compared to when the engine would start again… He fumbled to get the pads he'd brought into place to insulate his hands and knees in time, before the engine roared to life.

Holding on just takes balance, and willpower. The great shape thundered and buzzed against his body, as if it knew a human being didn't belong clinging beneath it—while Mark fought to picture himself as right side up and merely lying on the truck's roof. Reversed gravity let him press himself harder even against the metal, to anchor him there when the turns came. His arms and legs ached with the strain of holding that extra upward weight clear of the deadly spinning parts.

And if Winton could sense him by his magic anyway? *Winton can't. Too many times, that's been all that's saved us from him.*

Another turn, just a few more winding blocks…

* * *

The psychologist would have been the first stop.

Mark had changed his oil-stained clothes and walked partway to the campus, when he felt Angie again. He tracked her course soar over the blocks and veer to keep pace above him.

And he had to keep walking. The bright noon sun and the people on the street around him held him down, making him fight to keep his breathing even. A public street was no place to soar up and shout at her for some clue to her erratic comings and goings, or just a sign that she could still understand him. And she'd never found a way to answer.

She'd never tried, except by attempting to reach his mind. But, all he could do was trust her, and keep picturing how easily she'd trailed Winton all the way to the factory.

Five blocks later she spiraled up and out of reach. Gone *again.*

And he moved on. He kept walking, trying to picture her off following some tail that she might have spotted behind him. The streets gave him all the choices he needed to keep twisting his route and throw off anyone else that might be there.

An hour later, his phone chimed. The sender and text were simply:

W: You can't save her.

Mark heard a roaring in his ears, and knew it was his own breathing. The killer, the thing that had made *him* kill, was—

W: I can give her a body again.

Mark's hand clenched over the screen. Fingers shook, tendons strained, but he held his finger away from flinging curses back. *How, how, could this monster believe we'd ever let him near Angie...*

"You okay?"

A kid Mark's age had paused on the street, flashing an honest, concerned smile. He met Mark's gaze and that smile wavered.

"Hey, hey, whatever they sent, it can't be worth answering. Don't Feed The Trolls, you know?"

"I... I know, right," Mark forced out with a nod. At least he didn't sense Winton watching through anyone nearby. He nodded thanks and started walking again.

Trolls. Of course Winton was taking cheap shots, just to rattle him. Mark flicked through his phone's security settings, still strong, and thought of simply blocking anything that was forwarded through his old number.

Voices from the university hall ahead drew his gaze up. He knew the bright, careless sound of those crowds, most only a little older than him. Just this summer he'd been hoping he could scrape up enough of his own money to sign up for… something, somewhere.

He left the phone settings unchanged. The fight had cost him too much of his life already.

The right building was easy to find, with the maps and schedules on Mark's phone. The corridor was so quiet he wondered if he'd wandered into an empty wing, until he found Dr. Batiste's lecture letting out.

The articles' dates meant that Timothy Batiste would be pushing retirement age, but in person his face looked even more lined and sunken. Still, the pictures didn't capture how much energy he held himself with. Or how smoothly he waved aside questions from some of the dozen students around him and started to make his way out of the building.

After all, it's been decades since his mentor's "jade research" crossed paths with the older Winton. But he could still be a lead to understanding the Wintons, or even where the magic itself came from. Mark leaned back against the wall and reminded himself that Irene had given him all the tools he needed. So if he failed, it would be because he didn't sell the story.

And Batiste had already left the students behind. Mark stepped out to close with him, holding out his phone for the man to see. "About Edward Winton, Doctor."

Batiste's face didn't change, as he squinted at the image of the isolated English cottage where Roger Winton had grown up. Then Mark flicked from that picture to its burned-out ruin.

"Yes, I know it was years ago when Edward Winton died there," Mark went on, "and that was years after Dr. Samuel Chung died in his coma… after he funded his research with you, on all those new ideas in addiction treatment—"

Batiste's eyes narrowed, just for an instant.

Each of Mark's words came faster and sharper. "Doctor, I don't know if that still matters to you. But if you haven't heard, Roger Winton was taken away in an ambulance and vanished from the hospital. That's three times now, all connected with the Wintons—"

Batiste cut him off with a sigh. The old man glanced over Mark's shoulder, back at the students behind them. One woman was already starting forward to join them, concern on her face, but Batiste told her, "Just give me a minute."

"Of course, sir." She pulled back, and Mark braced himself for the doctor's reaction.

Batiste's hand came down lightly on his shoulder. In a low, dry voice, the doctor said "Let me save you some time. Whatever conspiracy journal sent you here, I'm not going throw them any bones. If you don't know what *no* means, you can talk to my lawyer."

"Listen, I've *seen* what the Wintons do." Mark leaned in closer, just an inch or two, so he could give his lowest voice the fierceness it needed. "I've seen Roger Winton look me in the face after he destroyed my life. You've watched his father work his tricks on your mentor. About that fire, do you wonder if it was set so the son could kill the father, or was the father trying to stop his son from becoming even worse? Either way, we know which one was ruthless enough to survive, and now Roger Winton's gone off the grid and free to target anyone he wants, and I've seen that too. His father covered up your findings but he left you alive. The son may not want any traces left."

Now it was taking everything Mark had to hold his voice down. Batiste's features flickered and twitched under the torrent of words.

But when Mark came back to their research, the doctor only shook his head, and his face began to smooth again. "No. There's no conspiracy, because there was nothing in our findings worth covering up."

Was that a lie lurking in his voice, or at least a hint of doubt?

"But there was," Mark flung back. "You know there was something more to your work, and you saw Edward Winton go after it. You still remember."

The students' voices were still mostly ten, twenty feet or more away. That might be far enough from view for him to tell Batiste to watch his shoes and then risk floating a few inches up, to make him listen.

The doctor said "There… there was nothing. I can understand you've suffered some kind of loss, and you may have your reasons for suspecting Roger Winton. But there's no need to look back and tie Ed Winton into it. He was the one who *saved* me from the dead-end path Chung was on. And I'll show you."

Batiste started walking, and Mark realized that exercise must be what kept the old man so energetic; he had to scramble a moment to catch up. In his head he kept turning over Batiste's words—Edward Winton had "saved" him? From what? Still, Roger Winton had twisted Mark around his finger once, so the father really might have been as slippery. Mark was learning something already, before Batiste even mentioned jade or secrets.

Then Batiste twisted around, and brought up a phone. His camera snapped a picture of Mark's face.

"That's so some friends of mine know who I'm going off with, in case there's any… misunderstanding," Batiste said quietly.

"Smart," and Mark forced a smile. "That's the kind of thinking that can keep you alive."

He tried to keep the embarrassment off his face, at being caught off-guard there. The whole scheme had always been a gamble, but that picture did raise the stakes.

Now I can't *let this turn ugly,* he thought. If Batiste sent it to the police, it might be one strike too many against Mark. So it all came down to convincing Batiste he was no threat… or showing him the magic, and risking Winton treating Batiste as the same kind of loose end that Iskander had been, and Detective Lee before him…

Was that risk what it took, to talk to anyone who might have been around any of the Wintons and their magic? Mark looked at the old man hurrying along ahead of him.

Then he thought of everything he—and Angie—had already paid in this fight. He'd *make* Batiste listen.

* * *

Batiste didn't head to some office in the college. He led Mark to a dull-silver BMW and, without a word, drove them across town. With every block Mark felt the facts and the theories in his head compressing themselves tighter, aching to strike out.

When they stopped, it was on one of the wealthy streets not far from Nolan's own Orchard Heights district. Mark's eyes caught the size and ornate old look of the house, and how the sharp-pointed roofs would make a rougher landing than most places he'd dropped onto. Batiste led him straight inside.

Within, the walls were crowded. Even while the doctor paused to scrape his shoes dry on the doormat, Mark saw a souvenir-shop's worth of trinkets and curios lined up in a perfect grid pattern over the walls. Old clocks ticked and chugged away in neighboring rooms.

Batiste marched inward, and their footsteps muted the ticking.

"There." The doctor halted and pointed a finger toward a picture on the wall. "There's when you say this started. That's my mentor and me, with the ideas he always said would revolutionize addiction therapy. It was easy to believe, then."

Mark glanced at the photo; a younger Timothy Batiste and the late Samuel Chung, crowded onto some tiny speaker's platform.

"You mean the jade." The word was out before Mark could catch it. *Slow down, let him talk,* he thought.

Batiste winced. "There was more than that. Sam had a whole range of small, feasible theories we worked with. But he could never keep from hinting at the 'soothing sleep properties' in that stone—Do you even know what it's like to have months of testing shot down when someone mocks a Chinese-American researcher for leaning on 'old country superstition'? But the real drugs we tested didn't do much better at fighting withdrawal symptoms, and the funding dried up. Until he came."

He took a quick, sharp step across the room, and waved at another section of the wall.

Edward Winton, Roger Winton's father. Mark knew it had to be, and he moved closer to search the set of tiny pictures. Off in the corner of one conference's shot, the almost-familiar face lurked. Just like in the other pictures he'd seen, this man had a whole different nose from his son, but the same eyes… and *the same way of sniffing around someone who might know another magic's secret… and if Chung had been working toward making sleep-magic public some day…*

A faint scrape of wood sounded behind Mark. Batiste's reflection moved against the picture's glass, and Mark edged to the side to see better.

The doctor was sliding a cupboard closed, and pocketing what had to be a pistol.

Mark's muscles locked. But Batiste wasn't pointing it at him—was it just a precaution against the stranger he'd let inside?

Softly, Batiste said "I'm sure you've been through quite a lot, and you blame Roger Winton for it. You can't even keep your eyes off a picture of his father. But there's no need to tie Edward Winton or me to it all, because he was never anyone's enemy."

Mark made himself swallow. "You sure about that?"

"The truth is, with research this is simply what can happen. If you look around behind you you'd see all the awards and the contacts I was making when I started medicine. And then, gone."

"Gone." This time Mark said it softly.

"Because I kept holding out hope that Samuel Chung was onto something. You know, he liked to do half his tests in the dark, said it was the best factor for helping people through the worst hours of withdrawal. No matter *what* it did to our test conditions, or what our enemies said we could be hiding with the lights out! But I made myself stay with him."

Batiste's voice was rising, echoing through the house. Mark tried to keep the thought off his face: *working in a dark room… like where Winton hid his talismans…*

"And then Ed Winton came. Not much of an investor, just a two-bit local entrepreneur—but he saved *me*. He listened to Sam, they started talking about new plans. And he *saw* I didn't believe in it like they did, and I swear it was his insisting that made Sam set me free."

Batiste waved Mark deeper into the house.

"He helped me make the right choice." Batiste's voice settled back to something almost calm again. He nodded into the room ahead: "You see that certification there, in the fourth column near the floor? I finally got back to doing real treatments. Half of the next column is mementos from patients, real patients I helped. And there are more pictures of me with Ed Winton than with my 'mentor'—hell, for six months I was married to the woman he introduced me to. He saved me."

Or, the older Winton had eased Batiste out of his target's life so smoothly that he never guessed—

"And then, the great Dr. Chung falls into a coma. A drug treatment specialist, in a coma! You should have heard the jokes… and that was before he died, and they confirmed how many meds he'd been testing on himself. My friends were telling me to not even go near his funeral. I looked up to the man once. I really did.

"But there's no conspiracy here. Just mistakes I've tried to learn from."

The words softened and faded, to let the ticking of clocks fill the stillness again.

But, there had been something in his voice.

Mark fixed his eyes on Batiste's. "Or Winton stole Dr. Chung's research, and then destroyed him. You keep saying there's nothing to it, but you *do* think it's possible, don't you? That's why you brought me here, to talk us both out of it."

"But Ed Winton *wasn't* a man like that, not then or ever."

There it was, the same haste in his voice.

"Son, I'm trying to help you accept—"

"So you do believe it," Mark cut in. "I heard that, you got a glimpse of what he was really like. And *I've* seen the son he raised, and maybe tried to kill, if that's what that fire was about. Roger Winton is a monster who'll have you doubting your own name and then kill a cop to keep his secrets—and he's got ways to—"

Mark pulled back the fury that rose in his throat.

Batiste shook his head. "Now you're talking about a man I never met. As for Ed Winton, he still couldn't have done what you say, because he had no reason to."

"Because the research was nothing? What if it wasn't?" Mark felt the magic in his belt, that only needed a thought to lift him up and prove everything.

Batiste looked at him, eyes wavering. His hand twitched once, near the coat pocket where he'd tried to hide that gun.

Then the doctor said "It *was* nothing, and I'll show you. This way."

He waved forward, and Mark let the gesture lead him across the room. *Don't hope, don't even guess what might be here about jade and magic...*

"You'll see," Batiste said. "Whatever you need to get help with, there are no clues to some Winton family conspiracy here. Because Samuel Chung's theories were nothing worth fighting over. I've had a long time to accept that, and I can show you line by line, until you're ready to face your own problems."

They passed another room and started up the stairs. The pattern of objects and memories continued along the walls, with the same precise, tight grid of rows and columns. Batiste must have had laid his whole life out using his walls as a regimented scrapbook, aging from the ground upward. When the walls partway through the hallway suddenly turned bare, Mark glanced over and saw that a picture in the final column was of this very week's snowstorm.

At the end of the hall stood a single door.

"It's all there, up to the moment I left those studies. The whole dead end." Batiste's voice clenched bitterly.

Mark swung the door open. A puff of dust washed out into the immaculate hallway.

A row of four green metal file cabinets stood pressed against the back wall. Mark slid the first drawer open.

Instead of notes, all his fingers found was a sheet of old, bronze-colored newspaper. *Of course. Why did I think this would be anything easier?*

"That's the first summary we wrote," Batiste said.

"This?" Mark held up the page.

"That's… not right." Batiste coughed in the dust, then said "Next file."

Mark pulled another drawer open, but he knew what he'd find. This time he spilled a stack of newspapers onto the floor.

"Those aren't mine. I had our lab notes here. Here!" Batiste stumbled into the room and dug into the drawer. His gun clattered to the floor, but his eyes never glanced after it. "I know I put them here years ago."

"Then you forgot where you kept them. Or that's how it would look, if you reported it."

Batiste slammed a fist on the top of the cabinet. "No, no—right in my own *home?* And they couldn't just rob me? They had to leave these, and make me look like some forgetful old… How *dare* they!"

"They?" Mark said. "We both know who it is."

Batiste coughed again. "We only know I was robbed. You think that proves someone put Sam in that coma?"

"Yes!" Mark wanted to shake him; of *course* it was another Winton coverup.

"But Ed Winton wouldn't… he'd never…"

"Roger Winton would!" Mark said. "He would if it covered up one trace of this. And his father was the man who might have tried to kill him in that fire, or that the son had to get rid of. See?" Mark yanked out his phone, and thrust the image of his enemy in front of Batiste again. "See? This is a young man who was raised to kill, and it even cost him a bit of his face until he had it rebuilt. And what he's done to the world since then…"

Mark's fingers jabbed the screen to flip from picture to picture, and in that moment he wished he'd loaded *everything* the puppetmaster had done into that sequence. Instead he skipped through pictures of the young Winton with bandages over his nose and covering his hands, the proud look on his restored face when he signed in to take over his father's businesses, the overseas cottage burned to the ground—

"Go… back—" Batiste gasped. He coughed, spluttering in the dust.

"What?" Mark started back through the images.

"There! But that's…"

Batiste broke off coughing again. His face was pale, so pale Mark wondered what a heart attack looked like.

"No, it's nothing," Batiste managed to say then. "I see, that's just the young Winton's face. It's only…"

Then Mark felt his own heart freeze up.

Knowing what the Winton magic could do… he couldn't bear to ask, to let this *new* horror be possible. But his mouth was already moving: "What did you see?"

"The way he's standing, and waving. Just… just imitating his father, I know." Batiste took a slow, hard breath. "But… that exact smile, even on the wrong face… I could swear I see Edward Winton looking out of those eyes."

CHAPTER ELEVEN

GATE AND CRASH

"Winton *took over* his son's body? Permanently?" Henry's voice had a restrained sound, hard to follow over the phone. "Is that what the doctor said?"

"Not what he said. He has no idea, he's never seen what…"

Mark swallowed, and glanced around the sidewalk. The late afternoon was quiet enough here, with only scattered people out enjoying the thaw, leaving this patch of street to him. And he couldn't hold the chain of thoughts in:

"I could be wrong. But, I mean… just when I thought I could stop feeling used! I was *carrying* one of those things for a night—it could be that the only reason there's a *me* left is because Winton keeps his options open… God, if he switches bodies all the way, why would he still be Winton at all any more, now that we know that name? We thought Angie killing his bird hurt him, but if he can ditch that body… and he's been texting me to say he can put Angie in a body—"

A text pinged.

A wave of coldness smashed through his stomach—but it wasn't Winton, it was still Henry:

Had to mute you. Listen!

Mark brought the phone back to his ear.

"—know what I heard! Winton's father and the son, and some kind of taking control." The voice was Irene's. As if she'd…

simply… walked… in…

"Of course it is," came Nolan's answer, calm. "I already asked you to look at decision patterns through the Winton family—"

"Like Roger Winton's face being *so much* like his father's, until the fire, and then he had his nose rebuilt to be just that touch different? What's that tell you?"

"Do you expect me to know that? I'm no mind-reader."

"You know *something!*" Irene flung back. "The face, the finger-prints—the ages are wrong for it to be old Ed impersonating his son, but why would the son have those changes *just to look different from his dad?*"

"To get out of his father's shadow?" Henry said. "Why else would he? Unless you think the father really did take over his son's identity—"

"At his age?" Irene snapped. "Stop insulting me! You tell me what's really going on, now!"

Nolan's voice could have frozen the phone it came through: "I'll tell you when you've earned it."

"And that's *your* choice, is it? I shut up and do the work? The cops would throw us both in a hole if I mentioned—"

"If you want to trade threats," Nolan said, "we two need to talk. Now."

Then… silence. Mark strained, trying to hear past the scattered voices on the street. He thought he caught footsteps, maybe moving away.

Finally he texted a silent: *Did I start that?*

Henry broke the silence with a low "I guess Irene was sure to overhear something. Maybe this means we can stop whispering in this house soon. Nolan's not happy about what you told Dr. Batiste either."

"He only knows Winton's a threat," Mark sighed. "And I told him I'd get back to him soon, and he let me put him off, so we've got some time before we work that out. And he's been lucky; Winton might have taken Dr. Chung's magic and his life and reputation, but Batiste was safe on the sidelines as long as Winton got rid of the notes. We just have to watch that we don't lead the killer back to him now."

"I don't think Winton's anywhere near you, so far. He's been mostly watching us up here. We know he saw Irene driving up."

Mark shook his head. "That settles it. There's no way Nolan's letting her leave the house this time."

"Here's something good from all this," Henry said. "I always thought the fact that Angie was trapped in one body means it's possible to give her another. If Winton did do that for himself, at least it's more proof that she can too."

Mark felt a smile stirring—when had his careful cousin started looking for the bright side? "Thanks. I guess all we have to do is find the secrets, deal with the enemy, and then keep looking until we find a body in the right kind of coma for her. If there is a right kind."

"One step at a time, we keep saying. So what's next? You're still leaving us alone with Irene?"

"I have to." Mark looked around the street again. "Can't waste the time that Winton's thinking I'm in there with you... I can look at the factory again, then on to that maid he had."

He slid the phone away, and broke into a quick stride up the quiet street.

The factory... was finding that really such a breakthrough? If Nolan was right, Winton could be gathering his magic from dozens of places and he'd never use that one again now that they'd found it. Or his power could be like the belts after all, and have only that one site where the energies formed right. As far as they knew.

He growled to himself. No matter what they did, it was always guesswork, trying to figure out the rules of Winton's magic and never knowing if they'd be *anything* like their own.

A presence in the sky drew his gaze upward. Angie.

She was already turning toward him, and that clear sudden twist in the air had drawn his awareness. But she'd simply *spotted* him from more than a block away, as if she always could.

Then he looked at the houses rushing past him. The belt's easy power had drawn him into a magically-lightened trot, ready to race through the streets all day… and that speed had to stand out to anyone searching from above. *And I let my guard down, and it could have been Winton up there. Stupid!*

Mark settled to a stop, leaning against a telephone pole, cold wood against his back. The street was empty nearby.

He pitched his voice the way he'd speak to someone next to him. "I think you can hear me. We found how Winton was controlling me, and I'm free now."

The confession spilled along the still sidewalk, tossed by the rumble of a passing car.

But he felt Angie gliding down. She settled above him, at the top of the pole.

The words were easier if he didn't look up. "Please… can't you search for Winton *with* us? You know we'll never, never stop until we get Winton and a way to bring you back to us. But you… even when you're here, we can't understand when you'll show up, or you find us and just fly away and we never—"

She flew away. She actually dropped from her perch and flew *away*—

But she moved directly above the street. He watched her brown and gray shape beating upward, moving so slowly along the way. So easy to follow.

Mark moved after her, and she gathered speed, bringing him up to a jog again with the belt letting some of his weight fall away. He slid around one passer-by, then more, as the streets moved deeper into the city.

A light snow began falling again.

* * *

By the time they neared the South Bend apartment, Mark knew where Angie was leading him.

He couldn't guess how an owl might have learned about Winton's maid. But he knew the address ahead would be the one they had found for their final lead, even before Angie settled at the building's top, five stories above most of the block's height.

Mark flipped through the phone's files on Sasha Lawrence as he walked closer, all too quickly. She was barely older than himself, and living a quiet life, so quiet that even their best searches could find little more than a smattering of different jobs she'd worked at before the several years she'd spent as Winton's occasional maid. They'd dismissed her once as not worth approaching.

And now? He could go in and openly ask her if her aunt had really moved away, and ask what she knew about the older Winton—or the same man—that her aunt was last seen working for. Or Mark could watch her for signs that she knew more than that... or Nolan could pay her for answers, gambling that Winton hadn't spun some of his lies or used his talismans on her...

Mark kept the phone at his ear as he walked closer, as an excuse to move slowly and steal more glances at the lobby door, the well-kept walls and windows, the number of people in view.

His phone vibrated.

The text was from Joe Dennard: *Score one for Kate's lawyers. The police let me go.*

A great grin of relief came welling up inside Mark.

Another text was already coming: *You there? Or in the middle of something?*

Mark stared at the screen a moment longer, trying to pick his answer. He could tell Dennard what a pleasure it was, but the man might be more at ease going straight to advising him about the security on the building here.

He almost missed Sasha Lawrence's face, behind the bags of groceries she carried along the street.

She was a dozen paces away on the street and closing. Mark turned aside toward the wall of mailboxes just outside her building's entrance. Was she someone Winton told enough to that she'd recognize him? The mailboxes there would give him an extra excuse to keep his face to the wall when she passed inside.

Better yet—discarded mail ads lay on the shelf under the boxes, and he caught up a page and hid his face in "studying" it. If he let her walk *right* past him, he'd be in range to feel if she had an inactive talisman on her. Except she'd pass right by his back, so close that if she shared Winton's magic she'd only need a step to brush against him and seize him.

He strained his senses, both for magic and to try to catch her footsteps on the street. Any second now…

A big man stomped past him and unlocked the door. As he stepped inside, Mark heard what should be Sasha trotting up to grab at the closing door—

Missed it! Was that a talisman or not? Mark moved away from the wall to step in closer as she caught at the handle—

He must have been clumsy. She spun around, and she slipped on the snow and stumbled backward against the closing door. Groceries flew from her bags and Mark felt something splatter against his coat.

"Whoah!" She caught her balance, her pale face round with what looked like ordinary embarrassment. "Don't startle people like that. Oh, sorry for the spill, you should get that cleaned—" Her hand reached toward where the tomatoes had hit his chest.

Careful! Mark ducked back a step out her reach, with a quick "I'm fine" that he tried to make sound like the same awkwardness she had shown.

And she simply turned away and started gathering up scattered cans. In that moment, he strained to catch any flicker of a talisman on her, but he sensed nothing.

She gave a faint mutter: "Well, you should do something. Before the stain sets."

He pocketed his phone and crouched down to help her.

"I've seen worse," he began. "I've done time as a waiter—okay, I tried *not* to spill the orders, but I've seen a few accidents—"

He shifted in his crouch. The move let his heel nudge a long plastic brush from where it had fallen, to wedge it under the closed door, and a trickle of his magic through the touch gave it a few more pounds of weight to jam the door. *Just keep the conversation going and get a read on whether there's something behind that harmless tone of hers.*

He added "I always thought that 'club soda fixes everything' line was just a way to calm customers down."

"I know. I've done some work housecleaning—"

She broke off there, and turned past him to tug uselessly at the brush. Just like the kind of caution anyone might show, remembering she'd begun chatting with a strange man. He hoped that was all it was.

Just then, he felt Angie drop from the roof and swoop up the block.

His eyes swung to follow that direction. That man right below where she'd just passed, rounding the corner, that was Rafe.

He heard himself replying "Housecleaning? That'd keep you inside where it's warm, anyway—"

Inside, I have to get her inside before Rafe reaches us, why didn't I sense him?

"—and you're right, I should try to save this coat, if I can. These days I'm either roasted or frozen depending on how my cab's working."

His mouth kept running on its own, not caring that she might have heard that Winton had an enemy who was a cabbie.

But Sasha only gave a sullen "At least you have a job."

She was still wrestling with the brush. Up the street, Rafe was only fifty feet away. His face didn't change, looking at Mark and Sasha, and his steps didn't slow.

"How about this…" Mark lunged around her to reach down, grab the brush and twist as he stripped its added weight away. It jerked free and he stumbled back, but a little embarrassment was nothing now. He handed it over with a smile. "Here. I should get moving."

"Thanks."

He turned away, ready to face Rafe again. Rafe must have left his belt behind—just to keep Mark from sensing him?—but he'd still have his guns. And he'd seen Mark shoot his men.

Sasha said "Sorry again. Look, if you want, you could come on up and let me try to fix those stains before they set too far."

"Ah, thank you—"

He found himself sliding in after her, watching the door click and lock behind them. Rafe could probably find other ways in, if he'd been casing the place the same way Mark was. And of course he knew about Sasha: it had been *Rafe* from the beginning who'd reminded Mark about Winton's home, that there was something—or someone—there that Winton had warned Rafe to stay away from.

The walls inside Sasha's lobby were painted a deep, odd red. The ominous line *Walk into my parlor* flashed through Mark's head, but Sasha felt less and less like someone setting a trap.

"By the way," she added suddenly, "I've got a boyfriend... or I did," and she looked away. "And, I'm Sasha."

So she was flirting, or pretending to. He nodded: "Marty."

He followed her along, still keeping an extra step back from her and his senses ready for the first flicker of magic that might reach for him. People moved here and there in the lobby—a woman with children, an older man. Those witnesses were one more sign that he was safe, so far.

He also noticed that the elevator moved with a stately whisper instead of rattling. And the neighbors looked more like people that could afford to call for his taxi than have to drive it. Sasha might act like a struggling housekeeper, but she didn't live like one.

Partway up in the elevator, he felt Angie turning and flying out beyond his range. Watching Rafe leave, he hoped.

He steadied his breathing, trying to open himself to his instincts. Sasha could be a tool of Winton's… or have just known him briefly and gotten free… at least until Rafe had shown up. If Nolan were here she'd have read the girl's face in one sharp glance.

When Sasha opened her door, the apartment beyond didn't fit her manner either. The first room was almost the size of his own place— what Rafe had left of it—with shining padded furniture. He saw a second room's closed door on one side, but a bed and dresser sat crowded into the main room, toward the back. The leafy smell of too many air fresheners pushed at his nose.

"Not bad, you know? Cleaning houses can pay better than you think," Sasha said. "My last boss helped me get this place." She set down her bags and knelt at the kitchen cabinet.

Then Mark *heard* it: the low, settled squawk of a resting bird—and then another chiming in near it, like in the pet shops he'd visited to learn about birds. All coming from right behind the closed door.

His gaze darted back to Sasha, just as she straightened up; he realized she could have pulled out a weapon in that moment, instead of the bottle in her hand.

"This should do it. Let's see that coat."

"No, let me do this." He edged back from her touch and stretched out his own hand for the bottle, smiling to hide the sudden dodge-away tautness in his muscles. But all his "shyness" earned him was a hurt look as she passed the bottle over, and he dribbled the cleanser over the blotches, still keeping one eye on her. "Now, wash it off?"

"Just give it a few minutes." She took the bottle, and added "Marty. That boyfriend I mentioned, he's long gone."

"Oh. The thing is, I'm already—" He reached for words that she'd believe.

Her face fell. "Oh. Sure."

The silence began to lengthen. Then she took a step toward him and said:

"Um, can I just ask you something? I just missed a job today—another one, when I was really living on severance from the last one. And here you are, and you talk like you've done everything... What do you do when you're out of work?"

Career advice, was what she thought of?

But Mark met her earnest look with a smile—holding down the urge to come right out and bribe her for anything she knew about Winton—and said "I don't know. They always say to pick some work you can really push yourself at, and to stay in touch with your friends for contacts. And your old bosses," he added, trying to work that prompt in casually.

Sasha looked at the floor. "I guess. At least for people that have that *thing* they always wanted to do. I mean, I like games, music, my friends... I just did whatever I could to keep the bills paid—"

Magic stirred.

Somehow Mark kept from dodging backward. The flare of power came from *behind* Sasha, a talisman like Winton's coming to life in the closed room, with the birds, just as she was saying:

"—you know? I wish I knew what to do now that it's gone."

Mark's eyes narrowed, locked on the woman slumped against the kitchen cabinet. *Could* she be triggering magic between one word and the next, and hiding it all behind *that* ordinary a mask as she lured him in? Or was it all Winton working behind her back?

Mark opened his mouth, then thought *Winton's listening, can't let him overhear my voice, if he's just checking in and doesn't know I've found her.* He tried answering with a muffled "Mmm?"

That got him a glare from her. "You think it's easy? I had a real paycheck for years. I started to think my luck had changed. Now all of a sudden it's gone."

Don't ask why it was sudden, just keep the conversation sounding ordinary and my voice low, he's listening... Mark took a step toward her, enough to say a hushed "You must have something."

"I tried. My last reference almost got me a place with one of those cleaning vans, but that's gone now. I haven't even told my mother I lost the other job yet—I was just learning to cook too…" She swept a hand around, almost hitting Mark as she waved it around the gleaming kitchen.

He could only whisper "Sorry. So, cooking's what you want to do?"

"Well, it's okay—" She looked up then, at how close he stood, and her face tightened up. "I'm sorry I read you wrong and wasted your time and everything. The whole day's been too crazy for me."

Then, before Mark could protest, the energy in the next room vanished.

Maybe even a manipulator like Winton only checks in on her for so long. Sasha's bland, mundane worrying might have just saved her from ending up like Ben Iskander the PI, if it had convinced Winton she couldn't be talking with anyone who threatened him.

"Some days… get pretty crazy," Mark said, and laughed softly. "I should probably get moving. Thanks for fixing the stain."

"Oh. Sure," she nodded. "And thank you, for listening to me rant."

Mark moved for the door, knees weak with relief. *Let* her think they'd almost been flirting, as long as he kept his visit off the killer's radar. Whatever she knew, whatever Rafe was up to, he couldn't talk to her here.

"Hey, you want to see something?" Sasha called after him. "The reason I can still afford this place? Birds."

Can't risk it. I can't get any closer to Winton's eyes—but still, he looked back. "What do you mean, birds?"

"My old boss said they were some kind of rare breeds. When he closed his house, he said he'd pay me to look after them a while." And she opened the side door.

There they stood. Three large birdcages, bigger than any suitcase. All were covered, but through one's folds he saw a small, sleek hawk, blinking drowsily at the door's motion. The others gave only the softest sound.

Mark took a step toward the doorway, drawn by the sight. Around the hawk's leg he saw a thick band, holding a silvery-gray metal shape—one of the talismans he'd just felt Winton using.

"He said they like to be kept fed and then left alone," Sasha said. "That works for me. I can use the rest of the room for storage."

She thinks that's how you care for birds? She's never read one *book to help her do this job?* But Sasha wasn't arguing with her paycheck. Mark could see a flimsy latch on that cage, light enough that a talon could slide it open any time a human mind wanted the bird to fly. Even the window outside had what looked like a delicate lever on the pane; she'd said Winton had helped her find the apartment, and he could have had the whole room built so his possessed birds could manage it.

"See?" and Sasha grinned. "And he pays me for it. That means I'm living on chicken feed."

"Good one! Thanks again." Mark spun away, chuckling, hoping that her joke would let him take those few steps to the door and Winton would hold off on peeking in again for just a *few more seconds*...

He shut the door behind him. Walking down the corridor he could still feel the risk that he'd been spotted, like an eye boring into the back of his head. When the elevator doors finally closed, he let out a breath that made the old woman next to him edge away.

I made it. He'd gone in and out right under Winton's nose, and Winton had no clue.

Mark shivered in relief. The birds were right there, he could come back any time and take their enemy's best weapons away… But Winton might blame Sasha for that, and they needed to draw her away from here and learn what she could tell them about her boss, then help her hide. And until then, there was Rafe lurking around—they had to keep watch for whatever *he* had planned for her.

The elevator opened again and a young couple stepped in, and they joined the old woman in edging away from Mark.

When they finally reached the lobby, Mark stepped out and leaned against the wall, eyes on the front entrance in case Rafe simply strolled in. At the corner of his eye, he saw an older man watching him from behind a door—a building super, with an eye for strangers who didn't belong? Mark settled into a corner to check his phone like anyone might, but the puzzles wouldn't let go of his mind.

How *could* Sasha be that innocent, with her family ties and how Winton was still using her? Or was Mark still misreading how deep in she was? He tried not to think about how Rafe would try forcing answers out of her… *Rafe might have been only guessing she knew something, until he saw* me *with her!* But Angie might have found Sasha through Rafe too, or else she saw the birds sneaking out…

Again and again he caught nervous glances from the people walking past him, and tried not to see if the man at the door was still eyeing him for loitering.

His phone chimed.

Mark took a moment to see Henry's name on it, and Dennard on the call as well, before he lifted it to his ear.

The tautness in Henry's voice stabbed at him. "Nolan's out there! She was driving out, but the car just *stopped* in the driveway. I heard something go bang! Then this fog came up in the yard, and she's not answering…"

Then Nolan cut through: "Someone's got me trapped in here. The first shots stopped the car. I tried slipping out under some fog, but he almost got me."

"Henry!" Dennard snapped. "Get down! Stay away from windows!"

Clang!

The harsh metal-cracking sound echoed through the call. Mark gasped "Hey, you there?" He heard Henry's voice shouting, and a booming like far-off thunder.

"Stop shouting, Henry, I'm okay," Nolan said. "When I crouch low enough, the car stops the bullets. But… did he bring a whole army? The cops must be on their way."

"Maybe not. That sound you just heard? Fireworks," Henry said.

Dennard added "Sure. And if the shooter threw in a sound suppressor on the rifle—yeah, he'd have it all set. The police won't be looking for a sniper until it's too late."

Nolan's voice cracked like a gunshot of its own. "Then don't call them! The cops have already noticed us too many times. Don't you 'save' me by ruining my life!"

When Henry started protesting, Mark brought up his locator app and dashed across the hall, to where the "super" was still watching him.

"I've gotta run!" Mark told the startled man. "But I think I saw a murderer outside looking for a way in. Rafe Martinez—look him up!"

"Hold on—"

Mark ran for the front door, hoping that would keep Sasha safe for now.

On the street, the scattering of potential witnesses up and down the sidewalk kept him on the ground—*it wouldn't matter, full jumping isn't faster, and Orchard Heights is too far unless Nolan can hold out… But I have to get there!*

Winton was really *shooting* at them? Or was that Rafe? Mark flung himself into his fastest run, and he felt the fear growing in him as he skimmed over the sidewalk. Something must have changed for their enemies.

Blocks later, Dennard's white Ford slid up beside him.

Mark was scrambling around for the drivers-side door even before he noticed Dennard squeezing over to let him take the wheel; of course it should be the professional driving now. *Just like Nolan taking me to save Dennard and Henry. Thank God for tracking apps.*

As Mark started twisting them through traffic, Dennard spoke into his phone: "Keep the engine running! –The car, I mean, and keep the fog up too. You said the sniper tried to shoot you through the fog? You need the car's heat!"

"The engine's dead!" came Nolan's voice through the speaker. "I get it, I wish I could run it—engine heat would cover something from whatever thermal vision scope he's got. But you think hot and cold air grow on trees?"

Is Nolan trying for one of her jokes or not? I can't tell—she must be worse off than she's letting on.

Mark slipped them through a yellow light, and then twisted at the next corner into a quieter road, closer now. He forced his foot to ease back on the gas, holding them back to making dignified swayings around the other cars instead of plowing blindly into the next turns.

"Come on, come *on!*" Henry's voice was shouting. "Oh—and I'm tracking Winton and Angie up there, but I'm not sure what they're doing."

Dennard laughed, with a confidence that warmed the car. "Angie will be picking her moments, I bet. She can't do much on her own."

Mark made another turn, and slowed again when he found they'd reached the first Orchard Heights road. Long estate walls streamed by beside them, turning the winding roads into a maze of graceful, maddening bends.

He told Dennard "You can't go in there either. When we get to Nolan's, you stay back—"

"You're kidding. What do you know about sniper tactics?"

It's been ten years since you were a cop. And two months since you could walk without pain. But Mark didn't say that, couldn't.

Dennard went on "Listen to me, Henry. Do *not* look outside. Is Irene there? Tell her to stay down too. But can you guess what direction the bullets are coming from?"

Nolan didn't lose a moment in answering. "Of course. Out in front, somewhere opposite my grounds. It's the front of the car that's shielding me."

"Irene should be somewhere here," Henry added. "Let me try the cameras. Some of them can reach out there."

As Henry spoke, Mark felt something else, prickling at the other side of his mind: the rough energy of Angie swooping toward them.

The road branched off ahead, and Mark felt Angie heading into the sky to the right and swung the wheel to follow her lead. Keeping the car speeding along the twisting roads in the twilight pulled at his attention enough without three other voices on the line and all the fears and guesses trying to buzz in his thoughts. *But I need to watch for magic too, Winton's here somewhere!*

When he cleared another turn he gasped "Angie's leading us. Into the upper hills, I think, don't know if she'll go a mile away from you or what."

"Not as far as that," Dennard said. "Not if the sniper's using an IR scope."

Mark didn't try to answer, just kept twisting the car along the road. The sense of Winton's presence came pushing through his scattered focus too, watching from somewhere above, keeping his distance.

Then Henry's voice came at a whisper:

"Is… Irene with you? Don't let her know I asked."

What now? It was one thing too many; Mark let the car slow to an amble so he could listen, though the hill road was straight enough to race through for now.

Nolan's voice was clear, steady. "She's not with me. It's… complicated."

"Complicated?" Mark heard himself growl. Where was Winton? What was Angie doing?

Henry pressed Nolan: "But you left in Irene's car. And she's not here. And I found—"

A ring of metal on metal broke through the phone line, making Mark wince. Another shot tearing into Nolan's car.

And Winton's presence vanished from the sky, and reappeared somewhere on the ground in the hills ahead.

"I'm alright," came Nolan's voice. "But holding the fog, after all the power I spent… just hurry."

A booming split the air, and this time it drew Mark's eyes right up above the car. A shower of light burst, like a giant dandelion head breaking apart in the dark sky, and then a second firework joined it. Those would be Winton's distractions from the gunshots—launching from up ahead, where his control had jumped to some body on the ground.

"I was *saying,*" Henry cut in, "there was a blank spot on the security views. It's okay now, but—"

Oh God. Mark's hands clutched helplessly at the wheel as Dennard said "Henry, look out! Hide somewhere, there could be another assassin coming for you!"

Nolan said "That can't be. The plan was Irene would sneak out while I was the decoy with her car—did she really cut the cameras—"

Mark dragged in a breath and shouted *"Quiet! Winton's here!"*

The blast of his voice in the car pushed away the chaos for one blessed instant. He peered through the darkness ahead, matching dim curves and estates with Angie in the sky ahead and Winton's presence somewhere beyond the next wall's corner.

At least Winton's focus was out here, not closing in on Henry yet. But the area seemed too far from Nolan's place, and too low on the ground to give anyone here a clear shot at it.

Dennard's voice was steady, as if he'd read it all from Mark's reaction. "How close is he? Do we sneak around or—"

Mark found his foot bringing the car roaring forward, skidding around the turn.

A whoosh of light made him flinch, but it was only another rocket soaring away into the sky, not a gunshot. Winton's magic was right there, controlling a small figure under it.

Then the power winked out. Mark pulled the car up, and stared at the shape of a boy sleeping beside the road, next to a bicycle and slumped against a long wooden box. It might have been what any kid might do with stolen fireworks, if he'd been awake.

"Winton was using him," Mark said. "He's dumped him—for now, but if he's got a talisman—"

Dennard was already opening the door. He scrambled across the grass in moments, then froze over the sleeping boy. "Where is it?"

Mark jumped to his side. *Focus, be still, no matter how your heart's pounding—* He pointed to the boy's front coat pocket.

"If Winton grabs me, you stop me." Dennard said it so evenly, with only a ripple of fear in his voice. His hand darted out, and he yanked out the bit of silver and flung it away into the night before Mark could answer.

Then Dennard scooped the boy up with a grunt of pain, that must be his stab wounds flaring up.

They set the boy in the back seat, still asleep. Mark said "I don't know how long he'll be out… maybe minutes, maybe more. Can we get him some help?"

Dennard gripped his stomach and grated "Now we head back. No more fireworks to cover them means no more shots, I hope. So, where would the sniper be? Any high ground, close enough to Nolan's for an IR scope to work?"

What do I know about infrared scopes' ranges? "Maybe over…"

Mark swung the car around, reaching for his memories of the estates' view by air. They couldn't be too many blocks away from Nolan, but with all those winding bends in the dark? He thought of soaring up for a look, but Dennard seemed to think staying low was safer. Still, Angie must already have a better view—where had she gone? *Something doesn't fit.*

Another shot crashed through the phone's speaker, sharp but loud only because Nolan's phone must be so close to the metal it hit. Mark sped the car up—then heard a curse from her.

Then: "Still alright," she said, but her voice sounded weaker. "One of those birds tried to get through the windshield."

"And you can't find the gunman?" Henry said. "That's it, I'm calling the police."

"Don't! I said I can hold the fog. Mark will get him."

But Angie should've already found…

Mark opened his mouth, as thoughts spun and clashed to fall into a different shape. Angie missed nothing, he'd seen that, and yet she had led them to save the boy that was Winton's cover, not to stop the shooter himself. Or she'd *led them away* from the shooter? To keep them safe? That could be it.

"We'll get him," he promised. "Henry, you stay out of sight there."

Dennard said "Mark, think of any hills or trees the shooter could be up in. He's got to realize he's lost his covering sounds."

Henry added "I'll try the front cameras. Those never stopped working."

Dennard's voice actually grew softer, but firmer. "Please, Henry. Just find a place to hide, and we'll be with you soon."

Another part of Mark's mind spotted the road crossing ahead, and he was pulling the car to the side before the thought came clear: "This is the next block before Nolan's. The sniper could be on one of these estates. But I can't home in on him—Winton's not controlling him."

With the car stopped, it took only an instant to search for magic around them. He spotted Angie in the sky, and Winton circling too, two bits of power that might be a quarter-mile apart in the dark. He swung the door open.

"Is Angie still up there?" Dennard asked.

"Yes. She could have missed where the sniper is," Mark added, as if saying it could convince himself.

"Keep your eyes open. Stay low, and hope he's looking at Nolan."

"Got it." He dug into his pocket, to pull out the two strips of leather that were the original backup talismans. He tossed them back into the car. "If you can keep up, come on." Then he ran.

The belt's magic buoyed him up, stretching controlled hops out to the gliding pace a little faster than a full-out sprint, and tireless. Behind him he felt Dennard's talismans start out behind him, then slow. He glanced back to see Dennard setting the boy down, at the side of an intersection, and still a block short of the threat ahead. At least Winton couldn't find him where he'd been, and if he didn't wake up soon, someone on the street would see him there.

The night's blur thickened—Mark felt moisture on his face and realized he was running into the fog Nolan had raised, and the shapes grew dimmer with every step. He swept a look along the trees, the walls, anywhere that might give someone a shot over Nolan's own wall. *Don't miss it in the dark, don't think about the gunman who might not miss* me, *or Henry or Angie or...*

"Henry says—" Dennard dropped into place behind Mark, moving in awkward, rusty bounds, but he still had his phone at his ear. "He says, watch for the windows!"

Windows? Mark could barely glimpse the houses back behind their walls. He glanced back; no, no house there, nothing but mist and wall.

Up ahead, a broad roof loomed out of the fog, almost at the foot of the wall around it. *Right, that place that was almost opposite Nolan's! If the shooter's eyes stay off us a few more seconds...*

Winton's magic bore in above him.

Mark loosened his stride, hoping he could leap clear as he tracked the bird diving in—

It didn't dive at him, but at Dennard behind him, the one who'd never sense it coming—

"Look out!" Mark yelled, and the shout ripped through the night.

He felt the bird plummet in. He tried to get his balance to leap at it, but Dennard was already diving away into the street. The bird swept down past him and pulled up again. Something about its angle was shallow, afraid of diving too quickly into fog.

Over the wall, something moved.

Mark stared up at the shadow in the high window. The long tube stretching out and training downward through the mist. Drawn by his shout. But it was aiming past Mark, toward where Dennard had dived away from the wall and lay helplessly sprawled in the street.

Then a streak of gray feathers and magic darted down through the window. Mark heard a scream of pain as Angie struck the sniper.

"Come on! In there!" he heard himself bark at Dennard, and flung himself at the top of the wall in one controlled leap. As he dropped to the grass beyond it he felt Angie already winging out into the night again, safe. *Just like she did when I first came out here—and saving Nolan too this time.*

Mark lunged across the yard in a straight jump that locked his momentum and tossed him up against the wooden front of the huge house. As he landed, he caught Winton's magic flaring out of no-where. That was a talisman up near the window, seizing control of the sniper.

The front door was within Mark's reach, so he grabbed at it before looking for a better way in—but the knob turned and the door swung open.

As he stepped into the dimness, the magic at the window dropped. It moved behind him, outside, straight down.

Winton's grip vanished in mid-fall. There was one dazed "What—" before a final *thud* on concrete.

Mark moved back outside again, knowing what he'd find.

Out on the walkway, Dennard was bending over the jumper's body. A lean, scarred stranger with hands clenched around a rifle—another of Winton's discarded pawns.

Hired and used and thrown away, like Ben Iskander. Like I *was, except the killer wants my magic too much to bury me.*

Dennard was reporting on the phone "Winton took out his own sniper. But that doesn't mean it's over tonight."

"It never is," Nolan's voice answered.

Mark felt Winton up above, back in one of his birds. But the moment showed him something else: the sound of a car moving slowly, purposefully by beyond the wall.

"Police, *now?*" Mark said.

"Private security, probably," Dennard said. "They're only checking for fireworks and shouts in the streets."

The car's rumble drew nearer the gate, where the wall had nothing but bars to hide them from it. They moved aside to shelter under the wall until it passed on by.

"Henry?" Mark raised his voice to reach through Dennard's phone. "Are you alright?"

"Still fine," came Henry's voice. "I've almost got the cameras back—the ones that were shut down. And I don't think anyone was trying to get in here at all."

Mark let out a slow breath. Henry had stayed at the security controls, no matter *how* many times they'd warned him there could be someone creeping up behind him…

Then Dennard said "About this house: the door was just open?"

Mark frowned. "That's right. Why does that matter?"

"Then the shooter didn't break in. Could be Winton left it open for him, after he cleared the owners out with some quiet possession. I'm hoping we'll find them sleeping in the basement, or not here at all tonight. Winton knows they'd get less attention alive than dead." Dennard took a slow look around the dim room.

Mark felt himself starting to smile. Dennard could be right, and the former cop had reasoned out the residents' likely survival before Mark had thought to be afraid for them.

Then they heard Nolan add "Except he had to leave his hired killer here. None of us need the police asking who the target was. If the body's still there, you have to get rid of it!"

"What?" Mark asked. *Just like that, that's what she thinks of?*

"It's your power. You know how," was all Nolan said.

Mark swallowed. He did know, the same way he'd removed Rafe's stash of shoes. But to just wipe out someone's death like that—

But it *would* head off more trouble, for once.

He walked back toward the figure on the grass. Gritting his teeth, he laid one palm—but not his fingertips, not his prints—on the rifle, and the other on the limp, sprawling thing that had been a man. And he let the energy flood in.

When Mark drew back, the shapes shot away into the sky, falling upward until... *Would they catch some current up there and come down in the lake, or keep going into space?* He swayed on his feet, suddenly dizzy. *Too much magic—or too long a day.*

They gave the security car another minute to leave the area, and Dennard glanced around the house to confirm it was empty. Then they hopped the wall to the road, and over Nolan's wall to land in the mist-smothered driveway.

They heard the creak of a car door before they saw the shape within the grayness. Nolan stepped out to greet them.

"So if a friend watches your back," she said, "and a real friend helps you hide the bodies—"

"Not funny," Dennard snapped. "Besides, you were lucky."

"What?"

"Doubly lucky. Driving out of a long, straight driveway like this? You're lucky the mansion that *was* opposite you didn't have enough height to shoot from. The sniper had to use a window off at an angle and track you driving out, and that's the only reason the first shot missed you."

Mark looked between the two, feeling a sudden urge to step between them—or keep clear. Instead, he brought up his phone. "Henry? You're still alright?"

"Still fine," came the familiar rasp. "And I think I've got the security recordings right here. First the cameras went blank whenever they swung toward the back door, and then that blank spot travelled out until it reached the back wall, and that was it. The gap only moved *out,* not inward. So nobody snuck in."

"She really did it." Nolan shook her head.

"What? 'She'?" Dennard said.

"Irene. Wait, is that bird still watching?"

"Winton's gone," Mark answered. Angie was too, with the excitement over. It *should* be over.

Nolan turned and motioned them back into the heart of the fog. In a few steps they could make out the blue Honda Irene drove, and then—

For a moment Mark thought he saw another corpse. But the shape in the passenger seat was a bundle of wadded-up clothes, stuffed into what looked like one of Irene's camo outfits. A dummy.

"I was going to drive this car out, to cover her sneaking away in the back, when Winton wasn't watching. And she… joked about hiding her tracks on her way out."

"So she screwed with your security to hide from *us?*" Dennard growled. "That's crazy. What was she doing—and was it setting us up for Winton or just for herself? Now we have to check the whole system, *everything.*"

"I *know!*" Nolan said. "Anything could be hiding there now. And Winton just tried to murder me. But first, let's get this out of sight."

She slid back into the car, careful of glass from the shattered windshield. Mark heard her mutter to herself as she struggled with the ignition, and finally coaxed the wheezing machine in a slow, slow crawl past her garage and on into a shed behind it.

At a wave from Dennard, Mark started back to collect their own car.

A sniper. Winton had sent an actual assassin, someone who could take the shots himself so that Winton only needed magic to let him take his position, and then to silence him. Their struggle had turned so deadly that even Angie was trying to lead them away from danger.

What had happened to Winton's long, patient games of manipulation?

We found out he's been playing them for generations. Maybe he needs us gone now.

And they'd left Sasha alone.

CHAPTER TWELVE

THE GIRL AND THE BOX

The pitiless cold of the roof numbed his feet, no matter how he kept shifting them. But Mark kept scuttling back and forth along its steep slope, staring down from points where he could see the shadows around the building's front door, then its side entrance, or its back. Hour after hour.

And Rafe could have gotten to Sasha before he even arrived. Mark's only reassurance was their hacking, reporting that Sasha had still been active on the net when he reached his perch. Nolan's weather magic took some of the sting from the air, leaving him hazy and sweating in his coat instead of freezing. But Mark had to force himself to only keep watch, and let his ears follow the intermittent churn of the car engines for any distraction to hold himself awake.

It would be so easy, I could just drag *her into our protection. Or take my knife and pry her window open so she'd call the police. Anything.* And moving in now would be safer than trusting his eyes to stay open all night. Safer for her, anyway.

But, if somehow…

He hung onto that hope, more delicate than his grip on the water-slicked tiles of the slope. *If,* Sasha somehow knew enough about Winton to help hunt him down. *If,* they could convince her to share it tomorrow, somewhere away from Winton's cages of spies. Every time Mark felt Winton's power peeking through one of the birds he ducked back behind the roof, but they never flew out from her apartment. And every time that presence faded peacefully, it told Mark that Rafe wasn't inside either.

Was this how Angie lived—alone and watchful and straining all her wits for one glimmer of a lead on their enemy? Sitting through a night was the least Mark could do, for *any* chance at turning one of Winton's associates around behind the killer's back.

Hours into the night, one of the birds flew up from outside, and he managed to sense it in time to shift behind the wall out of its sight. He felt its presence move to Sasha's window, open it, and it vanished among the others.

The first glow of dawn felt like the skyline turning against him, when he had to stumble down to the pavement before he was seen and hope Rafe didn't make his move in the morning crowds.

Nolan's voice on the phone sounded fresh as ever:

"A job offer under another name should get her. The girl's looking for money, and Winton shouldn't blink if she comes out for an interview."

Henry warned "You say that like getting her to trust us will be easy." He sounded like he was gulping down food, and Mark's stomach ached.

"It won't," she said. "But I'd hate to simply take out those birds and waste a chance at learning something more."

Mark could only say "Thanks. It just might change everything." Though now that the plans were forming, the other part of him wondered coldly, *Why* would *someone as ordinary as Sasha be anything but a bird-sitter to Winton?* She still didn't look enough like the Wintons to be some secret daughter of his.

"I believe you," Nolan said. "It's all in how we approach her. I can bribe her, scare her, trick her… I just need to watch her and get a read on which one she's responding to."

Mark forced a small chuckle. "Just watch her? You sure you didn't pick up some mind-reading magic with your weather?"

"I wish."

Mark heard the bite of sincerity in her answer, but before he could reply, Dennard spoke:

"But… there's still no answer from your friend Irene." He gave the words a measured, deliberate tone.

Nolan answered "Not a word. But that's also just how she is, sometimes. She's got enough to do. Right now, I'd say we all need to be nearby when I meet this Sasha, in case we need numbers to persuade her—"

"No."

Dennard's word knifed through Mark—*but we have to reach her, I sat up all night—*

Dennard went on "At least one of us needs to go check on if Irene made it home. I never met her, but I can't ignore that. Winton's had too many chances to see her with us. And why'd she screw with our security when she left? Besides, what good was all our reinstalling last night, if our enemy's captured the person who helped design the system? Or he's recruited her?"

"I know!"

Mark could almost see them facing each other: the hard-eyed woman with the core of paranoia, and the former detective who'd just redefined protecting a friend as covering their own weaknesses.

Nolan said "I know all that. But, *it's too late* to stop Winton from getting Irene, if you're right. What we need is to get through to Sasha before Winton can use that advantage—"

"If Irene hasn't told him we found her."

"Irene doesn't *know.* Sasha was only a blip on our research until Mark found her. But convincing her might need any or all of us. It could certainly need Mark, he's the one who knows her. And if you go to Irene's home without his senses, she could be under Winton's control and you'd never know it until he snared you too."

"Then it's a good thing I can spot it as well," Henry said.

Mark felt a rush of pride, warming him after the long night. Had his cousin planned that with Dennard, to face down Nolan together, or had Henry just jumped right in?

If he had, Dennard didn't say. He only said "We can keep it to investigating at a distance, for now. I'm still not a hundred percent from my wounds, and Henry can't strain his back. But if he spots Winton's power anywhere near Irene, I'll get us both out if our magic has to drag him."

* * *

The coffee helped. When Nolan drove up she brought Mark a whole thermos of the blessed stuff, along with a bag of bagels. And she said Sasha had agreed to the "interview."

By late morning, he and Nolan had settled her yellow SUV in an underground parking lot at the far end of the huge Beechwood mall. Mark felt no power around them, but he tried to keep his eyes alert too; Iskander and now Rafe had surprised him too often already just by approaching without magic.

They hadn't counted on the crowds. Mark and Nolan had to pick their way through shifting, chattering throngs chasing "early sale" signs up and down the stores, too thick even for mid-November. Every harried-looking shopper that passed within reach of Mark pressed at his bleary awareness that they were within knife range, and he felt the corners of his eyes straining to track anyone who looked less like they belonged in the crush. But in a mall crowd, nobody looked like they belonged.

Then Nolan waved him back as they approached a corner. The smell of coffee and fried snacks filled the air; they were at the food court, where Sasha would be.

"You keep out of sight," Nolan said. "She knows you as just someone she bumped into—unless she's in on it all—so she can't see you with me until I decide how to play this."

"Unless she's in on it?"

Mark had edged back from the corner and its row of Christmas-gold lights… but the open suspicion in Nolan's voice made him lean around to sneak a peek. Back near one of the exits, he saw the small form of Sasha, fidgeting with a set of papers on a tiny table. Her resume, for what she thought was a job interview at the mall.

Ducking back, Mark said softly "You ever think she might *be* what she looks like? Someone who's in this just for being blind enough to clean a killer's house and take in his birds without asking questions?"

"I think about it. I can't *assume* it." Nolan leaned closer. "Did you ever think she might be Winton's backup?"

Mark smothered a laugh. "You *really* haven't met her. Whatever she is, nobody would count on that girl to watch his back."

"No. She might *be* his backup, to be his next identity."

Mark froze.

Nolan's voice was taut. "You saw how Edward Winton—or whatever the man's real name was—might have swapped his mind into his own son. He may have set Sasha up to be next, if he needs an escape. Which means we'd be saving the 'poor, innocent thing' from a kind of death," she added with a grim smile.

Mark blinked, blinked again; the fast food scents in the air suddenly smelled thick and cloying. He pressed back against the corner, fighting the urge to peep around again and convince himself Sasha wasn't living under *that* threat.

"That… can't be true." He fumbled for reasons: "Why, why would he shift himself into such a, well, a nobody, after he's had money and respect all over town? I mean, even changing from a man to a woman would make everything harder for him, right?"

Nolan blew out a slow breath. "On that much, if ever words were true…" She stepped back around the corner then. "But if he just needs a temporary escape—"

She lunged on past the corner, staring. *"What?"*

Mark scrambled around her to see. Far across the court, his eyes picked out Sasha, walking away through the crowd with Rafe's hand on her arm.

One step flung Mark forward, but the next had to twist to the side and plunge between tables, dodging around a knot of squabbling kids. Far ahead, he could see fear spreading Sasha's features wide—*Rafe and his threats!* Mark swung around another crowded table, lightening his steps as much as he dared to let him maneuver.

He's still *got no talisman on him to sense, and we let him sneak right in! But that means I can run him down, if I can just get through...*

He stepped clear of another table and the big man standing up from it, but the man stepped into his path.

"Hold it, you almost *hit* me—"

"Sorry, have to get through—"

"I said *hold it*—" and he grabbed at Mark.

Mark dove away and bolted to the side, reaching the court's edge where the crowds were mostly thinner and skipping past a couple stepping out of the first shop front. Rafe and his prisoner were almost at the corridor to the exit.

Then two people ahead of Rafe skidded together and tumbled down. Rafe staggered a moment, then pulled Sasha around the patch of floor ahead. One of Nolan's ice tricks, Mark guessed as he charged closer.

For one moment, he saw a pair of women call out in concern to Sasha and the man who was not-quite-dragging her away. Then Sasha waved them off, face still pale, and she and Rafe disappeared out the entrance to the parking lot.

Mark dove forward, dancing between milling figures and startled voices, fighting the urge to leap onto a table—or higher—and the small thought warning him that Rafe might have something worse waiting for him. The open space around the ice patch let him risk one extended leap clear across it, and then he was out the door and in the open lot.

Fifty feet away, across a blessedly empty path between cars, Rafe was pulling Sasha along. Mark kicked away more of his weight to double his stride across the slushy pavement. *Can't give him time to react—*

Rafe looked back. He looked straight at Mark, still seconds beyond Mark's reach, whole seconds to let him reach for some weapon.

Instead, Rafe's jaw fell open like some panicky punk. He let go of Sasha and turned and ran.

Shock and relief thrilled through Mark. He lunged after Rafe, darting past the dazed Sasha. Rafe twisted between the cars, but a few barely-contained steps brought Mark up behind his prey.

Rafe spun around, fists raised. But it was his knowing, mocking smile that had Mark slowing and let Rafe sneer "I don't forget what you did to my boys."

The words slammed through him. *Q, Gunner, all the ones I killed—*"Not me, that was *him,* " he said.

"So hunt the bastard down. Get Sasha to talk, now that I just made you her big hero."

Rafe turned and ducked behind a parked van, and Mark tensed to chase after him.

"Are you alright?"

Sasha's voice. The opening Rafe had staged for him. For one instant Mark teetered on the balls of his feet, hearing Rafe's boots weaving away though the cars. Then he turned back to the girl he'd "rescued."

"He's gone." Mark found that his breath was as steady as if he hadn't run a step, since the magic had carried so much of his weight.

A motion made him turn. Nolan was jogging across the lot toward them.

Sasha said "He told me to come with him or he'd... Should we look for a cop?"

"You could," Nolan said as she stumbled up. "But he'll come after you again. I thought it was safe to 'interview' you here in a crowd, but now he won't stop until he finds out what you were told. Let's see if he left something on you to listen in."

And without a moment's pause, she pulled out her bug sweeper.

Sasha stumbled back a step, eyes locked on the small woman and the piece of spyware that Nolan openly played over her.

Mark moved in to reassure Sasha, but the sight of the scanner reminded him what else could be planted on her, and he held in his words and probed for any talismans.

Sasha's voice broke into his concentration: "What does that mean, what I was *told?* Wait, you mean the interview out here was with *you?* And Marty—what are you doing here?"

Mark managed a smile, to slow down her words and let him strain for focus.

Nolan was saying "Looks like you're clean. What you need to know is: your attacker's name is Rafe, and he was after you because of your history with Roger Winton."

"Mr. *Winton?* Do you know what happened to him? They said it was some kind of seizure, but now he's just missing."

The clear ring of simple concern pushed at Mark's control, and he took a slow breath to keep steady.

Nolan answered "I think you know better than we do. You're closer to the danger than that—since your 'aunt' worked for Winton's father. Or if she wasn't your aunt, and you're this Winton's sister. Or something else to him."

"No!" She shook her head, hard. "Why do people ask that? I worked for him, he was never like that with me, or did anything else wrong—he just knew I needed a job. And you, you saved me—Marty, you *lied* to me yesterday, you were spying on me! God, what kind of people *are* you?"

"Survivors."

Nolan said it with a small, bitter smile, as if the word explained everything.

"Just think," she added. "You know what it's like to be in Rafe's grip now. You know Winton must have made himself disappear, because he has information that Rafe and his... employers want. And they'll destroy Winton, and you, if we aren't able to stop them. With what you know."

For an instant, Mark felt his heart stop. She couldn't... Nolan *couldn't* have just claimed they were here to *save* Winton!

Somehow he kept the revulsion locked in his skull, back behind his face. *Think of helping Angie, and saving everyone else the killer can drag down.*

"I don't 'know' anything! This is all wrong, this can't be happening..."

He heard the fear in Sasha's voice, as if it shook her deeper than the trembling in her hands. Nolan's practiced eyes must have seen deeper than he did, but still—

He took a step toward her, between her and Nolan. "It's alright, we'll take you somewhere safe. And you're right, you should be careful what you believe from anyone, starting with us."

But Nolan pushed on. "Think! In all the time you worked in his house, what did you see about where he'd go? One memory of yours could save his life."

"I don't—" Sasha's voice broke off, but then she added "How can you save him? He's gone because that thug Rafe got him, isn't that it? And there's more of them?"

"But Rafe *doesn't* have him," Nolan said. "We know he can't find Winton, because he came after you, don't you see? No, Winton staged his whole 'seizure' to cover his escape."

"But... he kept a heart monitor in his bedroom." Sasha said it slowly, struggling to catch up. "He always talked like his medical problems were real."

Real risks, when he sent himself out in another body, Mark thought.

Nolan said "You know, that makes sense. We always thought there were dozens of places that would be easier for him to disappear from than a hospital. So you think he had an actual seizure, but then he used that to make his escape?"

"I didn't say… oh."

For a moment, the only sound was the slosh of tires in the snow. Mark held his breath… Had Nolan just led Sasha, step by step, into following their chain of logic until she had to make the last step herself? All without knowing what Winton really was?

Then Sasha said "If he really did… if that man was after him, and Mr. Winton needed to get away… There was another doctor at the same hospital that he worked with, someone who wasn't part of the service that brought Mr. Winton in…" She squared her shoulders and looked straight up at them. "I talked with him once. Dr. Tarnow."

The hospital where Winton vanished—and where I went with Rafe, the one place I might be recognized.

But Nolan was already moving closer, taking control again. "Could you introduce me? It could change everything for us."

* * *

It was a tense walk and a longer, tenser drive, with Mark trying to keep his eyes from meeting Sasha's. But every glance he saw his passengers making showed that Nolan wouldn't take her eyes off Sasha for an instant, and that the younger woman might not even be aware of that. Not even when Clearwater Hospital came into plain sight, and Sasha belatedly thought of phoning the doctor—and Nolan said only "Let's leave your phone in the trunk; it could be bugged. And we'll try to meet him unannounced."

Did Nolan think Sasha would warn Winton, somehow? Sasha had no talismans on her, Mark was sure now… Unless she was like Rafe, with magic that she had left behind to fool Mark. But even Nolan couldn't think *this* girl was playing them so completely, could she?

And all Mark could do was sit in the car and watch the two walk up the lot; any orderly who'd heard Mark's description from that damn night could ruin everything. *Trust Nolan, trust Nolan, nothing gets by her.* Except for Winton's magic—and Mark kept a finger on his texting button and his senses open for the first flicker of the enemy seizing a victim.

Nolan's phone was transmitting the background murmurs around her. Mark tuned it down. For now it was just too nerve-wracking to know the women were walking in alone.

A car honked, right at the entrance where Ben Iskander had run to his death. Somewhere above that sprawling building was the ledge Mark had clung to after Gunner had died, no matter how the sunlight washed over it now.

He cued up a warning text he could send Nolan at the first sign of magic, and called Dennard.

"Mark?"

"Hi. We couldn't check in before, not with Sasha right with us. She's willing to help, but that's because Nolan has her thinking that… God, thinking that we're trying to *save* Winton." Just saying it made one piece of the tangled, sleepless morning easier to face. "Don't suppose you've got any news to top that?"

"Nothing solid. It looks like Irene never came home last night."

Dull, half-expected fear pressed at him. "Winton *did* get her?"

"Or she was already going to him, or when she ran away she kept running. Henry says she and Nolan had quite a fight, before Nolan calmed her down—or thought she had. Looking at Nolan's grounds again might tell us how far she got."

"I see." And, Dennard didn't sound like anyone but himself, no matter how easy it might be for Winton to grab control of them both. And he had Henry right there to warn him, while Nolan only had Mark straining his senses at this helpless distance.

Then Dennard added "We're rethinking the leads we have. And answering a call from Henry's girlfriend now."

"Nolan's going to love that. But keep your eyes open," Mark had to say. "All your senses, and all of Henry's… but you know that, sorry."

"Mark, are you okay?"

Why was he asking that, out of the blue? *He's probably testing that I'm still myself, and he needs me to prove it.* Mark opened his mouth, feeling for words for how he felt about tricking Sasha, about losing track of Irene, about sitting useless in the car…

If I start I'll never stop. He tightened his grip on his senses, and said only "Just a long night. There's always a way, right?" Angie's motto was good enough for a password.

"If…" Dennard hesitated, then said simply "If you say so. Watch yourself too." And he hung up.

Mark heaved out a sigh, and switched to Nolan's call; still just more background noise in the hospital. He tapped on the seat, to help him focus. If Winton did have a way to know they were here, Mark might feel a talisman waking only a second before its puppet touched Nolan.

And what warning had Gunner had? *What did he see, my hand reaching out to him before he blanked out too? Did Q see me pick up his pistol before I pulled the trigger?* Mark hadn't even known their real names.

He forced a slow, steady breath, and held onto his sense for magic. He'd survived Angie's "death," he'd come through the belt's madness and kept control ever since; he could survive sitting in a car and watching.

Breathe. The parking lot, the buildings, were just more space he could run or jump through, even with the daylight crowds holding him to the ground.

Breathe. Listen. Sense.

Somewhere minutes later, a text came in.

W: I'll give you one chance. The keys to your magic in exchange for a body for Angie. It's the only chance she has.

Mark held his sense open. He checked the phone's security apps—they had to be holding. This had to be another random try to get a reaction from him, Winton *couldn't* have tracked him to the hospital after they'd fought to keep their enemy from getting even one warning… He cut the call from Nolan, just in case Winton could somehow tap into it.

Breathe.

Sense.

Ninety-seven breaths and two security resets later, a text came from Nolan:

Got an address. For the right warning, and the right price.

Breathe…

When Mark saw Nolan and Sasha walking up the lot, he was halfway out of the car before he remembered he'd only have to climb back in. What mattered was, they were there, they'd gone through unseen—Nolan even carried a set of coffees that he suddenly wanted more than any magic.

He held his sense open until the doors slammed and they settled in their seats.

Nolan jumped right into the news. "Lightning React just was the medical service that brought Winton in. It turns out," and a tight smile worked across her face, "Dr. Tarnow is part of another service, and they had arrangements to sneak him back out, and cover it up. And we know where they took him."

Sasha whispered "Because you just *bought* the answers from Dr. Tarnow… I mean, do you think Mr. Winton's alright?" and she looked straight at Mark.

He tried to loosen his throat, to make some kind of answer that wasn't a curse against the monster she thought she was protecting.

Before he could speak, Nolan said "So far."

Somehow she made that sound like a reassurance, not the threat it had to be. It seemed to fool Sasha.

Nolan went on "Dr. Tarnow looks like he's loyal to whoever pays most, and I think I made an impression on him. He won't be any trouble, for now."

"And you… you just walk in and do things like this?" Sasha breathed. "You really aren't with the government, are you? Are you some kind of security—"

"It's better if you don't know." Nolan's voice was actually gentle.

* * *

Nolan never sent Sasha away.

Mark had steeled himself for the tales Nolan might spin to let them chase after Winton without her. But instead Nolan only gave him the address she'd found.

Boll Street lay clear across town. Mark drove silently, wishing he could check their notes; he thought there'd been an apartment complex there on the list of properties that Winton might, just *might* have owned. But with Nolan keeping quiet, he kept himself still. In the mirror he saw how Sasha sat with the coffee perched on her lap, shooting wide-eyed glances at both of them but not breaking the silence.

Ten blocks short of the address, Mark spotted a motorcycle peeping around the cars behind them… for the second, no, the third time he'd seen it since the hospital.

Had Rafe been wearing biker boots when they'd "saved" Sasha from him?

Mark opened his mouth, but he could feel Sasha behind him, and imagined the panicked questions she'd ask about spotting Rafe again. He settled for saying "Looks like nobody's following us so far," but he gave Nolan a tiny shake of his head.

She answered with a small, slow nod. She got it.

So… now we're free to watch for if this is a trap, and if Rafe—or Sasha—are setting us up, they won't know we know. And if they're both who they seem, we still haven't told Sasha how the man she trusted is a killer and the one who kidnapped her is siding with us... His head hurt. The buildings they passed shrank and shortened, packing tighter together as they drew nearer to Boll.

His phone vibrated in his pocket.

Henry and Dennard checking in, probably—but he left it unanswered. Nolan still said nothing, and she had to know they were nearing the address. But she only glanced at Sasha, sitting in the back with her eyes closed.

As they stopped at the next light, he felt Angie in the sky, turning and changing course to follow them.

Her too? Mark forced his gaze back from staring up through the windshield. They had Sasha, Rafe, a call from their friends, and now Angie, maybe a block away from Winton? Was *everyone* on the move right this minute? Shaking his head, he edged the car over toward the right lane the moment the light changed.

"It's up at the next block, his address," he said. As he did, the biker roared on past them without a glance—it could have been Rafe under the helmet, but Sasha never glanced over.

Mark brought the SUV into a parking spot with a lurch.

Sasha tipped, and slumped limply over in her seat.

Nolan sighed "That coffee took long enough," and she snapped off her seatbelt and moved around toward the back seat. "We have too many unknowns here to leave her awake to warn Winton. Or let his mind escape into her, if we can finish him."

"But..." Mark looked at Nolan calmly propping Sasha up in her seat again, and spreading a blanket over her knees, to look like someone napping after a long drive. She simply *drugged* her like that? Even with all Nolan's explanations, the wrongness of it stuck in his throat, and he could only say "We just got her to trust us, and now you..."

He remembered the phone call; it gave him an excuse to look away. But, what the screen showed him was a text from Dennard, and it was blank.

He sent a question mark back, but no answer came. "Dennard sent me… something," and he sent another prompt. What was going on there, so far out of his reach? And just when he'd arrived at what might be the source of their problems.

The source. Mark looked out, down the quiet street of apartments, felt the afternoon stillness of a neighborhood almost soundless except for the passing cars.

If this was really the place…

He sighed. "Is that how you see it, stop arguing about Sasha and worrying about Dennard, because we're right where we need to be? And we've got Angie up there, and maybe Rafe nearby. What's the plan, check out if Winton's here now? Those are apartments full of people, so don't ask me to drop a battleship on him."

He winced; the battleship joke had been Angie's, and she had regretted it the moment she said something so bloodthirsty.

Nolan smiled thinly. "It wouldn't be *that* easy. Besides, we're only guessing he has notes about his magic in there. Our best chance of using this for Angie is to take Winton alive, if we can."

"Good." Mark flexed his fingers, trying to loosen the tension that had clenched them. *No, we can't crush him on sight no matter what he's done… even for using me to kill…*

But she'd said *if we can.*

"What was it, 14-D, fourth floor?" Was that one of the windows he could see, along the next block? Mark went on "Using the window by day's risky—we need to find a way in, but it could be a trap, if Rafe or anyone is setting us up… Rafe. That's one thing we can watch for."

All he had to do was tap the lever to slide the window down a few inches. Brisk winter air seeped into the car, along with the sounds of engines along the road.

"Angie?" He had to hope a normal voice was enough for her to catch. "Can you find Rafe, and warn us if he tries something? I think he was on the motorcycle that went by."

He felt her turn and fly up the street—finally, this time, working *with* them. And just when they had complications at every side to manage.

That was when his phone chimed again. He stared at the text.

"Dennard says... 'W's using Christa'."

The symbols shimmered in his eyes. The picture those three tiny words painted... Henry's girlfriend, Winton's power turning her against Henry... the curtness of the text, and the blank one before that just to ping him, as if Dennard could only sneak moments to warn Mark... and all of it far away where he *couldn't help*—

"We go in *now!*" Nolan said. "While he's distracted."

Mark shot off the fastest text of his life—*"careful! distract him!"*—and wrenched open the car door, trying not to think how they were charging into what might be Winton's own lair while Henry and Dennard were matching wits with the puppetmaster across town.

Nolan pulled on a wide-brimmed hat. It was to hide part of her face, Mark realized, and he scrabbled in his pocket for his own ski cap. The air cooled as they walked—her magic providing an excuse to cover their heads.

They reached Winton's block at a simple stroll. Mark took in the gated entrance ahead, the seven-foot brick wall around it. One of those windows on the fourth floor would be the perfect doorway if the hour were darker...

"I see two cameras," Nolan said. "Keep walking by and I'll freeze them—"

She broke off just as Mark saw the police car turn the corner ahead. It glided slowly down the street toward them, a quiet threat that made Mark fight to keep from looking away; innocent people wouldn't hide their faces.

If they keep patrolling here... or notice Sasha's not just napping...

He was drawing a breath to whisper to Nolan, when he felt the power grow heavier on the other side of the wall. His next step made it grow deeper still as he pushed into the currents. Currents he knew.

"Mark?"

Nolan's voice was low, a warning. The magic was thickening on his left, but the police car was drawing nearer on his right.

"It's here. Like the factory—Winton's got a talisman gathering power in there—" He broke off, clenched his eyes shut, and focused on the strongest energy ahead. "And, it's on the *first* floor. Not the fourth." He stiffened his stride, walking into the thickening waves of power as if there was nothing but empty air to feel.

"So Winton didn't even use the same room they brought him to." Nolan chuckled.

The police car reached them then, and moved on by, not even slowing. Cool relief washed through Mark.

His phone buzzed again, still in his hand.

He looked down, just as he heard the motorcycle roar, the sound of Rafe on his bike racing toward them.

On the screen was one word from Dennard: *hurry*

Mark's gaze flicked between it and the bike rushing at them, too fast for any city street—he tensed to dodge if it swerved over at him, but no, that would be leaving Nolan—he heard a siren squawk once from the police car behind them—

And Rafe rocketed past them, swept by in a rising and falling thunder of speed that had the police car blaring its siren and charging after the "reckless biker" until the sounds of both shrank in the distance. Now Mark could feel Angie flapping after them too, her presence almost lost in the currents of energy.

"Rafe *is* helping us, he's leading the cops away," he gasped.

"There'll never be a better chance. Come on!"

Nolan dashed for the wall. Mark ran after her, pushing away thoughts of who else might see them on a quiet street; *Dennard said hurry.* A moment of magic let him boost Nolan up the seven-foot wall and scramble after her.

They came down in what was almost an alley, a tight parking lot stretching from the wall and around the back of the building, lined with scattered cars but feeling silent, quiet... except for the invisible whirlpool of energy. The air whistled over the rims of the walls, called up by Nolan to cover any sounds they made. Mark gritted his teeth and led the way to the back window closest to the heart of the magic.

Locked, of course. Mark stole one last look around the tiny lot and the building's rear; Winton seemed to have picked the place more for privacy and to blend in than for security out here. He felt for the heavy pocket knife he'd bought yesterday, but, jimmying the window would take too long.

"Can you cover the sound?" he asked. "And, if it's all a trap, and that thing explodes when I touch it..."

"You ever wish you were like Winton, and you could send someone else to take the risk?" Nolan smiled, and Mark could hear a moment of real envy in her voice. Right now, he shared it.

Think of smashing through *the glass. No, think of Angie, and her father and Henry right now.*

He leaped up, in a twisting motion that brought his foot spinning in a wide roundhouse kick—and he locked gravity tight around him to brace himself in place just as his heel struck the glass.

And Nolan's winds surged to a frenzy, swallowing the noise and flinging the glass fragments into the room beyond. For a moment Mark fought to keep his perch in the air. Then the wind softened, and he dropped and leaped inside.

He knew the room would be dim, beyond the sunlight. It still took him a moment of blinking for the walls to take shape, while his shoes scraped on glass shards and the magic hammered at his senses... Then he saw the outlines.

Bare walls. No Winton, no furniture, nothing to break up the emptiness of the room. He scrambled through a doorway, but saw only the blocky shapes of an empty kitchen.

The wind softened outside, and he heard his footsteps echo, and Nolan rushing up beside him: "Where is he? Is this place really empty?"

"Well, it's still got the magic."

It was like walking against an intangible wind, the way the energy beat against his senses, Mark only had to close his eyes and move toward the center of it, back toward the room with the window. There, by the floor…

He knelt, and brushed glass away from the boards with his sleeve.

—Far off, a whisper pushing against a hurricane, came the sense of Angie winging toward them.

"Stand back," he said. "This time I just have to pull *up.*"

He laid a finger on the two boards—part of him wanting to flinch at the sizzling power below—and poured his own energy into them. The flooring trembled, creaked, strained as its many-times-less-than-nothing weight fought with the nails' grip. Then it slid free and he cut the power before the boards could slam into the ceiling. They drifted down like feathers.

In the space below, his fingers found a metal box. A tiny, smooth thing barely big enough for a piece of jewelry. And it was keeping the talisman within covered, safe from the light as it recharged. He lifted the box out.

"We've got it," he breathed, and somehow he could feel Angie sweeping closer even with the power blazing so close. "If we figure this out, Angie, we can help you—"

"Shh!"

Nolan's hiss made him stop, listen. Somewhere beyond the room came the sound of huge, heavy feet on floorboards, moving at a clumsy run.

Mark saw Nolan step to the apartment's door, with her gun in hand, behind her back. She clicked the latch off.

And he sensed two presences through the storm: Angie sweeping in toward the room… and the possession power that controlled the heavy-sounding shape just outside the apartment.

Mark gasped "That's *him*—"

Nolan flung the door open, one hand raising her gun and the other sweeping down in front of her with a wave of magic to stop the killer—

Then she halted with the gun still rising, staring in shock, as a figure careened into view in the corridor. It loomed more than seven feet even as it toppled, fell, and the most gigantic man Mark had ever seen skidded through Nolan's ice slick and crashed into her.

The next instant, something snatched the box from Mark's hands.

He turned, stared, but he could sense the presence bearing it away before his eyes focused on the feathered shape, on the talons twisting to wrench it open—

The magic vanished. The pounding against Mark's senses was gone, destroyed by the light, leaving a perfect awareness of Angie as he saw her flapping back toward the window and dropping the box that had sheltered the talisman. And the giant was pushing off against the doorway, rising to a huge height and flinging Nolan at Mark—

In the one moment Mark had to brace to catch her, he saw the shape tucked under the giant's other arm: the familiar face of Roger Winton, but instead of his usual bulk his body was wasted halfway to a skeleton of sunken flesh and flopping limbs, lying as limp as a man unconscious but still guiding the possessing power that drove his huge puppet.

Then Nolan slammed into Mark. Pain flared, a tangle of arms and legs and they went thudding down onto the floor… a floor with *teeth,* bits of glass stabbing at his fingers.

That pain drove the spots and the dimness from his eyes. He forced himself to his feet, staring… Had it been only seconds? How could he still hear the huge feet outside, escaping?

Escaping. With Winton.

While Angie had—

He lurched across the room after the enemy.

CHAPTER THIRTEEN

CROSS AND CROSS

The first jump went off target, and he crashed against the doorframe—more pain clashing with the dizziness as he fought for his balance. His gaze went to the floor and caught a shimmer running up the corridor; hadn't Nolan tried to stop the killer with ice?

Then the footfalls spun Mark's gaze up—heavy steps, from the enormous man moving for the corridor's largest door that had to be the way out, moving at a dead run even with Winton flopping under his arm. And staring at them all, a blue-haired old woman looking out from her own doorway.

Winton's puppet slowed, and glanced back. His arm started to swing up—and Mark wrenched back behind his own doorframe before the gun came up.

Think, how do I get to him? Think! He could hear the woman outside squawking protests, and the remains of the wind beyond the shattered window behind him… Ducking outside might be one way around the gun…

Nolan had pulled herself to her feet, leaning on the wall. She groaned "Go! Get them!"

Them. The word stabbed through Mark: get Winton and the body that carried him, or those two and the owl that had destroyed the talisman just at the instant Winton had needed a distraction, *why, WHY*—

His senses reached out, caught the signature raggedness of Angie's presence in the owl, winging away down the block... and Winton's puppet rushing off, his presence already too far to still be in the corridor. Mark's head was still swimming.

He lunged out, twisting around the woman in the corridor and her gasps for the police, to dart for the open front door Winton must have taken. He burst through it into the bright sunlight of the street and heard the squeal of rubber as a car peeled away. With Winton inside.

Because Angie let him get away—

Mark clenched the magic and shot after Winton, arching through cold air for whole heartbeats before his feet hit the pavement and let him spring onward again... but the nimble black compact was already revving its engine and pulling further away—

Can't lose sight of them, can't lose—

He leaped too high.

The moment he felt his burst of power he knew it, even before he felt himself arching high up and heard a gasp from someone along the pavement, before the rush of air swept the sound from his ears. He pulled himself up higher, too late to take the leap back, and he could only yank it into a bone-rattling flight up out of any more witnesses' view, a leap that blurred even the last fleeting glimpse of the car...

Somewhere in the sky, he remembered to slow, to stop. The grayness faded from his sight, and he hung in the vast blueness to drift soundlessly within the breeze.

I screwed up! Mark wanted to scream, to fill the sky with curses. Of course he couldn't catch a car without a jump someone would have noticed—but he'd tried to anyway, and had to escape straight into the sky. *Oh please let nobody else have seen me, let that one person not find anyone who'll believe them...*

He could have tried to get to Nolan's car instead. He could have sent Angie after them.

Angie. Mark sucked in a deep, cold breath, and clenched his fists, knowing he had nothing to pound against.

What had Angie *done?* She… she must have destroyed the talisman to protect him from some trap, he told himself, just like she'd tried to lead them away from Winton's sniper last night. "That's it, that's got to be it. It's just bad luck she moved at the one moment that made us look away from Winton…" he growled.

He floated in the sky, feeling the cold air burrow deeper into his skin. The city below was a blur of browns and blacks next to the lake's blueness—how had he gotten so high, shouldn't he at least see *some* motion below as he moved with the wind? He had to see below, enough to pick a landing spot to risk diving back down to, or else he was trapped up here until dark.

Finally he remembered his phone. He pulled it out to call Nolan, but the screen was covered with Dennard's texts:

look out!

W let C go

you ok?

Mark called back, suddenly hungry to hear a human voice. "Hi. Sorry I couldn't answer before."

"Sorry? Mark, are you alright?" Dennard's voice slowed and calmed even as he said it.

"Fine, I guess. We had Winton, we *found* him, and then he got away—" He broke off before he let slip just who had let the enemy escape. "We found where he had a talisman charging, like the one in the factory, but… I think he kept his body in a separate apartment…"

He paused for breath, and heard the pinging of another call. Nolan joined them.

"Mark, *stay up there!"* slashed into his ear. "Don't you *dare* drop down where anyone sees you. At least it looks like Winton's still too weak to move, if he needs someone to carry him. You can track that! Henry needs to get out scanning the streets, *now,* before Winton gets to some other hiding spot. And if there are any police left who owe you a favor, use them all! Find him!"

"I know," Dennard said. "Right now Henry's trying to calm Christa down—all she knows is she woke up and found him cutting her pocket open, to get rid of a bit of jewelry she'd never seen before. This is going to take a while."

"This is *our one chance!*" Nolan snapped. "Mark, don't let them see you, but get back here. Winton could try to get at me again, and you left me blind to his tricks. But I have to try breaking into his other room, the room he was listed in. Before the police get here."

"Okay." Mark felt knots loosening from his nerves, just from having a next step in the tangle they'd moved into.

Nolan added "But *do not* get clumsy, Mark. Nothing, *nothing* we do matters if someone gets a real look at you and the world finds out power like this exists. And, don't lose Sasha—if Winton's body is still weak, he may be desperate now. I'm sure she knows more than she's told us. Here, this has to be Winton's room—I'm going in."

The sound shifted, stretching out to a low murmur of what had to be the building and its background voices. Nolan had switched her phone to transmitting her surroundings again.

"That's… a lot of orders." Mark managed a smile.

"We'll do what we can," Dennard said. "Later—Christa's about ready to run off on us if we can't get through to her."

He hung up. Mark hung alone in the sky-drifting silence, with only the muffled sounds of Nolan's search in his ear.

Where is Winton, what was Angie doing, Winton's never once had control of her so why...

Mark forced his eyes to focus on the patchwork shapes below—a mottled, orderly blur, showing he hadn't passed beyond the residential streets yet, good. He sucked in a breath and dropped.

Pick a landing point and thump down onto the roof. Simple.

Rush right down the fire escape; he didn't waste a second.

Bounding up the street with magic's tireless, near-weightless run, he placed Winton's hideout on Boll at about half a mile ahead.

Mark was closing on Nolan's SUV when the sounds through his phone resolved into voices.

Nolan was saying "—just trying to understand why a man would get kidnapped like that. That brute simply dragged him away! And he burned some of his belongings too."

"Ma'am, this is a potential crime scene," came a patient, firm voice. "We're still trying to understand who lived here. Don't make me arrest you for interfering."

Mark's gaze darted ahead, to what cars he could see parked along the next block. That *could* be a police black-and-white behind that van... He slowed.

So Nolan was nosing around Winton's hideout even with the police there to catch her? *Well, we're all desperate now.* At least he didn't see Sasha outside; she must still be in her "nap."

Nolan's voice came again, and this time it was a sharp whisper: "Mark! The place Winton slept looks almost as bare as the other room, and Winton burned the rest. We need to make Sasha tell us what she's holding back, before he makes his next move on us."

"Sasha?" After Winton using Christa and escaping with what looked like Angie's help, the key was still Sasha?

"I tell you she knows more, and she doesn't trust us—"

She broke off, and a moment later the cop's voice came back:

"Olivia *Nolan?* We have a report of a break-in across the street from your home last night. And that was your Solar Sellers banquet that was robbed this week... and now you say you just 'coincidentally' come across a kidnapper breaking in a window, and instead of calling us you *come to look?"*

"I did," she said. "I suppose... my life has become insane. And when I saw one more piece of insanity happening, I tried to do something. It seemed crazy enough to work, at the time."

"Really? And this is no connection to your associate, Irene I-can't-pronounce-that? The woman who seems to have gone missing?"

"Missing? Oh, what's that girl gotten into now?"

"What does that mean?"

Mark heard the hesitation in the cop's voice, and felt a smile twitching—

But it's all falling apart. Winton escaped, he's already sent assassins after us, and Irene's missing. Sasha's still drugged, Dennard and Henry barely escaped... and Angie was taking talismans away from them. *She really did that.*

Mark looked at the street ahead, at the people here and there gazing across at the police car. At any moment one of them could turn and realize he was the one they'd seen flying away, just when they were talking themselves out of it...

A dark head reared up in Nolan's car window. Sasha was coming to.

No no not yet— Mark trotted toward the SUV. *Please let her not shout about being drugged... not that too.*

Just as he stopped at the car door, he saw Nolan and a cop step outside across the street.

Sasha was staring at him, eyes blinking wildly. Then the window slid down just an inch, and in a cracked, shaky voice she said "This... this is Mr. Winton's street, isn't it?"

"That's right." Mark stopped there, waiting for the rest to sink in with her.

Her eyes were already going wide. "I... didn't fall asleep, did I? There was something in the coffee." She fumbled at the door, and *snapped* the lock on. "You drugged me! How could you do that?! What did you do to Mr. Winton?"

"We didn't do a thing to him." Mark locked his eyes on Sasha's shocked face and tried to focus on her fear, not on how she still trusted the killer. "We thought going inside could be dangerous for you. And we were right—"

"So you *drugged* me?" At least her voice stopped rising. "Who are you people? What do you want with me anyway? God, I just clean houses, I, I'm nobody—"

That tiny hitch in her voice, like holding something back—

"Please. I just want to go home."

"Sasha… Listen, I didn't know about the coffee. I'd never have done that." A little of the tension on her face loosened, and more softly he went on "But please remember, you were already in danger."

"Not until you came—but, you did save me from that Rafe," she added.

"There's worse things than him out there." Like what Winton might have planned for her… but sharing his rage would only push her away again. He could only say "Think: we're here now, and Winton's still missing. And you're still just finding out about all of this. If you want to survive, you have to trust someone."

She didn't answer. Mark held his mouth shut, feeling the secrets and the doubts squirming to pour out.

Then she slowly nodded. "I… I do want to trust you."

Maybe you shouldn't, he thought as he said "Thank you," and finally stole a look around.

Up the street, Nolan was walking toward them—and she'd left the police behind. *Good.*

And down the street, another motion drew his eye. It was too far to see that face, but it could be Rafe leaning against a tree, watching the police car, the picture of casual curiosity.

Mark told Sasha "We'll get you out of this, I know it." He waved to Nolan.

I can't go to her yet, I have to work this out—

He spun away and marched toward Rafe. It took him away from what a fragile link Sasha might be, and away from his strongest ally, but somehow meeting Rafe was easier than facing the people Angie had… *betrayed…* His steps came faster, harder.

Rafe had ditched the motorcycle gear and could have been any young man from one of the buildings, lounging against the tree. Just as Mark reached the other side of the tree, Rafe hissed "Did you get him?"

Mark kept his eyes on Nolan and the car, and muttered back "No. But at least I don't sense him coming back for us now. And he looked like he could barely walk—but he still had someone else ready to carry him out."

"He ran away when he couldn't walk? The bastard's always ahead of us."

Like how he used me *against Rafe's men.* Except, Rafe didn't sound mocking, he spoke in the same calm, encouraging tone Mark had heard him use among his followers. *That I killed.*

For a moment, Mark wanted to turn and look at him, to search for the fury he was sure must be in Rafe's face, no matter how controlled the voice was.

Instead Mark closed his eyes. "Winton used you too." The words had a bite.

Rafe said slowly "He told me I'd own the streets. And then he turned on me, same as you said he would. And when I try to use what I saw about power, he starts killing everyone I take in. But you know about that." Then, at last, Rafe's tone sharpened. "He used you to wipe us out, and he killed one of yours too, and now you let him get away? You tell me, what would you do to pay him back?"

Mark couldn't answer. Fury was easy, his fingers were already clenching on their own with the need to crush Roger Winton and wipe away everything he'd done… but it had never been just for revenge. And yet Angie herself was blocking him?

His phone vibrated. He snatched it out.

"What are you doing?" Nolan demanded.

He could see the tiny shape of her up by her SUV, standing away from it, and away from Sasha inside it.

"I found Rafe," was all he could say.

"Good. Tell him, no more sneaking around us. What's his number?"

Just like that, Nolan was making Rafe one of them? But Mark found himself holding up the phone to him. "Nolan wants your number."

For one surreal moment he was sure Rafe would answer with a dirty joke. Then Rafe simply leaned over and tapped the digits in.

Nolan went right on, as Mark switched it to speaker: "We've lost too much time. I'll make sure the others keep the pressure on Winton, while Mark and I work on Sasha."

Rafe chuckled. "So you're giving orders?"

"You see anyone else thinking, right now?" Nolan's cold, calm words rolled out, ready to gather them all up and push them on without a moment's stalling.

"Okay," Mark said. "And, sorry about the timing in there… but who knows what kind of trap Angie may have saved us from?"

The phone was silent, long enough for Mark to wonder, *why'd I point that out just now?*

Then Nolan said "The trail's getting colder. Mark, you start searching for where Winton might have gone. Run, steal a car, whatever it takes to sweep the city."

"But you wanted me to talk to Sasha—"

"I can handle her. Every second you lose might be the moment *he* stops needing to keep control of his bodyguard puppet, and then we've got nothing to track."

"Got it."

Mark looked down the street the way Winton had driven, letting the maps and plans flood into his memory again. Winton could be long gone, but Mark could still move through the nearest streets and feel for any power within a couple of blocks.

"You want in?" he asked Rafe.

"I'll see what my 'orders' are," and Rafe smiled coldly. "Don't wait for me to grab my belt again. Go!"

Mark sprang away down the street. His tired legs fell into the gliding pace of a half-weight run; the first people he veered past on the sidewalk stared at him, and he eased the magic back to keep from bobbing upward in a way no runner could.

The first sidestreet seemed like the best bet, as the best start on covering the most ground. Nolan's car was already passing by behind him.

His steps wobbled, reminding him of all the sleep he'd missed. Rafe's words about taking orders kept swimming in his mind. Rafe's voice had been odd… but not as strange as Nolan hoping Mark would stumble over Winton's magic, after all the times they'd tried random searching…

A stoplight brought him to a clumsy halt. Just one more thing slowing him down… he could run all through Lavine before he found Winton, if the magic didn't drive him insane first… Better to get Sasha to trust them. But Nolan had sent him away…

She sent me away.

And the way Rafe had spoken about what his own "orders" might be—the coldness in that memory shot through Mark. *Nolan doesn't want me there to persuade Sasha. She wants me gone so* Rafe *can scare her. If he stops at a scare.*

The way Nolan looked at me after I was possessed, so close to shooting me… and she did *shoot one of Rafe's men, and yet Rafe's working with her too to get at Winton, and he'd left them both with Sasha…* But, how ruthless were those two?

A woman with a dog walked past Mark, and he realized the crosswalk was green again. He grabbed out his phone and shot a call to Henry and Dennard.

"Be careful with Nolan. You may want to steer clear of her for now."

"What happened?" Dennard said. "Did Winton get his hooks in her?"

God, that would have been an easy excuse. But Mark told the truth: "Not him. I could be wrong, but I have to see if she and Rafe are torturing Sasha."

"What, Rafe?!"

Mark didn't answer. He spun left toward Nolan's home. Except, he'd seen her car heading to the *right*... Her plans might not be about Sasha after all. The route she'd taken wouldn't bring her to her home's privacy, or to Winton's home where Sasha had known him... but the apartment he'd set Sasha up in was to the right. And they could kill Winton's birds too... *two birds with one stone... stay awake!*

He dashed for Sasha's apartment on South Bend.

He had to be wrong. Just because Nolan had sent him away so suddenly? She'd changed her mind right after he defended Angie... Angie must have destroyed that talisman to protect them... but what did Nolan think, that Angie had turned against them and that meant Mark couldn't be trusted either?

Please, please, let Angie just be saving us from the talismans...

Just a few doors from Sasha's building, a glint of the afternoon sun caught on Nolan's parked SUV, like the metal was smugly *winking* at him.

Mark's stride didn't slow. After all last night watching over Sasha, he knew every step to take to slip off the main street and out of any-one's view, and he flung himself up to a roof. Four more leaps brought him to the top of Sasha's building—even in daylight he had to risk a few moments where someone might look up and spot him. No-lan would never have risked that, not just to protect someone.

Climbing down the wall of Sasha's building was easier. He could imagine someone on the street looking up and wondering whether they were seeing a stuntman or a burglar at work. But all Mark needed was to find the right corners and cracks to brace his weightless body for the times when the breeze gusted.

The belt's power felt weaker. He had enough magic to climb, but not to keep dashing around town.

He felt the cold from the window before he saw the solid gray frosting over the inside of the glass. He felt for whatever latch the bird had used to enter last night—the frame's metal was stinging cold. But the window still swung open, with effortless, counterbalanced ease.

A wave of frozen air rolled past him like the blast from a freezer.

Worse than any winter, colder than the highest altitudes or the frenzied rush upward he might make to reach them… Mark stared into the silent room inside.

Three cages. Glancing between the covers he saw one was empty, two more held lifeless feathered shapes that would never be Winton's eyes again. Nolan had squeezed the heat and the life out of this room.

Deeper inside, he heard voices.

Mark swung himself through the window and plunged into the cold. His foot skidded a moment on the frost-slicked wood. He slid the window closed, and the frozen air hung thick with an overdose of air freshener—Sasha might have used it to smother the smell of the birds, but in this cold it stabbed the nose like the breath of some pine forest's ghost.

But through the next room's door, they were simply talking. Nothing more.

"Mr. Winton was curious about me, that's all," Sasha said. "My aunt had worked for his father—and he probably knew I wasn't finding a lot of jobs, so he hired me. Why would I argue?"

She sounded almost calm, like she hadn't seen the death in this room. Mark crept over the frost toward the door.

"Not even because that aunt had disappeared?" Nolan's voice could have been part of any awkward conversation. Even though at the same moment she must be freezing the air that had Mark's teeth chattering.

"Aunt Izzy didn't disappear. She left town. My mother got messages from her for months."

"Your aunt. This would all make more sense if she were your mother, and Edward Winton was your father."

"You said that before, and it's still wrong! She was my aunt. My father's dead—let me call my mother, she'll tell you. Just let me call her!"

That sounds like fear. Mark flexed his fingers in the cold, trying to hold off the numbness. *I can't sit here forever.*

"So our Winton isn't your brother? And you don't have some other tie to him? If he was so kind to you, it would be only natural if you developed certain feelings—"

"No! Why don't you just believe me?"

"I believe they told you all that, child. But... you do know more than that. Every time I've asked you about Roger Winton, I can see you holding something back. And we need to keep Rafe and the rest of them from finding him. So you need to trust me."

"Trust you? You *drugged* me!"

"But I'm the only way you have to help him."

"Please, please, just leave me alone!"

Mark gathered himself beside the door. But Nolan hadn't crossed any more lines, she'd only given Sasha more of her harsh "protection" and "advice."

"Will you think it over?" Nolan said. "For Winton's sake. I'll be back soon—I want to look around the building to see if we're safe here."

"Wait, you've got my phone—put my key back—"

Footsteps tapped across the room. A soft thump told him the door had closed, followed by a sharper thump like a frustrated fist on it and then the click of a lock. As if Sasha could shut Nolan out.

But Nolan had only rattled her, nothing more. Even if she'd taken Sasha's phone away, and a key too, none of that was what he'd come to stop. He glanced back at the window.

"Why, why, why..." Sasha's words were a sob.

That confusion in her voice pulled him back. Mark caught at the doorknob and forced his frozen fingers to grip it, and turn.

Sasha stood in the middle of the room, as if she had nowhere to go. A wave of cold washed out past the open door, and she looked up.

"Marty?"

"It's Mark, Mark Petrie."

"Wait, how'd you get back there?"

He waved that aside with a numb hand, not trusting his fingers to move. "Look, what matters is, you aren't alone. We aren't all like Nolan."

"She said…" She paused at just a step forward. Her voice dropped to a whisper. "Do you think it's true? Is Mr. Winton my brother?"

Or your father, or he needs your body, or both? "I don't know. But, you ought to see how dangerous this really gets." He stepped back, deeper into the cold. She needed to see what Nolan's power had done… and he wouldn't let her be like Ben Iskander, killed for finally seeing the magic…

The front door clicked open behind them.

Rafe's voice called "Now we can talk, girl."

The next moment Sasha scrambled through Mark's doorway, and her hands flailed and slammed the door behind her.

"Cute," Rafe laughed. "I know you've got no phone in there."

Because Nolan had told him.

And, Rafe hadn't seen Mark. Mark tensed to leap, at the moment the door would open. Rafe still had no belt, and Mark's had enough power left to crush him with a touch, if Sasha got out of his way.

Instead she stared madly around the frost-soaked room. "The b-birds…" Sasha's stutter could have been confusion, or simple frost-bite.

"Frozen solid," Rafe said. "Want to know how? If you try screaming I can do worse. And one more thing: guess how I got your key."

"Key? She took it…"

To give to Rafe, all setting the stage for him to force the answers out of her, Mark knew. So this *was* how far those two would go.

"There's no Miss Nolan coming to your rescue, that's how I got it. We're going to talk about Roger Winton—you can come out and give me what you know, or I can come in and start cutting."

Sasha gurgled, a strangled sound that tried to scream and failed.

Mark held up a finger trying to quiet her. If he could squeeze around her and surprise Rafe at the door... but Rafe might get a shot off, with him and Sasha right there. And where was Nolan, waiting to join Rafe? He felt for magic, hoping for some sign that she was out of earshot.

Instead he sensed Angie. Balancing in the air outside the building, watching them, her presence *mocking* him with all the questions she'd stirred up—

She'd destroyed a talisman... to keep it away from *Nolan?* With Nolan's ruthlessness on display, it made more sense now. *And fighting Rafe while Sasha's cringing in the middle makes no sense at all.*

Mark motioned Sasha to quiet again, and glanced around at the birdcages. Two had frozen bodies in them, both with silvery shapes on their feet. Talismans Nolan hadn't had time to take, the things that Angie wouldn't leave with Nolan.

He caught up one cage, opened the window, and sent the cage falling *up* into the sky. He spared it only a scrap of his remaining power, hoping it would drift enough blocks and be lost wherever it came down.

When he turned back, Sasha's face was ashen. "What are you— don't—"

He took two steps.

Those steps let him catch up the other cage—while he heard a quick footstep from Rafe nearing the door—and grab Sasha's arm. Now, finally, she flailed a punch at him, but he'd felt winds that hit harder, and he simply wrenched her weight away from her and yanked her through the air with him. She gasped again.

Please don't scream—

He heard the door of the room rattle, as he dove backward and arched out through the window with Sasha in his grip.

Far back inside, he caught one glimpse of Rafe and Nolan, side by side, staring after him. *That's right—I ducked out one more window to get away from you. So much for being partners.*

CHAPTER FOURTEEN

CRUSH AND WEIGHT

Just reach the building over there... Mark locked his fingers on the cage and his arm around Sasha's squirming body, and tightened the magic to push his leap outward. He lolled his head out to watch the roof rushing toward them. Sasha's fists beat in panic on his chest.

The faint air pressure against his side vanished. Nolan must have stilled the breeze to give him nothing to ride except his leap—he saw the street sliding by below, scattered people in the bright sun that could look up at any moment. Nolan wasn't going to risk forcing him out of the air here.

He felt Sasha trying to pull in a breath.

"Hold on," he hissed. And he let them drop.

For whole seconds they plummeted through the air, and Mark saw the rim of the roof rise up behind them to hide them from Nolan and Rafe. A surge of magic broke their fall and let them touch down gently on the wide, flat roof below.

Mark rolled free of Sasha. He could hear cars and voices rising below them, all the busy sounds of people who'd been just one glance away from spotting them in the air.

As long as Rafe and Nolan thought he had enough power to keep flying, and they couldn't *see* up to the many roofs he might be on... they were safe. He shifted his stiff hands to hold the birdcage at arm's length. Angie soared safe above them, the talisman in the cage was safe, Sasha was safe.

Except—he looked at the girl, still gasping where she lay. How could he "save" someone who was still loyal to Winton, who had no clue what the puppetmaster's plans for her might be?

Angie passed above him and moved on up the street, just the direction she'd take to keep watch for Rafe and Nolan.

Then Sasha stumbled away from him, looking back and forth between him and the roof's edge behind her. The leap had tossed her hair over her face so he couldn't read it. She drew back until she was within a foot of falling over.

Her breath hitched, like it was one gasp short of screaming.

"Would you like to get down?" His voice came out almost calm, steadier than the shifting city voices below. And the street below her was a quiet back street. He took a step toward her. "I'm not kidnapping you, I'm trying to protect you."

"Down? We… can do that?" She sounded like a child, needing to trust someone.

"Any time you want." He offered his hand. "All I ask is that you let me explain what Rafe—and Nolan, together—were doing. Either up here, or as soon as we're down."

She nodded, and reached out her hand. And closed her eyes.

Mark knew better than to ask her to step over the edge. He took her hand, reduced her to a feather's weight, and lifted her off the edge with him as they sank down, the birdcage in his other hand. Long seconds later they reached the pavement.

When he let her hand go, she kept staring at him. At him, not at the corner leading to the main street, an escape that was just thirty feet the other way. It was a start.

"You… you can fly," she said slowly.

"That's right. And Rafe can fly—but not right now, he won't be chasing us—and Nolan controls the weather, and Winton… it's complicated."

"Winton? He's one of you too?"

"He is—"

He took over his son's body, and you might be next, but I still don't know why Angie let him get away. Somehow Mark managed to keep that frustration from twisting his face as he looked at Sasha.

"Nolan's looking for Winton," he tried again. "And she thinks you know something about him and his magic. And Rafe's with her."

"I saw her beside him back there when we jumped... You said *magic?*" Sasha shook her head. Then she shook it again, and kept shaking. "No, no, I keep telling you people I don't know anything!"

There it was again, that secret catch in her voice.

"Maybe," Mark said. "But Nolan thinks you're hiding something, and she's usually right. And that's why she sent Rafe in, and I had to do something." But they wouldn't stay safe from Nolan, he needed help—

Henry, and Dennard! They only know a hint of what had happened. What could Nolan be telling them? Still holding the cage, he grabbed out his phone one-handed.

Only two rings later, Dennard answered, and he didn't even hide the uneasiness in his voice. "Mark?"

"Yeah. I think I just broke our deal with Nolan."

"Mark? Are you okay?"

That sounded like their usual caution over the phone, not like she'd gotten to them first. That was something.

"It's *me,* trust me, there's nobody pulling my strings. I told you, I had to save Sasha from Nolan." *If I'm not just setting her up for worse.* "First Angie grabbed a talisman—"

He heard a footstep. A slow, shuffling step moving away from his side, changing to a sudden patter as Sasha ran for the street.

Mark dove after her, one long step, as he thought, *I can't just drag her back—*

In a hiss of warning, a shape streaked down into Sasha's path, wings and talons spread to make her flinch back. Then Angie swept on past her, and Mark cleared another step to reach Sasha's side.

"You said you'd let me explain."

He made the words an accusation, and saw Sasha's eyes flick away, a hint of embarrassment. *Don't reach for her, she's still just steps away from the street.* Cars hummed past, so close.

He laid the birdcage down, gently. "I'm sorry I startled you. There just wasn't time, to tell you what Nolan and Rafe had planned for you. Or about Winton."

"What?" She took a step toward him. "He's one of you? What does that mean?"

"He—"

He kills people, and Rafe will cut you apart to find him?

His talismans are too dangerous to trust Nolan with—unless Angie really is siding with Winton now, because he can keep her alive?

"There's an invisible war, between spellkeepers." Saying that let him sidestep just which side Winton was on.

"And that's why that woman drugged me, and now you're telling me Rafe was with her all the time? I just want my life back!" She raked her fingers in her hair, trying to smooth it.

"It's not that simple. Nolan is sure you know something; maybe you *are* part of Winton's family, or it's something from your aunt, or—"

"You really think he's my brother? Does that mean I could have magic too?" Her eyes went wide, as if the thought had only just caught up with her.

"A second ago you wanted to get out." Mark tried a smile, a small one. "Believe me, nothing about this is that simple."

"But… if it's Mr. Winton that I'm connected to, then I should get to him and he'll protect me. If I could find him."

She added the last words a breath later, but Mark heard it again; she *did* know something. *And then Winton destroys her, one way or another... but she could still give me a shot at him, or at whatever Angie needs now...* And to start that, Mark only had to swallow the worries and nudge Sasha to use whatever she knew.

Instead he said "I said, it's not that simple. People have gotten killed in this fight, or someone turns their friends into weapons against them. You never know who you can trust, even if it *is* family. Hell, I should have known better—my own father's a drug-pushing waste of space who let my mother die, and that was long before any of this—"

His words choked up, and he tried to start again slower.

"What I mean is, think before you go trusting—"

"Like trusting you?" Sasha was edging back, an inch at a time. "You're not on Mr. Winton's side either, are you? Are any of you?"

That was the part she could latch onto? Mark throttled his voice back to a gentle whisper. "Just... you only think you know him. And whatever bond you have with him, he looked desperate—"

"You *saw* him? Marty, or Mark, if I hear any more lies..."

"No, I mean..."

I mean Winton could be desperate for a new body, and I think he's already taken over his son... and all the ways he's torn up our lives...

But if Angie does *need his help, if that's why she stopped us...*

He opened his mouth to make some warning about what Rafe and Nolan were, and how Winton was worse than any of them.

And that warning might be what ruined Angie's last hope.

"Please!" He looked up at Angie, toward the high cornice he felt her perching on. "What's your plan? What is it you want now?"

He felt her drop from the wall.

"Mark? There's nobody there—"

Angie glided down into view.

"The bird? You're talking to the *bird?*" Now Sasha could barely croak the words out.

"I *wish* she talked." Mark watched the owl approach. "Come on, Angie, there's always a way, right? What is it you need? To get rid of his talismans, or..."

He broke off and glanced at Sasha. With her listening, he couldn't even *ask* if Angie still wanted to keep her safe from Winton.

When his eyes swung back, Angie was settling onto his arm.

Sasha's voice fell away, and the night air could have been just a memory of cold, all pulled back by the touch of magic *inside* him.

She mustn't, this is some of the power that's keeping her alive—

Whirls of power around him, no, currents that were part of his thought, where her presence slid through and moved with quick purpose. Stirred by mind magic, like the magic they'd found and she didn't let them keep—

The box. He tried to form an image of the shape of the box she'd opened, and the "Why" question about her doing that, why, was she protecting the enemy now—

Hot, spiky rage trembled through the thoughts he sent, sending her flinching back—

Again he tried, just *Why,* stilling his self to a calmness that could accept any answer, still and ready and open to every motion of the message, the messenger—

Blueness… one clear image, blue paler than the sky… pale and fading, fading away too soon, shrinking and settling into a rounded shape and gleaming metal, forcing itself into form, but the image was fading, shattering itself with the effort of taking form, fading, *her dying—*

He *slammed* through the image and the connection and found his arm to shove the bird away. Too late.

He heard wings on air. That was the far-off sound of Angie catching herself… but too soft, too weak, she spilled onto the pavement and lay on her back. Her beak twitched, trembled.

The magic left in her talisman dimmed— *"No!"*

Somewhere, somewhere nearby, a woman's voice was saying something about "only a bird." But Mark's mind was stuck: *she's used up, she's used up… the power's fading—*

He had more power.

The birdcage still stood at his feet. His fingers clawed it open to spill out the frozen corpse of a hawk... *Don't stare at the awful, ominous thing, Angie herself is fading away right now.* He nudged it over to bring the silver shape on its foot next to the one on hers.

She reached toward him, ready.

Then he stopped, hunched over on the pavement. The damn talismans had already made him a murderer once, and if their maker could sense the moment Mark tried to use this one...

"Mark? What's wrong?" Sasha asked.

Something in her tone, doubt and simple concern, slid in among the desperation and made him ask "You want to help?"

She startled backward. "What?"

"Please!" *Every bit makes a difference, and something at the bottom of her voice sounds like helplessness, like she needs a chance.*

"I... yes. What are you talking about?"

"See that bit of metal there?" He pointed to the hawk's foot. "If I start acting like... not myself, try pulling it away from me. But don't touch it. Or if it's too late, just get away, and keep this away from me too." He stripped off his belt.

His fingers didn't want to let it go until she pulled it free. All of this was worse than a long shot; nobody made any magic obey them on their first try.

And I think I can control Winton's?

He forced the thought away and touched the death-cold side of the hawk. His other hand went to Angie. For a moment he brushed a knuckle along her feathers.

Then he brought the two squares of silver together.

Like some great shock, the power tore through him. No need to find some hidden mental trigger. Instead he locked his thoughts on the metal in his hands and the owl's flesh below it, as the world slid away.

All this is my mind, my thoughts, he told himself. The frantic swirl of power around him could be like any storm he'd ridden, or stood above... to know that was to create it, and that thought helped the winds steady and draw back into circling currents that left him float-ing, balanced.

Not all of it was him… something at the very center was *other,* was the throbbing core of force the rest were gathered around… and far away, a different ember of strength that showed a layer of the stubborn *someone* that he knew was struggling and squirming and fighting to keep from drifting away from that dimming beacon.

Not a beacon, it's like water, lifeblood, and I can pour it from its strong core into her fading one. He grasped the power, just a careful trickle to start with… she stirred, ready, and he willed it to flow.

It didn't move. Like water it refused to flow upward.

Up? The void *had* no up or down… but he felt the other presence growing and pulling and bending everything around it, and…

And the hungry many-limbed form that must be the magic's true master, sensing him, there, just as he feared and somehow rising up "behind" him and below his guard.

If I take my real hands off the talismans, I escape. But that was one small thought as he flailed wildly, uselessly at the power she needed, trying to scream *Just let me help her! She's not even fighting you now!*

The owl snatching the box from him—the image welled up in him, and with it the memory of the enemy charging by just as that dive drew all their eyes away, then her flying down to rejoin the killer after their escape—no, that last was only what he feared might happen, that the killer had somehow brought her over to his side… fury burned…

His rage trembled out through the currents, and the killer stirred in reaction… a kind of gravity swelled to draw him closer and drag the power farther away from her—

A touch. He turned around, saw that the first of the vast curved ten-tacles had already slithered *into* him from behind… shapes, words, tumbled inside him under the thing's blind groping.

It's for her! he tried to say. *She saved your talisman from us, you just let me help her or I'll have nothing left but hating you—*

The whole thought slipped from him and flowed out to the enemy, and the probe lashed brutally through spaces, through chambers of his mind that it could barely sense, if it had to fumble so callously… it was searching for

Sasha

He tried to plead, like speaking through vomit with the thing coiled in his thoughts, but he could strain to find his real hand and the power to break free—where had Angie gone in here—

Something whispered, not thoughts but far-off sounds, words that weren't his that made the world flow.

A trick, it must be a trick, and he flung his strength into following that flow toward her—

Emptiness in his grasp. Falling, pulled into the enemy.

Thunder, so far far away above—no, so close, shattering and fierce and shriveling the world, as the world split apart and fell away, pulled away by familiar talons…

He felt the hard surface first. The solid ground, smooth and cold—so cold—and the sound of real cars rumbling by along the street.

Mark couldn't *see*… no, the dimness and the pool of light at the corner told him it was simply night. No shadowy horrors. His mind was his own again. Cold ached in his bones.

He was alone.

Prying himself stiffly up, he looked around. He saw no owl beside him, no Sasha standing nearby. But that *had* felt like talons pulling the silver from his grasp and breaking him free—so Angie had to be alive. He felt for her presence.

The belt and his sense were gone.

Of course, he'd given it to Sasha. In case Winton got control of him again…

And she'd run off with them. That wasn't even Rafe's doing, no, none of the others would have left Mark unharmed. But the belt was gone, and so was the dead hawk and its talisman.

He rubbed his eyes, and scrabbled around the pavement. At least Angie was *missing,* so their struggle could have given her the strength to fly away… but that whisper that shook the void *hadn't been his*…

Mark stumbled to his feet. He'd *missed* it, Sasha had been with Winton all along, and *she'd* known how to unlock the magic and save Angie… or else she was still the trusting, frightened thing he knew, and Winton himself had saved her? But if Sasha was going to Winton, she'd bring the killer his belt and everything, and Mark had no magic, no answers. He hadn't even finished warning Dennard and Henry about Nolan—

His phone was missing too. And his wallet. Of course.

He sagged against the wall, feet slipping on a piece of trash. The girl had taken everything she needed to cripple him. "And I showed her how!" His fist beat on the wall.

Sasha could be anywhere, Angie could be anywhere, even with Winton—and without a belt he couldn't sense her if she flew right past him. No way to warn Dennard and Henry… or to help them, they had the only other talismans…

No.

His eyes slowly widened. Sasha could steal the belt, but she'd left him his knife. And his knowledge.

* * *

Somehow Mark knew it would be this shop. The same store window he'd once noticed on his twisting route back from the Youth Center, not so far from the park itself. Even when he knocked on a few late-night restaurants and convenience stores trying to borrow a phone instead, each time the desperation in his voice broke through and the people began backing away from him.

But this shop… His too-practiced eyes showed him no cameras around the back entrance. The door and its lock looked almost fragile, beckoning him.

So now I'm breaking into a place that's got nothing to do with our enemy... just like someone desperate for a fix... Mark's feet shuffled him forward, while his mind searched for some reason to turn away. Find a way to call Dennard and Henry, when he had no power left to help them? And hope nobody died during the time it cost him?

He slid the ski mask down and unfolded his knife. The heavy blade dug behind the doorknob's plate, but his trembling fingers only creaked in pain when he tried to pry it loose. He strained, gnashed his teeth, batted feebly at the knife.

At first he thought the blade had snapped—but the sound was the wood giving way, echoing and fading into the sounds of the night.

It was only opening a door, to take some belt or bag from somewhere beyond it. Mark dug the lock out and vowed he'd send the owner money for it all, if he got through the night. *This isn't stealing, it's survival.*

Inside was darkness. By the time Mark found the light switch, his nose had caught the musty hints of leather around the room. He stood in a storeroom, with one door leading forward and rows of different shelves and cases for coats, pants, and all the rest of the mix of clothes it offered. He wedged the door shut behind him with the stoutest piece of metal he could see, and stared around, trying to spot which of the scattered leathers might be made of real, magic-sensitive horsehide.

The shelf labels were meaningless codes. He settled for running his fingertips over the darker-toned pieces, hoping for some sense of recognition. These belts were too fine-grained, that coat too thin, that one too pale, this one might be…

The back door rattled.

No no no, of course they had an alarm—

The steps to the door forward were ready in his head. He dove through it with an armful of coat, as the back door creaked open behind him. The showroom ahead looked clear.

Then he saw the figure standing at the far end of its dimness, and knew he was trapped. He flung himself down behind a display case and crouched low. There had to be some way out. His fingers squeezed at the coat he'd grabbed.

Light flared; the storeroom door creaked open. Mark could only press himself lower, peering between the wallet displays; the glass case ran right down the middle of the room, so the guard in front or the one behind him had to spot him—

The unmoving front figure was only a mannequin, he realized just as the man behind him strode in.

Stupid, stupid, I'm doing everything wrong tonight! The sweat wafting around him felt like a swamp, enough that it ought to lead the big, slow-moving guard to him blindfolded. Boots scraped over carpet, closer.

The guard stepped past him, going the other way around the case.

Another step or two and I could hit him from behind... no! That could crack his skull, what's wrong with me... it's all *wrong now, I've got no chance left and nothing clean to hope for and it's all ending here... but Henry, Angie, Dennard—*

He leaped up. He ran, with nothing to lighten his weight. But, he'd used so many different strides and paces with the magic, now all the practice let his toes came down softly and roll his feet along the floor. He yanked open the storeroom door while the guard was still turning around.

"Freeze, damn you—"

Mark ran. Ran into the night with the black coat clutched in his hands, with street layouts flashing through his mind and desperation powering his steps. And knowing he'd simply been lucky—luckier than he deserved, with so little sense left of what side he was being lucky *for.*

* * *

The shop lay only five blocks from the edge of Rosewood Park. That put it almost at the center of the web of false turns, hiding places, and vantage points Mark had used for two months to hide his secret place from enemies more dangerous than a few security guards on a quiet night.

Twist here, hunker down and pause for breath… He'd *only* stolen a coat, they wouldn't search for long… The mechanics of evasion could almost keep his thoughts from coming back to how long he'd hated anyone who simply took what they wanted because it was easiest.

When he got a chance to look at the coat's tiny label, only the words *Genuine horsehide* helped him pull back from some scream of despair.

And then, suddenly, he found himself at the edge of the park, and certain nobody had followed him. Instead of slowing to make a plan, he dashed straight across for the thicket, and the power.

The owl's shriek split the night.

Mark raked a useless glance through the darkness above, as the thought thundered, *So she* is *alive!* before he cleared the last steps to the wood and slowed to grab at the first trees to yank himself to a stop. He twisted to steal a glance back.

From the trees at the far end of the snow, a figure was charging toward his wood. Of *course* Rafe would be watching the one place he had to come back to.

Mark dove between the trees, and a moment later he realized Rafe could have shot at him before he'd reached that protection. Mark hauled himself along as much by using his hands to push off and muscle him around the trees as by his feet clambering over the brush, anything to keep from crashing into trunks in the dark. Brush tangled at his feet and crackled like laughter at any delusion of him sneaking through. But stealth was pointless, when Rafe could simply wait at the spot unless he reached it first.

Instead Mark stumbled through, trying to match the little slopes he lurched over against all the times he'd picked his way along them at a sane pace. Could Angie even try flying in this thicket? One slope down, one more left—no, this should be the last one—

"Zha-Daruath—"

Nothing responded yet. He lunged up what had to be the last slope toward where the source really lay.

The impact on his back slammed him over and off his feet and sent him crashing down in a tangle of pain, then more pain as he fell against a tree, then his eyes clearing to see the foot sweeping in and sending him spinning.

Roll, keep moving, don't slow—

The sound cut through the fire in his ribs: the click of a pistol's slide, the gun in Rafe's hand.

Mark wheezed "You got me—"

"Shh!"

Rafe kicked at the horsehide coat—when had Mark dropped it?—sending it rustling away into the dimness.

Mark gasped in a breath through the bruises and tried to stand, but Rafe's hand waved him down. Then Rafe sank to one knee, his gun and the sharp sneer on his face never wavering from Mark… and Rafe's other hand dug into the brush below him.

A moment later Rafe stood, with a belt in his hand. *He hid his talisman right over the source, so I couldn't have sensed it was here even if I'd had my own belt—damn him—*

Rafe locked the belt around himself with one hand, never wasting a move. Then he advanced slowly on Mark with the gun ready. His other hand reached slowly out.

He whispered "Can't have his bird hearing this, can we?"

His bird? "That's *not* his bird," Mark hissed back. "She was just warning me! And she warned me about Nolan too—you think torturing Sasha is harmless, but wait till your new boss decides it's your turn—"

Then the hand came down on Mark's arm and drove the thoughts away.

First went his breath, forced out when the flood of weight pinned his chest. Waves of pain from the blows Rafe had landed flared up again under the pressure. And the brush, the ground, every root and wood chip under him dug into his flesh as the weight crushed him down, head swimming—

Then air rushed back in, but Rafe's hand held its place, and enough weight lingered to still chain him down.

Like he'd done to Rafe once, but this was no simple drowning…

"Where's Sasha?" came the voice above him.

Mark gasped. He held in his *I don't know!* out of some dim sense that stretching this out had to be better than letting Rafe win.

The weight slammed down again. Mark's fingers strained, couldn't even pull up from the brush, much less catch at Rafe's belt to fight his control. He could only stare through the haze at the dim trees above, wondering if some gap there was enough for Angie to dive through.

"Was the girl worth it?" Rafe hissed, and his grip slackened. "Sasha belongs to someone who's been killing us—and you pull her out and let her keep her secrets just to save her from a little… pressure?"

At that word he clenched the power down again, a single wrenching squeeze that made Mark's sight go gray in the heartbeat before it eased.

"Stupid! If you give us Sasha, we get answers, and we finally get Winton—how is that not worth it? And it beats what the weatherwitch has to do to Dennard and your cousin."

"Henry?" Mark croaked. "And—"

"So you missed all the plans she has for them?" Rafe's face, so close in the dimness, twisted into a sneer like a slash across his mouth. "With you gone, Henry's our only scanner now. And if they're traitors too, Nolan knows how to deal with them."

"What did she do—"

"Like you care! You should've thought of that when you turned on us. Where's Sasha?"

"I don't know!" Mark groaned. "She ran away… please, it's not Henry or Dennard's fault—"

"Liar!"

The word rippled through the dark, and Mark felt his eyes twisting toward the thin gap in the trees above again—

From the corner of his eye he saw Rafe's gaze twitch too. Was he watching, was he *ready* for the owl—

Rafe's voice was low again. "You *can't* be this weak, Mark. What happened to all that loyalty to Dennard, and Henry, and your own girl? One bitch you just met tries to cover up an enemy's secrets and you throw all that away for her?"

"Loyal?" The word hissed out on its own. "You sold out the Blades!"

"I gave them a *real* leader, and when the cops broke up that summit I got my own boys out. I made them the kings of the street—and I was just starting to show what the magic could really do. If they'd just let me—"

Rafe broke off then, and what might be a tremor of honest pain in his voice was swallowed up.

Mark flung back "But 'your boys' wanted it all, and I saw them turn on you. What'd you expect—they'd already turned on the Blades. Greedy backstabbers make the best suckers for you, right?"

Then, Rafe chuckled. Low, soft, and mocking.

"Oh, Mark… don't you tell me you were going to sell us to Winton and then betray him? You, fool *him?*"

"You did," Mark snapped. "You stole some of the belt's secrets so he couldn't get them, right?"

"Idiot! I stole them from you!" Rafe laughed again. "You think nobody can see you come and go here? And Winton never thought all his questions about you might tell me what he was looking for? Then I snap one picture…"

The last words were the softest whisper, and Mark could imagine the rest of it. So Rafe *had* snuck a picture of the belt, when he and Winton had forced Mark to take it off, and if Rafe was sure enough of his guesses to trust that the words on the belt were close to the right ones…

My God, I gave him this power—

"Yeah, I had to tell someone," Rafe said through a grin. "Now tell me again how *you're* twisted enough to beat Winton at lies? You think you can?"

"No…" was all Mark could say.

"But I still saw that bird warn you just now—so you *did* make the damn deal with him. You ready to die for him too? Where's Sasha, where's Winton? The truth!"

The force smashed down again, and Mark thought he heard bones creaking. Wet blood gushed from where his fingers were crushed into the bracken—

He forced his eyes away from watching the trees above, where she might be. He could do that much.

When the pressure ended, his body bending back into shape hurt worst of all. And Rafe hissed "All this, instead of giving me that nothing Sasha?"

"Not… her…" he managed to say.

"But you'll *die* for her? Pathetic!" Rafe's fingers tightened on his battered arm.

"Not… her…" Mark kept his eyes on the brush beside him, a maze of gray lines blurring as his sight faded.

"For Winton, then? All this for *that* user? Hell, you *deserve* this!" Rafe snarled.

"For… her," Mark wheezed before the weight crushed his breath away. No matter what, no matter what Angie might have done…

I shouldn't look. But his burning, aching eyes caught some motion above, and they moved on their own.

And Rafe's fingers shifted. The pressure lightened, Mark caught one eager intake of breath that had to be Rafe bringing his gun up *ready* all along for that one sign of Angie's dive—*no no NO*—

The power beat down on him like huge clutching hands even with Rafe distracted, but all of Mark's agony blasted out through one leg to wrench it up with a sound of something snapping and a feeble, flailing kick that barely brushed Rafe's body enough to touch the—

UP!

His thought burst into Rafe's belt, surging and forcing their way through its wearer's divided focus. The magic burst away with a great rush of air as Rafe was yanked into the sky.

Something thumped, rustled, down into the brush near him. That had to be Angie, pulling up from her dive.

And the weight was gone. Mark could move… if he ever wanted to again…

Finally he pulled in a full breath, and managed to turn his head. The disc of Angie's face twitched, just out of reach.

Chirrup, she hummed, softly, warmly.

"Guess you're alright." So he could speak now, too. But not move, not yet…

Angie jerked back. *Shreeee!*

This low cry was barely a yelp for her, but from this close the warning made his ears ring. He was dragging himself to his feet with the pain trailing behind his moves.

What did she spot? Rafe, getting control of his belt already? But none of that mattered, now that he had Angie to follow again—*I know that now.*

The coat lay only four steps away. The simple, ordinary space in the middle of the short upward slope was two steps more.

"Zha-Daruath!"

For one blinding, joyous moment the pain was gone, wiped away in the flood of power pouring in and filling the coat. *Into* my *talisman, all mine, this time. It's cost me enough.*

Then the first rush of power settled, and the pain crept back—he was still in danger, still too weak to fight, he had to remember. Straining, he could just make out the dim presence of Angie behind the storm of power at his feet. And… another pulse, of proper gravity magic, out in the park. Where Rafe must have landed.

But, that other power stayed in place on the ground, instead of coming closer. So Rafe was too hurt to move? Or he'd left his belt behind to sneak in again?

"Not this time. We're gone!"

The earth dropped away at last.

CHAPTER FIFTEEN

LEAP AND BOUND

The surging fire of magic swept around Mark as the endless sky drew him into its thin, moonlit coldness. And that cold was its own warning, like all the cuts and abuses in his weightless flesh—a reminder not to leap and soar and let the magic burn away his control.

He settled into the breeze, and let the whistle of air against him grow still. The ground below was a field of lights scattered over the darkness, with the blank space of the park already drawing away at his back. Rafe's presence was left behind; the thug must know better than to try searching the night without senses like Mark's.

And Angie… Mark squinted uselessly against the shadows, but finally he felt her nearing the height he'd shot up to. She winged toward him, and banked to circle slowly below.

Why did she really take that talisman from us? Who unlocked the power to restore her strength—Sasha, or Winton?

Still, one of Rafe's threats was clear, and urgent as the power that swept him up. "Henry, and Dennard!" he called. "What's Nolan doing to them? We need to know if it's true."

He stared around the lights below. The streets were close to endless, when he had no clue where to look, and no phone. But within a minute he passed over the beginnings of office buildings, and he had only to drop to a roof, with Angie following him down.

The door to the inside was locked. Mark laid his hands over the knob.

The power began as a testing flow, pressing the door downward and trying to find just where the locks held it. But when he felt the resistance and pushed harder, the coat's energy surged to match it and he heard metal shriek and give way. He yanked his hands back before the door could rip free of the frame, but the magic, the magic still rushed to his hands, wrapping unseen lightning around his arms, his chest…

"I… think I know why the Fletchers stuck to little belts," he told Angie, and the words helped him clear the fire from his head. "This coat pulled in so much power… control just got a whole lot harder."

He stripped the coat off and tucked it over his arm to get its throbbing off his skin. Letting the stairs echo under his full, normal weight, he trotted down into the building.

Dim corridors flashed into eye-hurting brightness, but that was only the automatic lights; the pale plastic cubicles were thick with silence. At least until some alarm went out.

I just trashed their door, when an hour ago I tried asking people for phones and thought of paying for what I'd stole—before I powered this coat up. Those are bad signs.

He grabbed at a desk phone, and tapped in Dennard's secure number. No answer. Nothing from Henry either.

For an instant, he thought of trying Nolan herself… no, what could he tell her that wouldn't end in shouting? He made for the stairs again.

Angie stood waiting on the rooftop. He said "They didn't pick up. All I can think of now is to try Nolan's home—"

She sprang into the air. Heading west, toward that estate.

Please let them be alright, let us find something. Mark leaped after her and fell into the quick quarter-block hops that could keep pace with her. Just leap, soar, aim, thump down and leap…

When they entered the side roads around Orchard Heights, Mark dropped and loped along the silent streets behind Angie. Fear grew in him, that whatever they'd find at Nolan's, they were only putting off dealing with Winton and Sasha—and whether Angie owed her life to one of them.

Suddenly Angie climbed, so sharply Mark glanced around for enemies before he leaped up after her. She led him into a glide with the wind, on a high path toward Nolan's estate. Mark watched the smooth open space of those grounds drift closer, far below. No lights were on. And, none of the other gravity talismans were there.

The longer he stayed high enough, the less warning the alarm systems would give Nolan, if she was even here. But he remembered Winton's hideout and the leather shop: empty or not, once he went in anything could happen. The dark, blocky outline of the house edged up.

He dropped. And Angie tucked into a dive—and he felt her rush down past him, cut *across* his path in one of her warnings, and twist onward along the wind.

Not the house, but up that way instead? Mark pulled up and let the current take him again, still a hundred feet clear of where the roof drifted by. He traced the pale line of the encircling wall ahead, the maintenance shed where they'd hidden Irene's car, and the open ground around it. The sight made him wonder again, what Irene had done after she'd shut those cameras off. Had Angie seen it?

Angie settled to the ground by the shed. When Mark landed beside her, the touch of his shoes on Nolan's land felt like ringing a starting bell.

They'd left the shed's door locked down, but Angie stood right beside it, watching him. Mark reached his hands slowly out to the plain, heavy wood. "Guess it's too late to worry about breaking Nolan's things, isn't it?" he heard himself say.

Angie's head rolled over, tilting sideways on her owl's neck in what might have been amusement.

Holding his breath, Mark let the coat's power flow, fighting to channel just enough to swing the door up. Wood splintered and it lurched upward three feet before it caught again—open enough. He stooped down and slid inside.

He had to edge around the rear of Irene's car; the tiny Honda almost filled the shadows. The tight, musty smell flooded his nose, with a hint of something odder… paint? Brushing back cobwebs, he wondered what Angie could show him in this cramped, dim space.

But the curve of the metal… His eyes turned back to the rear end of the car under his fingers. The blueness it should have was lost in the dimness, but the *shape,* the rounded lines and the crack of the trunk were the exact images Angie had risked her life trying to put into his mind tonight.

"Here? The car?" he said, as she flapped in to settle on its roof.

Something moved inside the car's shadows. A figure sat up inside it. Dennard.

A gag stretched across his mouth. And from the way he flopped in the seat—his hands were locked behind his back, with the cuffs threaded through the steering wheel.

Angie *hissed,* fiercer than any snake. She shifted from the car's roof up onto the front, watching.

The Honda's door wasn't even locked. Mark leaned in and pulled the cloth down from Dennard's chin, and saw him spit out a second wad of cloth it had held in his mouth.

"What happened?" Mark asked.

"You tell me." Dennard's words were slurred, like a man half-asleep, but there was nothing sleepy about the grimace of pain over his face. He strained his neck to look around at his transformed daughter on the hood. "Nolan said you and Angie were traitors."

"Not traitors, Angie didn't trust her with another talisman." That *had* to be all, he thought.

"Looks like she had Nolan right," Dennard growled. "Then our 'ally' said Henry had to sniff Winton out *tonight,* searching every last block, as the only way to finish this. Then I say that's too much magic at once, she hauls me aside and sticks a needle in me... Guess that makes me a hostage. *Again.* Henry's girl Christa might be one too."

"Hostages." Mark spat the word like he could force the facts away. He leaned in closer to study Dennard's handcuffs.

"Careful, those are my hands in there—"

Mark laid two fingers on where the chain ran across the steering wheel, and let the power flow. The coat's throbbing surged around him, metal links ground down against plastic-sheathed metal, he fought to strain the metal *slowly* and not let his vision blur away, but ohh *the joy of* making *something simply obey...*

The chain snapped before the wheel tore loose.

"How's... that?" he managed to say as his heartbeat settled. That ought to start making it right.

But Dennard only rubbed his wrists and said "Mark, you don't get off that easy. What did you and Angie *do?"*

"We..." Mark swallowed. Suddenly he couldn't look Dennard in the face. "We kept more of Winton's talismans away from Nolan. And—"

And Angie helped Winton get away, and I think he saved her. The words clogged his throat.

"And what?" Dennard's voice was rising. His gaze turned from Mark back to the car's hood where the owl perched.

She flapped from the hood, up and over the car, to settle on the trunk. The trunk that she'd tried to show Mark.

"In here?" Mark slid around behind the car again. "Can you find the trunk latch up there?" he called to Dennard, and heard a click as Angie hopped clear. He swung the lid up.

That smell's not paint.

It had been just a trace within the thick atmosphere of the shed. Now what the trunk released was still only a weak, alien scent, but those shapes tucked into the dimness of the compartment could only be a pair of folded-up legs. A body.

He leaned closer, bracing himself for what the smell had to be. Within the shadows, behind the camouflage print of the pants, he saw Irene's face… frosted in gray.

"She… Nolan *froze* her," he croaked. "To make Irene's body… keep. She hid it, because she did this." Mark stumbled back and ducked under the shed door, scrambling for clean air.

Angie glided out, with her father trudging after her.

"So…" Dennard said through gritted teeth. "I never did find a sign that Irene had left the grounds. Of course she never jammed the cameras to hide her leaving—Nolan must have done it herself, to hide that she *didn't* leave. And Nolan tried driving Irene's car out, so if the body was already in the trunk there'd be no real clue except that the sniper's shots crippled the car."

"So… Nolan had already killed…"

Dennard nodded. "Henry said Irene had heard some of Nolan's secrets, so she could have demanded more and tried to threaten her boss. And now we know how Olivia Nolan deals with threats."

The former detective's words, the step by step breakdown of the facts, could have come from some far-off, slowly growing distance. What filled Mark's head was, *She fooled me, just like Winton played at being my friend—No, I* knew *she was dangerous and I couldn't face it—*

When they got rid of the sniper, she'd said, *Friends hide the body.*

He heard Angie hissing again, and he turned to her. "You saw this, you *knew* we couldn't let Nolan have more power! So we just have to—God, how do we beat Nolan when we're still fighting Winton— But we have to stop both of them now, don't we—"

"Come on," Dennard sighed. "We see if Christa's here, then we go after Henry. And all the rest of them."

Entering Nolan's manor again was like stepping within some huge, dead fist—the building wouldn't close in around them itself, but Mark feared what might already have happened there. He followed Dennard in and they called out for Christa.

Her answer filtered down through the thick ceiling. "Joe? And… Mark, again? Can you let me out, finally?"

Upstairs, from the left? Mark dashed for the stairs. "Hold on…"

"Did you get him? Winton?"

Christa's voice led him down the stark gray corridor, to the second door. The knob held fast… *Leave it to Nolan to have a room ready to lock someone in.* "No keys, right?" he asked Dennard behind him. "You both better stand back. Way back."

When he heard her back away, the coat's power ripped the lock downward until the great wooden door split along the edge. This much energy made it easy… but his heartbeat couldn't seem to slow.

"What's going on?" Christa hung back at the end of the sparse bedroom, looking at the splintered door with the same steady look she'd given Mark at the bar with Henry. But her voice tightened with concern: "They said I could black out again if I left. And I could be a danger to everyone."

"You blacked out, they said?" Mark echoed. How much had they told her?

Then she sighed. "Relax, Henry and Joe already showed me the magic. But Nolan locked me in here, and Henry—*my Henry!*—said they had to, and they were going off to make sure Winton never got control of me again."

Dennard stepped around beside Mark. "So Nolan has him scared for you, instead of calling you her hostage. But she also left the dead body of another 'ally' in the shed… and you don't look too surprised," he added.

Christa did take a step back, but her voice was almost level. "Body? We should call the police… no, wait…"

Mark gritted his teeth. There it was again, the same invisible net that hung over them and blocked off any move that might draw attention to the magic. The *circus*, Kate once called it, of how the whole world could go mad fighting over their powers.

Then he heard Dennard say "No, it's about time."

"What—" Mark began.

"Get the police searching for her, now that she's leaving bodies," Dennard said. "I think I know how much we can tell them—I've covered for Angie's family long enough."

Christa took a step toward him. "What if you told them Nolan's deranged, as well as deadly? If you can't talk about her creating all these pocket storms, say she can't resist going to them. Ask them to look for her the minute one flares up."

"Because she's *been* seen at enough of them to 'prove' it?" Dennard chuckled. "Give them the pattern without the explanation. Not bad."

Christa was onto something. Mark was turning to congratulate her, when she looked straight at him: "But will they find her before something happens to Henry? Isn't there something else… Mark? You can look for their power too, can't you?"

There it was again, what had to be done, even with the whole city to search. Mark turned away from those demanding eyes. "I can fly, scan, start where Nolan might look for Sasha—I'll think of something. If she needs Henry for searching, she'll let him keep some of our magic. And I'll never miss that." The words and his first steps toward the door buoyed him up and pushed the doubts back.

"Hold on!" Dennard's voice stopped him in his tracks. "You sure you're safe to go out again? How long have you been flying?"

While you're afraid to fly at all?

Then Mark choked down the angry thought and drew in a slow breath; Dennard was right. "Not too long. It's this coat, this much power makes control… harder."

"Then stay on the ground." Dennard dug into his pocket. "Nolan took my magic and my phone. But she left my car keys."

* * *

Setting the throbbing, overcharged coat on the car seat beside him helped. Mark only needed its sleeve touching him to scan, and with that limited contact he managed to keep from flooring the gas and racing through the night streets. Thoughts jostled back and forth against the maps in his head: Sasha might be at her home or at Winton's house or other places Nolan might try, but all Mark needed was to pass near whatever talisman Henry had.

Angie flew behind him. He felt her narrowing the gap by cutting above the blocks when he turned, and falling behind whenever the car had a straight shot through the traffic lights. Back at that distance, her presence was a quiet ache that he couldn't call her down and demand whether her changes lately were still just a switch about Nolan, and not Winton himself.

He'd just turned onto the narrow lanes of Rowan when she swerved away from his wake.

Mark spun the wheel, weaving around cars to make the U-turn. Whatever she'd seen had to be close, but one block and then another passed without her changing from her new course.

Then he paused for a light, and he heard it: a whistle of wind against the car that hadn't been there blocks ago. Nolan.

When Angie turned again, he felt her flight buffeted by that wind. The shapes ahead looked like typical Valens Street apartment buildings—sprawling off from the street at irregular angles, small buildings crowded together. There had been *something* about a Valens address in their research, what was it? Angie's path began to tack left and right, either searching or just fighting through the wind.

One of their gravity belts pulsed ahead.

It lay somewhere in the tangle of streets to the right. It could be the belt they'd left with Henry, or else Rafe's new one, or the one Sasha took… Mark pulled the car over before he knew what he was doing.

Or that's the magic urging me to fly—but still, simply driving in would make him a sitting duck. The coat slid eagerly around him.

The wind shoved at the door as he opened it, and stung coldness against his face. He tightened the magic and bulled on through up to the roof, and then over to the next perch toward the talisman. Angie struggled through the air behind him.

Mark kept crouching low and watched between the buildings for some glimpse of the belt-wearer. He felt the power at ground level, at what must be a couple of these cramped Valens-sized blocks ahead, moving slowly along some cross-street, then shifting to reverse back down it again.

But above that area, Winton soared. Mark felt one of Winton's birds, flying an oblong curve over the street, wrestling to keep its position in Nolan's gale.

Mark gritted his teeth and leaped for the next roof. One block, maybe two ahead? The tiny twisting streets and their buildings had to give him a look at whoever had that belt soon.

Another talisman pulsed up beyond—another belt, unmoving on the ground, a block or more up along the first location's street. What was it, what had their research mentioned about a Valens address... Sasha's mother?

Winton swung in a wider loop, as if searching the streets.

Blocks ahead, Mark sensed a *third* belt lurking on the ground. On the far side of the first two's street.

Just as Mark's head turned that way, he felt the nearest talisman moving again. It headed up the cross-street—just beyond the ridge of the next roof now—moving with a brisk walking pace that its wearer hadn't taken before. Mark forced his way forward in a low leap to land atop the last roof that lay in the way.

Down below was the slight shape of a woman pushing through the wind, pulling her hand down from her face as if a phone call had spurred her into this rush. Sasha.

Mark crouched low and leaped along the roof's peak, keeping low and close to the tiles to slide under the worst of the gale. Angie was still too light and too many buildings back. But he was one jump from reaching Sasha's side or grabbing her, if he wanted. The second belt lay farther ahead, in the direction she was moving.

He settled on the building's corner—and the third belt's power drew his gaze back out along the street he'd left, as that belt drew nearer. It was still more than a block away in the dimness, and at that spot he saw a bulky vehicle that might be yellow if it came closer to the next streetlight. Nolan's SUV.

Which made that belt the one she had Henry using. Mark gathered himself, trying to think how to pull his cousin to safety.

A glimmer of light drew his eyes back toward the closer talismans. A doorway stood open onto the street, outlining a shape that looked like Rafe, right where the second-closest belt was. And Sasha was staring and running up the street toward him.

Mark glanced forward, back. Henry must be right ahead, his own cousin in a murderer's car… but Sasha was only a few doors away from Rafe, and she had some key to reaching Winton… and Nolan at least needed Henry intact to search…

"Damn, damn, damn," Mark snarled.

He flung himself over the street where Sasha slowed to a walk. She and Rafe didn't look up; two doors still stood between them. The building shot by under Mark.

A bird swept down. That was Winton's bird, diving at Mark's back—

Mark slammed himself *up,* away, wrenching through space to burst clear of the bird's path and halting a few stories up. *I was ready, this time I spotted it closing in, but I was so close to reaching Sasha.*

Far down in the door's pool of light, a second figure stepped out. A woman, pulled by Rafe's hand on her arm. As Mark dropped closer he saw Rafe waving Sasha toward them.

Winton's bird curved around, turning its dive into a rush at Rafe with a wild flapping of wings. Its presence cut through the night, then it spun away in a blast from the storm, and twisted right around in a struggle to dodge through… and the wind spun again to smack it down onto the street.

Its magic winked out before it could hit, bailing out.

Nolan's power had done that, probably with Henry's guidance—and Winton had made it *easy* with his reckless dive at Rafe. That left the sky clear of threats, except for the storm.

The next moment Mark reached the roof and landed softly on all fours, scrabbling in the wind before he got his grip. From below the roof's rim he heard a woman's voice:

"Alright, now you have my daughter. But you don't need to threaten her—what do you want from me?"

"She's not the bait, you are," Rafe said. "Inside, both of you."

The hostage and hostage-taker sounded as if they were right up against each other. Mark pulled himself in for a leap, trying to picture how he'd drop down around the rim and make a quick lunge in at them.

"Stop playing games," said the woman. "I don't know why you want me—"

Sasha's voice was shrill. "Mom, just let me—"

"You? *You* know something this animal wants?"

Mark peeped over the edge. He'd have to lean out and leap almost straight down, but they hadn't looked up yet.

A car moved onto Sasha's street, and Mark froze. White shone against black in the night, a police car, prowling up the street. *Here in the heart of the pocket storm. Christa's "storm-chasing Nolan" cover story brought them right to us!*

Mark flattened himself low. The approaching car was passing by the cross-street where Nolan and Henry were; he could feel Henry's belt already pulling further back, those two had seen the police heading by.

Below him, a woman screamed and footsteps pounded out of the building—*out* of it, when Rafe had wanted to take them inside. Now the older woman dashed toward the passing car, waving frantically.

As the police car slowed, Mark felt something wet on his face. The howling air began to darken with snow.

The police car slowed, and Sasha's mother waved it over. Rafe backed up the street away from them. Sure, with Nolan's snow for cover he could dash away for the shadows and then slip into the sky.

The police were climbing out of their car. Sasha and her mother were safe enough… Mark let a breath out and began crawling backward, up the slope of the roof, out of their view. Now he just had to catch Nolan and Henry.

Winton's magic caught at Sasha.

Its control pulled her back from the police, a soft grip clashing with the belt's solid pulse. She started up the street, away from Rafe but also away from the police.

Bastard! Sasha must still have the talisman from the caged bird—and now Winton was using it to force her away from safety when her own mother had just barely escaped from Rafe?

Rafe leaped.

Mark felt him shoot upward, then in a rush of shock he tracked him arching over and dropping straight onto the two police.

In another wild moment it was over. Rafe slammed down onto one cop's head, and the uniformed figure went flat—unnaturally flat, crushed by a wave of gravity. As Rafe landed, a gunshot smashed through the wind, and the other cop crumpled… all while Mark was trying to aim his own leap.

Rafe swung his gun around, toward the older woman. "Sasha! Get back here or your mother's dead!"

Sasha—under Winton's control—froze.

The van with Henry and Nolan was moving, circling around a block up the street. House lights flashed on up and down the street, roused by Rafe's gunshot. Mark felt them all, and the driving gray of the snow, as he flung himself upward.

With no time to plan, he borrowed Rafe's move in arching high to aim for a point straight above his target, above their blind spot. Wind hammered at him, but his leap balanced against it and let him move into place and drop straight down toward Rafe.

Sasha looked up.

Rafe's gaze followed hers and he started to spring clear, but Mark's foot was already lashing out. *Don't smear him over the pavement, the coat's too strong—* Instead he made his kick remove Rafe's weight and loft him away along the street.

The impact flung Mark back, floundering for stabilizing weight and balance before he tumbled down into a crouch ready to dive at Rafe again.

But the thug was spinning away… landing right near Sasha. Toward Winton.

The girl rushed toward Rafe as he flailed to get his balance, and tried to raise his gun. "Sasha" plowed into him, shoving him back. A tide of mind magic poured out that swamped him, left his limbs going limp and still.

"*What* is happening—" screamed Sasha's mother.

Mark glanced over at the woman, just for an instant. When his gaze flicked back, the possessed Sasha was charging at him, and he leaped upward as her pale face swept up and began to drop away below.

Something brushed his foot.

The world went black.

CHAPTER SIXTEEN

GRAVEYARD AND SHIFT

Cold.

Dead, numbing cold was part of his flesh, seeped in deep—

How high did I go?

He lurched backward, but he felt the solid ground and wet snow he lay on, not some freezing upper air. Voices babbled, two or three, distant in the stillness of the narrow alley. No more snow was falling. The worst, stiffest cold lay in his finger.

Just beyond where his hand lay, a drift of snow was piled against the bricks. Moonlight caught letters traced in it:

YOU OWE ME 2

And an arrow slanting away toward somewhere beyond the alley wall. All drawn with his own finger, before Winton set him free.

Chirrup?

Angie stood in the snow beside him… Seeing her there mingled warmth with the cold and the sickening shame of what Winton could have done with his body, *AGAIN—*

Mark staggered up and away from the words, on clumsy feet that needed a lift from the coat—still wrapping its power around him—to keep him from toppling as he fled from the alley and the arrow's direction. Instead murmuring voices drew him up the street.

To the wrecked car.

It was a squat, twisted shape at the curb. Not smashed in from the side or the front, it was the *roof* that had crumpled down, forced down to leave it like some oversized, sealed-over convertible instead of the SUV it had been. Painted in Nolan's gold.

Crushed by magic. Nolan's car, smashed by Winton using Mark's body.

Henry and Nolan would have been in there.

Two dozen swaying steps took *forever*, long enough for his stomach to lurch and settle, for part of him to think that seeing a mere two onlookers meant that even at night this couldn't have been long ago. If those two punks would just get their idiot asses out of his way…

He peered through the flattened remains of the window… *no bodies*. No bodies, and no magic except Angie watching above him. The roof had bent down to jam the doors but not crush the whole car. He sucked in a deep breath that smelled of spilled coolant, but no gasoline or blood.

On the other side, one end of the roof twisted *up*. Where Henry's belt could have forced it open to let him and Nolan crawl out of where Winton had trapped them.

"Is that wreck yours?" one of the kids was saying, eyes wide.

"No." *But it's my fault.*

Mark tottered away. Thoughts swam through his head: Winton had *let* Henry and Nolan live instead of grinding them into the street. And he must have been the one to save Angie when Mark couldn't restore her magic.

"I *owe* him?" he gasped. *And, how much does Angie already owe Winton?*

The voices fell away behind him. He was alone… maybe *all* alone. To think of Henry cowering down and watching "Mark" seal the car in on them…

Henry. "Have to see if, if he's alright," he said, latching onto the words. "And I stop Nolan, or use Sasha to get at Winton, make him save… if I find them…"

Ahead was the alley Winton had left him in, and that damn arrow the killer expected him to follow. Mark scowled at it, and instead leaned against the alley wall and sank to the cold ground.

Screw Winton's message. He had his own way to track them, if he could reach his sense beyond a few blocks. And the coat *crackled* with power.

His eyes closed. Feeling all the energy in the coat was like holding his balance in the heart of a storm… when just a *belt* had already twisted his mind before… but he drew in a slow breath. *I'm not* in *it, I'm balancing* above *the power, and every other magic out there resonates with it.* Somewhere in the city, beyond the restless twitching of Angie beside him, beyond the streets and borders he had accepted as limits.

There were no mind talismans on him, at least.

And, soft as the wind…

Deep between the heartbeats…

Magic pulsed, and he fought to hold that sense as he opened his eyes. Forward and right, southeast.

He lost the sensation as he stood, but the direction was clear. He sprang into the alley, out of people's sight, then soared for the roof and leaped toward his target. The air *welcomed* him; the cleaner cold of the snowless air brushed him as the magic let him ride his leaps, again and again as the belt ahead drew closer.

Only three blocks away he slowed. Blue lights flashed below, as police and ambulances clustered around where Rafe had held Sasha's mother. All Mark had sensed was *Rafe's* belt.

Mark slumped on the roof, and his feet scrabbled a moment before the magic anchored him. "Nice going," he growled.

The lights below hurt his eyes. Sasha's mother was waving the police around, and he could make out a motionless shape on a stretcher, with Rafe's belt pulsing around it.

Except… they carried Rafe with the sheet over his face.

Simple as that. One touch from a possessed Sasha, and…

The mastermind of two gangs, the thief who'd stolen magic out from under Winton's nose, the bully and the tempter Mark had tried to dodge for years…

Rafe. Dead.

The images blurred from his staring—but it was still the same silent, lifeless shape below.

And… and… Winton still had Sasha… and she was long gone, too damn *far* for him to sense Winton's grip or the belt's power on her. Gone, along with his best hope to help Angie, or *stop* whatever the next tragedy was. His fists clenched uselessly.

Angie settled beside him. He turned to her: "Where are they?"

Her only answer was to tilt her head—a quizzical look stretched into an owl's gesture that made his fist pound on the roof.

"I'll find something. I'll help you."

He leaped back up. Every stepping stone in the night was razor-clear in his memory, tracing the way back to the alley where Winton had left his arrow. *An arrow—why is Winton giving me directions?* But its path was already locked into his mental maps before he reached the arrow that should be his starting point.

For an instant he thought of Dennard's car, that he'd left back at the edge of the neighborhood. But the sky was faster. Better.

He picked a tall office building a quarter-mile down that direction to aim at, and dove into the air.

Riding his leap was easy—*too easy, too much magic,* came one prickling thought—and the long aerial path gave him time to be ready for any magic he felt, with Angie flapping along behind him. City layouts shuffled in his head, as he searched for a route ahead through downtown.

Every thought was shaken by the same aching worry: he was following Winton's direction for a chance to save Sasha, or stop Nolan's threats, that had to be all. Not because he "owed" Winton, or because Angie did.

I need Sasha to hunt down Winton, that's all. He kept telling himself that.

* * *

A few stubby inches of arrow was too crude a guide for navigating deep into the city. Mark zigzagged along its direction to stretch his scans for blocks to each side, and the maneuvers helped force his attention back from thoughts of what he might be chasing.

He only dropped to the streets when the air brightened with sunrise and dissolved the upper shadows. The first delivery and maintenance people filtered onto the pavements, and he dodged and sidestepped and ignored the coat's sheer power that would make it so easy to leap over those obstacles or smash through them. *Stay in control.*

Finally, he caught a hint of magic: one of the gravity belts, somewhere on the ground a block ahead. Mark spun up the street and charged toward it.

As he did, he felt a stronger presence beyond it: the other belt, on the far side, and closer to the first belt than to him. Mark stared up the street.

In front of the amber *Bank of Lavine* logo, a figure slumped on a bus-stop bench. Sasha.

What was she, asleep? As Mark closed in, he saw two men walking past her pause and rub their arms—shivering in a cold that struck out of nowhere. Nolan's power had to be gathering. Something wet brushed against his back.

He felt, then saw, Henry and Nolan step around the corner at the end of the block.

His foot hit sudden ice and flew out from under him. Reflex drew on the coat's power that could yank him up—*no, not out here!*—and he had to release what would have been a surge of power and crash down full along the pavement.

Lights flashed in his eyes. He blinked them back and stared through the thickening gray snow. People on the sidewalk were edging away from Sasha's bench, moving gingerly off a wider field of ice that surrounded it—and leaving Sasha isolated for Nolan.

Mark got to his feet. Nolan and Henry were talking with a man in a gray uniform, some guard from the bank, motioning at the still limp Sasha. Nolan must have said the right thing, because the guard let her start toward Sasha again. Mark saw Nolan's hand brush her coat where she might keep a hidden gun.

Mark charged across the distance toward her.

Henry stepped beside Nolan, raising his fists. His lip-curling glare stabbed through Mark, made him halt and scrabble on the ice.

"Guard!" Mark called, trying to face down his cousin. "Watch that woman there, you can't let her—"

Sasha jumped to her feet. "Please, give me a hand!" and she half stepped, half fell across the ice toward Nolan—with Winton's will controlling her again. As she fell her hand flailed out at Nolan.

Nolan dodged back from that destroying touch, and "Sasha" toppled down across the pavement. But as she did she looked over at the ice patch's edge where a young woman was squeezing around it, and her hand reached out to call for her help to stand.

"Um, sure, I got you." The woman shuffled forward, plump legs wobbling on the ice and shooting a reproachful glare to where Nolan and Henry were keeping out of Sasha's reach. Henry's mouth opened for some kind of warning, but Mark knew there was nothing they could say.

One woman's hand reached down to the other's, and the possession jumped. The abandoned Sasha stared up in surprise, and the other woman turned toward Nolan.

"It *is* you! Good to see you again!" and the possessed woman moved toward Nolan, reaching for a handshake.

"Don't you touch me. I don't know you at all." Nolan backpedaled, and a cold wind made the pawn stagger.

Sasha shuffled over the ice away from them, toward the building. Winton's new pawn sidestepped to cut Nolan off from her retreat. "Hey, don't be like that!" She reached out again.

"Pickpocket!" Nolan snapped. "This woman just robbed the other one, I saw it!" She scrambled back a few steps from the "thief" and her grasp—a perfect excuse.

"Miss?" The guard waved Sasha to come back, but she kept retreating with her back against the wall.

"That's not her own wallet on her," Nolan insisted. "It won't match… what's your name? Tell us your name, now!"

Nolan's got Winton trapped—of course he won't know his new pawn's name.

But, Nolan was the one Mark had to stop first.

"Miss, please wait!" the guard called to Sasha again. "She says you've just been *robbed!*"

"She's lying," Mark said, and he gave the guard his steadiest look. "That woman next to you is Olivia Nolan, and she's a murderer. If you check with the police, you'll know about the body they found at her home." He glared at Nolan, and at Winton's pawn; just mentioning the death aloud was his blow against all their coverups.

"Murder?" Winton's pawn squeaked. She jerked away from Nolan, and toppled over on the ice—

and shot Mark one *look,* a snarl of pure contempt as she fell—

against the guard's leg. The woman went limp, and the now-possessed guard reached toward Nolan.

Mark felt the air stirring as he began to leap away. He was in midair, hurtling after Sasha, when Nolan's gale slammed across the street and the gray air dimmed. Wet snow and eye-stinging wind ripped his view apart. Mark struggled along the wall, moving less by sight than by the memory of the buildings, and the presence of Sasha's stolen belt, heading for where the wall's corner must have been.

And he was leaving Henry behind *again.* But he was already closing on Sasha, on the one hint of striking at the real Winton.

He dove around the bank's corner. Outside the worst of the wind, he could see Sasha, pleading with two young men in suits that were unlocking the bank's side door.

She was saying "—no I *can't* wait for you to open. Can't you check—they're instructions about Sasha Lawrence, from Roger Winton?"

Instructions from Winton? Mark kept his face still, completely still.

The junior banker looked at her a moment. "We'll be open in another—"

"Please! Just check."

"I suppose we can't stand out in *this.*" He waved at the blizzard, then swung the door open.

Mark fell in behind Sasha, with two smooth, easy steps. The two bankers glared at him, until Sasha beckoned and waved him in with her.

The space inside was laid out more like an office building than a bank, but the polished floors and rich dark wood still made Mark look around for teller cages. Those were probably off by the front door, he thought. The pool of warmth and quiet after the chase had him sagging on his feet.

One banker gave Mark a cold look, maybe for the flight-stained coat dripping on the floor.

"If you'll wait here?" he said to them both. "This shouldn't take me long."

The bankers walked away. Mark saw one's head nod and signal a guard down the hallway to turn and watch them.

At least that guard hadn't heard an alarm from the excitement out front... Mark could feel Winton's control moving around outside, and Henry's belt drawing away from it. The windows rattled in Nolan's storm; Angie soared high up at a safe distance from anything she might have been flung onto.

Sasha smiled at him. "Thank you, for helping me out there. I guess I owe you a few more."

"Listen to me…" Mark leaned closer. "You need to ditch that talisman. The bit of silver you took from me, it's how—"

Winton's magic twitched in her. Mark jerked backward, but Winton only flicked Sasha's eyes around the room, a single, practiced glance. Then he was gone.

"Mark? What is it?" Sasha's usual worried look was back, and she looked around behind herself. The guard was still watching them.

Winton's gone again for now. I've got one chance. Mark took a slow breath, and stepped toward her again… too close, too hard to dodge, when he knew one touch of hers could put Winton in his head again.

"Please," he said softly. "Right this minute, drop that thing you took from the bird. Sasha, it *lets Winton take control of you.* You know *something's* happening to you, don't you—all the seconds you've blacked out since you picked it up? Trust me, get rid of it while you can!"

Sasha's eyes were wide. She said "You mean… but… every time I wake up, I'm out of danger. So he's the one protecting me?"

"Protecting—"

The outraged word rang off the walls, and Mark clamped his mouth shut. What was wrong with her—what was wrong with *him,* why couldn't he think—

A middle-aged man in a banker's suit was walking toward them. Mark forced his face to stillness again, and felt for the magic outside. Henry was a block away, he must not know Winton had abandoned his pawn to watch over Sasha again.

I'm using too much magic. But nobody here knows who the threats are, and still I have to hold myself back?

The banker gave them a guarded smile, one that crinkled his face but didn't reach his eyes. "Miss Lawrence? I'm afraid there's some kind of misunderstanding. We have no 'instructions' here about you."

"But… you have to!" She took a quick step toward him, hands reaching out—

Mark kept from flinching; that was an innocent gesture now that Winton wasn't controlling her.

She was saying "Mr. Winton said he'd arranged something for me. He said he didn't want it in his will, it was supposed to be just between us. And you."

"Miss, if this were connected to Mr. Winton's will, you should speak to his attorney—if he were confirmed deceased, at least. Whether we have had contact with him or not is beside the point."

"You mean… if he *disappears* but you don't know he's dead, you can't tell me if he set this up at all? That can't be how he wanted this to work!"

"I'm sorry, Miss Lawrence. I'm afraid there's nothing I can do." He walked slowly away.

Sasha spun back to Mark. "Do you think that's it? It's because he's in hiding?"

"Sasha…" Mark forced out a slow breath, fighting the urge to *make* her listen. "You don't know anything about this. You've seen what Nolan and Rafe can do… but Roger Winton is *worse* than any of them. He lied to me for years—he started a gang war—he would have killed Angie—she would have died again tonight if someone hadn't saved her when we were in that trance…"

"That wasn't me. If you're talking about the owl again."

"She's not an—" He swallowed, and forced down the thought, *So that* was *Winton who saved her?* But the words wouldn't slow down: "She's only an owl because she survived Winton's attack; I've been trying to save her for months! And you… you know he's been possessing you. Well, he did that with his own son, and never let go! And yesterday he couldn't even walk—"

"You *saw* him?"

"I mean, he needs a new body, a permanent one, maybe that's what this is all about—"

"You're crazy!" Sasha stabbed a finger at him, and he flailed backward to keep out of her reach. Her voice rose: "What's wrong with you? He's always been good to me—and he's *not* my father or my brother or whatever you think…"

She broke off. The banker was moving toward them again, and when their argument stilled he closed the distance with careful steps.

"Ahem. My apologies, Miss: we just received an email from Mr. Winton. His request is that…"

And he crooked a discreet finger to motion Sasha toward him.

She leaned in to listen. Mark stepped closer—and the banker stopped and turned a warning glare on him.

Mark had to pull back and let them whisper. *It's the magic, using all this power has me too revved up to slow my mouth down. But can't she see what Winton is? He contacted them just now to draw her in?*

Then Sasha yelped *"Graveyard?"*

The word didn't echo, but the banker gave her a pained look. "That was the whole of the arrangement, Miss. And that it was time to give you this."

He held out a brass key longer than his hand. Sasha snatched it.

"What about a graveyard?" The words poured out of Mark, even as he saw her frown tightening. "Sasha, please! Let me see if any of this is safe for you—"

"Just stop!" Sasha pulled back a step, back behind the banker. "You said Mr. Winton was too hurt to walk?"

And that's *what she remembers?* Mark felt another flood of protest rising in his throat, and all he could think was to lock his mouth shut.

Sasha's voice was cold, only a slight quaver as she looked at him. "Look, I'm going. Maybe I can help him. And don't worry, if he can help your friend with her… bird problem, I'll ask him to. But he wants this for me."

She turned to the banker.

"Can you show my 'friend' out? And find me a different way to leave?"

Mark held himself motionless, as she backed away, and the power he wore buzzed with the energy that could *make* her stop…

But the belt in her pocket still resonated, clear as any beacon to his coat's power. Sasha might be a trusting fool about Winton's schemes—and his body-snatching history—but she knew even less about what else she was carrying. Why fight through any more words when she'd lead him to the killer's work anyway?

He marched to the door they'd entered, with the guard closing in behind him. Sasha's stolen belt began moving deeper into the building, and he felt Henry's belt at what might be the next block over.

He stepped outside, and let Nolan's wild weather fling the door closed behind him.

Nolan, and Henry. They'd caught up with Sasha once, and Henry could still track her for whatever Nolan had planned. Mark trotted for the corner; he just had to reach Henry before Sasha was out of his own range, grab his belt to blind him…

The fierce thoughts made him slow, stumbling. *This is* Henry, *I just need to get him away from Nolan! Don't let the magic beat me!*

He felt Henry moving toward the corner to meet him, tracking him too. But when he turned it, he saw his cousin alone—no, Nolan stood apart in a small crowd around a car that had skidded onto the sidewalk. The figure in black facing her was a cop.

Henry walked hesitantly toward Mark. *He's* here, *away from Nolan. Finally some real luck!* Mark held a finger to his lips and moved closer.

Sasha was still in the bank; he had time. But, why wasn't that cop already arresting Nolan?

He looked at Henry, and the worry on his cousin's face anchored him against the magic's push to *move.*

"Henry, I'm sorry! Trapping you in Nolan's car—you know that wasn't me! Winton got me again."

Henry shot a glance around the street, at Nolan's group and the other people scattered around the street. He answered with low words, and Mark had to edge closer to hear.

"You could have killed us both, and you didn't. And you weren't possessed."

"I said that was Winton! When I woke up he said I owed him." *Like that'll save him if we catch him.*

Henry took a step nearer, hands rising up like he needed to fend him off. "No, Mark. I said you *weren't* possessed. I didn't sense any of his power in you when you attacked."

"What??" Mark heard the shout cut through the wind, and forced his voice down again. "That can't be true, you can't believe it... No, you *don't* believe it, or you wouldn't be here alone."

"I don't know what I believe."

Henry looked back again, at Nolan. She was gesturing at the cop, and the cop turned away.

"So, he *is* letting her go," Henry said. "What did you say to the bank guard before? There were murder charges against her?"

Up the street, Nolan looked straight at Henry and Mark. Mark braced for the attack... but she held her place. *She knows she's losing.*

Keeping his eyes on her, Mark said "Murder. Henry, we found Irene's body—frozen, by Nolan's magic. Call Dennard, you'll see—Wait, she took his phone—"

Sasha moved. Mark realized that all this time her power had been moving in cramped, indoor-scale turns, but now she broke into a quick, straight walk that had to be outside the bank and away up the street.

"Sasha's getting away!" he said. "She's going off to Winton's... something."

Henry frowned. "So you aren't defending Winton? You're doing all this to protect Sasha from Nolan?"

"Yes! And we need her, if she gets to Winton it's our chance to catch him. And his magic." He glanced up to where Angie was circling above the worst of the winds.

"You do… sound like yourself." Henry's eyes narrowed, and his voice grew gentler. "But, think about it, Mark. You're talking like you did months ago. When the magic was pushing you."

"I *know,* I know! I'm holding on, the coat's got too much power—"

Of course!

"That's why you didn't sense Winton controlling me! Our magic always feels stronger than his to us, so I bet my wearing all this power drowned out his touch, and you missed it! I told you it wasn't me!"

"That… could be right," Henry said. "So, you say I have to leave Nolan, and we follow Sasha so we can save her and Angie too? Because you're still you under that coat again? Prove it."

He held out his hand.

Mark slid the leather back from his shoulders. It felt more like putting something *on,* like adding layers of weights and grinding pain over his flesh. His fingers tightened on the power.

But Henry was *looking* at him, the same pained, disappointed look he'd used in the days after Mark had lost himself in the magic.

Sasha was gone. Out of range, and moving further every second.

"Mark?"

"I said it's still me!" He wrenched the leather off and tossed it to Henry in one motion—the thrill of power vanished and his bruises flared and doubled him over. He dragged in a breath, swaying against the wind.

Henry clutched the coat, eyes wide. "Now, what do you want next? We let Sasha go to Winton, and just the two of us catch him and finish this?"

"We… can beat him." Mark hauled himself upright. "Now that you know it's me. You and me—I know we can win this."

He reached out his hand, to take the power back.

Henry's fingers locked around his wrist. A flood of weight slammed him down, knees crashing onto pavement, bruises and aches flaring, burning, tearing, wracking through all the injuries he'd taken and the sheer helpless horror... Then the pressure passed.

All Mark could think was to force his head up. "Win... ton..."

"No, Mark," Henry said—it *did* sound like Henry. "This is what we need right now. You ought to know you're in no condition to fight. And Nolan's the only one left who has a chance to beat him."

He pulled on the coat, and Mark heard him gasp when all its energy slid around him.

Beyond Henry, Nolan was breaking into a run toward them. Henry turned and moved toward her, with his arms spread in warning. *Holding her off from me.*

Mark's vision blurred in pain. When he blinked it clear again, Henry and Nolan were jogging away after Sasha.

With his bad back, Henry shouldn't jog at all, but I showed the bastard how to float... Mark sucked in rage with the icy air. His muscles were empty, wrung out and battered and he couldn't even sense the goal so far beyond his reach. Snow, or his sight, dimmed the street.

They must be out there.

He dragged himself upward. Sasha needed him, Henry did, Angie did... The thoughts beat at him even without the magic. He stood, toppled forward, and staggered toward where Sasha had been.

"Save Sasha, before Winton takes her over..."

Something gray moved in the snow above; did Angie hear him? He wove forward, one foot after the next, faster. This was Winton's trail, this was the secret to saving Angie—no matter what Winton said about "owing" or how Sasha promised to persuade the killer. *This is Angie's chance.*

Walk, walk... He stumbled past people hunched in the cold, and knew he should be shivering too. *Graveyard*—Sasha's word from the bank echoed, and one piece of the maps in his head formed. Memory Grove, south, the same way Sasha had been going... the closest graveyard, but how far?

Glass storefronts wove in and out of the white. Olivia Nolan and her snowy smokescreens… but she'd murdered Irene, unleashed Rafe, been ready to shoot Mark to take Winton down with him… *And I really thought* she'd *share the magic with Angie, or let us live once she got it?*

Cars trundled across his path, forcing him to stop at the corner. He stared up at the sky; whirls of gray tore sight apart above the upper stories. Nolan and Henry as a team could float and ride a wind through that and home in on Sasha, all quick and camouflaged and inescapable…

The traffic cleared and he pushed himself to a trot. At least Nolan would save Sasha from Winton claiming her body. Let Winton offer all the "deals" he wanted…

A memory stirred: Winton in his last bird struggling to reach Sasha and her mother, staying in there to within an instant of being caught in the bird's death. Would he risk himself that far for someone who was just a tool?

"Excuses. He'll take Sasha over if he wants… or else Nolan will keep Angie's cure…" Or Winton just might keep Sasha's promise about it.

Through the whiteness far ahead, a patch of darkness dropped toward the street. He pushed on, twisting and teetering over snowy pavement.

A shape moved across on the sidewalk—pushing through the wind ahead—Sasha took shape out of the blizzard. She halted and stared at him.

Nolan and Henry will catch her soon, Nolan will end Angie's hope and everything…

The message formed on its own, deep in his frozen chest to rip its way up his throat and tip his world on its side with the choice: "They're tracking that belt you took!"

Sasha's eyes locked on him for one moment. Then she jabbed a hand in her pocket and sent a rolled-up shape flying over the cars and across the street, lost behind the snow and the crowd. The next moment she dodged past a knot of people and into a store.

Mark staggered after her. His side banged the man in the doorway, he tried to twist through, head spinning.

Long racks full of shirts stretched out before him. Shoppers, aisles, space going on and on to lead to hiding places and other exits... She could be anywhere among them.

And I told her how to get past Nolan and Henry. If she gets to Winton, if he takes her over...

Let *him. At least if those two owe me anything they've got more chance of helping Angie than Nolan does.*

He stepped back onto the street with that harsh thought in his head, and the cold air felt almost natural in his lungs.

—No, that feeling was wrong, and wasn't there something feeding his rage, some twisting worse than any of Winton's influences, something left behind by the power he'd been using...

Instead he moved across the street to search for the discarded belt.

He found nothing.

The memory was as clear as the frozen pavement under his feet, how the belt—the original Fletcher belt—had sailed across to the far sidewalk, but now he found nothing. It could simply have fallen behind something, landed in some corner... still, if he bent down now to search for it, he'd never get up again.

Sasha.

The graveyard. Memory Grove was the only graveyard near.

He ran down one block... Sasha could be heading there or it could be anywhere...

Think of Winton. Think of what I could be letting him do.

I have to *make it there.*

Another block. Another, and his feet grew numb. The walls of the buildings around him shrunk, dwindled down, as the street grew more and more still...

Finally, a wide gate loomed ahead. He panted on through it, and paused at a tiny hut just inside it. A warm light shone through the window. Mark stared through the frosted glass. One figure, a man, sat inside holed up against the storm. No sign of Sasha in there.

He started up the winding road leading in. Even under his numb feet, the sound told him it was rough dirt under the snow.

After the city walls, the open hills and shifting gray teased his sight. He'd come all this way on one word and the direction Sasha had fled in… Because something was *driving* him, some reason why he couldn't grow still, he should remember what it was… it pushed him even after he'd lost the coat's power…

Gray and white stones shifted in his view as he moved. Scattered trees lashed in the wind. On and on, he watched the trees and the larger monuments where some figure might be hiding behind them.

Footprints dented the whiteness leading toward the surrounding wall. The trail was faint, with fresh snow already swallowing it, but it had to be her, it *had* to.

Can I drag her away from Winton, or is this where he moves completely into Sasha's body and I see about those deals he offered me? Did I just save Angie by dooming Sasha?

The trail wound through the snowfall. His feet slipped, used to good smooth roads and now catching on dents and roots lurking under the snow.

One shape ahead was larger than any other he'd seen here: a mausoleum of gray stone, a simple block that might be large enough for one or two people inside to stand over a coffin. Its door hung open.

Shreee!

The owl's call yanked his gaze upward. Up in the snowy air, a faint shape slid through the swirls… and he saw the missing Fletcher belt dangling from Angie's grip.

She flew past him, well out of his reach.

The thought hit just as he heard the shout in the sky: *she didn't bring the magic for me, but it could lead the others here.*

Up in the gray heart of the sky, two shapes sank down toward him—Henry floating Nolan down through her storm. Mark could only stagger away, toward the stone shape ahead, thinking *I gave Winton his chance at Sasha, I bet everything on that leading to the cure, but Angie won't allow it.*

Her shriek could have been a curse, at him.

He turned to face the two spellkeepers as they touched down. When Henry let go of Nolan's arm and stepped clear, Mark looked straight at him:

"Alright, I'm here, Henry. Just… please, don't turn your back on Nolan!"

"Oh, can't I?" Henry's voice had a harsh edge Mark had never heard. The coat—the damn overpowered coat!—hung loose on him like it could swallow him up.

Mark looked at him, at Nolan silent beside him. *I need to step aside.* Angie *wants me to let them by and I can't even stand straight…*

A soft, sad voice came behind him. "Mr. Winton wasn't here."

Sasha stepped out of the open mausoleum, her eyes on the ground, her hands hugging her sweater.

"Sasha?" Nolan took a slow step toward her, and she used her gentlest voice. "Sasha, we have to know you're still yourself."

"It's me. This place is… where my aunt's buried. And Mr. Winton never told us. He never told me anything."

Mark could hear the pain in her voice. "I'm sorry," he said "I am."

She moved toward Nolan. "Please, can you just let me go—"

A roar of wind blasted across the field. Sasha flailed to stay on her feet, but a second blast against her other side spilled her to the ground.

"Winton's abandoned you?" Nolan raised her hand, and the air tightened with cold. "I risked my life, my reputation, everything I built, and there's still magic out there that can *control me?* Did you ever think how we could all use that power to start new lives, if you hadn't let it slip through your stupid fingers? Or how about, we could see if Winton's still ready to come save you again."

She stretched her hand forward. The cold deepened, and Mark saw Sasha's frozen breaths thinning and her body growing still.

Mark started toward Nolan. "Stop it! How many people do you have to kill?"

Henry's voice was louder. "Let her go!" He scrambled forward and threw himself across where Sasha lay.

Mark turned back to Nolan. The glacial look in her eyes made his teeth chatter, and she was still four whole steps beyond his reach.

Somewhere down across the field, a voice shouted "What is going on here?"

Two shapes moved out of the snow. The man in front looked like the chubby face Mark had seen in the entrance building. The smaller figure behind him—dark uniform and dark face stark within the white air—was a cop.

Something moved in the air above the two men. As if Angie had led them here too.

"Is one of them Winton?" Nolan snapped, as they closed in.

Henry gave a lopsided smile. "They *might* be."

"Might?" Nolan whirled on him.

"Figure it out. I'm not helping you." He turned back to Sasha, where she lay crumpled on the ground.

Mark held his place between Nolan and her victim; it saved him from having to move. Henry took Sasha's hand, and Mark saw a fierce shudder wrack through him.

"What happened to her? She alright?" The groundskeeper was right behind them now, and the cop with him.

Henry staggered up from Sasha, and moved out to meet the two authorities.

"She has to be." Mark managed to hold his voice steady, even with his lungs gasping for air. "This woman over here is a known murderer—"

Henry stumbled, and toppled forward, and fell against the groundskeeper. The plump man *spasmed* as if he'd brushed an electric line, until he sprang backward—

And bumped into the cop. In the next instant the cop jolted, and the groundskeeper slumped to the snow. Henry lay just as still. Both had been possessed, and abandoned with magical sleep, to leave only that last man standing and controlled.

Nolan's voice was smug. "I *knew* you'd picked up something, Sasha. Unless that's Winton to the rescue again."

"This time it's me." The cop's voice was male, but the tremor in it was pure Sasha. A possessed hand waved at the sleeping groundskeeper. "Doing that wasn't so hard. And now there's nobody to see us, just like it said to do."

" 'It' said?" Nolan's tight smile stretched wider. She turned to toward Sasha's body—the body that hadn't moved since Henry had touched it, when she'd shifted to seize control of him. Nolan added "So he left a talisman in there for you?"

"You're going to leave Mr. Winton alone. I'll show him. I'll make you!"

She, the cop, reached a hand down for the cop's gun.

Nolan dropped for the ground. Mark dove to get clear of her... and felt the air *tighten*.

The air pressure slammed down, the wind screamed and tore around them. Snow sprayed up from the ground, and all across the field, winter-darkened air spun in wild circles around them as more snow funneled in from the sky. With every heartbeat the hazy ground of the cemetery faded deeper into frenzied white—all battling with the sharp booms of Sasha's gunfire.

Mark crawled, twisting into a thicket of low headstones, away from where Nolan had been. Bullets cracked against stone, sounding all too close, clear even in the maelstrom.

He opened his mouth to shout, then shut it again; Nolan wouldn't back down, and Sasha couldn't let up. Instead he forced himself forward, hoping he could work his way around and pull Henry to safety with the coat he was wearing. Anything to keep from rooting through the snow like a helpless, grounded animal.

The gunshots stopped. Mark rose to his hands and knees… and the air went still.

Between one breath and the next the winds halted, and the churning snow was simply waves of powder settling to ground, *easy* to see through. Another gun fired—a higher-pitched blast, two controlled shots and then a third cutting through that moment of exposure.

As Mark flattened, the wind shrieked to life again.

Nolan doesn't just peep out from cover, she clears all the cover to shoot and then raises it again. Mark scrambled forward, to a gnarled tree-shape in the white ahead.

As he neared it, a second outline broke from behind the trunk and thrust a hand toward him.

Mark flung himself back from the "cop's" possessing touch. "Sasha! It's me—"

The air stilled again.

Mark gasped out "Down!" and flung himself flat before the bullets came. But the sound of *two* guns tore through the air, Nolan's quick shots and a frantic barrage from Sasha that drew back up the slope and continued shooting even while the storm sprang up again.

"If that body's hit you could die with it!" Mark called. Her flashes of light only kept blasting, from further and further away in the gray.

Useless! Mark pushed himself into a crouching run. *Why can't these hills be straight city blocks that let me find my way back to Henry?* He swerved around a motionless squirrel in the snow, twisted clear of a row of headstones.

A figure stretched out ahead. Mark dashed for it, even as he saw it crawling—

That man should still be asleep—

The groundskeeper spun around and his thrust a hand at him. Mark stumbled backward, feeling a scream of helplessness gathering in his chest and about to rise. *Not another one!*

His heel touched something soft. Not a stone.

Mark twisted down and caught at his cousin. His arms closed around the coat.

A roar of joy tore loose as he clutched the power tight and flung them both upward, away from the puppet's grasp and high, arching high and cutting through the storm and letting the gunshots boom away behind him. He arched down again, a hundred feet away—a tree loomed out of the snow below, and he shifted weight in an instant to stop their fall and let the wind blow them clear of the branches as they came down. So effortless.

Henry's breathing was fine, Mark felt that as he laid him down and stripped off the coat. Through the leather in his fingers he sensed Henry's belt beside him, and Angie with the other belt high in the sky... and two flickers of possession magic. So somehow Winton had gotten his own hooks into the groundskeeper, while Sasha held the cop...

And of course the immediate enemy, Nolan, had the one magic he couldn't zero in on. Mark gripped the coat and leaped for a blocky shape in the snow that could be the mausoleum; Sasha's body should be near.

In midair, he heard "Cease firing! Police!" somewhere in the distance. Then he slid through the thick of the storm and came down on the stone slab.

Sasha's body lay below. Nolan was rushing toward it, slowing and leveling her gun at it.

In the slow, trapped instant that Nolan aimed, Mark tossed the coat in his hands toward her.

It flew past her like a sprawling shadow, and the motion brought her gaze up and a barrage of bullets into the leather. Mark jumped for the ground—his body heavy and frail again—to sprawl across it, struggling to roll with Sasha toward some kind of shelter. Nolan aimed straight for him.

The gun clicked empty.

"Police, I said! Identify yourselves!" The voices sounded from out through the snow, but they had to be closing in fast.

Nolan bent down over Sasha. She yanked Sasha's sweater up from her stomach—just the spot Sasha's hands had tried to cover when she'd walked out of the mausoleum—and pulled out a small square shape. A book.

"So 'it' showed her how to use it. The girl just had to brag." Nolan held the leather-bound object up, with a fierce grin.

The next moment, Angie's shriek sounded just above them. Mark looked up… and saw the belt dropping toward him.

He braced for some howl of wind that would knock it aside, but instead the long black shape fell perfectly into his hand. Magic ready, he spun back toward Nolan.

She was bending over the fallen coat.

Mark leaped at her.

The wave of air caught him as he flew, the wake of the lifting power that blasted her upward out of his reach. He skidded and tumbled to the ground, and felt her stolen power rocketing away. Gone.

And around him… Mark sensed Henry's magic approaching, and Angie balancing on the winds above. And the magic that was Sasha's grip, and Winton's too, where the cop and the groundskeeper ran through the snow.

"That book? What was in it?" Mark asked cop-Sasha.

"Magic. Taking people over. It looked like it had everything about it." The cop's smooth black features twisted with Sasha's shame.

All of it? The ways to give Angie a body? Mark's eyes squeezed shut.

"You *lost* it?" Winton burst out.

Sasha looked up, stared at the groundskeeper's face and then stared harder. "That's *you?* Oh God... I... wanted to stop her for you..." Her stolen voice shriveled and died away in the wind.

Mark glanced back and forth between them. His first, most deadly enemy was *right there,* but inside the groundskeeper's body as his hostage... and Winton had saved Angie once, *but he made me kill—*

"All of you, raise your hands—Chuck? You okay?"

Two uniformed cops rushed up, with a third behind them. Their gazes and guns took in Mark, the unconscious Sasha, and the two possessed men. As they did, Winton's groundskeeper wobbled on his feet, and toppled over—asleep and abandoned.

One cop went to help him. Another went to where Sasha lay.

The third kept his gun on Mark, but stared at Sasha's pawn, the cop. "Chuck?"

"Don't shoot! It wasn't us—she got away!" The possessed hand waved outward, upward, vaguely in Nolan's direction.

"Chuck? What's with your voice?"

"I... I think I need..." Cop-Sasha glanced at the body Winton had left. Then she clutched at "her" head, and sank to the ground herself.

Mark sighed, left facing the police alone. His head spun, the belt pulsed in his hand so ready to lift him away...

He focused on Henry closing in, and Angie watching, to steady him. One slow word at a time, he said "Like he said, she got away. She was... she was breaking into the tomb here."

"Yeah? So what's broken? Looks like it was unlocked."

The cop stepped inside.

Mark edged up behind him. As he did, he felt Henry stumbling up and settling into place at his side.

Blinking into the dimness showed a long shape at the chamber's end that must be a coffin. Sasha's aunt, she'd said. And Sasha had been given the key. Nothing looked damaged—except Winton had hidden that book there for Sasha.

Everything Angie needed, maybe, and Nolan had it now. And she had all the gravity power in the coat too. *Because I trusted her.*

Angie shrieked a warning.

Mark turned, as one of the uniformed figures lurched into the narrow entrance. The cop's arms reached out at them.

…

When they woke, Sasha was gone.

*****

Mark's adventures continue in:

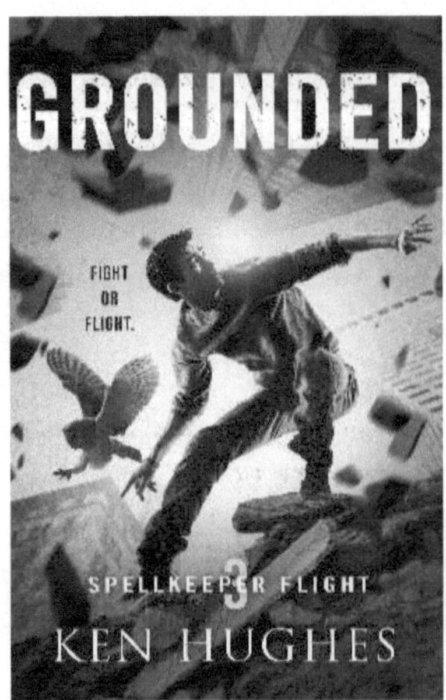

Grounded

from GROUNDED

Dammit, Angie! None of this is helping you!

Mark Petrie took another glance back up the police station corridor, but with all the cops moving about he couldn't even see the door they'd taken Olivia Nolan and her lawyers through.

He reached out with the magic in his belt again to search for her power. The weather energy Nolan carried was a primal force his gravity power could barely feel at the best of times… and using any more magic now stretched his frayed nerves and made the dull, shifting roar of the police station's constant crowd beat against his head. At least he could sense Henry's own gravity belt up in the room they'd taken him to.

"We should be done with him soon."

Mark snapped his head forward again. Was that *satisfaction* in the rail-thin detective's voice, about how shaken Mark's cousin clearly was, and how much he might let slip? *We can't even let them guess what's got us wired, the effects of our magic.*

One hint would bring Winton down on them all.

The cop was still blocking the corridor they'd taken Henry, and he swept his gaze between the remaining three of them. "Tell me again. It was Olivia Nolan who kidnapped you two," and he looked at Angie's father Joe Dennard, and Henry's girlfriend Christa, "and murdered

this deep-freeze corpse you found. That's your story about yesterday—

"And then this morning she chased *you,*" he looked at Mark, "and
Henry Maes through the blizzard, and broke into a mausoleum? And
that place's next of kin, Sasha Lawrence, can't be found. And yet,
none of it's got a connection to the gang bloodbath this week at Henry
Maes's house, that we already had *you* in for," and he glared right at
Dennard, "and you still say Henry wasn't even there when that happened—"

He broke into another round of his spluttering coughs, but Mark
thought he saw those eyes watching Christa. Henry's prim corporate
girlfriend had had a brittle kind of stillness around her ever since she'd
been dragged into their struggle, and she'd still only had a glimpse of
what they and now Henry had faced.

"And he wasn't." Dennard's steady, ex-cop confidence broke the
detective's insinuations apart.

—*But it's a lie,* Mark thought, *and even that was because we
couldn't risk being in custody and at Winton's mercy. And yet now
here we are with the police again.* What was keeping their lawyer,
Todd Gilbert?

Dennard went on "You've heard all our separate statements, except
you're dragging out Henry's. But Irene is still dead, Sasha is missing,
and I woke up in Ms. Nolan's garage in handcuffs."

He held up his wrist to show the bruises around it. The motion was
so quick Mark wondered how many times he'd done it today—
Dennard had always been the one hoping that this once the police
could lock up one of their enemies without getting too near the truth.

Did Nolan still have Sasha's book on her? Had she caught up with
Sasha again, before the police brought her in?

The detective snuffled once, then glared back at them. "But that
other time… you keep saying the gang came to Henry Maes's house,"
and he hooked a thumb back up the corridor where they had Henry,
"and the person they found there wasn't him, and wasn't his cousin—

" he looked at Mark— "it was the cousin's friend—" and he turned to Dennard— "And now it's Mark Petrie's boss Nolan who's kidnapped Petrie's— friend—" Dennard again— "and his cousin's girlfriend—" to Christa. Then his eyes locked on hers and he snapped "So, which of these cousins dragged you into this tangle—your Henry, or Mark?"

Christa didn't move, pinned by the detective's gaze. How had she kept quiet so long, just to protect someone she thought she'd known? For one instant Mark felt nothing but the cold fan humming away above them, loud in a sudden pocket of quiet after the cop's question.

Then Christa said, "Olivia Nolan drugged the two of us, and your tests will prove it. Along with the *dead body,* Irene." He voice wavered only on the last words.

But the detective's eyes were looking past her now, right on Mark, probably seeing how the nineteen-year-old kid in the weather-battered clothes must be the one that connected them all. *What was Henry telling them? How can he keep* anything *in after he saw the magic get me so crazy he had to side with Nolan against me, at least until he saw how deadly she could be? And now he has to keep his story straight in an interrogation twice as long as I got through...*

The chatter of voices around the police station pressed at Mark worse than the walls, all those people ready to throw Henry in the madhouse if he had said one word about magic. Henry didn't even have much magic left; he'd already swapped his belt for Mark's nearly drained one. But just one flex of the power Mark wore now could float himself upward and leave all the lies behind...

"Can you just let me see him?" Christa asked, and her voice wavered again.

"When we're done. These things can take... as long as they take," and the detective gave the tiniest smile. A bluff, it had to be.

"So you're stalling until the blood tests come back, and seeing if we change our statements," and Dennard chuckled. "When they do, you'll see Christa and I were drugged. Probably Irene too, before Nolan had her frozen."

"With what?" The cop coughed again, and that rasp added to his voice's contempt when he went on "An industrial freezer in her back pocket?"

"After all the deep cold snaps we've had?" Dennard shot back. "How is that a mystery?"

Except, it was Nolan's weather magic at the heart of these crazy months, that and Winton's possession and flying talismans like Mark's.

Just one push upward, to float him up against that damn fan's downdraft—

Mark could hear the regret in Dennard's voice, wanting to come clean with the police force he'd served with long ago. *But I'm the one who restarted the lies, just like I left Henry with Nolan, when she killed Irene, now maybe killed Sasha... I trusted her, just like I trusted Winton—*

And got Angie trapped—

He drew in a slow, steadying breath. One moment of magic could prove it all, but then they'd lose control of the hunt for Winton. He drew on the belt's power again, feeling for any other magic it would resonate with.

Angie was there. He caught no trace of Nolan's power brewing up some escape, but he could feel the solid gravity magic with Henry off in his own room, and the rough-edged flicker of the energy that let Angie hold onto her flesh. His sense placed her far above the building, just where a watchful owl could wing by.

Her presence centered him, better than floating in the sky himself. Mark turned to the detective again and let the frustrated tightness slip from his jaw, his eyes, his fingers. *I'll fight for Henry, for Dennard, but* nothing *will make me say one word that could take us away from the hunt for Winton. And for the magic to help Angie.*

The detective was studying Christa again. "Look, your boyfriend's been asking to see you. But he can't remember why you were both at

Ms. Nolan's home—what, some all-night brainstorming about her business?"

"Yes," Christa nodded.

Dennard added "We told you—"

"You *did,*" and the cop stabbed a finger right toward Christa. "Henry needs a doctor soon, but even he didn't pretend he'd drag you out to see his cousin's boss to talk marketing plans."

"What doctor? Is Henry—" Christa began. Mark opened his mouth to break in, saw Dennard move to step between her and the cop—

A buzz swept through the corridor. A whisper of voices, low but everywhere, and a ripple of movement as heads turned toward the space behind Mark.

Nolan was walking out.

Mark only caught a glimpse of the small, squat woman surrounded by the three sharp-suited lawyers. But none of the police pressed close enough to be keeping her in custody, and she wore no handcuffs.

A shocked gasp came from Christa behind him. Some other voice slipped above the corridor's murmur with "Is that the one—" and broke off.

Nolan paused at the far end of the wide area, talking to one of the police. She didn't look at Mark or her other victims, across the open space and the currents of startled cops and staff and visitors and all, but she didn't flinch away either. Instead Mark saw her motion one of her lawyers back, and he drew a step further from her, keeping the ring around her spread wide even as she kept talking with the cop.

What was she doing? Mark stared at her; Nolan never hesitated, but was there something... uncertain about the way she looked between the officer and her lawyers? Or her assistant at her side, Zeke Brent?

One grim-faced cop turned from her group and strode across to Mark's side of the area. He stepped past them, whispered in the coughing detective's ear, and then moved on beyond them toward where Henry was.

Christa tried to slip in behind him, but she only moved a few steps before their detective moved to block her.

"So you're letting Nolan out?" Dennard said. "What about the evidence?"

The detective laughed coldly. "The toc screens came back. You two weren't drugged, you were drunk."

"We were *not!*" Christa's voice rose.

"Drunk, the lab says. And the prelims say the dead girl may have stumbled out in the snow—" He coughed again. "Exposure can do worse. The files show other cases like it, natural enough."

A human popsicle, just from a crazy winter in Lavine? Mark thought, as he felt his feet moving to edge him clear of Dennard and Christa's sides, his eyes back on Nolan—as if his body already expected to have to leap across the room to stop some counterattack of hers at any moment.

She still didn't look at her accusers. Mark felt for her magic, and for a touch of Angie's presence outside…

Off there! Just for an instant Mark felt it, not the soft power that might be Nolan's magic but a fleeting familiar *twitch* off to the side like an eye peeking out. Which was what it had to be.

"So I imagined this?" Dennard was growling, waving his bruised wrists again.

"Those tiny marks, are those toy cuffs? Sounds more like you want to blame your host for the party you had."

"Party? What are you implying?" came Christa's outraged voice.

But all those sounds were back behind Mark, pushed away by the strain of keeping his face calm, his focus on the magic he should have been watching for every second. He felt the presence spark and vanish again, gone too fast for even its victim to feel Winton peeping through his eyes.

Like he did with me, when he planted one of his talismans on me. Like when he used me to kill.

Mark kept his face toward Nolan, as if he'd never sensed the killer's will lurking somewhere among the hundreds of unsuspecting cops. Another flicker came, and from the corner of his eyes he tried to pick out the face that matched it—

For one moment he thought he could see Winton's own eyes watching him, before the presence hid again behind the uneasy face of Osborn, the same ME who'd examined… Angie's body…

Think! Mark tore his eyes back to Nolan, before the red rage filled his vision. The tests and the evidence against Nolan… Winton had controlled Osborn before, he could have used him and other tools like him to cover the truth up again…

He's protecting Nolan? *After she chased Sasha all over town?* But Mark felt himself breathe again; Winton must be covering for Nolan just to keep attention away from any hint of magic, same as ever. He'd killed police to keep the secret, once.

"Is that—Christa?"

Henry's voice was hoarse, but still steady, and Mark saw Christa dash up the corridor to meet him and give him her shoulder to lean on. Henry was fine, of course he'd faced the police down and stuck with their story after all.

"You, you're letting her *go?!*" Henry stared straight across at Nolan, and his voice rang off the ceiling. "Where's Sasha?"

Nolan never turned away from her lawyers. But at her side, Mark saw Zeke spin and glare a challenge back at them, and he could hear a hush tensing in the precinct as if the police were waiting, watching for what they'd let slip now. And Henry hadn't even noticed the sense of Winton's power coiling here.

Dennard snapped "They're letting Nolan go, because Lavine's Finest have barely looked at their evidence. Not even how an 'accidental death' ended up in a car trunk. We can file a complaint for that."

Mark glanced from him back to Nolan—

At the corner of his eye, something moved. A shape slipping through the crowd, closing in—

"Osborn—" Mark gasped, a warning he would have shouted if he dared, but—

The possessed man reached through the crowd. He touched Dennard's back.

Mark felt the magic shift, and he saw Osborn pull back a step, mouth half-open to find himself across the corridor now. Dennard's possessed face didn't even twitch, but Mark had to choke down a scream of *let him go!*

One second later, Christa said "Filing a complaint sounds about right. We were *not* drunk."

And Dennard… slumped. His controlled defiance slipped away as the puppetmaster spoke through him: "No, we might as well admit it. Drunk."

"What?" Christa's shout burst across the space. "You were just demanding, how did Irene get in that trunk?"

She stopped then, and Henry whispered in her ear. He must have sensed it too.

But Dennard, Winton, took a slow step toward Nolan and her group. "Irene's death was a tragedy. But…"

Mark stared. He felt his side brush the heavy table there, and knew it would only take a moment to press it against the ceiling to prove magic was real, to *try* to stop whatever Winton was about to unleash. All useless.

Dennard's voice settled at a strong, low tone, almost like his real voice at the times when Mark had heard him exhausted. "We regret this happened. I suppose you want to sue us for false accusations next? You've got your lawyers right here."

And he clapped the lawyer in front of him on the shoulder.

Power jumped, leaving Dennard and seizing that lawyer and on to the colleague brushing against him, to make that one pull back and reach toward Nolan.

His hand touched her.

Nobody else could have felt it, only Mark and Henry, from the soft brush of Winton's magic resonating against their belts. The simple touch, the flick of power—the faintest curve of Olivia Nolan's lips as a second flicker of the same energy threw Winton's control back and left the lawyer drawing away as if nothing had happened.

"Ms. Nolan?"

The lawyer was free. Mark felt the power wink out, and saw Dennard staring but only edging away, in control of himself again.

Nolan had... her own possession magic now? God, *what was in* that book of Winton's?

Mark glanced back to Osborn—where Winton's control talisman must be—as Winton retook control of his real pawn here, and the man's jaw went slack in the same instant the power gripped him.

"I think," came Nolan's slow, confident voice—and Mark saw her eyes flicking toward him, and then to Winton in Osborn, before turning back to Dennard and the crowd—"I think that my life isn't as easy to ruin as you think."

Dennard took another step back. "And that's it? You just walk away?" The tight words were more a challenge than a thanks.

Silence hung thick around them, but murmurs began eddying. A smothered cough came from the police detective.

Mark forced the words out, stepping toward Dennard. "It's no use. If the evidence isn't helping us, we should just go, and be glad it wasn't worse."

Dennard froze, his opening mouth shifting to an *O* of surprise as he looked at Mark. Then his eyes darted past him—toward Osborn—and settled back on Mark with barely a hint that he'd noticed the man their enemy had already used once before.

The ex-cop let out a loud sigh. "All right. For now."

"You can't!" Henry's voice was rising again, his control slipping away.

"Are you both out of your minds?" the detective said. "You think you can make murder accusations and then just wipe them away?"

Nolan nodded. "I think I'd be happy to leave things where they are. I have too much to get back to."

"Then, thank you," Dennard said. He turned to the detective. "Looks like that's all there is to it."

The detective coughed, and spat to clear his throat. "For now. You know this is just Round One, and we'll keep digging into you and her both. Don't do something stupid."

Dennard grunted something back to him, and then raised his arms to herd their group down the corridor. Henry and Christa started dazedly across it, Mark and Dennard behind them, through the forest of watching eyes and whispers.

Mark felt his thoughts clearing from the shock. Of course, of course Nolan wouldn't want to double down on public attention to their fight, any more than Winton would.

Walking just ahead, Christa looked back to Dennard. "How could you just back down like that? It was just one blood test and a cop with blinders on."

"It wasn't that," Mark said. "Please, just keep walking…"

The human currents were moving around them now, and Mark's glance back could only catch a glimpse of Nolan's knot of people. He forced his thoughts away from what she must be saying about them, and all the eyes watching. *One step at a time, steady as Angie balancing on the winds outside…*

Winton's magic moved. It moved to follow them—not by walking, Mark felt the energy pulsing as it closed the gap, jumping from one person to the next to weave through the crowd like a spark moving up a twisting fuse.

Mark scrambled a step to stay with the others. And Henry's eyes went wide.

"You feel that moving? It's *him*—"

"Come on," Dennard cut in, low and controlled.

They pushed for the door—and the sudden briskness in their walk made an officer up ahead turn to watch, suspicious. Winton's presence worked its way closer.

Mark brushed Henry's shoulder. "Easy…" and he held himself down to a quick walk. Winton could only jump along between what bodies were there. That had to slow him down, didn't it?

Henry's face was pale and twitching trying to steal glances back; Christa kept her hand on his arm, but she couldn't *know* how it hurt him to use the magic too long.

Then Winton's presence fell back, and Mark realized they'd passed a wide room, where the people spread out and thinned Winton's supply of stepping stones. The crowd was tighter ahead, but that was the door outside.

Mark strode forward and slid boldly between the people ahead, and the others kept pace behind him. The door stood just ahead, Winton was still hanging back, Angie's owl presence waited in the air outside—

He felt Angie being flung across the sky, two steps before he shoved the door open, into the blast of arctic air.

The clouds piled above the station were a heavy gray piled as high as his eyes could see. The air bit into his lungs, and wind rolled against his face as the afternoon light darkened with a growing whirl of snow.

God, Nolan had hours *to gather this storm, and I missed it all!*

A young woman behind them called "Trust me, you don't want to go out in—"

Instead they pushed across the parking lot, wrapping their coats against the whistling wind. Mark could feel Angie struggling back across the block above them. Out there Nolan could only freeze them slowly, but Winton could still send a puppet after them at any moment. Or Nolan could.

Mark's phone buzzed in his pocket.

He glanced down, as Henry gasped "It hurts… to breathe…"

Was Nolan *focusing* her cold on Henry? Mark clawed out his phone with numbed fingers, to see Nolan's text on the screen:

we shouldn't be enemies

And Henry heaved in a breath, and another, smoother now.

Mark looked back across the pavement. Just behind the glass door he could see a knot of people there—what had to be lawyers, an oblivious cop or two, and the woman who had just loosened her weather's grip on Henry.

Two uniforms trotted past them, heads down as they made for the shelter of the station. The air was growing dark.

wheres sasha? Mark threw back at Nolan.

I'd still welcome your help Nolan answered.

Help? She had her weather magic, and now she'd blocked Winton's attack too. What did she need with them? Mark felt Winton's energy hanging back beyond the entrance, watching too.

Wind slammed against them again, fiercer than ever, and Henry gasped.

Christa yelled "Get to the car!" She pulled Henry forward, slipping a moment on the slick pavement.

"No, back to the police!" Dennard said. "Winton let us go once."

Mark looked between them, and back across to Nolan, untouchable with her untraceable weapon. His belt was *useless*—everything about cancelling gravity was easy prey for Nolan's winds, ideal for allying with her but suicidal against her.

I could increase my weight to help me push through to get to her... no, down is the wrong direction...

The wind was blowing right in his face, leaving no shelter from the cars at his back. He took a step toward Nolan, then with a flex of thought he cut most his weight to let himself skip backward along the blast, twisting around and flinging up his arms as he *slammed* into a van.

Then, as he leaned against its grill, he sent power through his touch.

The van *lurched* upward—just for one creaking instant before it slid from his grip and slammed down with its full weight again, suspension straining to take in the impact. Car alarms ripped through the howling air, and Mark saw figures all around the lot spin to stare at what the wind had started to slide across the snow.

Mark's phone was still in his hand, and his aching fingers managed to text:

dont make me go over the top

Only two icy breaths later, the winds eased back.

He slid the phone away and stumbled toward the others. Dennard had wrenched open the back door of his Ford, waving Henry and Christa in.

Mark dove into the blessed shelter, and found his hands had closed on the seat belt and the ignition before his mind finished savoring being out of the storm. He eased the car out of its space and through the mostly-still lot, with all the care of a cabbie with too much practice driving in a city under Nolan's power.

"Did that van *float?*" Christa said, sounding out the words. "That was you, Mark?"

One car? Angie knocked over a whole junkyard stack of cars, once, Mark thought. The memory stabbed at him, and kept him silent until he felt Angie soaring safely above them again. Along the street he saw cars pulled over to the roadside, drivers leaving more of the street open to the fast-gathering snow.

Then he said "The threat made Nolan back down. Just like everyone did with the arrest—she'd never let anyone realize magic is real. I think keeping that edge hidden is the only thing she won't stomp over if it gets in her way. Her and Winton both." Even her texts had been careful, nothing the police could have proved were threats.

"They'll still be watching her, and us," Dennard said. "Keep an eye on that car that pulled out behind us."

Mark glanced in the mirror and saw Henry take a startled look back. A shape moved through the snow behind them, but the outline looked too trim and elegant for a police vehicle.

Coldness brushed through the enclosed air around them.

ABOUT THE AUTHOR

"Whispered spells for breathless suspense."

Ken Hughes dreams of dark alleys and the twenty-seven ways people with different psychic gifts might maneuver around each corner. He grew up on comics and adventures before discovering Stephen King and Joss Whedon, and he's written for Mars mission proposals and medical devices, making him an honorary rocket scientist and brain surgeon. Ken is a Global Ebook Award-nominated urban fantasy novelist, creator of the Shadowed Steps series, the Spellkeeper Flight, the Mirrorman, and many more series of supernatural thrills.

Don't get him started on puns.

Find more books and join the Overview newsletter at:

KenHughesAuthor.com.